DOWN IN THE COUNTRY

A Carlow Valley Mystery

James Bowring

The Book Guild Ltd

First published in Great Britain in 2021 by
The Book Guild Ltd
9 Priory Business Park
Wistow Road, Kibworth
Leicestershire, LE8 0RX
Freephone: 0800 999 2982
www.bookguild.co.uk
Email: info@bookguild.co.uk
Twitter: @bookguild

Copyright © 2021 James Bowring

The right of James Bowring to be identified as the author of this
work has been asserted by him in accordance with the
Copyright, Design and Patents Act 1988.

All rights reserved. No part of this publication may be
reproduced, transmitted, or stored in a retrieval system, in any form or by any means,
without permission in writing from the publisher, nor be otherwise circulated in
any form of binding or cover other than that in which it is published and without
a similar condition being imposed on the subsequent purchaser.

This work is entirely fictitious and bears no resemblance to any persons living or dead.

Typeset in 12pt Adobe Jenson Pro

Printed on FSC accredited paper
Printed and bound in Great Britain by 4edge Limited

ISBN 978 1913551 698

British Library Cataloguing in Publication Data.
A catalogue record for this book is available from the British Library.

To Polly
With grateful thanks

One

Wednesday 16 August

With half-closed eyes, Gareth Adamson shuffled into the gloomy kitchen. Although a few narrow rays of sunlight were penetrating the small gaps in the drawn-down Venetian blind, the room felt dank and cold, and he shivered as he continued to tie the cord of his threadbare, blue dressing gown untidily around his ample midriff. Yawning, he picked up the kettle and ambled slowly over to the sink.

"Welcome home," he muttered as he tried to unscramble his malfunctioning brain while he carelessly filled the kettle, splashing liberal quantities of water over his dressing gown and onto the tiled floor, which felt icy cold to his bare feet. He and his wife, Elizabeth, had returned from their Italian holiday the previous evening and had enjoyed a relatively good night's sleep in their familiar, slightly lumpy bed and yet, somehow, he felt disorientated and confused this morning. Admittedly, it had been late into the evening when they had finally returned home after a predictably wearying day of travelling and the interminable periods of frustrating inactivity at the airport, but, even so, they had only to cope with an hour's time difference so they couldn't really claim to be jet-lagged. Yet his normal thinking processes remained stubbornly numbed as he yawned again, plugged the kettle in, coughed, scratched his stubbly chin and rubbed his bleary, bloodshot eyes. He was in desperate need of a generous infusion of caffeine.

While he waited an eternity, it seemed, for the kettle to boil, he shambled over to the kitchen window and slowly raised the Venetian blind. Despite years of practice, he had never quite mastered the delicate art of raising and lowering the blind smoothly and evenly, and, as a result, he left one end dangling lower than the other. The sun was already rising in a clear blue sky, presaging the start of yet another hot, sunny day and Gareth Adamson was forced to squint at the sudden intrusion of bright light that coursed into the kitchen and exploded into his eyes.

Partly shielding his eyes from the blinding light, he peered out into the back garden, surveying with dismay the parched beds of wilting flowers, the drooping leaves of his perennials and the withered remains of his lovingly cultivated vegetable patch, all of which bore indisputable witness to the unusually prolonged spell of dry, warm weather which had arrived, largely unheralded, while they had been away, suffering violent storms in the Bay of Naples. The lawn, too, looked scorched, although, to his surprise, there were still some lush, green patches in the area furthest from the house, immediately in front of his vegetable patch. Then, as he studied the mottled lawn in more detail, his eyes gradually growing accustomed to the bright light, he noticed something lying on the ground towards the far end of the garden, half-obscured by a shrub border. Puzzled, he unlocked the back door and, still in bare feet, strode with gathering pace and an increasingly perplexed gaze towards the object that had aroused his curiosity. As he got closer, he stopped momentarily, stared in bewilderment at the sight that faced him, then turned and raced back towards the house.

Coughing from the exertion, he rushed through the kitchen, ignoring the boiling kettle which was billowing angry plumes of steam towards the ceiling, ran into the hall and called upstairs to his wife.

"Elizabeth! I'm going to call the police; there's, erm, something in the garden…"

Two

Friday 18 August

The trademark of Clive Walsingham's long and relatively successful career in the police service had been his detached, analytical approach. It was therefore something of a surprise, not least to Clive himself, when, acting on no more than a whim, he and his vivacious wife, Clare, had invested virtually all of their savings into the purchase of the Follycombe Hotel.

The hotel was a substantial, brick-built Victorian edifice, with a wing at one end which protruded both to the front and rear. The building comprised three floors, with solid bay windows at ground- and first-floor level, an imposing entrance with a moulded cornice hewn from local limestone and a solid grey slate roof from which a series of small dormer windows projected at regular intervals. Originally constructed as a lavish country house, it had been converted into a luxury hotel between the wars. The entrance now led into a spacious reception area and foyer, with a lounge, bar and corridor leading to the downstairs guest rooms to one side and the kitchen and office to the other side. From the foyer, the main staircase curved up to the first-floor guest rooms, while a narrower, more modest staircase, hidden behind the kitchen, led up to the attic, which had originally housed the servants' quarters. Largely unaltered over the years, this floor was mainly used for storage, with the exception of a handful of small rooms which had been cheaply converted into basic bedrooms which could accommodate members of the hotel staff who needed to stay overnight. A previous owner had constructed a substantial conservatory, running almost the full length of the rear of the building which served as the hotel dining room. It also provided convenient access both from the bar and the kitchen. Double doors led out from the conservatory onto the extensive terrace and gardens. At some stage in its history, the ground-floor brickwork had been rendered and the plaster painted in a disconcerting shade of pink.

When Clive and Clare bought the place, it had been losing money for years and, although Clare's parents had briefly run a hotel when she was much younger, neither she nor Clive had any relevant experience of modern hotel management, a failing which frequently caused them to doubt their combined wisdom in taking on such a daunting challenge. But they did at least inherit a small group of experienced staff, about whom they knew disturbingly little, the previous owner having had only a transient regard for accurate record-keeping, but who clearly had some relevant skills and a helpful smattering of local knowledge.

The reception area and the small team of part-time staff that ran it were presided over by Debbie Oxton, a hard-working individual with a calm, assured, occasionally self-important manner, a suspicious nature and a less than reliable memory. Debbie did not suffer fools gladly and could be brusque with both her colleagues and the occasional recalcitrant guest, but there was no doubting her loyalty and honest endeavour.

The chef's real name was Peter Wendlebury, but he preferred to be called Pierre and tended to speak with a phoney French accent. He was a short, stocky individual with light brown curly hair, an excitable temperament, a penchant for experimentation, not all of it successful, and a tendency towards flouncy petulance whenever Clive or Clare ventured to suggest that his menus were becoming too exotic or esoteric for the more traditional palates of most of their regulars.

Jamie Coulton worked variously as a porter, handyman, waiter and occasional barman. Tall, thin and darkly handsome, he was blessed with a serene temperament, an exuberant sense of fun, a flashing smile and a lightness of foot that enabled him to glide silently around the hotel, dispensing cheerful courtesies and, whenever he could, flirting outrageously with the more impressionable female guests. It was a trait that was, unsurprisingly, disapproved of by his girlfriend, Zoe, with whom he enjoyed a volatile relationship, but which did, from time to time, earn him lavish gratuities. Though generally outgoing and garrulous, he always seemed strangely reluctant to discuss his background, his family or his employment history.

And then there was Simon Verwood, who was responsible for maintaining the extensive grounds and gardens. He was a tall, sinewy man with an unruly mop of silver-grey hair, a deep, leathery tan, cultivated over many years of working out of doors, a capricious temperament and a booming, educated voice. The immaculately cultivated grounds and gardens were a fitting testament to his hard work, achieved mainly in the hours between breakfast and lunch as, towards the end of most afternoons, he had usually succumbed to one or other of his principal vices – whisky and attractive young men.

The hotel also came with a resident cat; a portly, middle-aged ginger cat called Archie, who would occasionally venture up to the attic to sniff around in its dark, dusty recesses, but who spent most of his time snoozing in a cosy corner of the bar or lounge or, when the weather was sufficiently benign, in one of Simon's lovingly cultivated herbaceous borders or in a sheltered spot on the terrace. When stirred into life, he would occasionally make a forlorn attempt to intercept the flight of an itinerant butterfly or low-flying bird, and when enticed by the aromas emanating from the kitchen, he would sometimes linger by the kitchen door and attempt a poor imitation of an emaciated, starving stray.

Through hard work, latent business acumen and a touch of good fortune, Clive and Clare were, to their surprise, making a success of the Follycombe Hotel. Clive had harnessed his analytical mind and sound judgement into successfully augmenting the hotel's regular, steady income by promoting it as a top-quality "Country House Hotel" venue for weddings and conferences, securing regular block bookings from a couple of "prestige" coach holiday companies and organising highly popular quiz evenings and murder mystery weekends. Once established, the hotel's burgeoning reputation quickly gathered momentum.

Clare, for her part, was a personable, hard-working and efficient hotel manager, organising and supporting her team and pouring copious amounts of energy into ensuring that all their guests had a memorable stay.

*

It was another unusually hot day. Clive Walsingham took a long, slow sip of ice-cold white wine, eased himself back in his chair, stretched out his long legs, rested his feet on the chair opposite and gazed absently out across the lawns and gardens. To his left, the lawn sloped towards a rustic gate from which a path meandered through a gap in the trees down to the River Carlow, snaking its way gently through the bucolic rural valley. To his right, there were some formally cultivated gardens mainly comprising beds of roses and a couple of herbaceous borders. At the far end of the gardens were the remains of the original Victorian walled kitchen garden, derelict and overgrown when they bought the place, but which Simon was increasingly taming in order to grow vegetables for use by Peter the chef. Nestling against the high brick walls were a lean-to greenhouse and a solid wooden shed which doubled as Simon's retreat when the weather closed in or the need for refreshment, in its many guises, became an irresistible priority. Several gravel paths led through the gardens and alongside the walled garden to the car park beyond.

Clive was wearing a crisp white, short-sleeved shirt, pink trousers, no socks and a pair of lightweight deck shoes. He was alone on the terrace, half shielded from the hot afternoon sun by a large, dark green parasol protruding vertically from a hole in the middle of a nearby wooden table. Apart from the gentle rustle of leaves in the faint summer breeze, intermittent distant birdsong, the sporadic hum of traffic from the minor road that passed the hotel and the occasional clatter of kitchen utensils as Peter set about preparing dinner, there was total silence. Across the brown lawn, Simon, wearing only a pair of venerable, faded blue shorts and a floppy hat perched precariously on his unkempt mane of silver-grey hair, was dead-heading the roses.

As he surveyed the tranquil scene with increasingly heavy eyelids, Clive suddenly became aware of busy footsteps approaching from the conservatory doors behind him. He looked up and smiled as Clare approached with her usual jaunty stride. She was wearing a light, billowy yellow summer dress and her short brown hair seemed to shimmer in the hot sun. She looked at him with her intense grey-green eyes and smiled indulgently, well aware of her husband's indolent disposition.

"Ah, I see you're working hard again," she teased.

Clive craned his neck, looked up sheepishly as Clare stood over him and gave a nervous cough. "Mmm? Ah, well, there's nothing much to do at the moment – at least nothing that's very urgent on a lovely afternoon like this. The office work is pretty much up to date, all the rooms have been cleaned and I've replenished the bar. Our guests are all out somewhere, no doubt enjoying themselves in the sun. Chef is busy in the kitchen preparing God knows what for this evening's meal and I'm not due to open the bar for another couple of hours. So I thought I'd take a short break, you know, just sit here for a few minutes and watch Simon pruning the roses."

"Well, don't stare at him for too long, or he might think you fancy him."

Clive laughed. "Oh, I've no doubt Simon knows where to draw the line, thank you very much."

Clare's face, always expressive, suddenly assumed a more serious appearance. She shook her head. "Oh, I'm not sure he does! Maybe now, Clive, but later in the bar, when he's had his usual skinful, you know what he can be like. Remember that poor young man he tried to proposition a few weeks back. I've never seen anybody skedaddle from the bar so quickly. You're really going to have to speak to him, you know; he's getting worse."

Clive took another sip of wine. "Yes, okay, I'll speak to him," he agreed reluctantly.

"I mean," Clare continued, warming to her theme, "he's so embarrassing in the evening when he's drunk, wandering about the place making coarse remarks in that loud, fake, plummy voice of his. Don't forget, we've got that coach party arriving next week and we don't want any unpleasant incidents. And I'm not sure that letting him have permanent access to that room in the attic helps matters. It just makes it too easy for him to get drunk, make an exhibition of himself and then go up to bed and crash out until the morning."

Clive raised his hands in a defensive gesture. "Yes, I know, you're right, of course, but it's a bit difficult at the moment, isn't it? Apparently he's been thrown out of his old place in Crowdale because the lease has run out and I just offered him use of a room here until he can find somewhere else. In any case, you've seen the state he can be in by the end of the evening. I'd feel guilty about forcing him to drive home. He'd be a danger to himself and any unfortunate motorist or pedestrian who happened to get in his way. You never know what might happen. I mean, I know he's a pain, but I do feel a bit sorry for him. He's a middle-aged, gay alcoholic with no close friends or family that we know of and I think he gets quite lonely."

Clive looked up at Clare's tense, unsmiling face.

"But I will have a word with him about his behaviour, I promise," he added quickly.

Clare smiled again, reached down and gently rested a hand on Clive's shoulder.

"Yes, right, that's sorted then. I'll leave that with you. But that wasn't really what I wanted to ask you." She could feel Clive's shoulder tense slightly. "What I really wanted to ask you was, well, we've just had this guy turn up at reception to check in – he says he phoned a couple of weeks ago to book, but we've got no record of the booking and he can't seem to remember who he spoke to or even if it was male or female. I've spoken to Debbie and she doesn't remember him phoning, but she'll probably come and have a word with you herself when she has a moment. Anyway, Jamie says he didn't speak to him and I just wondered if you might have spoken to him – he gave his name as Ralph Dalton."

Clive scratched his head of thinning light brown hair and pursed his lips. "No, no recollection of anyone of that name. Of course, Simon has been known to answer the phone if he happens to stagger through reception and then forget all about it. I'll speak to him about that as well." He paused as he heard more footsteps approaching, heavier and more bustling than Clare's. He looked up to see Debbie Oxton heading purposefully in his direction. She had short, dyed blonde hair, neatly parted in the centre, round, black-framed glasses and alert pale blue eyes. She had a pear-shaped figure, due in no small part to her unbridled enthusiasm for the chef's exotic, rich desserts, and wore an unflattering black skirt which was so tight around her legs that, when she walked, she was forced to take small, heavy steps.

"I was just telling Clive about Ralph Dalton," Clare said, defensively.

"Yes, that's right," Clive agreed, looking up at Debbie. "How long is Mr Dalton staying for?"

"He said for about a week, on business," Debbie replied briskly.

"I hope he paid in advance."

"Yes, in cash. He's paid up to tomorrow week. I've put him in Room 25." Debbie paused for a moment, half-expecting a response from Clive but he just nodded. "It's just that he seemed a bit shifty, a bit evasive," she continued. "He spooked me a bit, turning up out of the blue like that, claiming he'd got a reservation…"

"Shifty? In what way?"

"Well, for a start, he didn't look me in the eye at all. And, as he was registering, he kept looking back over his shoulder as though he thought he was being followed, or he was frightened of something or someone. And he couldn't remember the registration number of his car. He had a bit of paper with the number written on, which he kept looking at."

"I see. Has he been violent or abusive in any way?"

"Oh, no, not at all! He hardly said anything. It's just that, well, you know I'm a good judge of character and there's something about him…"

Anxious not to pander to Debbie's overly suspicious nature, Clive tried to smile reassuringly. "Okay, I'll keep a look out for him and if he says or does anything that you're not happy about, then you must let me or Clare know."

"Oh, I will, don't worry!" Debbie replied before turning on her heels and walking briskly back, in short pitter-patter steps, towards the conservatory doors.

Clive waited until Debbie was out of earshot before he reached out, squeezed Clare's knee and muttered, "I might introduce this Ralph Dalton chap to Simon later on…"

He broke off as though suddenly distracted by something and began to stare transfixed into the distance beyond the flowerbed where Simon was working.

Clare waited for Clive to finish what he was saying, but he didn't. Instead he continued to gaze ahead unblinking, a hint of a frown beginning to form on his high forehead. Clare tried to see what Clive was looking at that had so transfixed him, but she could see nothing unusual. She bit her lip, sensing that it was time to say what she had been thinking for some time. "There's something wrong, isn't there, Clive? You're very distracted and that's not like you. You're not really happy, are you?"

Clive continued to squeeze Clare's knee while still staring into the distance. "Ah, erm, no, I'm fine, darling, honestly," he replied unconvincingly.

Clare felt Clive's grip on her knee tighten. "No you're not. I can tell something's wrong. Is it my fault?"

Clive looked up, more anxiously this time, licked his dry lips and swallowed hard. There were times when Clare was uncomfortably perceptive. "No, no, it's not your fault," he finally replied. "You've been brilliant. I wish I'd met you much earlier in my life. No, no, if you must know, it's just that, well, I never thought I would miss life in the police force – all the hassle, all the paperwork, all the bureaucracy, the chief constable's management-speak drivel, all the insults, all the frustrations – but there was something about it, I don't know, the thrill of the chase, maybe, the pleasure to be gained from piecing the clues together, solving the crime and nicking the villain. You were always on your toes, always on an adrenalin surge, never quite sure what was going to happen next. But here, well." He shrugged. "Here everything runs like clockwork most of the time, thanks mainly to you and the team, and it can all become a bit, I don't know, a bit routine, I suppose. Oh, we get the occasional unpredictable guest, a bit of a tantrum from the chef sometimes and Simon's eccentricities, but that's about it. I think I'm missing the uncertainty, the challenge and, yes, occasionally, the danger. Sometimes, on days like these, I start to feel that there's not enough to occupy my mind. But don't worry, darling, it's still early days and I probably just need a bit more time to adjust. I'll get used to it, I promise."

Clare leaned forward and kissed the top of Clive's head. "I don't know about your mind, but I just might be able to occupy your body for a while if it helps." She gently prodded Clive's stomach. "And you could do with losing a few pounds, otherwise you won't be able to squeeze into those appalling pink trousers and that would be a great pity!"

Clive laughed as he allowed his hand to wander up the inside of Clare's thigh. "Hang on! You're not wearing any…"

"No, well, it is so very hot. But it's a lot cooler indoors, in the bedroom, and I can offer you a bit of a distraction for a while if you're interested."

Clive laughed again. "I daresay I could force myself."

"Good, I'll just pop upstairs then. The pleasure palace will be open in five minutes."

*

It was early evening and the multitude of day-trippers, sated on sanitised heritage, overpriced souvenirs and bland mass catering, had long since loaded themselves into their cars, clambered aboard their coaches and driven away, leaving Chartfield Castle standing proudly silhouetted against the crepuscular skyline, like a lone sentinel, on a ridge of high ground overlooking a graceful curve in the River Carlow, while the sun's fading light cast a mellow glow on the castle's imposing facade and crenellated ramparts and threw lengthening shadows across the dark recesses of its impressive stone walls.

Chartfield Castle had been home to the Earls of Westleigh since the thirteenth century. It was originally constructed, using locally quarried limestone, as an intimidating, impenetrable fortress from which successive earls controlled their volatile territories in the Welsh marches and defended themselves against the frequent incursions that characterised medieval life in the borders. Over the centuries, however, as the political environment changed and local turbulence slowly eased, each succeeding earl had made modifications to the castle, slowly transforming it from a military stronghold into a prestigious, luxuriously furnished stately home. These days, the remnants of the original castle walls, keep and fortifications were no more than a romantic embellishment, offering a pleasing choice of photo opportunities to impressionable tourists.

As he was being driven down the long, straight, private road that led to the castle entrance, past the extensive deer park and through sprawling, lavishly landscaped grounds, Richard Edgton could not suppress his feelings of envy and antipathy, and his swarthy face bore a deep scowl as his limousine came smoothly to a halt by the towering entrance and he hauled his large frame out of the back seat.

"Thanks, Dean. I don't think I'll be very long!" he growled at his attentive chauffeur as he strode towards the solid oak doors of the castle entrance. Richard Edgton was an imposing presence. Bearing, a little too obviously, the trappings of a successful, self-made businessman, he had immaculately styled, short, dark, almost black hair, expertly tinted to disguise the increasing and unwelcome incursion of grey; he wore an expensively tailored, heavy pin-striped suit, which he augmented with a royal blue handkerchief in his breast pocket and unnecessarily garish cuff-links. Clutching, in his left hand, an expensive briefcase with his initials "GRE" prominently embossed in the leather, he rang the bell with his right hand and was, almost immediately, shown inside.

Once inside the grand entrance hall, with its polished marbled floor and frescoes in the Renaissance style, he was escorted by one of the Earl's coterie of loyal retainers, who led him up the Palladian Grand Staircase and ushered him, with due deference, into the large oak-panelled library, where numerous rows of learned volumes, mostly in their original leather bindings, were arranged neatly on the hand-crafted shelves which lined the walls of the large, rectangular room. Above the shelves, on the burgundy walls, portraits of previous Earls of Chartfield looked down unsmiling. In front of the ornately carved marble fireplace, on an expensively woven carpet, several antique armchairs, upholstered in the finest brown leather, formed a neat semi-circle. Behind them, two mahogany escritoires were placed symmetrically either side of an elaborately carved cabinet on which a cut crystal decanter stood, together with two matching glasses. Anthony Granard, personal secretary to the Earl, was waiting, standing with his back to the fireplace which was partly obscured from view by an ornate tapestry fire-screen. Anthony Granard was a small, dapper man with curling, slightly untidy grey hair, alert blue eyes and a pair of mock horn-rimmed spectacles perched precariously on the end of his aquiline nose, giving him an avuncular, school-masterly appearance. He was wearing a checked shirt, green tie and grey trousers. He strode forward and proffered his hand to Richard Edgton, who seized it and gripped it so firmly that, when his hand was finally released, Granard instinctively examined it, as though fearing some serious damage to his small, bony fingers. With his undamaged left hand, he gestured towards one of several leather armchairs that surrounded them.

"Richard, thank you so much for coming," Anthony Granard began in a quiet, gentle voice, while smiling benevolently at his visitor. "A glass of port?" Without waiting for a reply, he moved over to the cabinet and poured two generous measures of vintage port from the decanter.

Richard Edgton eased his heavy frame into an armchair and, as he was handed his glass, made a point of looking around the room. "I take it his lordship won't be joining us," he observed gruffly.

"Ah, er, no," Anthony Granard confirmed as he perched lightly on the edge of an adjacent chair. "As you know, Lord Westleigh always re-locates to the south of France at this time of year, but he asked me to arrange this meeting. It's ironic in a way," Granard continued, swilling the port around the inside of his glass and laughing nervously. "I'm half-French, I've still got some family out there, and yet I have to stay here and look after his estate while the Earl is away."

"My heart bleeds. So why have you invited me here out of the blue, as if I didn't know?"

Anthony Granard adjusted his pose on the edge of his chair and coughed self-consciously. "Yes, of course, of course, you're a busy man and, er, I'll get to the point."

"I wish you would!" Richard Edgton replied brusquely before taking a generous swig from his glass.

"Well, er, as you know, Lord Westleigh is very concerned about your plans to turn the old quarry at Fearnley into some kind of theme park." Granard could not conceal the distaste in his voice as he uttered the words "theme park". "As you know," he continued in measured, precise tones, "Lord Westleigh owns the farm next to the old quarry – he's got a lot of rare breeds and a trout farm there – and, as I am sure you can appreciate, he's very concerned about the possible adverse ecological and environmental impact that your theme park would have, quite apart from the obvious disruption that would be caused by all the noise and the extra traffic. As you know, the local roads are really no more than country lanes and he's sure they won't cope and—"

Richard Edgton held up a large, muscular hand. "Yes, yes, I've heard it all before," he replied impatiently. "But, frankly, the quarry is no good to me in its present form and I've got to get a return on my investment. Of course, if his lordship hadn't been so vocal and so... so obstinate in his opposition to my plans to turn the quarry into a heritage museum, we wouldn't be sitting here now, would we? And on the subject of the local roads, I don't notice his lordship complaining when they get clogged with traffic visiting this place."

A smile flickered across Anthony Granard's benign face. "Ah, yes, but opening up this place has been good for the local economy – the shopkeepers in the village haven't complained. And it brings in some much-needed revenue which allows us to employ a good many local villagers, some of whom, incidentally, were made redundant when you shut the quarry down. Anyway, Lord Westleigh accepts entirely that you've got to get a return on your investment, as you put it, and he really doesn't want you to suffer financially, so he is prepared to make you a good offer for the quarry."

He rose nimbly from his chair, went over to the nearer of the two escritoires, opened a drawer and produced a plain white envelope which he held delicately between his index finger and thumb before handing it, with great ceremony, to Richard Edgton. Richard Edgton opened it, removed a piece of paper, unfolded it, studied its contents briefly and then snorted. Allowing the envelope to drop to the floor, he screwed the sheet of paper up into a ball and tossed it contemptuously onto the expensive carpet.

"Is that really the best you can do?" Richard Edgton hissed as he leaned forward aggressively. "I don't know how much his lordship is worth, but this place is one of the most visited stately piles in the country, he has a private yacht, his own helicopter and a large villa in the south of France. He manages a profitable farm, he owns a successful chain of garden centres, he's got a controlling interest in a big frozen food company, he's a director of a flourishing publishing house and all he can manage is a derisory offer like that." He pointed a stubby finger towards the screwed up ball of paper on the carpet.

Anthony Granard fingered his tie edgily. "I think you'd be surprised at how much it costs to maintain this house and the estate. I doubt that Lord Westleigh is nearly as wealthy as you think he is. Nevertheless, he has carried out a full market appraisal of the quarry and the offer he's prepared to make is based upon the best of the independent valuations."

"Huh! Well, you can tell his lordship, when he deigns to reappear, that he is going to have to raise his offer substantially before I'll even consider it and if he doesn't, then my plans for a theme park will go ahead. As a matter of fact, I shall be flying out to America on Tuesday week to meet some people out there who know how to run a successful theme park and who might be persuaded to invest in my little venture. And if they do invest, I can tell you now that the theme park we build will be brash, it will be noisy and it will be very successful."

Anthony Granard made one last attempt at persuasion. "Of course, if you do decide to go ahead, you must appreciate that Lord Westleigh will vehemently oppose your plans."

"Oh, I'm sure he will. He was quick enough to oppose my plans for a heritage museum, but you can tell him that I'm ready for a fight. And I usually win my fights – even if I have to fight dirty."

"I hope you're not making threats to…" Anthony Granard began, his voice sounding uncharacteristically harsh, but, before he could continue, Richard Edgton swigged down the rest of his vintage port with unseemly haste, stood up, placed his empty glass firmly on the cabinet, picked up his briefcase and, without further acknowledgement, strode briskly from the room.

Anthony Granard continued to finger his tie as he waited a moment or two while the sound of Richard Edgton's heavy, echoing footsteps receded into the distance and until his normally calm demeanour returned. He then lifted the phone by his elbow and spoke, coolly and quietly.

"Hello, this is Anthony here. May I speak with Lord Westleigh, please?"

*

Crowdale was originally little more than a hamlet. It had a church, St. Peter's, which lay only a few yards from the banks of the River Carlow, a short walk from the village green. It also had a pub, the King's Arms, a general store and a scattering of cottages built around the green. In more recent times, however, there had been some modest and not entirely sympathetic expansion and a small number of modern housing developments straggled along the main road leading away from the centre of the village. It was in one of these developments that Jamie Coulton and his girlfriend, Zoe, rented a cramped first-floor apartment.

It was late in the evening when Jamie climbed the stairs and opened his front door. He was weary after his day's work at the hotel but was whistling contentedly as he anticipated the welcome that awaited him inside his modest, unpretentious home. Zoe, he felt sure, would be there, probably in her usual position, cheerfully sprawled on the threadbare sofa watching something undemanding on the television. But she wasn't. Instead, as he looked around, all he could hear was a series of dull thuds and clattering noises emanating from their tiny bedroom. Puzzled, Jamie put his head round the door and flashed his engaging, toothy smile. Zoe was standing with her back towards him, her auburn hair trailing down over her shoulders. On the bed was a half-packed suitcase of clothes.

"Hi, Zo! Everything alright?" Jamie asked, nervously.

"No, everything is not alright," Zoe replied, her voice quavering with emotion. She turned to face him with swollen, pink eyes. "Where the hell have you been?" she asked plaintively.

"I've been working, Zo. It took ages to clear up after dinner and—"

"Bollocks! I phoned the hotel and they said you'd finished work over an hour ago. And it takes about fifteen minutes to get here at this time of night so I repeat, where the hell have you been?"

"Well, I, er…" Jamie Coulton hesitated.

Zoe did not wait for Jamie's vacillating reply. "I know what you've been up to, you sod, so don't bother to deny it. I've been asking around and I know. You've fallen back into your nasty old habits, haven't you? And you promised me you wouldn't."

"No, Zoe, that's not fair!" Jamie Coulton protested limply.

"Well, I've had enough; I'm moving out. I'm going to stay with my aunt in Buckham while I think about my future and… us."

Quickly throwing a few more items of clothing into her suitcase, she zipped it up and, while Jamie Coulton attempted an incoherent, spluttering apology, she stormed past him. As she opened the front door, she half-turned and called over her shoulder. "And I'm warning you, don't try and contact me! I'll be in touch when I'm ready."

She slammed the door and was gone.

Three

Saturday 19 August, morning

Clive Walsingham studied his visitor with the practised eye of a former detective inspector. The man was of average height, but his gaunt physique and perpetually hunched shoulders made him seem smaller. He had short, dark hair, liberally flecked with silver-grey strands, heavily lidded brown eyes and a mouth that turned down at the edges, giving him a permanently crestfallen expression. He was carrying a white, slightly dented bicycle helmet and was wearing a yellow shirt and black Lycra shorts that were tight enough to reveal any anatomical inadequacies. Panting and sweating profusely, he almost fell into the chair that Clive had offered him.

"Are you a keen cyclist?" Clive asked, quizzically.

"Oh no, not really," the man gasped. "Although it can be the quickest way of getting around at the weekend when the sun is shining and the roads are clogged. If it's still hot like this next weekend, it being the bank holiday, it'll be chaos on the roads. No, no, actually I was advised to take some more exercise by…"

"The doctor?" Clive enquired. As he was to discover, his visitor had an annoying habit of not quite finishing his sentences as though enervated by the effort of talking.

"No, well, my partner, really – I'm sure it's doing me good…" The man paused, seemingly gasping for air and apparently unable to speak.

"Are you alright?"

"I will be," the man gasped. "I just need a few minutes."

"I'm sorry, I didn't quite catch your name when you phoned," Clive remarked innocently, knowing full well that his visitor had not identified himself but worried that he might have to provide a name if an ambulance was needed.

"Er, well." The man spoke slowly and quietly as his breathing gradually improved. "It's Beauregard; Acting Detective Inspector Beauregard."

Clive tried but failed to stifle a giggle, something he often found difficult. "I'm sorry, but I'm not going to sit here and call you 'Acting Detective Inspector Beauregard' all morning. I take it this is an informal visit?"

"What? Oh, yes, yes – quite informal. I'm, er, Caspar; Caspar Beauregard."

Clive Walsingham heard himself laugh out loud. "Holy shit! That's one hell of a name for a policeman to carry around."

"Yes, it is rather," the acting inspector conceded, sheepishly. "It's French, of course."

"Of course! And Caspar? Didn't your parents like you very much?"

"Oh, I think they just liked unusual names. That's why I've got a brother called Lucius and a sister called Venetia."

"I see; at least I think I see," Clive spluttered as he tried to quell his instinct to giggle again. At that moment, Clare and Jamie Coulton emerged from the shady interior of the hotel carrying a tray of coffee, biscuits and a generous selection of cakes. "Ah, Clare, I'd like you to meet, er, Caspar?" He looked across at the acting inspector. "Is that what people call you?"

"Er, well actually most people call me Dick."

"Dick?" Clive heard himself laugh out loud again. "Why do they call you Dick?"

"I've no idea," the acting inspector replied with an apologetic shrug.

Clare, who was by now having nearly as much difficulty keeping a straight face as her husband, placed the tray on the table, carefully studied the acting inspector's sweat-stained, tightly fitting cycling gear and shook his clammy hand. "Pleased to meet you… Dick! I don't know if it's too early in the day for cakes, but you look as though you're in need of sustenance so I've put a few on the plate in case you're peckish."

The acting inspector's sweaty, hangdog expression lightened briefly. "Oh, I think I could be tempted if that's…" he replied hesitantly as he reached out for a large cream slice.

"Well, er, if you'll excuse me, I've leave you to it," Clare announced, as she turned to leave. Jamie, however, who did not seem to be his usual insouciant self, lingered briefly as though curious to know the purpose of the acting inspector's visit. Catching Clive's eye, he coughed, self-consciously. "Will you be requiring anything else?" he asked solicitously, hoping, no doubt, for a positive response, but Clive shook his head emphatically.

Clive watched as Clare, clutching a hand to her mouth, disappeared rapidly inside the building and waited for Jamie to make a more reluctant exit. "You said 'Acting Inspector' when you introduced yourself," Clive observed as he started to hand out the coffee.

"Yes, that's right. My inspector – Detective Inspector Morris – had a very nasty accident, the Thursday before last," the acting inspector announced solemnly before taking a generous if messy bite from his cream slice.

"Oh dear, no! What happened? Was he on duty?"

"Unfortunately, nobody quite knows what happened – there are no witnesses or… We know he was out riding across Willowmere Heath that evening – he often goes riding in the evening and we think he must have been thrown from his horse and… He was conscious long enough to phone for help but, by the time help arrived, he was unconscious – he still is. They had to airlift him to hospital. They found his horse nearby, apparently unharmed."

"Is he an experienced rider?" Clive asked, his attention momentarily distracted by the sight of a large blob of cream on the end of the acting inspector's nose.

"Oh, very experienced. He was in the mounted police for a while. He loves his horses."

"Oh, well that is bad luck! I am so sorry. Do you know when he'll be fit enough to return to work?"

The acting inspector's mouth which, until a moment or two earlier, had been filled with a substantial portion of cream slice, took a more pronounced downturn. "I'm not sure. I mean, I'm not sure if he ever will… He's still in hospital in a coma, with massive injuries and…" He paused to wipe some moisture from his eyes. "He's been so helpful to me and I've learned such a lot from him…" The acting inspector covered his face with his hands and started sobbing, his hunched shoulders heaving with emotion.

Clive observed the acting inspector's unravelling emotions with some discomfort. Sorry as he was at Caspar Beauregard's obvious distress, this was not how he had planned to spend his Saturday morning. Besides, Clare was far better at dealing with emotional turmoil and far more sensitive and understanding than he was, especially as his overwhelming emotion at that moment was one of amusement at seeing Caspar Beauregard's damp face smeared in cream. After a polite pause, he tried to change the subject.

"Um, you said, when you phoned, that you wanted to discuss something with me."

The acting inspector produced a crumpled handkerchief from the pocket of his cycling shorts and blew his nose loudly, louder in fact than Clive thought possible from such a quiet, melancholic man.

"Yes, that's right, I did," he snuffled. "You see, we – that is my, er, partner and I – came to one of your murder mystery weekends here a few months ago and we were very impressed and I remembered you saying you used to be a detective inspector."

"Ah, yes, of course!" Clive tapped his forehead gently with his fist as though annoyed by his oversight. Frankly, he had no recollection of the acting inspector attending one of his murder mystery weekends but he wasn't going to admit it. "I remember you now. You were quick to solve a lot of the clues – must be the detective in you."

"Oh, I don't know about that," the acting inspector replied, trying to sound modest but secretly pleased that he had apparently made such a good impression on Clive. "Anyway, I made a few enquiries and discovered you used to work at Inglemouth on the south coast. I understand your superiors were very impressed with your work and were sorry when you decided to leave the…"

Clive was taking a sip of coffee and spluttered as he heard Acting Inspector Beauregard's account of his departure from the police force. "It's kind of you to say so, er, Dick, but I don't think—"

"And I really need your help," Acting Inspector Beauregard interrupted, looking earnestly at Clive with his deep brown, pleading, moist eyes.

"In what way?" Clive asked, suddenly sounding defensive, and glancing over the detective's hunched shoulders in the vain hope that Clare or Debbie might emerge from the conservatory with an urgent message for him.

"The thing is, I was delighted when they appointed me as acting inspector after Inspector Morris's accident – I thought it would be a great opportunity for me to show everyone what I could do – but, if truth be told, I'm a bit out of my depth. I mean, I haven't been a sergeant for that long and Inspector Morris took me very much under his wing and was very protective and… Obviously, I don't want to admit that I'm struggling – that would pretty well be the end of my career – and I had hoped that I could get away with things as long as nothing too complicated or high-profile turned up, which is usually the case around here. That was until last Wednesday when – just my luck – this body turned up and—"

"Hang on, er, Dick, hang on a minute," Clive protested. "What are you asking me to do?"

"Ah, yes, I'm sorry, I should've explained. You see, I was wondering if you, erm, you might be able to help, you know, if I could pick your brains a bit. We are allowed to use civilian advisers and consultants these days, if a case can be made and provided they are not too expensive. But… but, don't worry, there is some money available to pay for your time. I mean, I know you've got this hotel to run and you probably haven't got any spare time and—"

"You mentioned a body?"

"Oh, yes that's right."

Clive leaned forward in his chair, suddenly intrigued and, for the first time, more than mildly interested in what Caspar Beauregard had to say. "Tell me more!"

Acting Inspector Beauregard dabbed his eyes, thrust the last piece of the cream slice into his mouth and stared longingly at an unclaimed slice of chocolate cake before taking a deep breath. "There's this couple who live in Morstock; they're a perfectly ordinary couple as far as we know. They'd been on holiday in Italy for a couple of weeks and they arrived back home late last Tuesday evening. Anyway, on Wednesday morning, he went into his garden for the first time since they returned home and discovered the body of a woman lying naked, face-up, on the lawn near the bottom of his garden. As far as we can establish, he didn't know the woman and his garden is enclosed on three sides by a six-foot-high solid garden fence. The only access to the garden is through his house and that had been locked up for the previous two weeks while they were away on—"

"What's on the other side of the fences?"

"Neighbours on two sides and school playing fields at the bottom."

"Ah, that'll be Polbury Manor school, I imagine."

"Yes, that's right. You know it?"

"No, not personally, but my wife went to school there. She's still got friends around here. That's the main reason we moved here. Could someone have got into the playing fields and over the fence?"

"Obviously, we've examined the site, but there's no evidence to suggest that anyone got into the garden that way. The school is closed for the summer holidays and they don't exactly invite the public to use their fields. There's a large wrought-iron gate at the entrance that is locked, high fencing all the way round and cameras all over the place and—"

"And the boundary fences are all in a good state of repair? No sign of any recent damage or any panels having been replaced?"

"No, nothing suspicious at all."

"And no sign of the couple's house having been broken into?"

"No. They say everything was just as they left it."

"Do any of the neighbours have a key? Did they hear or see anything untoward?"

"No, not as far as we know." Finally succumbing to temptation, Acting Inspector Beauregard reached out for the slice of chocolate cake and took a hasty bite.

"Do you know who the dead woman is?"

"What?" The acting inspector answered, spraying crumbs down his yellow shirt. "Oh, yes, of course, I should've said! Dental records have identified her as Mary Pullman, aged sixty-four. She disappeared back in April – her husband reported her missing. There's been no sign of her, or her car, since then until her body turned up last Wednesday."

"And do you know how and when she died?"

"The pathologist said she'd been strangled and he reckoned she'd been dead about three or four days when she was found, although he did seem a bit confused – muttered something about some inconsistencies; he said he'd have more information when he'd done the full post—"

"So unless the full post-mortem tells you something different, you reckon she was strangled and that she died sometime last weekend when the owners of the house were away on holiday?"

"Correct!"

"Mmmm. Any evidence of broken bones, a violent assault, a sexual assault?"

"No, nothing – no bruises, no fractures – nothing. Just the strangulation marks around her—"

"Where did she live?"

"In Buckham village, several miles away."

"And the guy who found her body; no connection with her, you said?"

"No, not as far as we know. His name is Gareth Adamson,

but he says he's never seen her or heard of her before. He sounded genuine, but—"

"And Mary Pullman; she has a family?"

"Yes, she has a husband, Gregory, who reported her missing, and two daughters, neither living at home."

"Mmmm."

Acting Inspector Beauregard had raised the nibbled slice of chocolate cake halfway to his mouth before his eyes began to water again. Replacing the cake on its plate, he dabbed at his eyes. "I just don't know what to do next. I've got a woman who has been missing without trace for about four months, who then suddenly turns up murdered in a stranger's back garden. We don't know how she got there or why, or who murdered her or why, or where she's been for the past four months and I'm just at a complete loss. The chief constable wants a quick result and I just wondered if you would be able to help in any way."

Clive pursed his lips and exhaled gently as he pondered the dilemma. "The thing is, I've got a coach party coming in on Wednesday and we'll be very busy then, so I can't really help after Tuesday and—"

"But could you help over the next couple of days or so? Any help would be appreciated."

Clive leaned forward and spoke in a low, conspiratorial voice. "Mmmm. I'm intrigued. I think I'd like to see where she was found and look at the 'scene of crime' photographs. Finish your cake first!"

Four

Saturday 19 August, afternoon

Gareth and Elizabeth Adamson lived in one of the middle houses of a terrace of four which were originally constructed to accommodate workers employed on building the ill-fated local railway, although the houses themselves had been much modernised over the years. Their back garden was rectangular in shape, enclosed on one side by the back of their house and, on the other three sides, by a solid six-foot-high fence of wooden panels. Subtle changes in colour and grain suggested that some of the panels had been replaced over recent years, but none of them looked brand new.

At the rear of the garden, where it backed onto the school playing fields, was a large, ramshackle wooden shed and, in front of it and to one side, were the parched remains of Gareth Adamson's treasured vegetable patch. Nearer the house was a neat lawn, on both sides of which were beds containing mature shrubs, perennials and the remains of some summer annuals. Roughly halfway down the lawn, its symmetrical, oblong shape was broken by two irregularly shaped flowerbeds which protruded into the lawn from each side, permitting a small central route through to the far end of the garden and the vegetable patch. It was just beyond these central beds, slightly to one side, that Mary Pullman's body had been found.

Clutching a couple of police photographs, Clive Walsingham strode busily around the garden, stopping occasionally to look across at the neighbouring properties, or to examine the garden fences, or to scrutinise the ground around the area where the body was found, or to assess possible angles and trajectories, rather like a ballistics expert, while all the time being quietly observed by Acting Inspector Beauregard, who was standing in the centre of the garden with his hands thrust deep into his pockets. When he had finished his detailed inspection, Clive studied the photographs he was holding and moved a couple of feet to one side.

"So this is where the body was found?" he asked, pointing to the ground.

Acting Inspector Beauregard nodded his confirmation.

"It's very odd, don't you think?" Clive continued, waving the photographs in front of Inspector Beauregard's heavy eyes. "The way the body was discovered. For a start, Mary Pullman is naked and yet there is no sign of a sexual assault of any kind. So why remove her clothes?"

"To get rid of some kind of incriminating evidence?" Acting Inspector Beauregard suggested.

"Possibly! And then we've got Mary Pullman lying neatly on her back with her legs together and her arms down by her side. Now, if she had been thrown over one of these fences, she would have landed in a much more untidy heap and probably much closer to the fence in question. But she was several feet from the nearest fence. You see, looking at these photos, it looks as though the body has been very carefully and very tidily laid down and yet its position seems fairly random. There's been no attempt to hide the body – it was only partly concealed from the house – but it's not been placed in the middle of the lawn either. It's odd that the murderer went to the trouble of removing her clothes and arranging her body so neatly and then effectively abandoned it rather haphazardly in this part of the garden."

He paused briefly, hoping for a contribution from Acting Inspector Beauregard, but the hangdog policeman remained silent and brooding. Clive's keen eyes, meanwhile, had focused on a couple of broken twigs near where he stood. He stooped to pick them up, stared for a moment at the nearby shrub from which they had come and looked at the photographs again.

"Do you think she was murdered elsewhere and her body brought here for some reason, or was she murdered here?"

Acting Inspector Beauregard shrugged his hunched shoulders. "There's no sign of a struggle, so our thinking is that she was murdered elsewhere and her body was brought here but, of course, we can't be sure and we've no idea why or how."

"Okay, so let's run with that hypothesis for the moment. If her body was brought here, and we don't know why, then she must have been brought through the house, or somehow been lifted over one of the fences, or carried or dragged through a gap that's now been repaired, or she fell from the sky!"

Acting Inspector Beauregard shrugged again and nodded.

"And there were no injuries on the body consistent with her falling from a height or being hurled over a fence?" Clive asked.

"No, absolutely none! Just the strangulation marks around her throat."

"Were there any scuff marks on the ground, or any damage to any of the fence panels?"

"No, absolutely not," Acting Inspector Beauregard repeated. "You can see why I'm puzzled."

"Mmmm, yes I can. We've had quite a long spell of very hot, dry weather. Mr Adamson obviously spends a lot of time tending to his plants, so did he arrange for anyone to water the garden while he and Mrs Adamson were away?"

"He says not."

"Mmmm. I think I need to talk to Mr and Mrs Adamson."

The Adamsons' lounge was small and quite cluttered. Against one wall, which was painted in mint green, was a sofa, upholstered in garish pink and green stripes and, close to the sliding glass door leading out into the garden, was a battered armchair, its threadbare upholstery liberally covered in a variety of mismatched cushions. A fussily assembled collection of cheap, porcelain ornaments adorned the window sill, the mantelpiece and a wall-mounted shelf unit, and several framed prints – the sort that are produced in bulk and sold to tourists in tacky souvenir shops and foreign markets – hung from the walls.

Gareth and Elizabeth Adamson sat attentively on the sofa while Clive arranged himself as comfortably as he could on the lumpy, cushion-strewn armchair. Gareth Adamson was short and stocky, with a muscular physique, a heavily lined face, a balding pate and a restlessness that caused him to fidget incessantly. His rough hands and dirty fingernails suggested that he spent a lot of time fidgeting in his garden. His wife was beanpole thin with straight grey hair, round spectacles and a serious, slightly disapproving demeanour.

Acting Inspector Beauregard pulled out a creaky, upright chair from beside a small table in the corner of the room and perched awkwardly on it. He looked expectantly towards his new temporary colleague. Clive cleared his throat nervously. He felt uncomfortable having his somewhat rusty detection skills and interrogation techniques so carefully scrutinised.

"Errm, Detective Inspector, erm, Beauregard has asked me to help with this investigation, so I'm sorry to have disturbed your Saturday afternoon and I hope you don't mind me asking you some questions you might have been asked before."

Gareth and Elizabeth Adamson exchanged glances before Elizabeth spoke in a rather severe, matronly tone. "I think we've told your colleague everything we know, but if it helps to get to the bottom of this… It's been most unsettling, you know."

"Yes, I'm sure it has. Now, as I understand it, you were on holiday for two weeks and you got back home last Tuesday evening?"

"Yes, that's right," Elizabeth Adamson confirmed. "We'd been to Italy; Sorrento actually. We've provided Inspector Beauregard with details of our flights and hotel." She looked across to the acting inspector, who confirmed her statement with a dilatory nod. "Anyway, we got back home quite late on Tuesday."

"And when did you discover the body?"

Elizabeth nudged Gareth before he spoke. "Let me see, that must have been on Wednesday morning around 8.30. I got up to make some coffee, pulled up the blind in the kitchen window and there she was."

"I see, thank you. We've identified the body as Mary Pullman. She lived in Buckham. Did you know her at all?"

Gareth Adamson glanced at his wife again and fidgeted. "No, not at all!"

"I see. Now this next question is very important. Did you arrange for anyone to come in and water your garden while you were away?"

Gareth Adamson fidgeted again. "Er, no, no, I didn't. To be honest, it has always rained quite a lot when we've been away – until this year, that is."

"Does anyone else have a key to your house – a neighbour or a friend or a relative; anyone at all?"

"Absolutely not!" Elizabeth Adamson replied with conviction. "We did give our neighbours a key when we went away two or three years ago…"

"Your neighbours?"

"Yes. Mr and Mrs Footner." She sounded contemptuous as she uttered the words. "We just wanted them to keep an eye on the place for us, but they rather abused the privilege, I'm afraid. They've got three young children who are a bit out of control, if we're being honest, and they allowed them to come in here and, well, they made a bit of a mess – a vase got broken and things got moved around – so we haven't given them the key since."

"And they returned the key?"

"Of course they did."

"But they could have had another key cut while you were away."

"I suppose so, but there's never been any suggestion that they did. I mean, why would they?"

"What about the neighbours on the other side?"

"Donald and Margaret?" Elizabeth Adamson laughed sarcastically. "Have you met them? I mean, they're very sweet but, well, you'll see what I mean when you meet them."

"So there were no signs of any disturbance or intrusion when you got back from holiday?"

"No, none," Gareth Adamson replied firmly, "apart from the body in the garden, of course."

"And no damage to your fence or plants or anything?"

"No, nothing at all!"

"And how long have you lived here?"

"Let me see; just under four years," Gareth Adamson replied, suddenly jumping to his feet and pacing the floor. "I used to work at Fearnley quarry and we moved here so that I could have a shorter, easier journey to work. Then that bastard, Richard bloody Edgton, bought it and almost immediately closed it down."

"So where do you work now?"

"I don't. I haven't been able to get another job. There aren't too many openings for a fifty-eight-year-old quarryman around here. Elizabeth works part-time in the local supermarket and we get by – just!"

As the two men left the house and walked the few paces along the front path to the pavement, Clive turned to Acting Inspector Beauregard. "Shall we see the Footners first or start with Donald and Margaret?"

Acting Inspector Beauregard smiled for the first time that afternoon, though his lugubrious features seemed ill-equipped for the task. "Oh, Donald and Margaret first, I think. We'll save the best till…"

"Strange, don't you think?" Clive asked as they walked the few yards to the neighbouring house. "Gareth Adamson has been out of work for probably three years or so and his wife works part-time in the supermarket and he said they got by – just. So they haven't got much money coming in and yet they can afford a fortnight's holiday in Sorrento, which is not cheap."

Acting Inspector Beauregard shrugged again. "Savings, maybe, or a legacy of some kind?"

"Maybe," Clive replied uncertainly. "And you're quite sure that there's nothing that connects either of them to Mary Pullman?"

Acting Inspector Beauregard sighed. When he spoke he sounded frustrated. "No, nothing at all; nothing that we've found."

"Mmmm." Clive pursed his lips. "Did you tell me what Mary Pullman did for a living?"

"Err, did I? Maybe not! She'd been retired for three or four years or so, but before that she worked in a bank."

Five

Saturday 19 August, afternoon

Donald and Margaret Holt were an elderly, rather frail couple. Donald had wiry, untidy, white hair, a weary, solemn demeanour and a stooped appearance. When he moved about, he did so slowly and shakily, with the aid of a stout walking stick. His wife seemed more robust physically, but she appeared quite confused. She wore a fixed smile, but her eyes showed little emotion beyond a flicker of panic whenever she was asked a direct question. Clive was sure that they were lonely, as they seemed delighted to see him and Acting Inspector Beauregard even though, as Donald Holt was quick to point out, they had already told Acting Inspector Beauregard all they knew. The acting inspector nodded his confirmation with some enthusiasm, as though grateful for the chance to demonstrate to his temporary new colleague that his investigation, though not yet productive, had at least been thorough.

The Holts' lounge was identical in size and layout to their neighbours. It was furnished with three high-backed, unmatched chairs, a well-polished sideboard of mature vintage in dark wood and a cheap-looking cupboard that had, no doubt, started life packed flat. An old radio took pride of place on the sideboard and a small television occupied one corner of the room. Any available surface was liberally covered with an assortment of faded photographs, mainly mementoes, Clive guessed, of a younger Donald and Margaret Holt in the company of friends and relatives who they had, long ago, lost touch with or who had passed away. A compact conservatory to the rear had been commandeered as a makeshift dining room and the room next to the kitchen, originally designed as the dining room, had been converted into a bedroom containing two single beds and a modest assemblage of cheap furniture. A door led through into a small bathroom. Although the weather was hot and sunny, all the windows were closed and a pronounced fusty smell pervaded the lounge.

As Clive began to question the Holts, gently, about the mysterious appearance of a dead body on their neighbour's lawn, it became clear that, in addition to being elderly and frail, they were both rather deaf and had only a vague recollection, if any, of when certain events had occurred.

"We think the body had probably been there since sometime last weekend," Clive shouted. "Do you remember seeing anything or hearing anything unusual?"

"No, not a thing," Donald Holt replied, slowly and loudly, carefully articulating every syllable. "I expect we sat out in the garden quite a bit last weekend – it was such lovely weather – but we didn't see or hear anything out of the ordinary."

"And in the evening or during the night?"

"Ah well, I'm afraid we do have the television up rather loud in the evening and we take our hearing aids out before we go to bed, so…"

"Do you have many visitors?"

"No, we live quite quietly," Margaret Holt replied uncertainly. "We have a nice lady – I forget her name – who comes in a couple of times a week with our shopping and helps us with chores and things and our son, er…"

"Christopher!" Donald Holt prompted.

"Yes, that's right; Christopher comes to see us when he can."

"Which isn't very often," Donald Holt added, his voice tinged with bitterness. "He's always far too busy!"

"And what about your garden?" Clive asked, gently. "Do you have any help with that?"

Donald nodded sadly. "Yes we do, unfortunately. I've always loved gardening, but these days it's all too much, I'm afraid. So Gareth from next door comes in every so often to mow the lawn and tend to the beds. He wanted to buy part of our garden from us – he mentioned it a couple of times. He said he wanted to expand his vegetable plot but…"

"He didn't have the money?" Clive suggested.

"Oh no, I think he had the money. We thought he made quite a generous offer but, when we mentioned it to Christopher on one of his rare visits, he wasn't keen. He said losing part of our garden would affect the value of the house if we needed to move, so we told Gareth that we weren't interested."

"And when was that? Can you remember?"

Donald Holt scratched his nose and thought for a moment. "Oooh, I should think it was probably back in March or April sometime."

"Can you see into Mr Adamson's garden at all?"

"What? Oh, er, no," Donald Holt replied, hesitantly. "That is, we could if we went upstairs, but we don't. I'm afraid the stairs are rather too much for us now. As you can see, we have our bedroom and bathroom downstairs these days."

"Would you mind if we take a look upstairs before we go?"

"Ah, er, no, I suppose not, although I'm afraid it's rather neglected up there…"

The upstairs rooms were bare, cold and dank. There were a few mildew-speckled cardboard boxes stacked against the wall in what was once the main bedroom and, in a second bedroom, there was a wooden wardrobe, with its door half-open, containing some old clothes. Here and there, wallpaper was peeling from the musty walls. A tap dripped echoingly in the bathroom. Clive wandered over to the rear bedroom window, his footsteps echoing on the bare, creaking floorboards, and looked out. Small sections of the Adamsons' garden were visible between some overgrown shrubs, but the part of the lawn where the body had been found was frustratingly obscured by a rowan tree and the sloping roof of Donald Holt's neglected garden shed.

Clive tried to open the window, but it was jammed. "Mmmm. Well, the body certainly wasn't thrown out of this window."

While Clive had been speaking to Donald and Margaret Holt, Acting Inspector Beauregard had remained silent, aloof and increasingly brooding, but now they were upstairs and out of earshot, he felt unable to contain his obvious frustrations. "I had already asked all those questions," he suddenly exclaimed, sounding unexpectedly tetchy.

Though taken aback by the acting inspector's sudden outburst, Clive smiled benignly. "Excellent! And did I miss anything or were any of their answers different this time around?"

"No, I don't think so. But I hope you understand that this is still my case." Acting Inspector Beauregard spoke as though trying to convince himself more than his new colleague.

"Of course it is," Clive replied benevolently. "But you did

ask me to help and I thought I might unearth something new; you never know. It was interesting what Donald Holt said about Gareth Adamson's interest in his garden. It might be worth trying to find out a bit more about that. Anyway, I think it's time we went and talked to the other neighbours. I don't think we can make much more progress here. I do wonder, though, whether the Holts are entitled to a bit more help. Maybe someone in authority could have a word with the local social services."

They returned downstairs, thanked the Holts for their time and strode out of the house into the hot, glaring sun. The Holts' house had been so dank and cool that Clive had temporarily forgotten how hot and sunny it was outside and he had to hold a hand in front of his face to shield his eyes from the glare.

As they walked past the front door of the Adamsons' house and up the short path to their other neighbours, Clive turned to his colleague and spoke quietly. "And what do you know of Mr and Mrs Footner?"

The acting inspector stopped and hesitated for a moment before answering. "Erm, nothing much," he said unconvincingly, while giving another of his dramatic, apologetic shrugs. "They have three young children and, I'd guess, not a lot of money. They were away when the body was found, so they couldn't tell us much."

"You've checked their story?"

"Of course!" Acting Inspector Beauregard sounded tetchy again.

The door was answered by Tracey Footner, a plump woman, probably in her late thirties, with long, tightly combed-back hair, dyed mainly blonde but with a hint of pink along the sides, and an attitude that suggested she was no lover of authority figures. Her tight black leggings served to accentuate the plumpness around her midriff and bottom. She was holding a mobile phone in her hand, which she kept glancing at. Behind her, from somewhere in the house, three young voices were bawling at each other as they thundered up and down the uncarpeted stairs.

Tracey Footner turned and shouted at them. "Oi, oi, you lot, will you just shut that row for a minute? Go and annoy your father in the garden for a few minutes." She turned back to her visitors and glared at them. "This isn't a good time! I hope this won't take long; we're going out soon and I've already told you what I know."

"Yes, er, thank you," Acting Inspector Beauregard replied diffidently. "May we come in?"

With some reluctance, Tracey Footner held the door open, stared at the men as they walked past and then followed them into the house. The living room was cluttered with the tell-tale ephemera of bored children. Some soft toys lay abandoned on the laminate floor, in uncomfortable proximity to a large plastic football. An assortment of cheap, plastic playthings were scattered across the shapeless sofa, together with a discarded games console. Through an open door, Clive could see that the kitchen surfaces were strewn with soiled crockery and a couple of empty crisp packets. A faint smell of stale nicotine pervaded the air.

"I'm sorry about the mess; it's the school holidays and you know how it is…" Tracey Footner's apology sounded more defiant than regretful. She stood in the middle of the living room with one hand on one of her wide hips, while the other continued to clutch her mobile phone.

Not knowing how it was, Clive picked his way carefully between the discarded toys, made his way over to the rear window and looked out into the garden. A large man with a shaved head, a substantial stomach, heavily tattooed arms and, wearing dirty jeans and a grey vest, was apparently building a patio and was heaving some large stone slabs into place, while two young boys, called Bradley and Ethan, and a younger girl, called Tiffany, were racing around the garden shrieking and pretending to fire plastic guns at each other. A large workshop, built from grey breeze blocks, ran part of the way down the side of the garden closest to the Adamsons' fence and, beyond that, there was a child's trampoline.

"We're really interested in last weekend," Clive observed as he continued to look into the garden.

"Well, like we said to your colleague," Tracey Footner replied impatiently, "it's the school holidays and we took the kids away for a few days. We left on the Thursday before last and got back this Tuesday."

"Where did you go?"

"We went to Radholme down on the coast – we rented a caravan."

"And you must have been very lucky with the weather," Clive remarked before turning and scrutinising Tracey Footner's pale complexion.

"Yeah, we spent quite a bit of time on the beach, till the kids got bored. It saved us a bit of money!"

"Yes, quite. Of course, your neighbours have been away for two weeks. Do you have a key to their house?"

"No, why should we?" There was an air of defiance in Tracey Footner's reply.

"No, no reason, it's just that we've been talking to your neighbours, Mr and Mrs Adamson, and they mentioned that they gave you a key when they went on holiday, two or three years ago, I think they said."

"Yeah, that's right. They wanted us to keep an eye on the place, water their plants, that kind of thing."

"And you returned their key when they got back."

"Yeah, of course we did! Look, I don't know what you're implying…"

Clive held up his hands in a gesture of apology. "I'm not implying anything, Mrs Footner, I'm just trying to establish the facts. Anyway, I gather Mr and Mrs Adamson didn't give you the key again."

"No, they didn't. There was a bit of an accident. A vase got broken; it was only a cheap vase, but they made such a fuss. I mean, have you seen their place? It's full of cheap bloody ornaments—"

"I see. Thank you! Do you mind if I take a look in the garden?"

"I'm not stopping you; the back door is open."

Clive wandered through the back doorway and out into the unkempt garden, neatly sidestepped a marauding child, and studied the trampoline in forensic detail. The grass beneath it had been mowed recently, but an area closer to the Adamsons' fence, circular in shape and approximately the same dimensions as the base of the trampoline, had conspicuously longer grass. Clive turned towards the man, whose grey vest was drenched in sweat.

"I'm sorry to bother you," he ventured.

"I doubt it," the man replied querulously.

"Yes, I'm sorry, I didn't catch your name."

"And I didn't catch yours."

"Ah yes, very rude of me. I'm Clive Walsingham. I used to be a detective and I'm helping, er, Inspector Beauregard with his investigations into the body that was found next door…" He paused, waiting for a response, but the man continued to move a large stone slab into place. "And you are…?"

"Footner. Dean Footner."

"I gather you were away last weekend."

"Yeah, we took the kids away for a few days, trying to keep them amused, fed and out of trouble."

"And you got back on Tuesday?"

Dean Footner stood up and mopped his sweating brow with the back of his sweating hand. "S'right!"

"The dead woman's name is Mary Pullman. Does it mean anything to you?"

Clive Walsingham thought he could detect a slight flicker of recognition on Dean Footner's rugged, sweat-soaked face, but it was so transitory that he couldn't be sure.

"Nah – 'fraid not."

Clive turned round and glanced up towards the bedroom windows. "How much of next door's garden can you see from those windows?"

"Not much – my workshop obscures most of the view. We can't see the area where the body was found, if that's what you mean."

"Oh, I see; that's your workshop. Is that what you do for a living?"

"Nah, not really! I build model aircraft in there – it's a hobby mainly, although I do sell a few. No, I work for Richard Edgton; you may have heard of him. I'm his driver and security adviser."

"His enforcer!" Acting Inspector Beauregard barked the words in such a way that Clive sensed he was deliberately trying to provoke Dean Footner. Predictably, Dean Footner stared at the acting inspector; it was a cold, intimidating stare, but he went no further. Clive felt sure that he and Dick Beauregard were old adversaries, despite Dick's earlier protestation that he barely knew the man.

"Now you be careful what you say, *Acting* Inspector," Dean Footner responded at last, his voice sounding harsher and more menacing. "I'm no thug or 'heavy'. It's just that sometimes, as you know, Mr Edgton has to go to places and see people who don't much like him and I just accompany him to make sure he comes to no harm."

"Richard Edgton has a number of 'interests' in the area." Acting Inspector Beauregard relayed the information to Clive in a sneering voice. "Including the quarry at Fearnley. He plans to turn it into a theme park of some kind or—"

"Yeah, someday, maybe," Dean Footner added, cynically. "You see these stone slabs here? They were some of the last to be quarried at Fearnley before it closed down. Beautiful limestone, it is. Mr Edgton let me have a few slabs for my patio."

"Your next-door neighbour, Gareth Adamson, was telling us that he'd been made redundant when Richard Edgton closed the quarry," Clive said. "I don't think he's Mr Edgton's number one fan."

"Yeah, that was a shame, but Mr Edgton had no choice but to close it down. It was losing money and then there were the accidents—"

"So are there any tensions between you and Gareth Adamson? I presume he knows you work for Richard Edgton?" Clive asked.

"Yeah, he knows, but we haven't really spoken for a couple of years – not since the broken vase episode. We manage to live our lives without getting in each other's way, but we don't exactly go to the pub together."

"I see. Well, thanks for your time and I'm sorry to have disturbed you on a Saturday. Oh, just one more thing. I was looking at that trampoline over there. Have you just moved it there? Judging by the long grass, it looks as though it's recently been much nearer to your neighbour's fence."

"Yeah, I move it around to keep the lawn fresh. I moved it when we got back on Tuesday but I haven't got round to mowing the lawn since – it's not growing much at the moment."

Sensing that there was nothing to be gained from prolonging their visit and craving an early escape from the turbo-charged junior Footners, Clive signalled his readiness to leave to Acting Inspector Beauregard, thanked the Footners for their time and retreated rapidly to the relative calm of his colleague's car.

"I rather think we should be finding out a bit more about the Footners and their background," Clive suggested to the tight-lipped acting inspector. "I've a feeling that Dean Footner may know more than he's told us. I'd be really interested to know if any local locksmith cut a key for him while he was looking after his neighbour's house. And I'd like to know a bit more about his boss, Mr Edgton, whom you've obviously stumbled across before. Meanwhile, I think it's time we arranged to visit the dead woman's husband."

Dean Footner waited until the detectives' car had pulled away before making a phone call. It was answered quickly. "Hello, it's Dean," he announced. "I thought you should know that there's a new man on the Mary Pullman case… He's an ex-cop called Clive Walsingham and I don't think you should underestimate him."

Six

Saturday 19 August, late afternoon

The dining room at the Follycombe Hotel occupied the large conservatory, which ran almost the entire length of the rear of the building. Although it made a pleasant, capacious and practical dining area, particularly when it was warm enough, outside the wasp season, to throw open the doors that led out onto the terrace, Clare had been unhappy about the huge, echoing open-plan space from the moment she and Clive bought the place. She wanted dining to be a cosy, more intimate affair with diners able to enjoy their own space and not feel that they were on view to the other diners, and to have private conversations without being overheard. So, by interspersing the rows of tables with intricately decorated screens and trellis frameworks festooned with climbing indoor plants, Clare had managed to create a series of artificial nooks and alcoves. No doubt miffed that his flashing smile and easy charm could be seen by fewer people, Jamie Coulton had initially complained about Clare's new layout, claiming that it took him longer to serve the food as he had to weave in and out of the various recesses, but he soon discovered how many more personal conversations he could overhear from behind a screen and his protests soon subsided.

Clare was in the dining room preparing the dinner menus. It wasn't her favourite task, particularly when Peter, the chef, insisted on using obscure, pompous French phrases to describe a traditional British dish, but at least she could shut herself away from other distractions and play one of her CDs of organ music while she moved from one table to another, each immaculately laid and presented in matching shades of pale blue and white. On this particular afternoon, she was playing her music so loudly that she didn't immediately hear the door open and visibly jumped when Simon Verwood suddenly emerged from behind a strategically placed screen and shouted, "Where's Mr Clive?" from only a few feet away.

As she turned round, struggling to recover her composure and still looking startled, she could see immediately that he was greatly agitated about something; he never tried to hide his emotions. He was hopping up and down, causing small pellets of dried mud to drop from his sturdy boots onto the recently cleaned floor, his untidy mane of silver-grey hair looked more wild than usual and his perpetually bloodshot eyes were open so wide that they were threatening to explode from their sockets. He was clutching a pair of secateurs – well-used but razor sharp – which he was brandishing in a wildly erratic fashion, causing Clare to take a precautionary step backwards and, in doing so, nearly tripping over Archie the cat, who was beating a hasty retreat from the kitchen door, having been left in no doubt that Peter found his presence unwelcome.

Though surprised to see him in the hotel on a Saturday and temporarily disconcerted by Simon's thunderous, theatrical entrance, she was not greatly concerned by his histrionic behaviour; in her experience he was often prone to serious over-reaction, especially when he had had too much to drink. Once safely out of range of his flailing arm, she smiled, as she always did, at the way Simon called her husband "Mr Clive" as though he couldn't quite decide whether to be deferential or familiar.

"I'm afraid Clive's not here at the moment," she replied calmly as she switched off her music. "He's off somewhere playing at being a policeman again."

"Is he, indeed? Well I need to speak to somebody," Simon boomed, his excitable demeanour showing no signs of calming.

"Alright, why don't you calm down and tell me what's wrong?" Though well used to Simon's behaviour, Clare hated it when he got melodramatic about something and Clive wasn't around. She well knew that Simon would normally respond better to Clive's firm, calm authority than to her own gentler, more feminine qualities.

"I've… I've just seen this man coming out of the hotel," Simon continued, his arms still flailing about extravagantly.

"It happens quite a lot in a hotel," Clare replied, not quite able to disguise the sarcasm in her voice.

"Yes, but this isn't just any man," Simon continued dramatically. "I asked Debbie about him and she said he was staying in Room 25."

Clare smiled again. Normally Simon could barely conceal his predatory instincts if he discovered a passably presentable single man in the hotel, especially if he was seen drinking on his own in the bar, but not, it seemed, on this occasion. Simon's reaction seemed more one of fear than of pleasure.

"Oh, you must mean Ralph Dalton."

The mention of his name seemed to inflame Simon still further. He clasped both hands to his head, nearly removing part of his ear with the secateurs, and started to pace around.

"Oh, my God, no, no, not Ralph Dalton!" He pointed towards the car park from where Ralph Dalton had recently driven away. "I'm telling you, that man is trouble – big trouble."

"What on earth do you mean?"

"I… I can't say any more. I could be in big trouble already and so could you. You need to get rid of him as quickly as possible. He's… he's very bad news for me and he could be bad news for you and Mr Clive."

"Look, it isn't as simple as that. I don't think we can simply 'get rid of him' just because he's spooked you in some way. We're going to need a bit more information than that and—"

"How long is he here for?" Simon interrupted, still pacing about agitatedly.

"What? Er, I think he's here until next Friday or Saturday; I'm not quite sure. Debbie will be able to tell you—"

"Oh, God, no! That long? Oh, God! I wonder… do you think I could take the next week off? There isn't that much to do in the garden at the moment and I just don't want to be around when Ralph Dalton is here."

Clare hesitated. With a coach party due on Wednesday she couldn't pretend to be heartbroken at the prospect of Simon absenting himself. At least he wouldn't spend every evening in the bar, getting drunk and behaving boorishly, but she didn't feel able to make a decision until she'd discussed it with Clive.

"Listen, Simon, I'll speak to Clive as soon as he gets back. I don't think he'll be very long and I'll ask him to have a word with you. But, for the moment, I suggest you keep out of the way whenever you see Ralph Dalton's car in the car park. If he's here on business, he's probably going to be out during the day, so you should be okay, but it might be better if you keep out of the way during the evening. And by the way, what are you doing here? It's Saturday afternoon and you don't normally work at weekends."

Simon stopped pacing about briefly, scratched his head and looked vaguely around him. "Is it Saturday? Oh dear, I seem to be getting very confused these days."

"Of course, it might help if you didn't get through a bottle of whisky every evening!"

"Yes, quite!" He glanced at his watch. "Still now is not the time to change the habits of a lifetime."

Somewhat taken aback by Simon's ostentatious performance, Clare watched with relief as he left the room, his fist clasped melodramatically to his forehead, like a hammy Shakespearean actor departing the stage, and listened as his theatrical groans receded slowly into the distance. She sighed. Perhaps Debbie had been right to be concerned when Ralph Dalton first arrived. He was beginning to sound like a pernicious presence. She would speak to Clive again when he finally got home.

Seven

Sunday 20 August, morning

Although Acting Inspector Beauregard had taken the precaution of phoning in advance, Gregory Pullman appeared somewhat unprepared when he found the detective and Clive Walsingham standing on his doorstep. He looked behind him into his hallway and then gazed down the road as though hoping that an unexpected visitor or sudden mishap would provide him with an excuse to deny the two men access to his house.

"Oh, I suppose you'd better come in," he said grudgingly and led the way through into the tidy living room of his 1950s house. Clive Walsingham glanced quickly around the room as he settled into the armchair that Gregory Pullman had gestured him towards.

The room was decorated with the kind of swirling floral wallpaper that contemporary interior design experts would call dated, and a couple of cheaply reproduced rural prints hung from the walls. On a solid wooden table beneath the bay window, Gregory Pullman had spread out what looked like a cricket scoring book, together with a pocket calculator, a couple of pencils, an eraser and a neatly arranged collection of lined notepaper on which he was obviously working. Framed photographs filled the window sill and mantelpiece but, as far as Clive could see, they were of members of a cricket team – there were no photographs of either Gregory or Mary Pullman or any other members of the family. Clive tugged his earlobe – it was a mannerism he had developed whenever he was trying to arrange his thoughts into some kind of coherent pattern – as he mulled over what he was seeing. Maybe Gregory Pullman had quickly erased all trace of Mary Pullman's presence once he heard that her body had been found, or maybe he knew that she was never going to return as soon as she went missing.

Gregory Pullman was of medium build. His dark brown hair, greying at the temples, was thinning, he sported a pair of spectacles in heavy, dark brown frames and he had a neat moustache that was conspicuously greyer than his hair. The deep lines on his face suggested a man who took life seriously. He was wearing a white shirt, open at the neck, a baggy, brown knitted cardigan and grey trousers. While Acting Inspector Beauregard settled into an armchair next to Clive, Gregory Pullman sat in an upright chair next to the table where he had been working.

At Clive's suggestion, and to avoid Caspar Beauregard displaying any further signs of disgruntlement at being sidelined, the acting detective inspector, who was at least vaguely familiar to Gregory Pullman, commenced the questioning. He began quietly, almost apologetically.

"I'm sorry to bother you again, especially on a Sunday, but my colleague, Mr Walsingham, has recently joined the investigation into your wife's, er, death and he would like to check a few facts…"

Gregory Pullman pointedly looked at his watch and then glanced across at his scoring book and sheets of paper. "Yes, well, I hope this won't take long. I'm scoring for Buckham Village Cricket Club this afternoon. And we've got our annual general meeting soon so I was hoping to spend a bit of time working out the club averages and preparing my annual report and summary of results."

Clive, who, in his youth, had been a fast bowler of considerable potential, seized upon Gregory Pullman's comments. "You're involved with Buckham Village Cricket Club?"

Gregory Pullman forced a half-smile. "Yes, I do the scoring for them every weekend."

"Ah I see. I must get along to see them play one of these days. I see you're using the old 'pencil and paper' method. You don't use a computer to compile the averages?"

"Er, no, I've always just used a calculator and done everything else by hand. I think I'm a bit set in my ways."

"Yes, of course; I see. Anyway, we'll try not to keep you long and we're sorry to intrude on your grief." Clive tried to sound appropriately sympathetic.

Gregory Pullman shrugged. "I'll be honest with you; Mary and I weren't close. Over the years, we gradually grew apart and, although we lived under the same roof, we went our own way and followed our own interests."

"I see. But you didn't separate or file for divorce?"

Gregory Pullman shrugged again. "There was no point, really. There was no-one else involved, as far as I knew – no third parties – and this house was perfectly big enough for the two of us. We didn't have any big arguments or anything; we just ran out of things to talk about."

"So tell me a bit about your wife. What kind of person was she?"

Gregory Pullman sighed heavily. "Well, to be honest, she wasn't the easiest of people. She could be quite obsessive and pretty abrasive when she wanted to be – and she often did."

"She fell out with people?"

"All the time! For example, she had a big argument with one of our neighbours a year or so ago. I can't remember what it was about now, but there was a lot of shouting and I think the police got involved. And she was organising a petition to fight the plans for turning the disused quarry at Fearnley into some kind of theme park. I think she got a couple of abusive phone calls about that and a letter or two that seemed to upset her."

"She was due to attend a protest meeting about the plans for the quarry, in Buckham Village Hall, on the night she disappeared," Acting Inspector Beauregard added, importantly. "The main access road to the quarry runs through Buckham and feelings were running high. Nobody wanted the volume of traffic that a theme park would have generated, jamming up the village—"

"I see," Clive replied. "She was expected at the meeting?"

"Yes, I believe so," the acting inspector confirmed.

"And did she turn up?"

"No!"

"Did she contact anyone to say that she wouldn't be there?"

"No-one that we've spoken to."

"And the owner of the quarry is Richard Edgton?"

"That's right!" Acting Inspector Beauregard replied, barely able to conceal the contempt in his voice.

"So we can assume that Mary Pullman was not the best of friends with Richard Edgton. I take it someone spoke to him at the time of her disappearance?" Clive asked innocently.

"Of course," Acting Inspector Beauregard's response was edgy; he suspected that Clive was patronising him again. "DI

Morris spoke to him at the time. He denied any involvement and we couldn't find anything to link him to the disappearance. Of course, we were only investigating a disappearance at the time, not a murder."

"Mmm, so maybe not the highest priority," Clive reflected as he turned to Gregory Pullman, who was showing signs of disinterest. "I take it your wife was retired."

Gregory Pullman scratched his head. It was more a mannerism than an indication that he was thinking hard about his answer. "Yes, that's right. She worked as a cashier in the local bank – Nicholls Bank. When she was a bit younger, she worked in the bank's head office as a financial adviser – she was always good with figures; it's about the only thing we had in common. But, as she got older, she decided that she wanted a bit less responsibility and the bank agreed to her transferring to her local branch as a cashier. She retired about four years ago."

"And how did she spend her time?"

"You mean when she wasn't going around looking for trouble and upsetting people?"

Clive nodded while trying to stifle his highly developed instinct to laugh.

"She read a lot. She used the local library and was a member of a book club. History was her passion... and witchcraft, of course! And she liked pottering in the garden – growing hemlock and deadly nightshade, most probably – and she spent quite a lot of time researching her family history; it was one of her many obsessions. She was probably trying to prove she was descended from royalty, or witches. She spent quite a lot of time on her laptop and making notes in her exercise book."

"Yes, that's right," Acting Inspector Beauregard agreed, nodding enthusiastically. He was keen to make a telling contribution to his colleague's investigation. He reached into a cardboard box that he had brought with him and which he had placed by his feet. "I've gathered up all her personal possessions that I thought might help us to get to the bottom of why she was murdered. There's not much here, to be honest. It's mainly her books, some paperwork on the quarry that she was gathering, Richard Edgton's outline proposal for a theme park and a copy of the petition she'd been organising – we've checked some of the names, but nothing very promising. And this is the exercise book she was using to make notes on her family history research." Acting Inspector Beauregard brandished the dog-eared, spiral-bound notebook and offered it to Clive, who quickly flipped through it.

"What was her maiden name?" Clive asked.

"Borgia!" Gregory Pullman replied flippantly, before quickly correcting himself. "It was Hayward, actually."

"I see. May I hang on to this for the moment?"

"Of course," Gregory Pullman and Caspar Beauregard replied in unison.

Clive turned to Gregory Pullman again. "You said that she'd had a letter or two that upset her when she was organising her petition about the quarry?"

"Yes, that's right. She mentioned it over breakfast one day, but I never saw the letters and I don't know who they were from."

Clive looked quizzically at Acting Inspector Beauregard. "And there was no sign of the letters when you searched her room?"

The Acting Inspector looked thoughtful. "No, we didn't find anything. At least, I don't think so. DI Morris was in charge when we first searched her room."

Clive turned back to Gregory Pullman again. "And you mentioned some abusive phone calls."

Gregory Pullman waved a hand airily. "Yes; she'd said she had a couple but didn't say who made them and she didn't tell me what they said."

"And nothing was reported to the police?"

"We have no record of any reports," Acting Inspector Beauregard confirmed, rather formally.

"Now, Mr Pullman, perhaps you could tell me about the day your wife disappeared, if you would."

Gregory Pullman shrugged again. "What is there to tell?" he replied unhelpfully.

"Well, for a start, do you remember what she was wearing?"

Gregory Pullman scratched his head again. "I told Inspector Morris all I could remember, which wasn't much. She was up in her bedroom for a while before she went out. I only heard her go out – I didn't see her – so she could have been wearing anything, really."

"We believe she was wearing a dark blue jacket – it wasn't in her room – but that's about all we know for sure," Acting Inspector Beauregard added. "We noticed at the time that she had recently bought quite a few new clothes. A couple of dresses in her wardrobe still had their price tags attached."

"I see. Did she say where she was going or how long she'd be?"

"No," Gregory Pullman replied emphatically. "She often popped out, but I never asked where she was going. As I said, we led separate lives, really. I think she might have said that she'd be two or three hours, but I can't really remember."

"She drove a car?"

"Yes," Acting Inspector Beauregard replied. "A silver-grey hatchback; we've got all the details – make, model, registration number. We circulated them at the time, but there hasn't been a single sighting that we know of."

"What time did she leave the house?"

Gregory Pullman exhaled. "Not too sure; it was just after lunch, probably around 1.30ish, I think."

"Did she say if she was going to meet anyone?"

"No, but then she never told me where she was going or if she was going to meet anyone, and I never asked."

"Was she behaving any differently from usual before she left?"

"No. I'm sure she was just as cantankerous as usual."

"Did she take anything with her?"

Acting Inspector Beauregard exchanged glances with Gregory Pullman before he replied. "We think she must've taken her laptop with her. It wasn't here when we searched the place and we know she had one; plus her mobile phone, her diary, her handbag with her purse and her debit and credit cards. And before you ask, they haven't been used since she disappeared."

"And there have been no sightings of her between the time she disappeared and when her body was found last week – no letters, texts, emails, phone calls?"

"Absolutely nothing!"

"And when did you report her missing?"

Gregory Pullman scratched his head. "The following morning – there was no sign of her and when I checked her room; her bed hadn't been slept in."

"You waited until the following morning?"

"Yes," Gregory Pullman replied defiantly. "I've already told you, we led separate lives and had separate bedrooms. I think she had mentioned going to the protest meeting at the village hall that evening, so I wasn't worried when she didn't show up. I thought the meeting would probably finish after I'd gone to bed, especially if Mary was allowed to speak her mind. I go to bed quite early as a rule and she wasn't always in when I went to bed, but she was always there the next morning; until that particular day."

"Alright." Clive slapped his knee with his hand. He was getting frustrated. The discussion with Gregory Pullman was, at best, stilted and he seemed unable or unwilling to offer any particularly illuminating insight into his wife or her disappearance. "Alright," he repeated. "We are now investigating a murder, so tell me, Mr Pullman, can you think of anyone who would want her murdered?"

Gregory Pullman shook his head slowly. "Well, she'd made a fair few enemies over the years, but would anyone want to murder her? I don't know. I suppose Richard Edgton might have wanted her out of the way – she was being a bit of a nuisance to him over his quarry and he's the kind of man who would be able to recruit an efficient hit-man if he wanted to – but apart from…" His voice tailed off.

"You mentioned a neighbour?"

"Ah yes! Martin Carslake. She and he were always having an argument about something or other, but I don't see him as a murderer. He's always seemed quite pleasant to me – not violent in any way."

"What about your family?"

"We've got two daughters, Sarah and Alice. Sarah lives in Bailbridge, about twenty miles away. Alice is in Cambridge these days. The inspector has got their addresses and phone numbers. We keep in touch, but we're not especially close."

"And how did they get on with their mother?"

"Let's put it this way. They were both quite keen to move away as soon as they could, but there wasn't a major row or anything – they just didn't like her very much."

"And what about you?"

"Me?" Gregory Pullman looked briefly shocked, but his expression soon turned to one of evasiveness. "I, er, er, well, I didn't always get along with her, but why would I want to murder her?"

"Why indeed, but when a woman is murdered, it's often her husband or partner who's guilty – there's usually a good motive and plenty of opportunity. Where were you last weekend?"

"I was here." Gregory Pullman sounded resentful. "I scored for the cricket club both days. We were at home on Saturday and playing away at Morstock on Sunday. The club will confirm that."

"I assume they were afternoon matches?" Clive asked. Gregory Pullman nodded. "So what about the mornings?"

"I was here on my own, enjoying a bit of peace and quiet, like I was this morning until you turned up. I wandered down to the White Horse for lunch both days; it's my normal routine, I'm not very proficient in the kitchen. The landlord will confirm I was there, I'm sure."

"Do you drive?"

"Yes, my car's outside."

"And do you work?"

"No, I retired a couple of years ago."

"What did you do?"

"I was an estate agent."

"Where were you based?"

"I worked for, er, Blaby and Quixhill in Morstock."

"Ah, that's interesting. As you know, we found your wife's body in the garden of a Mr and Mrs Adamson – Gareth and Elizabeth. They live in Morstock; do you know them at all?"

"N-no." Gregory Pullman hesitated. "As I told the inspector here, I don't recognise their names at all and I can't think of any reason why Mary would be in Morstock. I don't think there was anybody there that she knew."

*

There had been a clammy oppressiveness about Gregory Pullman's house, and Clive exhaled with relief as he and Acting Inspector Beauregard stepped outside into the warm sunshine.

"Why don't you tell me about Mary Pullman's argument

with Martin Carslake?" Clive suggested as they walked the few yards to his front door. "Gregory Pullman said the police had been called." He looked quizzically at the acting inspector.

"What? Oh, oh, yes," Acting Inspector Beauregard replied after some hesitation. "It was Constable Pawlett who went to see her; you haven't met her yet, have you?" Acting Inspector Beauregard asked with a slight smirk. "Now, I'd need to check my notes, but, as I recall, Mary Pullman complained that her neighbour used to spy on her when she was getting undressed in front of the bedroom window. She claimed he even took photographs of her. We, that is Constable Pawlett, interviewed Martin Carslake and he confirmed that she used to stand, naked, at her bedroom window. He claimed she was deliberately trying to provoke him for some reason. We even confiscated his camera, but there were no pictures of her on the card, so we dropped the…"

*

Martin Carslake was a tall, thin, athletic-looking man with an unruly shock of ochre hair. His appearance, though casual, had a well-heeled look to it, his pale blue cotton shirt neatly matching his flawlessly laundered casual trousers.

Like Gregory Pullman, he seemed less than pleased to see Acting Inspector Beauregard and Clive Walsingham standing on his doorstep but politely invited them in. He ushered them into his smartly decorated, obsessively neat, starkly furnished lounge and waved his hand in the direction of a pair of matching armchairs, upholstered in a black synthetic material, while he perched on a low, swivel-topped stool, apparently upholstered in the same material.

"I take it you're here to talk about Mary Pullman," he observed with an air of resignation.

"Yes, that's right, I'm helping Inspector Beauregard with his enquiries," Clive replied, glancing around the masculine-looking room. "Do you live here on your own?"

"Afraid so! I'm divorced, you see. I have a, er, lady friend who comes to stay when she's in the area and my two sons pop in to visit from time to time, usually when they're short of money."

"I see. Anyway, I'll get to the point. Your neighbour, Gregory Pullman has told us that you and his wife had a bit of an argument. As I understand it, she accused you of spying on her through her bedroom window."

Martin Carslake chuckled as he gently swivelled his stool from side to side. "I wouldn't call it spying exactly – quite the reverse, really. You see, I like to potter in my garden when the weather is kind; it helps to keep me fit – that's where I was going when you called. Anyway, I was pretty sure she used to look out for me from her bedroom window; she could see a lot of my garden from up there. And, as soon as I ventured into my garden, she'd quite often do something to attract my attention – slamming the window shut, or making a sudden movement and I'd instinctively look up and there she'd be at the window, stark naked and staring out at me. It wasn't the prettiest of sights, if I'm being honest, and I found it quite unnerving. I tried going out into the garden at different times of day, but it didn't seem to make much difference – she was usually there with that defiant look on her face. I got so fed up with it that, in the end, I got my camera and pretended to take some photographs of her. That's when she reported me."

Clive looked across to Acting Inspector Beauregard, who was staring out of the window and seemingly taking little interest in the dialogue.

"And what did the police say and do when they spoke to you?"

"Oh, it was a rather frigid woman detective, if I remember correctly. She confiscated my computer and my camera, which I thought was a bit heavy-handed, but the police didn't find anything suspicious, of course, so they returned my stuff and dropped the case. Incidentally, I don't remember getting an apology…" He paused and looked towards Acting Inspector Beauregard, but he continued to stare out of the window.

"Why do you think she was doing what she did?" Clive asked.

"Good question. She knew I lived on my own and it was common knowledge that her marriage was over in all but name. Maybe it was a genuine 'come-on', but it seems unlikely. You see, she started disporting herself just after we'd had a row over her fir tree."

"Her fir tree?"

"Oh, I cut some branches back, as I was entitled to do because they were overhanging my garden, but she complained that I'd ruined the shape of the tree. She got very aggressive. Maybe her, erm, displays at the window were her way of trying to unsettle me."

"And after she reported you and the police, er, came round, did her behaviour change?"

"Eventually it did, but I suspect that was mainly because I made sure I never looked up at her bedroom window, no matter how hard she tried to attract my attention. Sometimes, when I was out in the garden, I felt sure she was standing there, naked, at the window with that bolshie look on her face, but I didn't dare look up. Anyway, I think she just got bored and gave up eventually."

"You said it was 'common knowledge' that her marriage was over. How do you mean?"

"The rows mainly; you could hear her and Gregory shouting and swearing at each other all evening sometimes – I don't know what about. And I'm pretty sure there was some violence, but I couldn't prove anything. I remember Mary shouting, 'Ow, ow, ow, you're hurting me,' on a couple of occasions, but I'd learnt not to get involved."

"I see. Were you asked, at the time, where you were on the day Mary Pullman disappeared – April 5th?"

"I was here, I think. I don't remember the day as anything special. It was only when the police turned up the following day – DI Norris, or Morris, or some such – that I realised something was wrong."

"Now, as I think you know, Mary Pullman's body turned up in a back garden in Morstock last Wednesday. Have you any idea why it was found there?"

"God, no! Mary Pullman and I hadn't spoken for months before she disappeared. I've no idea what she did with her time when she wasn't standing up at her window annoying me."

"And we think she was probably murdered about three or four days before her body was found. That would be around the Saturday or Sunday of last week. Where were you then?"

Martin Carslake had continued to casually swivel his stool from side to side as the interview had developed, but now, suddenly, he pressed his feet against the floor, stopping his stool from swivelling, and leaned forward aggressively. "Do you think I killed her?"

"We have to explore all possibilities."

"I was here. My, er, lady friend came to stay last weekend. We, er, didn't get out much, if you know what I mean."

"And your lady friend can corroborate your statement?"

"Now, look here!" For the first time, Martin Carslake looked rattled. He jumped to his feet, towering threateningly over Clive, and wagged a long, bony finger in his face. "It's not that simple. I mean, her husband doesn't know she was here for a start and it could get quite awkward."

Clive smiled. "I'll be as discreet as I can be, but, at this stage, you are a suspect and I'll need to know her name. Where does she live?"

"Morstock!"

*

As they left the house, Clive stopped momentarily and rested his hand firmly on his colleague's hunched shoulder. "Is there somewhere quiet we can go and share our thoughts?"

"We can go back to the police station; it'll be—"

"No, no, not a bloody police station!" Clive protested. "I hope never to see the inside of another police station. Do you want to come back to the hotel for an hour? I can guarantee you some delicious cakes."

Eight

Sunday 20 August, early afternoon

While Acting Inspector Beauregard made his lugubrious way out onto the hotel terrace, which was swathed in warm afternoon sunshine, Clive Walsingham stopped at the reception desk, wrote something on a piece of paper and handed it surreptitiously to Clare. "Darling, would you mind humouring me and checking that on the local street atlas and maybe just looking it up on the internet?"

Clare narrowed her grey-green eyes and stared intently at her husband. "You're really enjoying being a policeman again, aren't you?"

"Me? Oh God, no!" Clive protested. "You see, the great thing is, I'm not a policeman, so I can have a bit of fun, mainly at Dick's expense, while trying to help him solve his crime – all of the fun and none of the responsibility."

Clare seemed unconvinced by Clive's protestations, so he fled the scene and made his languid way onto the terrace, clutching Mary Pullman's notebook, and sat down opposite

Acting Inspector Beauregard, stretching his long legs out to the side of the stout, wooden table that separated the two men.

"So, what's your theory, Dick?" Clive asked as Acting Inspector Beauregard emitted one of his mournful sighs and mopped his perspiring brow with his grubby handkerchief.

"Oh, I don't think anything has changed. I've always thought that Richard Edgton was behind Mary Pullman's murder. I mean, she was a vociferous opponent of his plans for the quarry and she turned up dead in the garden of one of his former employees and next door to one of his present employees. It's just that we haven't been able to prove it yet! That's why I asked you to—"

"Tell me more about him," Clive interrupted. "His name seems to crop up a lot."

"Yes, and you'll hear a lot more about him too. He's a very rich and very powerful businessman. He moved here from London and came with a shady reputation. He has fingers in a lot of pies, mainly in the leisure industry – theme parks, leisure centres, golf centres, that kind of—"

"You don't like him?"

"No, not at all, but then I'm not sure who does. He's a villain of the most dangerous kind. We're pretty sure that a lot of his business dealings are crooked in some way or another. DI Morris and I spent a lot of time investigating his affairs, but we could never get enough evidence. Whenever we thought we had a good witness, he would buy them off or threaten them into silence. We thought he was bribing the more influential members of the local council's planning committee, but, again, we could never prove anything. And he's got some pretty intimidating heavies working for him – you've met one already."

"Dean Footner?"

"That's right, and there are more where he came from. I wouldn't fancy the chances of anyone like Mary Pullman who tried to take him on. She would have been way out of her depth and he is seriously sinister. He wouldn't hesitate to eliminate people like her if they made too much of a nuisance of—"

"Mmmm, but that's the problem, isn't it, Dick?" Clive announced, half-turning in his chair, resting his elbows on the table and looking earnestly at his colleague. "I mean, from your description of Richard Edgton, if he had wanted Mary Pullman out of the way, he'd have got one of his heavies to make her disappear without trace. But let's just consider the facts for a moment." Clive pressed the fingers of both hands together, stared thoughtfully at his colleague and half-smiled. This was the "bit of fun" he had just mentioned to Clare. "According to all the evidence you have, Mary Pullman was murdered about a week ago and yet she disappeared on 5th April; that's over four months ago and, in that time, there have been no sightings, no phone calls, no emails, no texts, nothing. There has been no trace of her car and nobody has tried to use her credit cards. So where has she been?"

Acting Inspector Beauregard sat back in his chair a little uncomfortably and averted his gaze. "Er, well, the most likely explanation is that Richard Edgton was holding her captive somewhere."

"Yes, that's possible, I agree," Clive acknowledged. "But why would he do that?"

"Perhaps he wanted to hold her to ransom or—"

Clive shook his head. "I'm not convinced, Dick. If he wanted to hold her to ransom, and I don't see why he would if he just wanted to get rid of her, why was no ransom demand received? And who would pay a ransom for her safe return? Gregory Pullman was probably glad to see the back of her and he didn't strike me as someone who could raise a lot of cash to pay a substantial ransom anyway. And then, out of the blue, four months after she disappears, she turns up neatly arranged and naked in a stranger's back garden – why would Richard Edgton do that? Why would he go to so much trouble? There was no evidence of sexual assault and nothing to connect Gareth Adamson with the murder, so it makes no sense."

While Clive had been talking, Jamie Coulton had arrived, almost silently, carrying a tray of tea neatly balanced on one arm and a plate of assorted cakes on the other. He placed them both carefully on the table, winked at Clive, produced a folded piece of paper from his pocket and handed it to Clive.

"Clare asked me to give you this," he beamed.

"Thank you, Jamie," Clive replied before unfolding the piece of paper and scrutinising its contents. He was about to say something to the acting inspector, but when he looked up, he saw that Jamie Coulton was still hovering at his shoulder as though expecting a tip or, more probably, trying to eavesdrop on the conversation. "Thank Clare for me," Clive added, hoping that his hint would be sufficient to persuade Jamie to leave. It wasn't. "Now, please, Jamie," Clive added firmly. Jamie Coulton smiled fleetingly, but as he turned and walked back towards the conservatory, occasionally glancing back over his shoulder, Clive noticed that he was frowning with unusual intensity.

"I just don't see how Gareth Adamson could be involved," Acting Inspector Beauregard mused, returning to Clive's theme. "We know he was on holiday when Mary Pullman was murdered, so—"

"Well, that's not quite true, is it?" Clive gently contradicted his colleague as he poured the tea while Acting Inspector Beauregard made his first foray into the generously loaded plate of cakes. "You know that he and his wife flew out of the country and you know where they stayed in Sorrento and you know they flew back last Tuesday. But have you checked to see if Gareth Adamson, or his wife for that matter, made an unscheduled return trip last weekend? They could have flown here and back in a day, just about."

The acting inspector looked doleful – something at which he excelled – and shook his head.

"And the same could be true of Dean Footner for that matter," Clive continued. "He said the family were away for a few days at Radholme, but that's only, what, fifty miles away? He could easily have driven back here, disposed of Mary Pullman and returned to Radholme within the day. And, despite what he said, he might have had a key to Gareth Adamson's house cut while they were looking after it. And he's got a big workshop in his garden; he could have kept Mary Pullman locked up in there."

Acting Inspector Beauregard had been hell-bent on devouring a large slice of chocolate cake, but, on hearing Clive's latest piece of speculation, he placed what was left on his plate and became suddenly, strangely animated.

"But Dean Footner works for Richard Edgton!" he exclaimed, slapping his hand on the table for emphasis. "So Richard Edgton could be behind the murder after all!"

"Mmmm, maybe," Clive replied enigmatically. "So I take it you'd be quite happy to go and interview Richard Edgton again." Clive made the enquiry sound like an instruction.

"I intend to!"

"Good! And it might be worth searching Dean Footner's workshop."

"I will, I will. I'll arrange for a search warrant." Acting Inspector Beauregard seemed positively buoyant by his own miserable standards and he attacked what was left of his slice of chocolate cake with renewed zest. Clive watched him devour his way through the cake with an expression that was both amused and repulsed. Then he spoke. "Still, we mustn't close our minds to other lines of enquiry."

"Meaning?"

"Well, I accept that Richard Edgton may have had a motive of sorts to murder Mary Pullman and I imagine Dean Footner would be more than capable of it, but, from what I've heard, she was no more than an interfering busybody. I'm sure Richard Edgton must have more powerful enemies than Mary Pullman."

"Lord Westleigh for one," Caspar Beauregard conceded, reluctantly. "He owns Fearnley Farm, which is next door to the quarry and, as you might imagine, he's made it very clear that he opposes any kind of development there."

"Right! So, unlike Mary Pullman, I imagine he's got enough power and influence to make life really difficult for Richard Edgton, but he hasn't been murdered, has he?" He paused, unable to suppress a mischievous smile, and studied Acting Inspector Beauregard's ever-changing kaleidoscope of facial expressions; mainly gloomy, occasionally elated and often simply perplexed.

"I wonder," Clive continued when his own facial expression had assumed a more enigmatic appearance, "have you considered Mary Pullman's relationship with her husband?"

"How do you mean?" Acting Inspector Beauregard asked quizzically while transferring a slice of Victoria sponge onto his now empty plate.

"Well, if you recall." Clive was trying hard not to sound patronising but wasn't entirely convinced that he was succeeding. "Gregory Pullman said that he and his wife just grew apart; 'we didn't have any big arguments or anything,' he said. But Martin Carslake, on the other hand, told us of heated arguments and, he thought, some physical violence…"

He looked questioningly at Acting Inspector Beauregard over the top of his slice of cake.

"What? Oh, yes, I see," Acting Inspector Beauregard replied doubtfully. "We need to look into that."

"Mmmm. And then, of course, there's Mary Pullman's notebook." Clive picked up the notebook and casually thumbed through the pages.

"Ah, yes, but there was nothing much of interest there," Acting Inspector Beauregard replied dismissively.

"You saw the scribbled note in the margin of one of the pages near the end?"

Acting Inspector Beauregard suddenly seemed to develop a strange fascination with his feet, which he studied intently while continuing to chew, albeit increasingly slowly. Eventually, he swallowed enough cake to enable him to speak without showering his colleague in crumbs.

"I think I might have seen the note," he replied defensively, "but DI Morris told me that he had checked it all out and there was nothing worth following up."

"Really? On what date did Mary Pullman disappear?"

Acting Inspector Beauregard studied his colleague suspiciously, as though he had just asked a trick question. "Ah, em, let me see – it was Wednesday April 5th."

"Correct. And this note in the margin of her notebook reads '*APRIL 5 2 VERNON COURT*'. Now, according to Gregory Pullman, his wife left the house around 1.30 on April 5th and was never seen again." He paused for effect while studying the piece of paper that Jamie Coulton had handed him. "Now it appears that there is an address in Stowbrook called Vernon Court and that would be, what, no more than ten or twelve miles away from Mary Pullman's house? Now we know that she was planning to attend a protest meeting about the quarry in the evening, but what about the afternoon? Isn't it possible that, when she left home, she was heading for 2 Vernon Court, for whatever reason? And you say there is nothing worth following up?"

"Look, you've got to understand," Inspector Beauregard spluttered, his normally ashen face taking on a blotchy, scarlet hue. "I was the junior officer at the time Mary Pullman disappeared. DI Morris told me that he'd been through the notebook and there was nothing worth following up. I didn't know anything different. I… I had no reason to question his judgement…"

Clive went pensive, gazing briefly across the parched lawn towards the rose garden. "I've been a policeman too, Dick, so I know the pressure you work under. When Mary Pullman went missing and didn't turn up, it would have been easy enough to assume that maybe she'd just done a bunk. Her home life was pretty miserable and maybe she just created a new identity for herself somewhere else. Perhaps she scrapped her car or hid it in a secure garage or lock-up somewhere and built a new life for herself. Maybe there was someone else in her life; after all, she'd just bought some new clothes, but you had no evidence and no concrete leads so…" He looked at Acting Inspector Beauregard with another questioning expression.

"I must admit," Acting Inspector Beauregard conceded, "that when our initial enquiries got nowhere and we couldn't get anything on Richard Edgton, she might have slipped to the bottom of the pile and—"

"Highly likely, I'd say! So do you know anything about Vernon Court in Stowbrook?"

"Ah, er, no, not really, but I do know there's been quite a bit of new building on the outskirts. It sounds like it could be part of the *Admirals'* Estate. It's mainly flats and apartments for retired people, I think."

"But you haven't checked on who lives at number two?"

"No, like I said—"

"And I presume you haven't noticed that there are some pages missing from Mary Pullman's notebook?"

"Pardon? How do you know?" The acting inspector's expression had become familiarly saturnine.

"Well, for a start, there are some shreds of torn paper trapped in the spiral binding, and if you read the notes, it's quite clear that one or more pages are missing." He flipped through the pages until he found the entry he was looking for, which he then jabbed at with his long, thin index finger. "Look, here, the last note on this page ends *she had a daughter, Emma, born in…*' and the next page starts *at the end of World War Two, he married…*'. The writing at the top of the right-hand page doesn't follow on from what was written at the bottom of the left-hand one. Something has been torn out."

Uncharacteristically, Acting Inspector Beauregard seemed to be losing his appetite. He placed the half-eaten slice of Victoria sponge on his plate and pushed it slowly away. Clive sensed that he was trying to say something but the words wouldn't come.

"And then, of course," Clive continued, while the detective tried to restore the link between his brain and his mouth. "We must return to Gregory Pullman. You'll recall he told us that he didn't know Gareth and Elizabeth Adamson, yet he told us he had been an estate agent in Morstock. Now I don't know Morstock that well, but it's only a small place, so I doubt that it has more than a couple of estate agents. You remember, Gareth Adamson told us that they moved into their house just under four years ago. It is possible, of course, that they didn't buy it through a local estate agent, but it's also quite possible that Gregory Pullman was involved with the sale. And if he was, why is he pretending he doesn't know Mr and Mrs Adamson?

And while the house was on the market, did Gregory Pullman get a spare key cut? I'm not sure what his reason would have been, of course, but we have to consider the possibility. Do you think that might be worth following up? And then, of course, there's the question of where Mr and Mrs Adamson found the money to go to Sorrento for a couple of weeks and to offer to buy part of Donald and Margaret Holt's garden when he hasn't had a job for four years and she only works part-time at the local supermarket. Do you think it might be worth taking a closer look at their financial situation?"

"God, what a cock-up!" Acting Inspector Beauregard muttered as he hunkered down in his chair as though trying to make himself disappear. "I'm so glad I asked you to help."

Clive smiled a little mischievously. "Do you know, I'm beginning to see why everyone calls you Dick!"

Nine

Monday 21 August, morning

Clive could tell immediately from the look on Clare's expressive face that something was wrong. Her eyes always had a penetrative quality but, this morning, they seemed wider and more intense.

"It's Jamie," she announced as she put her head around the office door. "He's not turned up this morning."

Clive pursed his lips and whistled quietly to himself. "Oh, that's not like him. Have you tried to contact him?"

"Yes, of course. I've phoned him at home, but there's no answer, and his mobile is switched off. And, you may have noticed, he hasn't been quite his usual self recently. Clive, I'm worried."

Clive stood up and placed a protective arm around Clare's slim shoulders. "Yes, I see what you mean. Look, I'm off to meet up with Dick in Stowbrook in a few minutes and I've got to drive past Crowdale. I'll drop by his place and see what I can find out. I'll give you a call. Meanwhile, keep trying his mobile."

"Yes, well, okay." Clare sounded doubtful. "But don't be too long; I'll have to rearrange the schedules and get some extra help in if Jamie doesn't show up soon."

Clive was about to leave when his phone rang. It was the duty sergeant at Stowbrook police station.

"Jamie Coulton asked us to call you," the duty sergeant began. "He's been in one of our cells overnight."

"Bloody hell! What's he done?"

"He got very drunk last night. The landlord at the King's Arms said he'd been drinking heavily all evening and, by closing time, he was barely able to stand and was getting quite abusive. So we collected him and shut him away for his own good. We've cautioned him and he's probably going to face a 'drunk and disorderly' charge."

"Have you let him go?"

"Well, he's still in a pretty bad way and we can't send him home like this. Would you be able to come and pick him up?"

"I suppose I could. I was about to set off to Stowbrook to meet with Acting Inspector Beauregard, so I could drop by, perhaps on the way back."

Clive thought he heard the duty sergeant snigger slightly at the mention of Caspar Beauregard's name, but he couldn't be sure.

*

As Caspar Beauregard had correctly surmised, the *Admirals'* estate, on the outskirts of Stowbrook, was a recently constructed development, consisting of groups of modern bungalows, intended primarily for the retired, built around a number of small communal courtyards. Each bungalow was identical in size and layout, with a small rear garden and a front door opening onto one of the courtyards. Vernon Court, separated from Drake Court by a car park, comprised twelve bungalows, four on each of three sides of the courtyard.

The occupant of number two, the Reverend Gerald Ashburton was thin and, despite his advancing years, had a tall, upright, military bearing. His full head of silver-grey hair was precisely parted and brushed down so severely that it was difficult to detect a hair out of place. His face bore a tolerant, well-disposed appearance and there was the hint of a mischievous sparkle in his elderly, blue eyes. He was wearing a cream shirt, beige jumper and baggy, brown corduroy trousers.

He seemed delighted to discover Clive Walsingham and Caspar Beauregard standing at his front door – a distinct change from the frosty reception they had received elsewhere during their investigation – and cheerfully ushered them into his small living room. As he always did when entering someone's house for the first time, Clive glanced quickly around. The room was relatively sparsely furnished, with no evidence of personal touches, no photographs, mementoes or souvenirs – just countless shelves, all filled to capacity with books, mainly on religious, historical or classical themes.

"Would you like a cup of tea or coffee?" the Reverend Ashburton asked expectantly. "I've just put the kettle on."

Acting Inspector Beauregard, who clearly felt that their visit was an unnecessary waste of valuable police time, looked across at Clive and pulled a disdainful face. Clive smiled. "Yes, that would be great! Coffee, please," he replied as he settled down next to his colleague on the small two-seater sofa.

"How long have you lived here?" he asked, as Gerald Ashburton pottered unseen in his kitchen.

"Let me see, it must be about five years now," the reverend replied in a gentle, articulate tone. "I came here not long after my wife died. The house we had was far too big for me and it had too many memories of one kind or another. These places had just been built so I came over and had a look and I was quite impressed. I must say, I find this place perfectly satisfactory for my needs. It's easy to look after, cheap to maintain and the town centre is within walking distance."

"I'm sorry about your wife," Clive replied.

"Well, yes, thank you. But she hadn't been well for a while, so it was probably for the best; a merciful release, as they say."

The room fell uneasily silent for a moment or two as Caspar Beauregard fidgeted nervously and Gerald Ashburton continued to potter in the kitchen.

"Do you still work?" Clive asked at last.

"Ah, er, no. I haven't worked for a little while now. I've been retired for a few years."

Eventually, the Reverend Ashburton wandered carefully back into the living room with a metal tea tray, on which was balanced a silver coffee pot, a milk jug, and three porcelain cups and saucers which he placed on a low coffee table in front of his two visitors. He then busied himself pouring out three cups of coffee before easing himself, a little stiffly, onto a high-backed chair in front of his antique bureau.

"I hope we made clear why we wanted to see you when we phoned earlier," Acting Inspector Beauregard said, anxious to get to the purpose of their visit as quickly as possible.

"Yes," the Reverend replied gently as he started to stir his coffee, "although, from what you said, I'm not sure I can help you very much."

"We're investigating the disappearance and subsequent murder of a lady called Mary Pullman." As he spoke, Clive was watching Gerald Ashburton carefully and noticed that he briefly stopped stirring his coffee at the mention of Mary Pullman's name.

"Anyway," Clive continued. "We found an entry in a notebook she was using at the time of her disappearance. It read 'APRIL 5 2 VERNON COURT'. April 5th was the day she disappeared."

"Yes, I see," the reverend replied thoughtfully. "Most intriguing, but I'm afraid I can't help you. I don't know this lady and I cannot imagine why she wrote that note. Mind you, I expect there's more than one Vernon Court around."

"Certainly – quite a few in fact – but this is the only one that's within easy distance of where Mary Pullman lived. But then I suppose, in his line of work, a vicar would come into contact with a great many people that he wouldn't necessarily know by name…"

Gerald Ashburton gave a wry smile. "Maybe once, but not now, not around here! As I say, I haven't worked since I came to Stowbrook and these days I have a very small list of acquaintances and this lady, Mary Pullman, isn't – or wasn't – among them. It's a bit of a mystery, isn't it?"

"It certainly looks that way. Did anyone come to see you, or phone you, about Mary Pullman's disappearance in April? A detective inspector, for example?"

"Oh, no, definitely not!" Gerald Ashburton's denial seemed excessively emphatic. "I don't get many visitors these days, so I am sure I would have remembered a policeman coming round."

"Very well, so perhaps I can ask you what you were doing on 5th April." Clive's request sounded uncharacteristically brusque. He felt sure that there must be a connection between Mary Pullman and Gerald Ashburton, but the retired clergyman was giving nothing away and Clive was getting frustrated.

"Ah, well, I'd need to check; it's quite a while ago." Gerald Ashburton half-turned, pulled down the flap on his bureau and reached inside for his diary, which was bound in black cloth. Slowly and methodically, he turned over the pages, holding the diary up in front of him, thus preventing his two visitors from catching sight of any of the entries. Eventually, he appeared to locate the correct page and studied it briefly before slamming the diary closed. "No, it is as I thought. I've got no entry for 5th April at all."

"So you can't tell us anything about Mary Pullman, or why she had this address in her notebook."

Gerald Ashburton smiled, slightly nervously, Clive thought, but he just shrugged and shook his head. Clive looked across at Acting Inspector Beauregard and noticed the merest hint of a smile on his normally down-turned features.

*

"He knows more than he's admitting," Clive remarked quietly as they left the house.

"He seemed quite genuine to me," Acting Inspector Beauregard countered. "No, I think we're wasting our time—"

"Mmmm. Humour me for a few minutes more, would you? I'd quite like to talk to the vicar's neighbours."

The interior of number three Vernon Court was identical in layout to number two but, as it was occupied by an elderly lady, it had a rather more feminine appearance, with pink walls, frilly floral-patterned chair covers and a generous scattering of cushions.

The occupant, Joan Glendale, a short, frail lady, seemed as lonely in her own way as Gerald Ashburton and was more than happy to receive the two men into her modest living room, though she could not disguise her disappointment when they declined her offer of a cup of tea.

"I'm sorry to bother you," Clive began in his usual, gentle way while Acting Inspector Beauregard sighed pointedly, crossed his arms and stared blankly out of the window. "We've got a little puzzle and wondered if you might be able to help."

Joan Glendale chuckled and said, "Oh, good, I like puzzles," before adding more gloomily, "but I'm not very good at them these days – too forgetful, I'm afraid."

"Anything that you can tell us would be helpful, I can assure you. You see, we're investigating a murder and—"

"A murder? How exciting!"

"And the lady who was murdered had written something in her notebook that suggested she might have been planning to visit someone here on the day she disappeared. We thought it might be your neighbour at number two, but—"

"Ah, yes, I saw you arrive. Well, I'm not surprised!" she announced gleefully before chuckling so much that she began to cough wheezily. Clive looked across at Caspar Beauregard, who had stopped staring out of the window and was now taking a keener interest in Joan Glendale's remarks.

"Tell us more," Clive encouraged.

"Well, of course, I'm not one to indulge in idle tittle-tattle…"

"No, of course not, but this is a murder enquiry!"

"Exactly! Now the Reverend Ashburton used to receive a lady visitor, regular as clockwork, every Wednesday afternoon and then, a few months ago, the visits suddenly stopped."

"Can you describe the lady?"

"Not very well, I'm afraid. My eyesight isn't what it was, but I do remember that she always looked very furtive, as though she didn't want to be seen visiting the vicar. She always wore a hat or scarf over her hair – which was dark, I think – and she wore large glasses; sometimes, in the summer, they were dark glasses. I remember, she usually arrived wearing a long blue coat and carrying a handbag and—"

"And did she come by car?"

"Oh, yes. I'm hopeless with makes and models, but it was a small grey car."

"How long did her visits last?"

"Not that long; about an hour or so, I should think." Not wanting her visitors to get the idea that she had been spying on her neighbour, which she had, Joan Glendale tried to sound vague.

"And when did the visits stop?"

"Oooh, let me see, it must be several months ago. Probably around Easter time, I should think."

"Well, that's really helpful. Tell me, how well do you know your neighbour, the Reverend Ashburton?"

"Oooh, not very well at all! I mean, if we bump into each other, he's always very polite and pleasant and he'll always raise his hat, but he never wants to stop and have a little chat. And I know I shouldn't say these things, but he does behave a little mysteriously sometimes. Often he'll go out alone in the evening; a couple of times a week, on average, usually on a Wednesday and a Saturday. He sets off, regular as clockwork, around eight o'clock. He often wears a hat – a trilby kind of hat – which he pulls down low over his eyes. He skulks off towards town and returns a couple of hours later. I've no idea what he does or where he goes. I mean, this is Stowbrook; it's hardly Las Vegas. I wondered if he had a fancy woman somewhere, so I asked him once where he went of an evening, but he didn't really say. He just muttered something about 'things to do, people to see'. He seemed a bit shifty and—"

At that point, Acting Inspector Beauregard's phone rang. Looking flustered, he excused himself and disappeared into the kitchen, returning a few moments later.

"I'm sorry, I'll have to go, I'm afraid," he announced gravely. "Lord Westleigh has just reported that his daughter has gone missing and he wants a senior officer over there straight away."

*

Clive Walsingham was quite shocked by Jamie Coulton's appearance as he sat beside him in the car. When he was at work in the hotel, his appearance was immaculate – well-groomed, gleamingly clean and impeccably laundered – and his demeanour was unfailingly outgoing and charming, often flirtatious and occasionally unctuous. Now, however, his eyes were red-rimmed and heavy, his face was stubbly and his dark hair was bedraggled. His casual clothes were crumpled and stained and his demeanour was surly. His breath smelled strongly of stale beer.

"So what's been going on?" Clive asked, as he drove back from Stowbrook.

"That's my business," Jamie replied sourly.

"Well, yes, that's true to an extent, I suppose," Clive conceded. "But it becomes my business if you're not at work when you should be."

Jamie Coulton sighed heavily. "Alright, if you must know, Zoe has walked out on me. We had a bit of a bust-up and she moved out. I thought if I turned on the charm, I could persuade her to come back, but when I phoned her yesterday after I finished work, she made it very clear that we were finished. So I went down the pub to drown my sorrows and, well, let's say I got a bit carried away."

"That's one way of putting it. You were 'carried away' by a couple of policemen, from what I've heard. So what was your row about?"

"Oh, the usual," Jamie replied bitterly. "I'd been late back from work a couple of times and Zoe assumed I'd been seeing somebody else. Now I'll admit that there was a time when that might have been the case, but not anymore, not lately. But Zoe had made her mind up and that was it!"

"So why were you late back?"

There was a long uncomfortable silence before Jamie spoke. "I, er, I, er, was meeting someone. I can't say who and I can't say what about. I couldn't tell Zoe and I really can't tell you."

Jamie held both hands up to his face and started to sob.

Ten

Monday 21 August, early afternoon

There was a certain aura about the Earl of Westleigh. It had nothing to do with any kind of imposing physical presence – he was barely over medium height with a middle-aged plumpness, a consequence, no doubt, of years of lavish business lunches. His hair was grey and wavy at the front, but no more than wispy at the back, revealing a large natural tonsure. His skin, regularly exposed to the hot Mediterranean sun through numerous summers, had a tanned, leathery texture. But there was something about him that rendered those who surrounded him reverential, to the point of being awestruck. His evident aristocratic breeding contributed in no small part to this aura, of course, and he was clearly accustomed to being the centre of attention, surrounded, as he usually was, by a coterie of deferential flunkeys. But he also had the confident, assured manner and easy charm of a successful and respected businessman, able to command a rapt audience with a polished flair and gentle good humour, always delivered in rich, clipped tones.

Acting Detective Inspector Beauregard was ushered, with hushed reverence, into the large, opulently decorated library, where the Earl was standing importantly in the middle of the room, fiddling anxiously with a chunky signet ring on his little finger, while nearby, Anthony Granard, his private secretary, loitered expectantly. A couple of young men in working clothes hovered uncertainly on the periphery of the room. One was a tall, thick-set young man with a mop of untidy fair hair and affable expression, the other was shorter and thinner with closely cropped dark hair, and a restless demeanour.

"I came as soon as I could," Acting Inspector Beauregard began, apologetically. "You've reported that your daughter has gone missing."

The Earl greeted him with a brief nod and a perfunctory wave of his aristocratic hand and gestured towards an empty chair, close to the large marble fireplace. He well knew that the necessary police protocols and procedures would have to be observed, however tiresome and bureaucratic they seemed to be, but he would make it clear that he expected rapid, decisive action from the acting inspector.

"Yes, that's right," the Earl confirmed calmly, as he sat down opposite the anxious policeman, who had already opened his notebook and was starting to write. "She was out riding her horse on the estate, early yesterday evening, after the public had all left, and Matthew here," he waved his chubby, well-manicured hand in the direction of the taller of the two young men, "he's one of the estate workers, found her horse wandering alone up near the deer park. The horse was fully saddled up, but there was no sign of Lucy." Matthew nodded respectfully, if a little hesitantly.

"Lucy – your daughter's called Lucy?"

"Yes, Lucy Jeffries, that's her married name. She lives down at the lodge with her husband, Alex."

Acting Inspector Beauregard glanced doubtfully across at the other, shorter, more restless young man. "And you are Alex?" he asked.

"What? Good heavens, no!" the Earl replied with a mixture of disdain and amusement. "Alex will be out in his Land Rover looking for Lucy. He's terribly distraught. They've got two young children too, so you can imagine how they must all be feeling. No, this is Tom Chewton, the groom. He saddled up Lucy's horse, as usual, before she set off."

"I see and what time was that?"

"About six thirty," Lord Westleigh stated firmly before looking towards the groom for confirmation. "That was her usual routine."

"So she rides at the same time every evening?"

"Most evenings when she's here. Sometimes she's away on business or she and Alex are visiting friends, or they're hosting a gathering, but she rides most evenings when she can. She finds early evenings are the best time. The estate is relatively quiet at that time of day and she can fit in a bit of riding between finishing work, having dinner and spending some time with the children before they go to bed. I don't want to imply that she has obsessive rituals or anything, you understand, but she does quite enjoy her routines, which makes her disappearance all the more worrying."

"And when did, er, Matthew, spot her horse?"

The Earl looked across at Matthew and, with a brief wave of his hand, invited him to comment. Matthew shuffled uneasily and looked down before replying, stumbling over his words in his anxiety to say what he had to say as quickly as possible.

"Er, I r-r-reckon it was about eight o'clock. I was on my way back to my, er, my place, my, er, cottage. I live on the estate, see, and I noticed Lucy's, er, Mrs Jeffries' horse, grazing beside the lane, but there was no sign of Mrs Jeffries."

"Lord Westleigh said you found her horse near the deer park. Was that part of the estate where she usually rode?"

"She didn't have a specific route," Lord Westleigh interrupted, "but it wouldn't have been unusual for her to be riding there."

"And who did you report what you'd seen to?" Acting Inspector Beauregard asked Matthew.

"I phoned Alex, er, Mr Jeffries and he came straight away."

"Yes, and then Alex phoned through to Anthony." The Earl took over the narrative, nodding towards Anthony Granard, who was still hovering attentively, several feet behind him.

"But he didn't speak to you?"

"Me? No, not then, not immediately! I was still at my villa in France. Anthony phoned me as soon as he heard the news and I flew back straight away. God, this is a terrible business!"

"And there's been no sign of your daughter since she disappeared."

"Absolutely nothing – no sight, no sound!" There was a hint of irritation in the Earl's fruity tones. "You may assume we would have told you if there had been."

"Of, course," Acting Inspector Beauregard replied quietly. "Has anything like this happened before?"

"No, nothing at all! As I said, Lucy likes her routines. She is very ordered and very reliable. She and Alex do an excellent job, as a matter of fact."

"What is their job exactly?"

"They run my chain of garden centres; I expect you've heard of them – Chartfield Nurseries. Alex is managing director. He has been for the past five years or so and Lucy is in charge of all the publicity and the marketing – she seems to have a flair for it. The business was in a mess after, well, let's just say it was in a mess when they took over and they've really turned it around."

"I see," Acting Inspector Beauregard replied. Like many others before him, he was beginning to feel intimidated by the force of Lord Westleigh's personality and bearing. "Well, er, I trust it is okay for my men to search the estate. There must be plenty of buildings, stables, barns, outbuildings, cottages."

"You must do what you think is right," the Earl conceded benignly, "but I can assure you you'll be wasting your time. My people have been all over the estate and they've searched all the buildings. In any event, we all know what's happened."

"And what has happened?" Acting Inspector Beauregard sounded puzzled.

"She's been kidnapped by that unprincipled rogue, Richard Edgton."

Acting Inspector Beauregard nodded, knowingly. "Do you have any evidence?" he asked hopefully.

"None at all, but it must be him."

"Why do you say that?"

"Look, Inspector, it is common knowledge that I dislike the man intensely. He's a jumped-up petty gangster from London who thinks he can make his dubious living by depriving decent and respectable people of their livelihoods and riding roughshod over their protestations. He bullies and intimidates people until he gets what he wants. Frankly, I'm surprised that your people haven't been able to put him away. You know, ever since he bought Fearnley quarry, he's been trying to redevelop it in some inappropriate shape or form. First it was some kind of quarry museum, and then, when that fell through, he proposed a ghastly theme park. It was basically the original plan for the quarry museum but made bigger, tackier and noisier. Well, the fact is that I own the farm next door to this damned quarry. I've got a valuable trout farm there and some nationally important rare breeds and I couldn't have a damned theme park next door, with all the noise and disruption blighting my land. And that wouldn't be the end of it either. Once he'd ruined my farm, he'd try to browbeat me into selling it at a ridiculous knockdown price and turn it into another one of his exclusive golf centres – it would be Carlow Bridge Farm all over again. No, no, I couldn't have that, so, last week, I asked Anthony to set up a meeting with him and to offer to buy the quarry from him."

"And he refused?"

"He called my offer derisory. Now I do not consider Richard Edgton to be worthy of a charitable donation, but I did offer a fair market price. Anthony, you take over."

As though emotionally distraught by the conversation, the Earl reached into the breast pocket of his tweed jacket, extracted a linen handkerchief and dabbed his eyes, while his private secretary continued the account, with frequent glances towards his employer for reassurance and confirmation.

"Yes, well, it was a very fractious meeting," Anthony Granard began. "Mr Edgton made it clear that we weren't offering nearly enough money and he started to make veiled threats – he said he was prepared to take Lord Westleigh on and that he always won his battles. I did get the impression, though, that he would have sold the quarry if the price had been right but that he was holding out for a better offer. So we think he's taken Lucy either as a warning to Lord Westleigh to stop interfering in his plans for the quarry or he intends to ransom her for, I don't know, whatever he thinks the quarry is worth and then, with the ransom money safely pocketed, he'll graciously accept Lord Westleigh's offer for the quarry – that way, he'll be 'quids in', as they say."

"So that's where you need to be looking." The Earl took over, having re-composed himself sufficiently. "He probably knew that Lucy rode alone at that time of day – probably even saw her when he came to meet Anthony – so he's taken her somewhere and hidden her."

"I see," Acting Inspector Beauregard answered, although he wasn't sure that he did. "But can I just ask why you didn't buy the quarry when it first came onto the market?"

"It didn't come onto the market. The first thing I knew was that Richard Edgton was introducing himself as the new owner of the quarry. I expect he used his usual charming mix of blackmail, bribery and intimidation to persuade the previous owner to sell it to him – probably at a rock-bottom price. So, you see, I didn't get a look-in."

"And, forgive me for asking, but how much did you offer for the quarry?"

The Earl fiddled with his signet ring. "I do mind, actually, but I suppose you need to know. I got a full market appraisal done and, on that basis, I offered half a million – it's a very fair price for a disused quarry, I can assure you."

"And you said he might be holding out for a better offer. How much might that be?"

"I have absolutely no idea," the Earl replied tetchily, "but knowing Richard Edgton, I'd guess it'd be much closer to a million."

The acting inspector closed his notebook and stood up. "Right, thank you, Lord Westleigh, for your help; we'll get on with things. I'd like a recent photograph of your daughter and I'd like to know what she was wearing when she…"

"Shouldn't be a problem; Anthony can arrange the photograph for you and Tom can tell you what she was wearing – her usual riding gear, I imagine."

"And I'd like to examine the images from your security cameras. I assume there are some?"

"You're welcome to take a look. There are cameras at the main gates and the entrance to the castle, but it's a huge estate. We can't put them everywhere, I'm afraid."

"Thank you, and I'd like to put a listening device on your phone in case Ric… in case the kidnapper tries to contact you."

"If you must, you must," the Earl replied with a resigned air. "Anthony can liaise with you on that."

"And I'd like to interview Alex Jeffries and everyone who lives or works on your estate – somebody might have seen or heard something."

The Earl sighed. "If you must, you must, but I don't want you delaying things with a whole string of pointless interviews; we know who's got Lucy and we want her safely back with us. I shall expect results and I'll expect them soon."

It was some twenty minutes after Acting Inspector Beauregard had left Chartfield Castle that he had a phone call from the chief constable.

Eleven

Monday 21 August, early afternoon

It had turned into another hot day, the heat tempered only by a slight but unpredictable breeze. Clive Walsingham was sitting beneath an expansive parasol on the hotel terrace, a cold beer and a tuna sandwich by his side and, on the table in front of him, a folder of assorted documents, precariously anchored by a glass ashtray to prevent them from blowing about in the capricious breeze. He was mulling over the demise of Mary Pullman, occasionally allowing himself the distraction of watching Simon Verwood moving amongst the garden beds, pruning the dead flower heads with a delicacy that belied the muscularity of his arms and hands, whilst frequently glancing nervously towards the car park. Clive looked up and smiled as Clare emerged from the conservatory. She was wearing a thin, summery, salmon-pink cotton dress and carrying a glass of mineral water. Taking a sip, she pulled up a chair, sat down next to him, hitched up the hem of her dress, smiled and fixed him with her piercing grey-green eyes.

"So how's Jamie?"

Clive exhaled. "Not too great at the moment. He's nursing a hell of a hangover and feeling very sorry for himself. I've taken him back to his place, made him some strong coffee, given him a bit of a lecture and told him to take the rest of the day off – he's owed some time off anyway. I'm afraid you'll need to arrange cover for the rest of the day."

"Already done – I guessed he wouldn't be in today. Is there a particular reason for the drinking binge?"

"Apparently his girlfriend, Zoe, has walked out on him and he's taken it badly. She thinks he's been seeing somebody else. He vehemently denies it, although…."

"Although what?"

"Although he got home late a couple of times, but he won't tell Zoe where he was or what he was doing and he won't tell me either, so he's not really helping himself."

Clare rubbed her hands together with relish. "Ooooh, I'll have to try and winkle something out of him when I get the chance."

"Mmmm – I wish you luck. Whatever it is he's up to, it's not going to be easy to prise it out of him; you know how secretive he can be. But we will need to keep an eye on him. I've never seen him as low as he was today."

"Righto! I'll do what I can." Clare paused and studied Clive for a moment or two. He was staring into the distance again as though preoccupied with some thorny problem. "No policemen to play with at the moment?" she enquired teasingly.

"Mmm, no! Bit of a crisis up at Chartfield Castle, I gather. Lord Westleigh's daughter's gone missing and Dick has been summonsed."

"Oh dear! Poor Dick!"

Clive laughed. "Huh, poor Lord Westleigh, more like!"

"I see! You and Dick not getting on?"

Clive scratched his head thoughtfully. "Oh, okay, I suppose but I have to keep reminding myself that it's his case and I'm only being seconded to try and help, but it's so difficult; honestly, I have to keep biting my tongue! I mean, for a start, when Mary Pullman first disappeared, it looks as though Dick and his boss simply decided, without any actual evidence, that she had just walked out on her husband, with whom she clearly didn't get on and who was probably violent towards her, and they didn't follow it up seriously. And now she's turned up murdered, Dick is so convinced that Richard Edgton is the guilty party, he won't listen to alternative suggestions and—"

"Richard Edgton?"

"A local businessman; very powerful, apparently, with influential friends and a reputation for blackmail and intimidation – I've met one of his heavies already – but apart from the fact that Mary Pullman was one of the leading campaigners against his plans to redevelop Fearnley quarry, there's no real, direct evidence against him. I really think that's why Dick's involved me; he wants me to find the evidence to nail Richard Edgton, but—"

"Should you be telling me all this?" Clare asked suddenly.

Clive looked surprised. "Should I? Not sure, really. I'm not bound by police confidentiality and I haven't signed anything, so I suppose it is okay, but, on reflection, you'd better not say anything to anyone else, just in case."

"I promise! So you don't think this Richard Edgton is the killer?"

Clive shrugged. "Well, he could be. He certainly has a reputation for being more than a little dodgy. One of his heavies – the one I've already met – lives next door to where the body was found and he could have had a key to his neighbour's house. He's also got a workshop which is big enough to hide a body in, but if he did murder her, why would he leave the body on next door's lawn? Surely he'd dump it somewhere miles away, or even bury it in his garden – he was building a new patio when we went to see him. But what Dick doesn't get is that there are several other suspects worthy of further investigation."

"Like who?"

Clive tugged his earlobe. "Well, her husband for a start. He was hardly grief-stricken when he heard about his wife's murder and his neighbour thought he might have been violent towards her. And he used to be an estate agent in Morstock and probably handled the sale of the house where his wife's body turned up, so he'd know about the place, and yet he denied it."

"So he could have had a key to the house?"

"Quite possibly! Dick was going to check it out before he got side-tracked. And then there's Mary Pullman's next-door neighbour. He'd had rows with her and she'd accused him of being a peeping tom so there was no love lost there. And he was a bit shifty when we spoke to him. And, of course, we need to speak to her two daughters. They don't live at home but kept in touch so they might have some useful information. And then there's this."

He lifted up the ashtray, rummaged amongst the documents on the table and produced several sheets of stapled, photocopied, handwritten notes which he handed to Clare. "These are copies taken from a notebook Mary Pullman was using when she disappeared. Apart from the fact that at least one page is missing, which might in itself be important, you can probably see the note she's written in the margin."

"Yes, I see. '2 VERNON COURT'. That was the address you asked me to look up. It's in Stowbrook."

"Yes, that's right, and the date she wrote next to it is the 5th April – the day she disappeared. Now Dick and I went to Vernon Court this morning. The occupant of number two is a retired vicar who seems – superficially at least – to be totally innocuous and claims not to know anything about Mary Pullman. But there was something about him that I wasn't sure about – just an ex-policeman's hunch, maybe, but he certainly didn't want us to see his diary – so, against Dick's wishes, we went to see his neighbour and she told us that the vicar used to get a regular visit each Wednesday afternoon from a woman who seemed quite keen to disguise her appearance. And the neighbour thought that the visits stopped around Easter – that would be about the time that Mary Pullman disappeared."

"So you think the mystery visitor was Mary Pullman?"

Clive shook his head. "Well, she wore a blue coat, like Mary Pullman, and she drove a silver or grey car, like Mary Pullman, and she had dark hair, which Mary Pullman had, although it was probably dyed. But she also wore glasses, which Mary Pullman didn't do. That could just be a disguise, I suppose, but there's something else that's not right."

"Couldn't she just have been a cleaning lady or a friend or something?"

"Quite possibly, but the neighbour described her as furtive, and, if she was a cleaning lady, why has there been no sign of one since April?"

"I don't know, but if Mary Pullman was a regular visitor, for whatever reason, she'd be unlikely to write the address in her notebook – she'd already know it…"

Clive sighed and carefully lifted Archie the cat from the table, where he was beginning to take a keen and persistent interest in the contents of his sandwich. "Exactly, that's the bit that's not right! Oh, it's all just speculation, which is why it's so frustrating and nothing quite… fits. I mean, Mary Pullman disappeared on 5th April and then nothing. She didn't use her phone or laptop, both of which we think she took with her, there have been no sightings of her car, no withdrawals from her bank account – nothing. And then, quite suddenly, she turns up four months later, having just been strangled. And she was naked, but there was no sign of a sexual assault, so—"

"Do you think she'd been held hostage somewhere?" Clare asked dramatically.

"Possibly – Dick and I discussed that scenario – but we're not aware that there has been any kind of ransom demand, although Gregory Pullman wouldn't necessarily have told us, of course."

"And he wouldn't necessarily have paid the ransom anyway, from what you've said."

"No, true, but four months is a long time to hold someone – the longer you hold someone hostage the greater your chances of being discovered. And if Gregory Pullman wasn't going to pay the ransom, my guess is the kidnapper would have known that quite early on. But here's something else that's quite interesting." Clive jabbed his finger on the table a couple of times to emphasise the importance of what he was about to say. "It transpires that Mary Pullman had bought quite a lot of new clothes in the weeks before she disappeared, although some at least were still in her wardrobe when she vanished."

"Another man?"

"Possibly, but who? Her next-door neighbour, who lives alone, has a theory that she was giving him the come-on, standing naked at her bedroom window while he was in his garden, but he says he wasn't interested, certainly not after she reported him to the police for being a peeping tom. And we don't have anything to link her to another man, so—"

"What about her children?"

Clive tugged his earlobe. "She's got two daughters, apparently, neither living at home. I haven't spoken to them yet. But, you know, the biggest mystery is how the body was found; naked with her arms by her side and her legs together, in a secure garden, to be discovered by the owner when he came back from holiday."

"Did the owner know Mary Pullman?"

"No, there's absolutely nothing that we know of to connect Mary Pullman to the house or its owner, except that they both disliked Richard Edgton, along with a lot of other people, and Gregory Pullman might have handled the sale of the house when the present owners purchased it."

"So what was she doing there?"

"Not a lot, really, but why and how did she end up there?" Clive shrugged again. "Was she killed somewhere else and then taken to that house for some reason, or was she alive when she arrived at the house, in which case, was she meeting someone? Does the fact that she was naked mean that she had an amorous assignment which went wrong in some way? Or was she taken there under duress?"

"These notes of Mary Pullman's." Clare hadn't been fully listening to the last couple of minutes of Clive's out-loud deliberations. She had been studying the papers that Clive had given her. "It looks as though she was doing some family history research."

"Yes, but I'm not sure what she was researching or how relevant it is. Her husband didn't seem to know or care and I haven't had time to look at the notes in detail."

"Didn't you come across a genealogist during your last case in Inglemouth?"

"God, yes, what was her name, Julia something? She was very prickly as I recall."

"Still, from what you said at the time, she was good at her job. She might be able to help. You said there was a gap in Mary Pullman's notes and—"

"Mmmm, yes, good point! I think I'll speak to Mary Pullman's two daughters first – they might be able to shed some light but, if not, I might give her a call."

Setting Mary Pullman's notes to one side, Clare's eyes alighted on some photographs among Clive's collection of documents. "Oooh, are they the photographs of the crime scene?" she asked excitedly.

"Yes they are, but—"

"Can I take a look?"

"I suppose so, but I don't—"

Clare picked up the photographs and studied them intently. "When were these taken?"

"Last Wednesday, but—"

Clare peered at the photographs and then glanced quickly around the hotel grounds. "You know, there's something a bit odd about—"

Her musings were interrupted by the sudden and unexpected arrival of a tall, young woman who had marched purposefully onto the terrace. She had dark, almost black hair, cut short, bright red lipstick, which partially disguised the thinness of her lips, and was dressed from head to toe in blue denim.

"Excuse me," she interrupted impatiently. "I'm looking for Clive Walsingham."

Clive rose to his feet and eyed his visitor with customary thoroughness. "Yes, you've found him. I'm Clive Walsingham and this is my wife, Clare. And you are?"

The woman advanced towards Clive. "I'm DC Alison Pawlett. Dick, er Sergeant, er, Acting Inspector Beauregard asked me to come and introduce myself. As you know, he's been called away to investigate the disappearance of Lord Westleigh's daughter and he thought you could use some help…" She paused as she noticed the photographs that Clare was holding.

"Aren't those police files you've got there?" she asked, assertively.

"Yes, copies of some of Dick's files, a few photographs…" Clive replied.

"But they're confidential. I'm not sure you should have them and you certainly shouldn't be handing them around." She had moved aggressively towards Clare as though she was about to snatch the photographs from her when her mobile phone rang. Clive immediately identified the ringtone as 'The Ride of the Valkyries'.

"Excuse me," she muttered as she turned away and answered her phone.

"Hello, Colin. Yes... yes, I'm sorry, but Dick has reallocated me... yes, yes. I'm helping with the murder case... yes, yes... a complete waste of time, of course, but... Look, there's no need for that, you know what police work is like. We're a senior officer down, we're investigating a murder and a high-profile disappearance and all leave has been cancelled. I can't just drop everything and rush home... No, I don't know when I'll be home... no, well, that's just tough... get used to it. Now listen... hello, hello..."

"The bastard's rung off," she announced to no-one in particular. "God, men!"

"Look, if you need to go, that's okay," Clive soothed. "I'm not going anywhere this afternoon, but I'd like to visit Mary Pullman's daughter Sarah in the morning."

Constable Pawlett sighed heavily. "Alright, I'll make the arrangements. I'll be here at nine," she replied with a hint of truculence, before turning and heading rapidly towards the hotel entrance.

"And I'll look forward to that," Clive mumbled when Constable Pawlett was safely out of earshot.

"Have you still got your bullet-proof vest?" Clare asked as she dissolved into giggles.

Clive was about to reply when he happened to glance across the lawn and noticed Simon, who had been dividing his time between pottering in the flowerbeds and casting nervous glances towards the car park, suddenly drop his secateurs and bolt towards the house, a frightened look in his eyes. He didn't even look at Clive and Clare as he scurried quickly past them into the conservatory. A few moments later, Ralph Dalton strode casually across the parched lawn from the car park, nodded and half-smiled at Clive and Clare, and disappeared inside the hotel.

"I take it you haven't managed to speak with Ralph Dalton yet?" Clare asked as her gaze followed the visitor.

"No, I'm sorry, darling. I've been a bit immersed in this case, but I will, I promise."

"And have you spoken to Simon? He had asked me for the week off."

"Briefly; I thought I might find him in the bar yesterday evening, but there was no sign, so I had a quick word when I came back earlier. I'll speak to him again later when, hopefully, he'll have calmed down a bit and before he gets too far into his daily bottle of Scotch. But I backed you up; I told him he can't have time off just because a guest has spooked him. I did also say that if there's any unpleasantness of any kind, he's to tell one of us straight away."

"So you haven't given him the week off?"

"No, why, should I have done?"

"No, no, you're right, of course, but he did look very frightened when he rushed past us just then. Oh, God, I hope he's not going to make another scene in the bar."

"With a bit of luck, he'll keep out of the bar…"

Clive stopped talking as soon as he heard the familiar, rapid, pitter-patter steps approaching. "God, what now?" he muttered under his breath.

"I'm sorry to interrupt," Debbie interrupted. "But I thought you should know that I've been doing the cashing-up for the last couple of days and there's a discrepancy between the takings and the till receipts. I'm pretty sure some money has gone missing."

While Clive muttered something under his breath, Clare turned to Debbie. "Oh, no, that's terrible! How much do you think has gone missing?"

"Oh, not that much, I suppose – about forty pounds in total – but I thought you should know before any more goes missing," Debbie answered importantly.

"And do you have any idea who's taken the money?"

Debbie gave Clare a knowing look. "Well, I haven't caught anyone with their fingers in the till, but I reckon I'm a pretty good judge of character and you'll know who I think it is!"

*

Acting Inspector Beauregard arrived at the lodge just as Alex Jeffries was alighting from his Land Rover. He was tall and thin with wavy dark hair partly hidden beneath a tweed cap. He had finely chiselled classical features, somewhat dissipated by a couple of days' growth of stubble. He sported a checked shirt, open at the neck, and a pair of well-worn but expensive-looking jeans. He was marching briskly towards the lodge as Acting Inspector Beauregard called to him.

"Are you Alex Jeffries?"

Alex Jeffries stopped in his tracks, tutted loudly and turned to face the acting inspector, a rugged scowl betraying the irritation he felt at being interrupted.

"Yes, and you're the police, presumably," he replied brusquely.

"Correct. I'm Acting Inspector Beauregard and I need to ask you a couple of questions."

Alex Jeffries pointedly studied his expensive watch. "Can't it wait? I've only just got home, my wife is nowhere to be found, our nanny is in there looking after two extremely distressed kids and I need to see them."

"I understand, sir, but I do want to find your wife and I need your help."

Alex Jeffries glanced at his watch again. "Alright, but be quick."

"Your father-in-law, er, Lord Westleigh, has given us his account of what happened when your wife disappeared, but it appears he wasn't in the country at the time, so I'd like your first-hand account, if that's okay."

Alex Jeffries removed his cap and stroked his luxuriant dark hair. "Yes, yes, I suppose so, but I can't tell you much, I was, errrm, working in the office."

"You were working on a Sunday?"

Alex Jeffries looked rather disdainfully at the detective. "Yes, of course I was working. Sunday is one the busiest days in our garden centres." He half-turned and pointed towards the top floor of a whitewashed, castellated tower which a previous Earl had indulgently appended to the original, solid-looking lodge. "We've got a small office up there – it's quiet and I can get on with my work without too many interruptions – and I looked out of the window and saw Lucy walking towards the stables for her usual evening ride; it was sometime after six o'clock, but I'm afraid I can't be more precise. And then, later, just after eight o'clock I think, I got a phone call from one of the estate workers, Matthew, to say that he'd found her horse all saddled up, but there was no sign of my darling Lucy. And that's about all I can tell you. I've been driving around all over the place, looking everywhere I can think of, but there's no sign—"

"Your father-in-law said that your wife usually went riding before dinner."

Alex Jeffries spluttered and then gave a nervous laugh. "Yes, that's right, whenever she could."

"And what time do you normally have dinner?"

"Normally, we sit down around eight o'clock. Our housekeeper usually prepares the meal. She does an excellent job, but her time-keeping can be, errm, a little unreliable."

"So weren't you worried when your wife hadn't come home by eight o'clock? I assume she'd change for dinner so she'd aim to get back here a bit before…"

Alex Jeffries suddenly looked flustered. He flicked his cap nervously from one hand to the other. "Look, Inspector, I was, errrm, working in my office. I often work quite late at this time of year – there's a lot to do – and, errrm, I often lose track of time. I didn't realise what the time was until Matthew phoned. It's normally Lucy who comes and drags me off to dinner."

"Has she ever disappeared like this before?"

"What? Errm, no, of course she hasn't."

"And was her behaviour in any way different or unusual in the days before she went missing?"

"What? Oh, well, she'd been a bit on edge recently. Our youngest starts school for the first time next week and it's a stressful time for them both, but, no, she wouldn't just disappear, especially not at such an important time." Alex Jeffries managed a forced half-smile.

"I see, and have you any idea where she's gone?"

"Yes, obviously," Alex Jeffries snapped. "That's why I've been driving around everywhere, out of my mind with worry, looking for her."

"Yes, of course, I'm sorry. Lord Westleigh is of the view that Richard Edgton is responsible for your wife's disappearance."

Alex Jeffries nodded. "Yes, that's what he's told me. I'm afraid I don't know Richard Edgton that well. I mean, I know of his reputation and I know that Lord Westleigh hates the man and is firmly of the view that he's responsible for Lucy's disappearance, but I don't know him that well and, if she has been, errm, kidnapped, there are other people who might've done it. You see, running the Earl's garden centre business doesn't make us universally popular. The Earl likes to see a tidy profit, so sometimes we have to squeeze our suppliers' margins, as we've been doing recently, and that leaves quite a few disgruntled people out there who don't like us very much. I'll tell you this, though – whoever is responsible, he must've known that Lucy rides round the estate alone at that time each day."

"So you're quite convinced that she's been kidnapped?"

"Of course she's been kidnapped," Alex Jeffries snorted. "She hasn't had an accident and she's not on the estate anywhere, so what else could have happened? What the hell are you implying?"

"I'm not implying anything," the acting inspector replied defensively, slightly taken aback by the vehemence of Alex Jeffries' protestation. "I'm just trying to eliminate other possibilities."

"Such as?"

"Well, that she might have gone off voluntarily with somebody or to meet somebody or—"

"Let me assure you, errm, Inspector, that Lucy would never go off without telling me and she would certainly never go off without stabling her horse properly. And I think you've got a damned cheek suggesting—"

"Presumably there's no public access once the castle is closed for the day?" Acting Inspector Beauregard asked, keen to change the subject.

Alex Jeffries stroked his stubbly chin while he let his emotions calm. "Technically, I suppose – the main gates are certainly closed – but it's not Fort Knox here and there are often vehicles coming and going, estate workers popping out for the evening, that sort of thing. If you know where to go, you can get into the estate by following one of the lanes that lead up to some of the workers' cottages. So it's not that difficult if you know how to do it."

"I'd like the names of anyone you can think of who might be responsible for your wife's disappearance, and obviously if you get any ransom demands or any other information, you'll let me know."

"Of course, why wouldn't I?"

"And I'd like to monitor your phone."

"Now look here—"

"Lord Westleigh has agreed."

"Has he? Oh, well, if the Earl has decreed then that's the end of the matter, isn't it? God help us if we dare to step out of line."

Twelve

Tuesday 22 August

As soon as Clive got into the car, on the dot of nine o'clock, it was clear that a glacial atmosphere prevailed. As they began the twenty-mile journey to Bailbridge, Constable Pawlett's facial expression was tense, distant and unsmiling. The strained atmosphere was not ameliorated by Constable Pawlett donning a pair of dark glasses, holding the steering wheel in a vice-like grip, staring resolutely ahead and manoeuvring her vehicle at terrifying speed through narrow country lanes and around blind corners. After several minutes of brooding silence, during which Clive's foot had repeatedly slammed hard on an imaginary brake pedal, he ventured a comment.

"It's good of you to help me out. Thank you."

Constable Pawlett jerked her head back slightly and sniffed. "Inspector Beauregard asked me to help," she replied coldly.

"Good. I hope I'm not taking you away from more important duties."

"No, only catching criminals," she responded with a surliness that Clive would not have countenanced were he still a detective inspector.

"So is a murder enquiry of no interest to you?" he asked with an air of resigned frustration.

Constable Pawlett jerked her head back again. "Well, we all know who murdered the poor woman, we just haven't got enough evidence, but this particular visit isn't going to provide it. We've spoken to her daughter before and she's got nothing helpful to say."

"Oh well, I'm sorry if I'm wasting your time, but Dick, er, Acting Inspector Beauregard has asked me to help and he seemed to think it might be worth talking to her daughters again. Sometimes, somebody fresh—"

"We're not a load of country bumpkins here, you know, we know our job."

"Yes, I'm sure you do," Clive soothed. "So I promise I won't make this visit last any longer than is absolutely necessary."

*

It was a matter of considerable relief to Clive when they safely screeched to a halt outside Sarah Tildesley's functional but unexciting modern, semi-detached house on the edge of a functional but unexciting housing estate and he was able to quickly extricate himself from Constable Pawlett's mercifully static car and stand briefly on the pavement, appreciating the delights of the warm summer's morning and the unexpected joy of being alive.

Sarah Tildesley was an inch or two above average height and thin, with a long, bony face, rimless spectacles and a solemnity that seemed to be a family trait and which made her appear rather older than her thirty-five years. Her long dark hair was tied in a tight bun, she wore no make-up and her clothes, mainly grey in colour, were frumpy. As she stood back to allow her visitors to pass over the threshold and into the living room, she emitted an audible sigh.

Despite the lack of warmth in Sarah Tildesley's greeting, she must at least have gone to the trouble of tidying up her living room because there was no obvious sign of her temporarily absent children or their playthings.

As always, Clive surveyed the room before sinking into a cream-coloured, modern armchair that formed part of a three-piece suite, which was festooned with matching cushions. Three of the four walls of the room were painted in a neutral cream colour, but the fourth wall was decorated in an exuberant grey and white patterned wallpaper. In one corner, there was a fussily cluttered display cabinet with a glass front and fake black wood surrounds. A salmon-pink carpet covered the floor.

"I hope we haven't called at a bad time," Clive said, apologetically. He was by nature courteous, most of the time, but in addition, he was only too aware that his lack of any official status required him to be unusually obsequious.

"It's the school holidays and my two are playing next door at the moment, but I could be needed at any time," came the prickly response.

"I'll try to be brief—"

"Mr Walsingham is helping us with the investigation into your mother's murder," Constable Pawlett interrupted.

Clive nodded his agreement. "Yes, that's right, so—"

"And I've explained to him that you've already told us all you know," the constable interrupted again.

Clive smiled. In a verbal battle of wits with the surly Constable Pawlett, he felt confident of ultimate victory. "Do you have any theories about who murdered your mother?" he asked innocently.

"You told us about your mother's very vocal opposition to Richard Edgton and his plans for Fearnley quarry, didn't you?" the constable encouraged.

"Yes, that's right," Sarah Tildesley agreed. "My mother was extremely vocal and extremely persistent in her opposition to Richard Edgton and his plans for the quarry and…"

Clive smiled again. The conversation was being heavily orchestrated and risked frustrating him. To use his favoured cricket parlance, it was time to bowl a googly. "Who benefits from your mother's will?" he asked suddenly.

"What?" Sarah Tildesley clearly had not expected such a direct question. She looked anxiously across at Constable Pawlett and bit her lip nervously.

"Sorry! I'm sure Constable Pawlett or Inspector Beauregard will already have asked you that," Clive observed, wryly.

"Ah, er, I expect so," Sarah Tildesley stuttered. "Although, since you mention it, I'm not sure they did."

Clive glanced at Constable Pawlett who was resolutely focussing her pale blue eyes on part of the cream-painted wall opposite her which, for some reason, seemed to have a particular fascination.

"So who does benefit from your mother's will?" Clive persisted.

Sarah Tildesley sat bolt upright and accompanied her response with a series of extravagant and apparently random hand gestures. "Well, er, I don't really know. Er, I mean, my mother fell out with each of us at, er, some time or another and was often threatening to change her will. I can remember her threatening to cut our father out of her will at one time, but I don't know, er, if she ever did and what, er, her present will, that is her last will, actually said."

"I see," Clive replied, though of course he didn't. "And would you describe your mother as wealthy?"

"Wealthy?" Sarah Tildesley snorted. "My mother? No, I don't think so, although, thinking about it, she might have inherited a bit of money from her parents; they seemed to enjoy a comfortable retirement. And now I think about it, she often spoke about 'Grandad's little legacy' and laughed. I'm afraid I don't really know what she meant. She certainly didn't give the impression of having lots of money."

"Your mother worked for Nicholls Bank, didn't she?"

"Yes, until she retired, but she was only a humble cashier."

"And you – what do you do?"

Sarah Tildesley shot another nervous glance at Constable Pawlett. "Me? I, er, I er, I used to run a hairdressing salon here in Bailbridge, but it went out of business about a year ago."

"And you haven't worked since?"

"Er, no, no! I'm divorced and my ex pays maintenance for the children, but, no, I haven't been able to find another job."

"So a legacy from your mother would be very helpful, I imagine."

"What are you implying?" Sarah Tildesley's hand gestures were becoming increasingly extravagant.

"I'm not implying anything. I'm just trying to find a motive for her murder. We think, incidentally, that she was doing a bit of research into her family history when she disappeared. Did she say what she was researching and why?"

Sarah Tildesley bit her lip again, regained some limited control over her flailing arms and thought carefully for a moment or two before replying. "Er, no, I don't really know. I think it was just a hobby for her, really – something to fill her time when she wasn't organising petitions or picking a fight with someone – although I recall at one time she was intrigued by her grandfather's middle name. I don't know what it was, but it seemed to puzzle her. I remember our father suggesting that his middle name was probably 'parsimonious old git' and laughing, but, er, that's all I know, really."

"I see! And how would you describe your mother's relationship with your father?"

"Huh! Non-existent, I'd say. I don't know how they put up with each other."

"Was there any hint of violence? Did your mother ever mention your father lashing out at her?"

"What?" Sarah Tildesley's arms began to flail around again. "What?" she repeated. "No, I don't think so. She never spoke about my father that much, but I never saw any evidence, any bruising or anything."

"I see! And did your mother get on well with her neighbours?"

"I don't think she got on well with anyone after a while." Sarah Tildesley laughed nervously. "I remember her having big rows with one of her neighbours, Martin somebody, I think he was called. I remember her calling him a 'perverted little voyeur' or some such, but I don't really know what the rows were about – there were so many of them."

"Can I ask where you were on the day your mother disappeared – 5th April?"

Sarah Tildesley shot another anxious glance in the direction of Constable Pawlett. "Ah, well, er, I don't really remember, but it was during the Easter school holidays, so I was probably here with the children."

"We think your mother was murdered sometime during the weekend before last – around the 12th or 13th of August. Where were you that weekend?"

"That's easy. I was here with the children. We went out to do a bit of shopping on Saturday, but it was lovely weather so they played in the garden quite a bit."

"Thank you." Clive looked across at the inscrutable constable. "One last question from me for the moment; we think she might have been intending to visit an address in Stowbrook on the day she disappeared – Vernon Court. Does it mean anything to you?"

"Vernon Court?" Sarah Tildesley's cheeks turned pink and her hand gestures became more excitable again. "Vernon Court? No, I, er, don't think so. No, no, er, I don't think I've heard of Vernon Court."

*

As they sped away from Sarah Tildesley's house and in the brief intervals between flinching and slamming his foot to the floor, Clive began to muse out loud.

"Well, Alison, I'm really grateful to you for bringing me here and I do hope it hasn't been a complete waste of your time. It certainly hasn't for me." He paused to allow Constable Pawlett to reply, but there was no acknowledgement. Instead, she continued to stare resolutely ahead from behind her dark glasses, as the scenery whizzed past at an alarming speed.

"Of course," he continued as his foot slammed into the floor again, "you may well be right in suspecting Richard Edgton of murdering Mary Pullman; after all, he appears to be an obvious candidate, but it seems to me that there are a few other leads that are worth following up." He paused again, but Constable Pawlett maintained her hostile silence. "For example," he continued, "we now know that there might be some kind of family issue or dispute involving her will, we now know that she might have been more wealthy than we first thought, we now know a bit more about the family history that she was researching, we now know that Gregory Pullman knew more about her research than he led us to believe and we now know that her daughter, Sarah, is a very bad liar. Now I know that your boss, Dick, er, Acting Inspector Beauregard, shares your view that Richard Edgton is the guilty party, but it seems to me that there are some fresh lines of enquiry that might be worth following up. They don't entail any more face-to-face interviews – not yet anyway – although I'll need to call Mary Pullman's other daughter, so if you want return to your normal duties that's absolutely fine by me – I'd quite understand. On the other hand, if you want to help me with some of these other lines of enquiry while your boss is cow-towing to Lord Westleigh then that would be great. You know the people and you know the places much better than I do. Obviously I'd have to clear it with your boss."

He paused and looked at Constable Pawlett. After a moment or two's reflection, she smiled for the first time, eased her foot off the accelerator and replied, "I'm sorry about my attitude earlier, it's just… Well, anyway, I'd really like to help you if that's okay."

*

Carlow Bridge Farm had been an established sheep and cattle farm for generations, but, in recent times, blighted by rising costs, dwindling returns and the occasionally climatic calamity, it had struggled to make a profit. Eventually, when the owners could take no more, Richard Edgton purchased it from them with the intention of turning it into a prestigious riverside golf venue. Initially, there was much opposition to the proposed scheme, with local residents deeply anxious about the adverse impact on their tranquil landscape, the increased volume of traffic and the disruption likely to be caused by the development, but the local planning committee seemed strangely malleable and gave its unequivocal assent.

Richard Edgton commissioned two of the best golf course architects to create what he called a "championship course", although no championships of any note had ever been staged there. The original farmhouse was almost completely gutted before being transformed into an upmarket clubhouse and some of the previously derelict outbuildings – mainly barns and stables – were converted to provide conference facilities and a suite of offices, some of which Richard Edgton himself occupied, together with a number of his most important acolytes. On a ridge of higher ground overlooking the river and safe from the risk of flooding that had so blighted the farm, Richard Edgton constructed a luxurious and exclusive spa hotel. Despite the initial opposition, Carlow Bridge had become a hugely successful venture for its owner. Clive and Clare Walsingham had even contemplated becoming club members when they first moved into the area, but the fees were high and the waiting list long.

It being another hot afternoon, Richard Edgton had removed his green and red striped tie and rolled up the sleeves of his blue and white striped shirt. He greeted Acting Inspector Beauregard with a distinct lack of cordiality and grudgingly offered his visitor a low-slung aluminium framed chair, upholstered in a vivid red fabric. It was positioned so that he could look out of the large first-floor picture window down to the eighteenth green teasingly sited close enough to the shimmering, tranquil water of the River Carlow to present the average club golfer with a pitch shot of disconcerting precision.

The aggressive office colour scheme, using bright hues of red and orange, coupled with the straight lines and hard edges of the furniture, were clearly designed to intimidate the unwelcome visitor. Acting Inspector Beauregard leaned back inelegantly in his low-slung chair and peered awkwardly over his knees at the imposing figure of Richard Edgton perched above him in his conspicuously large office chair, behind his conspicuously large, specially commissioned oak desk. Behind him, the office walls were lined with framed photographs of Richard Edgton in the company of famous businessmen, politicians and sportsmen.

"Er, I'm making enquiries," Acting Inspector Beauregard began tentatively as he adjusted his position, "about the disappearance and possible kidnapping of Lord Westleigh's daughter, Lucy Jeffries, and—"

"And of course you think I'm responsible," Richard Edgton replied, his icily calm voice betraying no hint of anger or outrage.

"We're exploring a number of lines of enquiry," the acting inspector replied disingenuously. "But Lord Westleigh did mention your name. He referred to a meeting you had recently with Anthony Granard, his secretary, when he offered to buy Fearnley quarry from you and—"

"And no doubt he mentioned that I declined his less than generous offer and that I suggested he might have to raise his offer substantially before he could interest me and that, if he didn't, I would go ahead with my plans to turn the quarry into a theme park. No doubt he said that I had made threats."

Richard Edgton smiled. It wasn't a warm, friendly smile; it was a smug, self-satisfied, almost sinister smile. At the same time, he raised his dark bushy eyebrows as though challenging the acting inspector to contradict his interpretation of the meeting with Anthony Granard. The acting inspector half-nodded in reply, but before he could say any more, Richard Edgton held up a muscular hand. "Hang on a minute, before you start accusing me of anything…"

He reached out, picked up his red telephone, gripped it tightly in his large hand, pressed a button and waited. "Ah, Duncan," he announced at last. "I wonder if you could join us. A police inspector of sorts has arrived." He replaced the phone with a clatter, continued to smile his supercilious, self-satisfied smile, placed his hands across his chest so that their fingertips touched and waited. After a moment or two, the heavy, wood-panelled door swung open and a tall, thin man with short, light brown hair and a smart light-grey suit entered the room. Richard Edgton turned and addressed the acting inspector.

"This is Duncan Brewham. He's my solicitor. Duncan, this is Acting Inspector Beauregard. I think he's about to make some unfounded accusations that you might want to make a note of, for future reference." The solicitor betrayed no emotion. He simply nodded, drew up a chair alongside his boss and opened his notebook.

"No, no, I'm not making any accusations," the acting inspector replied defensively. "I just want to find out what has happened to Lucy Jeffries."

"Of course you do, that's your job, for the time being anyway," Richard Edgton agreed, so chillingly unemotional that he sounded quite menacing. "But I bet my name is at the top of your very short list of suspects." He raised his eyebrows again.

The acting inspector coughed nervously. He was, naturally, unwilling to divulge that there was only one name on his list. "Well, er, I understand that Fearnley quarry hadn't been put on the open market when you purchased it and…" Before the acting inspector could finish his convoluted question, Richard Edgton interrupted him. As he spoke, he leaned forward in his chair and repeatedly jabbed his desk with his forefinger. His voice was less calm, more gruff and strident now.

"Let me tell you something, Acting Inspector Beauregard, or may I call you Dick? When I first heard that the quarry was struggling, I went straight to the owners and made them a generous offer which they accepted – a bit like I did with this farm. His lordship no doubt feels aggrieved that he didn't get the chance to buy it, but he only wanted it so that he could shut it down straight away, sack everyone who worked there and annexe it to his substantial portfolio of property."

"Whereas you didn't close it down," the acting inspector observed caustically.

Richard Edgton smiled again and spoke slowly and deliberately. "Whatever you might think of me, Dick, I really wanted it to succeed. I really thought I could make it a commercial success, but, despite my best efforts, it continued to lose money and then we had a couple of accidents – two workmen were killed – and I had the health and safety people on my back, so I was forced to close it."

"But running a quarry doesn't quite fit with your image, does it?" Feeling increasingly irritated by what he perceived to be Richard Edgton's concerted attempts to browbeat him – no doubt a well-practised business ploy – the acting inspector was becoming more emboldened. "I mean, we all know that your interests are in the leisure industry. Come on, you always wanted to turn the quarry into a theme park and those two accidental deaths were just what you wanted—"

Richard Edgton slowly rose to his feet, glared at the acting inspector and then suddenly thumped the desk with his powerful fist. When he spoke, his voice was harsh and edged with anger. "I think you'd better make a note of that, Duncan. If I understand him correctly, Dick has just accused me of arranging those two deaths." He stood for a moment or two, glowering at the acting inspector, before slowly subsiding back into his chair.

"I tried, you know," he continued, slowly rediscovering his icy calm voice, "to keep the quarry going as a tribute to all those men who had worked their entire lives there, often in appalling conditions and for little reward. I wanted to make a kind of living museum out of it – it would have been a lasting memorial to all those men. We would've had some interactive displays, some tableaux, some re-enactments, sculpture workshops, an adventure playgroup, a restaurant, a shop. It would have been a real shot in the arm for the local economy and it would've given me the chance to re-employ some of the people I had to make redundant—"

"Like Gareth Adamson?"

Richard Edgton looked puzzled. "Gareth Adamson?"

"We're also investigating the murder of Mary Pullman. He found her body in his back garden when he returned from holiday. He used to be a quarryman until you made him redundant."

There was a glint of recognition in Richard Edgton's eyes. "Ah yes, of course. Yes, I probably would have re-employed him – him and a number of others – but his lordship just wanted to sabotage my plans. He threw up all kinds of objections, so, in the end, I just gave up. But he won't thwart me again – the theme park is going ahead and even someone as influential as his lordship won't stop me this time."

"There's been a lot of local opposition—"

"Of course there has; there always is. There was local opposition to this place." Richard Edgton spread out his arms and looked around him with obvious pride. "But we dealt with it then and we'll deal with it now. We've got a three-year waiting list for membership here, you know."

"One of the leading local opponents to your quarry plans was Mary Pullman…" Acting Inspector Beauregard continued stoically.

Richard Edgton leaned forward in his chair. Although there was a brief flicker of uncertainty in his eyes, his voice remained calm. "Ah, I see, Dick. I think I've misjudged you; you don't give up as easily as I thought you would, do you? So now you're going to accuse me of murdering Mary Pullman, are you? You'd better make a note of that too, Duncan. Tell me, Dick, have you got any evidence that I murdered Mary Pullman, or anything that links me to her murder?"

Acting Inspector Beauregard shifted a little uneasily in his increasingly uncomfortable chair, partly to ease the numbness in his left buttock. "No, not yet, not directly, but one of your employees, Dean Footner, lives next door to where her body was found and you've got to admit that silencing her would've been in your interests."

Richard Edgton eased himself back in his chair, smiled smugly and wafted his hand dismissively in the air. "Mary Pullman was nothing. She was just an interfering local busybody. I've been dealing with them all my working life. She was just a minor irritant – no more than that – and she didn't have any power or influence. As I've just said, there was plenty of quite vocal and very determined opposition to this place, but it didn't stop me going ahead and I didn't have to murder anyone." He stood up again. "So are you going to arrest me, Dick? If not, I think it's about time you were leaving."

"Hang on, just a minute," the acting inspector replied. He was going to have one final attempt at unnerving his adversary. "Where were you on Sunday evening between the hours of 6.30 and 8.00?"

Richard Edgton gave an impatient sigh. "Is that when Lucy Jeffries disappeared? I was at home. My wife probably remembers me being there. She wasn't quite drunk by eight o'clock."

"And where were you on Wednesday April 5th – the day Mary Pullman went missing?"

"For God's sake!" Richard Edgton replied angrily. "I told Inspector Morris at the time. It'll all be on file, but if you need to check, my secretary will be able to tell you."

"And where were you when Mary Pullman was murdered around the 12th and 13th of August?"

Richard Edgton sighed again. "Like I just said, my secretary looks after my diary. She'll be able to tell you—"

"No, no, but the 12th and 13th were a Saturday and Sunday."

"Ah, then you'll have to talk to my wife again, I'm afraid. I expect we were entertaining, or being entertained; we usually are at the weekend. And now it really is time you were leaving."

The acting inspector struggled inelegantly to his feet and, feeling some cramp in his legs, stamped them on Richard Edgton's plush office carpet. "I'd like to search all your premises – your house, your offices, the old quarry buildings…"

Richard Edgton walked slowly and deliberately towards Acting Inspector Beauregard until he was only inches away. Bending his knees slightly, he stared directly into the acting inspector's wan face. "Then you're going to have to get a warrant, aren't you? Let me show you out." He moved over to his office door and held it open. "I was sorry to hear about your boss, Inspector Morris, by the way. I hear he's in a critical condition. He came off his horse, didn't he? Just like Lucy Jeffries!"

*

It was a perfect summer's afternoon, the golf course was busy, with several groups of members queuing expectantly for their turn to tee off at the first hole and practising their swings while they waited, and the car park was crowded. Acting Inspector Beauregard waited in his dark grey saloon car, parked inconspicuously in the middle of a solid row of other vehicles, his eyes focused on the entrance to Richard Edgton's offices. After no more than twenty minutes, just as he had anticipated, a vehicle drew up outside the office entrance. It wasn't a limousine this time; it was an estate car being driven by the ever-loyal Dean Footner. After a moment or two, Richard Edgton emerged, glanced around nervously and got in. His passenger door had only just closed as the estate car pulled away in a squeal of tyres.

Acting Inspector Beauregard followed at a safe distance. The road leading from Carlow Bridge golf club snaked alongside the river before meandering up the side of the valley. After about a mile, there was a crossroads. Although he was some distance behind the estate car, the acting inspector saw it turn left, taking the road to Buckham. It was his turn to smile smugly. He knew where Richard Edgton was heading.

Fearnley quarry lay at the foot of Fearnley Hill. The approach road ran down the side of the hill and then curved round in a half-circle towards the quarry entrance; the road only served the quarry, Fearnley farm and the neighbouring hamlet, but it was wide and well-surfaced, a legacy from the quarry's commercial heyday when heavy lorries would regularly trundle in and out. Acting Inspector Beauregard parked about halfway down the hill, his car hidden from view by some overgrown bushes, grabbed his binoculars from the glove compartment and crept over to the low dry-stone wall which ran alongside the road. From there, he had an uninterrupted view down the hill escarpment to the quarry entrance. Just inside the open gates were the remains of the original quarry buildings – the main building, large, brooding and imposing, stood idle, its doors and windows boarded up as a sentient reminder of a bygone age, while two smaller buildings – little more than stone huts – stood alongside. Both were still in use, although only for storage. One contained a number of exhibits that Richard Edgton had planned to use in his aborted museum project – wax mannequins, tools of the trade, rock samples – while the other contained an archive of various old files and records that he needed, or wanted to keep but which could not be accommodated in his main office. Beyond the small cluster of buildings, the original quarry workings undulated and meandered along the underside of the hill, occasionally pockmarked by caves and tunnels where the limestone had been chiselled away or exploded out of the hillside by generations of quarrymen.

Acting Inspector Beauregard continued to scrutinise the small complex of buildings for at least thirty minutes as the sinking late-afternoon sun threw increasingly long shadows across the hillside. At last, the two men emerged from the one of the smaller quarry buildings, both clutching what looked like large boxes, although the encroaching shade made it difficult for the inspector to make out the detail, and placed them in the back of the estate car which was parked alongside. The acting inspector had seen all he could safely see. He raced back to his car and had accelerated away before the heavily laden estate car began its climb back up the hill.

*

Alice Innes worked during the day, so it was early evening before Clive Walsingham could make contact with her. To his considerable surprise, Constable Pawlett had accepted his invitation to return to the hotel with him and, while most of the hotel guests were at dinner, he ushered her into the unoccupied bar where Clare was tidying up before the evening rush. Naturally inquisitive, Clare was keen to hear how the investigation was progressing and how Clive had fared with his erstwhile taciturn, truculent companion, but Clive knew that he was under forensic scrutiny by the constable and was the model of circumspection. He recalled with a shudder the eruption of anger that the sight of Clare holding some photographs of the crime scene had generated in the prickly policewoman, so, after a surreptitious exchange of knowing looks with Clare, he glanced at his watch.

"Look, Alison, I think Alice Innes should be home from work now and I don't want to keep you longer than necessary. If Clare will look after the bar for a few minutes, we'll pop into the office and I'll give her a call."

Clare thought briefly about making a flippant comment about Clive behaving himself while he was alone with the constable in his office, but Alison Pawlett's censorious expression dissuaded her.

"Okay, I think I can manage," was all she felt able to say as she looked around the empty room. "But try not to be too long."

Alice Innes, younger than her sister by a couple of years, sounded as guarded and defensive on the phone as her sister had been in the flesh and Clive fancied that she was probably deploying a similar repertoire of expansive hand gestures. At first, she merely confirmed, without any embellishment and with about as much conviction, what her sister had said about their mother, but then, suddenly, the conversation changed.

"Of course," Alice Innes announced, "I live a long way away from Buckham these days and I don't get back home very often – not very often at all if I can help it. But Sarah lives a lot nearer and she and our mother used to meet quite regularly; and Sarah's got the same dogged perseverance and manipulative streak as our mother. I'm pretty sure that she was trying to persuade our mother to cut our father out of her will – and probably us, er, me as well – but I don't know whether she succeeded."

"How do you know about the will?" Clive asked, suspecting that her elder sister had already been in touch with her.

"Oooh, whispered conversations when they didn't know I was within earshot, a copy of her original will lying around on the sideboard, a clandestine appointment to see her solicitor, my suspicious nature; that sort of thing…"

"Was your mother worth a lot of money?"

"Oooh, not very much, but probably a bit more than she let on, I think. She hadn't always been a humble bank clerk. For many years, she held quite an important position at Nicholls – 'Senior Financial Adviser' or some such grandiose title – and I expect she'd squirrelled quite a bit away over the years. And I think her parents were worth a few quid. They lived quite well in their retirement, but I don't really know what she was worth; all I know is that nothing much came my way, unlike…" Her voice tailed off.

"And do you have any theories about her disappearance and subsequent murder?"

"Oh, what? No, not really, although I should think half the village had a motive of some sort from what I hear, but I tell you something a bit strange. I thought, for a while, that our mother was having an affair and—"

"What made you think that?" Clive interrupted, remembering the new clothes in Mary Pullman's wardrobe and suddenly taking a keen interest in what, until then, had been a torpid conversation.

"Oh, I've got no proof and, if she was having an affair, I have no idea who the unfortunate man was but, on one of my last visits before she disappeared, she had to pop out for a few minutes – I can't remember why or where. Anyway, she left her diary on her desk, next to her laptop and I'm afraid that curiosity got the better of me…"

"And?"

"And I noticed she'd made a number of entries in her diary, usually once or twice a month. All she wrote was a time, usually in the afternoon, and the letter 'G'. Very mysterious!"

"'G'? Your father's first name is Gregory. Couldn't it have been him?"

"What? Oh, no! I don't think she'd put a note in her diary if she was meeting with my father – they lived under the same roof, after all. No, no, the entries that I saw were always at times when my father would have been away doing other things – scoring for the local cricket team, for example."

"I see. And you've no idea what the letter 'G' meant?"

"Er, no, no, not at all; I've got no idea. But she had started to dye her hair. Her hair had been quite grey for some time – it must be several years – but she didn't seem bothered by it and then, in the months before she disappeared, she started to dye it, or rather Sarah dyed it for her. Sarah told me it was an interesting shade of chestnut shortly before she disappeared."

*

As Clive accompanied Constable Pawlett to her car, he thanked her for giving up her time and assisting him.

"Are you sure you won't stay for dinner," he asked. "Chef's doing something with a long French name."

"Ah, no," Alison replied primly. "Thank you for the invitation, but I need to get home."

"Of course! I know you're not convinced about my involvement and you still probably think that I'm wasting your time, but I think we've made some progress today."

The constable turned and looked up at him. There was a slight redness about her eyes that Clive had not noticed before. She half-smiled. "Don't worry! I've quite enjoyed today actually and, yes, I think we have made some progress and, yes, I'll try and follow up on some of the things you mentioned earlier."

Clive held the car door open as the constable got in. "That's good. Um, I don't suppose I could ask another favour of you, could I?"

Thirteen

Wednesday 23 August

Clive Walsingham was a passionate advocate of the hearty breakfast. Early in his police career, he developed a convenient theory that his powers of logic and deduction could be badly impaired by gnawing pangs of hunger so, from then on, he had been regularly sustained by an ample early-morning spread, usually at Chloe's Cafe in Inglemouth. And now, although his analytical powers were deployed less often and less intensively than in his police days, he still could not resist partaking, occasionally, of the generous helpings of breakfast that he insisted the chef made available to his guests, even though the impact on his burgeoning waistline had not gone unnoticed by Clare.

Breakfast was also a time when Clive would often saunter through the restaurant and exchange bland courtesies with his guests as they laid ravenous waste to the contents of their breakfast plates; he usually found them in a good mood when they were fresh, well-fed and eagerly anticipating the day ahead. On this particular occasion, however, Clive was more single-minded than usual. Trying, with limited success, to look casual, he strolled with deliberate intent over to the table where Ralph Dalton was sitting alone, enjoying a plate of scrambled eggs and studying his morning paper.

Ralph Dalton had a young appearance, though he was probably around forty years old. He had a slim build and wore red trousers that were more tight than comfortable, emphasising the trim shape of his calves and thighs. His parched fair hair was unfashionably long and he sported large spectacles with pale brown frames. He glanced up with no more than mild interest as Clive approached.

"Good morning!" Clive greeted him heartily. "Is everything alright?"

"Er, yes, yes, fine thank you," Ralph Dalton replied, obviously slightly disconcerted by Clive's unannounced and solicitous approach, and apparently disinclined to enter into extensive conversation.

"And are you enjoying your stay?"

"Er, yes, I suppose… although I'm here on business, really, so I haven't been able to get out and enjoy this wonderful weather very much." He half-smiled, before his features assumed their usual, more solemn countenance.

"I see. I just thought you might like to know that we've got a coach party arriving this afternoon. They're on a bit of a cultural tour, so I don't think they'll be rowdy or anything, but obviously the place is going to be a lot busier and noisier for a few days. I hope they won't disturb you or anything."

Ralph Dalton shrugged. "Nah, not a problem. I'm usually a heavy sleeper and I'm out most of the day, so… Anyway, I'm only going to be here for another couple of days. I'll be checking out on Friday evening."

"Fine, fine," Clive replied, disappointed that he had gleaned so little information from his mystery guest. "Well, I hope you enjoy the rest of your stay."

"Thanks, I'll do my best," Ralph Dalton replied uncertainly.

As Clive reluctantly turned away, he heard the familiar sound of Debbie Oxton's pitter-patter footsteps approaching.

"Sorry to bother you, Clive," Debbie whispered as Clive ushered her into the office and out of earshot of their guests. "It's just that I've been looking at the till receipts from yesterday and I think some more money has gone missing."

"How much?"

"Thirty pounds, I think."

"And do you know who's responsible?"

Before Debbie could reply, they were distracted by a strange scuffling noise in the corridor just outside the office door. Clive tiptoed to the door and opened it just in time to see Jamie Coulton scurrying into the dining room.

*

It was mid-morning when Acting Inspector Beauregard received a phone call from Richard Edgton. There had been a break-in at Fearnley quarry and Richard Edgton expected him to attend immediately.

Feeling pleased with himself, following the success of the previous evening's espionage, Caspar Beauregard delayed his departure for as long as he thought he could reasonably justify and then drove, at a sedate pace, to the quarry. The entrance gates were open, a familiar-looking estate car was parked close to the main building and Richard Edgton was standing, hands on hips and legs apart, waiting impatiently for the acting inspector to get out of his car.

"You took your bloody time," Richard Edgton greeted him with his customary charm.

"I came as soon as I could," Acting Inspector Beauregard replied disingenuously, fortified by the knowledge of Richard Edgton's clandestine visit the previous evening. He looked across at Dean Footner solemnly standing guard at the entrance to the main building, his shaved head glinting in the sun. Although the acting inspector clearly posed no threat to his boss or to his property, Dean Footner seemed reluctant to surrender his normal security role. "You reported a break-in."

"Well done!" Richard Edgton replied sarcastically.

"When did the break-in occur?"

"Very early this morning, about seven o'clock or so, we think. One of our security guards got an anonymous call to say the intruder alarm had gone off so he came straight over."

"Did you get the number of the caller?"

"Hardly! The caller wasn't going to leave his number. I assume it was from a pay-as-you-go mobile or payphone."

"How did the intruders get in?"

Richard Edgton beckoned the acting inspector over to the perimeter wire-mesh fence and pointed to a large hole. "It looks as though they've cut through the fence, just here, and then, once they got in, they've obviously kicked the doors in." He pointed in the direction of Dean Footner still standing to attention in front of the open building door.

"I see. Any security cameras?"

"No, it's not worth it, really. We don't use the main building at all – the roof leaks and it's structurally unsound. We use the other two smaller buildings for storage, but there's not much of any great value here, just a few exhibits we were planning to put in the museum and some old bits of equipment. We have a security guard who visits regularly, but he's never seen anything untoward, until this morning, that is."

"So what were the intruders looking for?"

"I've no idea, really. I don't know if they thought there was more in the buildings than there actually is."

"Have you been able to identify if anything's gone missing?"

"I've had plenty of time while I've been waiting for you. In the far hut, amongst all the old junk, we keep a lot of old company records and quite a few have gone missing. They seem mostly to be about five or six years old, although I haven't been able to identify every document. My company secretary will need to do a detailed inventory before we know for sure."

Acting Inspector Beauregard stifled a smile. He felt sure he now knew what was in the boxes that Richard Edgton and Dean Footner had spirited away from the quarry the previous evening, no doubt realising that the acting inspector, armed with a search warrant, would shortly be turning the place over.

"Anything else?" the inspector asked airily.

"Well, as I said, we use the near hut for storing a lot of the exhibits we were going to put in the museum until Lord bloody Westleigh interfered – a few mannequins, some old quarrymen's clothes, tools of the trade, some memorabilia; that kind of thing. Now the place is in a mess and a lot of things have been moved about or knocked over – but I can't tell you what, if anything, has gone. I'll need to get someone over to do a detailed check."

"I see. And have you any idea who might have been responsible?" the acting inspector asked. His slight smirk did not go unnoticed.

Richard Edgton glowered at the acting inspector. "I do hope you're taking this seriously. There were some important company files in there. They're not valuable as such and wouldn't mean much to your average burglar, but there's some sensitive information in them and if they were to fall into the wrong hands—"

"Are you suggesting some kind of industrial espionage?"

"I'd be lying if I said I hadn't made a few enemies over the years and there are some people out there who might be looking for payback. If they targeted specific records about certain deals – and I suspect they did – then we might be able to work out who would most want to get their hands on them. Then, of course, Lord Westleigh himself might be looking for some leverage, if you know what I mean."

Acting Inspector Beauregard nodded and began to walk in the direction of the two outbuildings. "I'd better take a look in there."

Richard Edgton moved surprisingly nimbly for a big man and quickly manoeuvred himself between the acting inspector and the outbuildings, while Dean Footner took up a new position in front of the nearer of the two outbuildings and stood guard. "Have you got your search warrant yet?" Richard Edgton asked, raising his eyebrows into a quizzical expression.

"Nnno, not yet, but you did ask me to help catch your intruder and we do have a crime scene."

Richard Edgton stood impassively for a moment or two, staring unblinking at the acting inspector, before reluctantly stepping aside to let him pass. "You won't find her in there, you know; Lucy Jeffries is not here. I've got nothing to do with her disappearance."

"I'll get our forensic people to take a look and we'll need to take your fingerprints," Acting Inspector Beauregard continued. "Together with any of your employees who have been inside the building recently – just so we can eliminate them from our enquiries."

As he walked past Richard Edgton, the acting inspector smirked again. Immediately Richard Edgton moved close to his shoulder and spoke quietly in his ear. "How is Inspector Morris? I hear he's still in a critical condition. And I hear you like to ride your bike when you're off duty. You want to be very careful on these narrow country lanes. Accidents can easily happen and we wouldn't want that, would we?"

*

Later that morning, after Ralph Dalton had driven off on whatever business he was attending to, Simon Verwood emerged slowly into the garden, slightly later than was customary, and began pottering about in the flowerbeds, casting occasional glances in the direction of the car park. Wearing an off-white T-shirt and khaki shorts, he was kneeling, his silver-grey mane of hair flapping untidily around his ears, extracting some recalcitrant late summer weeds from their entrenched positions among the hardy annuals, when Clive approached.

"Morning, Simon," he boomed. "Another lovely day!"

Clive's unexpected, loud arrival had the desired effect. Simon jumped and, looking alarmed, rose unsteadily to his feet. "Morning, Mr Clive," he replied hesitantly. "I didn't hear you creeping up on me. You gave me quite a shock!"

"Sorry, I didn't mean to startle you," Clive replied inaccurately. "The gardens are looking very nice. You've done well!"

Slowly recovering some composure, Simon mopped his perspiring brow and looked around. "Yes, thank you, Mr Clive. Mind you, we could do with a bit of rain, really, everywhere is so dry. Some of these flowers will go over unless it rains soon."

"You can water them, you know. There's no hosepipe ban here yet."

Simon mopped his brow again. "Yes, Mr Clive, of course, of course, but you should never water the flowers in direct sunlight and by late afternoon, when the sun has moved round…" He fixed his bloodshot eyes on Clive and shrugged.

"And by late afternoon you're usually far too plastered to do any gardening," Clive thought to himself but resisted the temptation to say anything.

"Never mind," Clive replied. "I hear the weather might break at the weekend." He paused briefly as his agile but occasionally scattergun mind suddenly went to something that he had been puzzling over for two or three days. "Which reminds me," he continued. "I saw Ralph Dalton at breakfast this morning."

Simon's demeanour changed dramatically. In a predictably theatrical gesture, he held both hands up in front of his face as though trying to shield himself from some unidentified threat to his wellbeing and began to back slowly away. "Oh God, no, not Ralph Dalton again! I mean, er, oh God, did he say why he… er, did he say what he's doing here?"

When Simon Verwood was at his melodramatic worst, it was sometimes hard to keep a straight face and often quite difficult to gauge the true seriousness of the latest tragedy to have befallen him, but Clive had seen enough to convince him that his fright, if a little exaggerated, was genuine.

"Simon, you must tell me about Ralph Dalton – you look really scared," Clive pleaded.

"I can't, I can't say anything to you, to anyone, really. All I can tell you is that he is bad news. He's dangerous and you should tell him to leave!"

"Simon, Simon, calm down! You know I can't ask him to leave without good reason. It's not the way to run a successful hotel."

"Yes, yes, of course. Did he say when he was going…?"

"All he said to me was that he was here on business – he didn't explain the nature of his business – and that he was leaving on Friday evening and—"

"Friday evening; I see. Did he mention me at all?"

"No, why? Should he?"

Simon didn't answer. He just stood, eyes bulging, with his hands still shielding much of his face, and started to tremble.

"Listen, Simon, we've got a big coach party coming in today and I'll be too busy to keep much of an eye on Ralph Dalton, so I suggest you lie low until he's gone. There's not that much you can do in the garden until it rains and I suggest you keep well out of sight. You can still use that room in the attic for a while if you want to, and you can come and go by the back stairs so you don't need to be anywhere where Ralph Dalton might be – the dining room, the bar in the evening. And as soon as he's checked out, I'll let you know."

Clive felt pleased with himself, knowing that his suggestion was nowhere near as altruistic as it might have sounded. The last thing he wanted was Simon Verwood taking up drunken residence in the bar with a coach party of discerning holiday-makers, intent more on enjoying a cultural tour of some of the region's finest country houses than of suffering an evening of alcohol-fuelled histrionics and loud, boorish behaviour.

"I'm sure everything will be fine if you just keep out of the way," Clive continued, trying to sound as reassuring as he could. "But if anything happens that, you know, worries you, come and find me or Clare."

As Simon continued to cower in the flowerbeds, muttering to himself, Clive turned and walked back towards the hotel, followed by Archie the cat, whose quiet doze in the flowerbed had been disturbed by the raised voices and who was clearly under the mistaken impression that a tasty snack was about to be proffered. There were some photographs Clive wanted to take another look at.

*

Fortunately, when the coach party arrived, towards the end of the afternoon, Simon was nowhere to be seen, having already sought solace in a copious quantity of single malt. As Clive and Clare had expected, the party comprised mainly middle-aged and elderly couples, and, as always, Clive observed them closely as they eased themselves from the sleek structure of the coach, with its smart if garish livery of yellow and orange, and wandered, with varying degrees of agility, down the path to the hotel entrance and through into the foyer where Clare and Debbie were poised with their best smiles and a tray full of room keys. Behind them, the driver, middle-aged, balding and seriously overweight, assisted by the enthusiastic Jamie Coulton, began unloading the weighty and expensive luggage from the hold.

Clive was so intent on scrutinising his new guests as they filed patiently up to the reception desk that he had, uncharacteristically, failed to notice the tour manager, smartly attired in her official company uniform of yellow blouse, orange jacket and black trousers, who had led the way resolutely into the hotel. It was only while she was standing in reception, with an assured, practised smile, clutching a clip-board and discreetly observing the checking-in process, that Clive really noticed her. She was much younger than almost all of her clients, with lustrous, dark, flowing hair, expressive dark eyes and a gleaming smile. As she chatted animatedly with Clare, taking a maternal interest in the wellbeing of her brood of travellers, Clive studied her more closely. He felt sure he recognised her from somewhere, but, irritatingly, he couldn't remember where. Eventually, he moved behind the reception desk and glanced surreptitiously at the room list and then he recognised the name – Miranda Bellamy.

As was the custom at dinner, the tour manager and driver sat apart from the rest of the coach party, sharing a small table in a partially screened recess, where they could discreetly reflect on the trials and tribulations of the day and plan their strategy for the next day's excursion. Both had discarded their official uniforms and were dressed casually. Miranda Bellamy was wearing tight navy blue trousers and a loose turquoise top with a low-cut neck. As Clive wandered casually amongst the tables, chatting informally with his new guests, receiving approbation for the three-course meal, a pleasing exercise in culinary restraint from the occasionally excessive imagination of the chef, helping to clear away empty plates and delivering the occasional order of drinks from the bar, he kept a careful, discreet eye on Miranda Bellamy and her rotund travelling companion. Then, as the remains of the dessert course were being cleared away and Clare and Jamie Coulton began drifting effortlessly between the tables, dispensing fixed smiles with the tea and coffee, the driver excused himself and left, presumably to attend to some routine maintenance procedure with the coach, leaving Miranda sitting on her own, no longer smiling but looking distant and pensive. Sensing his opportunity, Clive strolled over to where she was sitting, pulled out the chair that the driver had just vacated and asked, "Do you mind if I join you for a moment or two?"

Miranda looked up, a hint of uncertainty in her expressive, deep brown eyes. In her experience, the hotel manager normally only asked to have a word if there was some actual or perceived problem. "Yes, of course," she replied guardedly but with her professionally polished smile back in place.

"It's just that I've seen you before," Clive remarked. Miranda's expression changed briefly to one of alarm and then of puzzlement. "You won't know me, of course," Clive continued. "When I last saw you, you were flat on your back, in a coma in Inglemouth Hospital, attached to all kinds of tubes and monitors."

He paused briefly while the look of alarm returned to Miranda's face, only this time far more pronounced and far less transitory.

"And who the hell—?" she began to ask, her voice charged with emotion and her eyes looking haunted and afraid.

"I'm sorry, I didn't mean to alarm you," Clive interrupted quickly, anxious to dispel Miranda's obvious unease. "I worked for the local police. I was the officer who led the investigation into the assault on you."

Miranda suddenly relaxed and her smile slowly returned. "Oh, you must be Inspector, er, er, let me think, Framlingham?"

"Close, well, close geographically anyway. I'm ex-detective inspector Clive Walsingham."

"Ah yes, of course, I should have remembered; I'm so sorry. I didn't realise you ran a hotel now."

"Oh, yes, that's right. I resigned not long after we'd dealt with your case. It's a long story and I won't bore you with it. I'd just met Clare and let's just say my priorities started to change and, well, anyway, here I am. I must say I'm delighted to see you've made such a good recovery," Clive enthused. "The doctors weren't sure you'd pull through for a while."

Miranda shuddered at the memory. "Yes, it was terrible at the time and I was pretty buggered for quite a long time afterwards. But I went to stay with my mum in Italy for a while and her nursing and the warm sun got me back on my feet."

"And you're fully recovered now?"

"More or less; I've got a nasty scar," Miranda pointed to her scalp just above her left ear, "but nobody can see it, fortunately. And I get some bad headaches at times and some panic attacks at night, and I'm still on medication, but I'm getting better. I guess I'm quite lucky to be alive, really."

"When I last heard of you, Trevor Cockrell had plans for you to work at his conference centre."

Miranda smiled, ran her hand over her hair and, now much more at ease in Clive's company, leaned forward, displaying an impressive embonpoint, and began to pour out her recent life history. "Yes, that's right, he did. I couldn't start for quite a while because of my, er, accident, but he kept the job open for me. I enjoyed it to start with, but, after a while, I started to get restless. And it was quite difficult to work so closely with Trevor." Miranda noticed Clive's quizzical look. "I mean, I couldn't exactly hide the fact that Trevor and I had had a, well, er, we'd had a bit of a fling, especially as Julia, his wife, more or less caught us in the act. I mean, I knew Trevor's marriage had been going through a rocky patch – Julia walking out on him halfway through their holiday was a bit of a clue – and we were kind of thrown together by circumstances, but when he and Julia got back together and then baby Grace came along, I started to feel, well, uncomfortable. Julia can be a bit neurotic, to put it mildly, and very jealous, and I sensed she was watching me all the time. Every time Trevor and I chatted, I half-expected her to leap out from a cupboard or from behind a bush. So, anyway, when this opportunity arose, I took it. I mean, I haven't fallen out with Trevor or anything, he gave me a good reference and, when I'm not on tour, I still help out at his conference centre if he needs an extra pair of hands."

"And Julia? Is she still working as a genealogist?"

"Ah, Julia!" Miranda raised her eyebrows, sighed and fell silent for a moment. "Well, I think she still does some work, but not as much, obviously, as she did. She's only really working from home these days and only when Grace lets her. I'm not really too sure she's enjoying motherhood very much. She gets quite tired and when she gets tired, she tends to explode, and when she explodes, you don't want to be anywhere near…" Miranda shrugged. "To be honest, I try and keep out of the way when she's around."

"Mmmm. Can I get you a drink?" Clive suddenly asked. "On the house! I'm not trying to chat you up or anything. My wife's over there keeping an eye on us and I'll ask her to come and join us, if you don't mind. We'd like to know a bit more about your coach party."

Miranda hesitated for a moment. "Yes, why not? That would be nice. A glass of white wine would be lovely – not too dry!"

"Right then, a glass of white wine, not too dry. Leave it to me!"

Clive rose from the table, exchanged a few brief words with Clare and, as she wandered over to where Miranda was sitting, he disappeared into the bar. Clare eased herself into the chair opposite Miranda, focussed her penetrating grey-green eyes on Clive's new acquaintance and smiled. "Clive's just told me who you are – I had no idea. It's wonderful you've made such a good recovery. I know Clive worried about you at the time."

"Did he?" Miranda emitted a girlish giggle. "I didn't think he'd even remember me."

"Oh, he's got a good memory, believe me! It comes of being a good detective, I suppose. So tell me about your party."

"Well, the tour's called '*The Stately Homes of Britain*'. It's tailored to the 'more mature' traveller who has an interest in history and a bit of money to splash around. The clients aren't usually very exciting, but they're normally well-behaved and the tips can be quite generous. We spend a fortnight travelling around the country. We spend a few nights here and a few nights there and go out each day to see a different stately pile in the area; sometimes more than one in a day." She paused, looked up and smiled as Clive returned with a bottle of wine and three glasses. He dragged a chair from a nearby table, sat down and filled each glass in turn.

"Anyway", Miranda continued. "We go to these stately homes, have a look around and have a guided tour. Often we're allowed 'a privileged look behind the scenes' and we usually have lunch and…"

"So where are you visiting while you're staying here?" Clare asked while Miranda took a small sip from her glass.

"Well, tomorrow we're going to Ambury House in the morning and Hackmoor Manor in the afternoon. It's supposed to be haunted, but I've never—"

"Oh, that old trick!" Clare laughed.

"And then," Miranda continued, "on Friday we're spending the day at Wickmorstead Hall and then, on Saturday, it's Chartfield Castle."

Clive and Clare exchanged looks. "Ah, I don't expect you've heard," Clive ventured. "The police haven't released many details yet, so I can't tell you much, but Lord Westleigh's daughter disappeared earlier in the week and there's talk that she's been kidnapped. She lives on the Chartfield estate, so, if she hasn't turned up by Saturday, I expect the police will be crawling all over the place so there might be some disruption to your plans. You'd better check before you leave and have some sort of contingency plan up your sleeve."

Miranda clasped both hands to her face. "Oh, shit! Oh, hell! That's all I need. Do they know what happened?"

Clive shrugged. "As far as I know, she went riding on the Chartfield estate, which she did most evenings and, sometime later, they found her horse wandering about, but she'd gone – completely disappeared."

"Oh, God! How awful!"

"Do you know who is supposed to be showing you around on Saturday?"

"Yes, it's somebody called Anthony Granard. He usually does our tours for us. He can be a bit solemn, but he knows his stuff and he's very informative and very helpful."

"You've done this tour before?" Clare asked.

"Oh, yes, a couple of times."

"But you haven't stayed here before."

"No, we used to stay at the Carlow Bridge Hotel, but they kept putting the prices up and it wasn't really that good. To be honest, we thought we were being ripped off. And then someone recommended this place; I must say that if the evidence of our dinner tonight is anything to go by, your hotel is much better!"

"Oh, that's nice of you…" Clive broke off as he was distracted by a shadow moving on the wall facing him. Out of the corner of his eye, he detected a sudden movement and turned round just in time to glimpse Ralph Dalton walking briskly away. Though he couldn't be sure, his instincts, honed by years of detective work, told him that Ralph Dalton had been loitering close by, shielded by one of Clare's carefully positioned screens, and listening in to their conversation.

*

The visitors' car park that separated Vernon Court from Drake Court afforded good views of the residents' bungalows across the open side of the courtyard. Alison Pawlett did not have much experience of discreet surveillance – whenever some form of surveillance was required, Caspar Beauregard was always keen to volunteer – and, although she was grateful for the opportunity to hone her skills, she was feeling uncharacteristically nervous. Anxious to avoid letting Clive down and keen to secure a parking space that would give her an unimpeded view of 2 Vernon Court, she had arrived much earlier than was necessary.

Still feeling strangely apprehensive about what should have been a routine assignment, her throat felt uncomfortably dry as she began her lonely vigil. So, not daring to avert her gaze from Gerald Ashburton's front door and desperate to remain alert, she regularly reached across to the passenger seat, grabbed a bottle of mineral water and quaffed liberally from it.

Eventually, at just before eight o'clock, the door of number two opened and an elderly gentleman, whom she presumed to be Gerald Ashburton, emerged. He was tall, upright and sprightly and, as Joan Glendale had intimated, he sported a trilby hat pulled low over his forehead. After a brief, furtive look around, he marched off in the direction of the town centre. Anxious to avoid arousing her quarry's suspicions, Constable Pawlett suppressed the strong desire to follow him immediately. Instead she replaced the bottle of mineral water on the passenger seat, took a couple of deep breaths and waited a moment or two. When she was confident that Gerald Ashburton was on his way to his destination – wherever and whatever that was – and was unlikely to turn back, she eased herself quietly out of her car and began her pursuit on foot.

The Reverend Ashburton was surprisingly spry for an elderly man and, as he strode down the road, his stride gradually lengthened and his pace quickened, so much so that Constable Pawlett had occasionally to break into a trot in order to keep him in her sights. South Street was an unremarkable road, lined on both sides by solid, unremarkable pre-war housing and, apart from a late commuter or two returning home, was largely deserted, most residents having already retreated behind their front doors for the evening. The natural light was fading and, as the street lights gradually came on, strange shadows were thrown across the street, highlighting narrow, dark alleyways between the houses. At the same time, the sounds of Alison Pawlett's footsteps seemed to grow louder as they rebounded from the solid, impassive walls.

After about ten minutes of brisk walking along the largely unpopulated street, Gerald Ashburton arrived in the town centre. Stowbrook was an old market town where once livestock, farm produce, wool and leather were freely traded. These days, much of its historical heritage had been swept away by a series of unsympathetic, modern developments. The town still retained its original layout, with four main roads converging on a square which, at one time, contained the old market cross. The square still remained the main focal point of the town, but the market cross had long since disappeared and, in its place, there was a small, uninspiring shopping centre with a few general shops, all closed, several sparsely populated restaurants and a pub, from which the sound of loud music was emanating. As she walked on, Alison Pawlett noted with some sadness that an Italian restaurant that she and her partner had often frequented in happier times had closed down, its shuttered frontage dark and unloved.

On reaching the square, Gerald Ashburton turned right into East Street and, still marching briskly, headed towards the oldest surviving part of the original town where a number of large, sturdy old houses straggled along the bank of the Stow Brook, a tributary of the River Carlow. After two or three hundred yards, he arrived at St Mary's Parish Church, a typical example of late sixteenth-century church architecture with a slightly overgrown graveyard and a couple of venerable yew trees. Constable Pawlett stopped and swore quietly under her breath. She had been hoping to uncover some dark, maybe sleazy, secret about the Reverend Ashburton's private life and was acutely disappointed to discover that she had given up her evening only to follow him to his local parish church. But, just as she was reluctantly thinking of abandoning her mission, Gerald Ashburton strode purposefully past the church and, with one final surreptitious look around, disappeared into the large, creeper-covered old house next door. Waiting until she was sure that her quarry was safely inside the house, Alison Pawlett crept up to the front gate. A sign announced that the house was called 'The Old Vicarage'. Cursing quietly for the second time, she had sidled quietly away into the shadows and was again considering aborting her mission when she noticed another man – shorter, stouter and slightly younger than Gerald Ashburton – approach, look nervously around, and disappear inside.

Darkness had now descended and, although the days were still warm and sunny, the evenings had a dewy chill that presaged autumn's capricious arrival. Suddenly realising that her usual denim outfit was scant protection against the rapidly falling temperature, Constable Pawlett shivered as she took refuge beneath a mature oak tree on the opposite side of the road from 'The Old Vicarage' and continued to watch the front of the house unobserved. After about twenty minutes, another man, no more than an indistinct silhouette, approached and quickly went inside.

It was at this point that Constable Pawlett's lack of surveillance experience, combined with the evening chill and the effects of imbibing nearly a full bottle of mineral water, reminded her that her bladder was uncomfortably full. After several minutes of shuffling restlessly from one foot to the other and the occasional grimace, she could avoid the inevitable no longer – she needed to pee. The only public conveniences that she knew of in Stowbrook were back in the square next to the shopping centre. Setting off briskly and gathering speed with every desperate step, she reached the welcome sanctuary of the ladies' convenience with little time to spare. When, a little later, she emerged onto the square with a look of undisguised, sublime relief, she faced an awkward dilemma. She had effectively been "off watch" for some minutes now and it was quite possible that Gerald Ashburton had, by now, left 'The Old Vicarage' and was returning home.

Unsure of the best course of action, she hesitated for a moment or two before striding back towards 'The Old Vicarage' and resuming her vigil beneath the tree. There were no signs of anyone arriving or leaving, however, and the heavy, opaque curtains and blinds drawn securely across the windows betrayed no secrets. After several minutes of dithering uncertainty, Constable Pawlett crept up to the gate of 'The Old Vicarage', hoping to get at least some hint of what was going on behind the heavy curtains and whether Gerald Ashburton was still in attendance. Almost immediately, the front door half opened, allowing a shaft of pale light to illuminate the footpath leading up to it, and she heard a male voice, one that she thought she recognised. Although she couldn't hear what was being said, something was suddenly making her feel vulnerable and, although she would not admit it, even to herself, slightly afraid. Without a moment's hesitation, she turned and set off quickly back up East Street. As she approached the square, she could hear loud, heavy footsteps behind her. Not daring to look round, she turned into South Street and, with ever more rapid steps, headed back towards Vernon Court and the sanctuary of her car. As she hastened on, and in a state of increasing fright, she began to imagine that there might be more than one set of footsteps close behind her. She couldn't be sure – it might simply be one set of footsteps echoing on the pavement – but, as she continued onwards, listening intently, she thought she detected two different stride patterns, one shorter and heavier than the other. It was then that her mobile phone rang, causing her to jump visibly. Afraid to stop, she reached anxiously into her pocket and studied the illuminated screen as she continued to walk. Recognising the caller's number, she shouted, "What the hell do you want?" into the phone. As she did so, she turned round and saw Gerald Ashburton striding towards her. Now frozen by fear, she stood and watched as he approached her, trilby hat still pulled over his eyes. Then, as he passed, he raised his trilby, smiled and said, "Good evening," loudly, his words reverberating down the quiet street.

"Phew, sorry about that," Alison Pawlett spoke quietly into the phone as she turned and continued walking, less hurriedly now. Then she heard the footsteps, the shorter, heavier ones that she thought she had heard before, approaching rapidly from behind. Panic-stricken, she turned round and, suddenly, a heavy, muscular fist smashed into her face.

Fourteen

Thursday 24 August

As Clive Walsingham followed Caspar Beauregard onto the hotel terrace, he paused briefly at the entrance to the bar, where Clare was piling an assortment of sandwiches and cakes onto several china plates. She looked up and gave Clive a reproving stare.

"You know, if you carry on inviting your new chum round for lunch, he's going to bankrupt us. He's eating us out of house and home!"

Clive smiled. "Don't worry, darling! My consultant's fee will more than cover the cost – I'll make sure of that."

Clare reciprocated Clive's smile. "Alright, I'll believe you. Are you expecting anyone else? There's a lot of food here, even for you and Dick!"

"Mmm, I was expecting Alison Pawlett, but there's no sign of her and I can't raise her on her mobile. It's a bit disappointing, really; I wanted to know how she got on last night. But give me a few minutes before you bring all the food out. I don't want Dick speaking with his mouth full more than I can help."

Clive strolled out onto the terrace and sat down opposite the acting detective inspector, who was wearing what appeared to be his best dark suit, together with a smart pale blue shirt and dark blue tie, and his usual crestfallen expression. Though still pleasant, it was a cooler day than of late, and Clive didn't feel the need to seek out the shade of a parasol to protect the top of his thinning head of hair, although Caspar Beauregard was carefully removing his jacket and tie.

"So," Clive began amiably, "I'd say, by your appearance, that you've been up at Chartfield Castle again this morning. How's the search for the missing heiress going?"

Caspar Beauregard stared wistfully into the distance. "Not very well, I'm afraid," he finally answered, shaking his head. "There's been no sign of Lucy Jeffries, nothing on the security cameras, her mobile is permanently switched off and there's been no contact with her family or… There's been no ransom demand – nothing. And meanwhile, Lord Westleigh is leaping up and down; he keeps phoning the chief constable and demanding to know why we haven't made any—"

"So you've got no leads?"

"Well, nothing definite, although we have uncovered something that might be of interest. When we started asking around the workers on the estate, we kept getting hints that Lucy Jeffries had been having a bit of an affair with her groom, Tom Chewton. No-one was prepared to say anything too definite, it was all a bit 'nudge, nudge, wink, wink', but we got the strong impression that when Lucy went riding, she didn't always have a horse."

Clive chuckled. "And do you think her husband knows?"

Caspar Beauregard shrugged. "I've no idea; he doesn't give much away. There have been some veiled hints, though, that he's playing away as well, although nobody is prepared to elaborate. There is a suggestion that he's a little closer to the children's nanny than is entirely appropriate and proper, but again, there's no proof, just gossip—"

"But if Lucy Jeffries' husband did know what his wife was getting up to, then he could be implicated in her disappearance."

Caspar Beauregard sighed. "Yes, I know. I'll need to talk to Alex Jeffries about the rumours, obviously, but it's a sensitive area and it's not going to be easy—"

"No it won't," Clive agreed with a slight smirk. "And Lord Westleigh; do you think he knows what's going on?"

"No, I'm pretty sure he doesn't – that's why no-one's being very forthcoming. No-one wants him to find out; he's very close to his daughter and if he thought she was having an affair, he'd be very upset. No, Lord Westleigh is absolutely convinced that Richard Edgton is behind his daughter's disappearance, but we've turned over his house, his offices, his quarry buildings and we've not found her. The forensic team are currently going over the quarry buildings in the hope of finding something relevant, but nothing's turned up yet. But what is quite intriguing is that I went to see Richard Edgton the day before yesterday and then followed him to Fearnley quarry where he and his minder, Dean Footner, were skulking around loading some boxes into the boot of his car and then, next morning, he phoned to report a break-in at the quarry. I'm sure he knew that we were going to turn up sometime with a search warrant and I reckon he staged the break-in so that he could remove all the incriminating stuff before we pitched up."

"I see." Clive tugged his earlobe thoughtfully. "Mind you, if Richard Edgton has kidnapped Lucy Jeffries, I doubt he'd be stupid enough to hide her anywhere you might easily find her. He'd have hidden her somewhere where you wouldn't think of looking."

Acting Inspector Beauregard emitted another sigh, much louder and heavier this time. "I suppose so," he agreed reluctantly, "but we're really chasing shadows now. I'll speak to Alex Jeffries again and maybe talk to the groom again, but I don't know what more I can do. We've circulated Lucy Jeffries' details, published her photograph, spoken to known friends and relatives, and got nowhere. I suspect either she will suddenly turn up or we've got to wait for a ransom demand to be made, or we discover a body." He shuddered. "It's very frustrating, especially with Lord Westleigh so involved."

"Tell me," Clive asked. "I never hear any mention of a Lady Westleigh. Is there one?"

"No, there isn't; it's all quite tragic, really. A couple of years after Lucy was born, Lady Westleigh gave birth to a boy, but there were complications and the boy was born severely disabled. He died when he was seven and, apparently, Lady Westleigh took it all very badly. By all accounts, she became very depressed and, one afternoon, they found her body in the lake on the estate. A verdict of suicide was returned. Lord Westleigh has never re-married and, as far as we know, there's been no other woman in his life since."

"Oh dear, that's terrible!" Clive concurred. He looked up as he heard Clare and Jamie Coulton approaching. They were laden with plates of sandwiches and assorted cakes, and trotting behind them was Archie, his keen sense of smell having already detected the presence of prawn in some of the sandwiches.

Svelte and elegant as always, Clare placed her plates on the table and gave the slightly automatic smile that she reserved for the hotel guests. "There, that should keep you going for a while. We'll go and fetch the drinks." She turned and marched purposefully back towards the conservatory, with Jamie Coulton plodding uncharacteristically slowly and solemnly behind her.

Caspar Beauregard surveyed the generous spread, his heavy eyes suddenly wide and alive. "Is this all for us?"

Clive nodded. "Yes. I was expecting Alison Pawlett but—"

"Ah yes, that reminds me. We got a message earlier on to say that she was off sick, but I haven't had time to follow it up yet. I don't know what the problem is or how long she's going to be off for. Was she alright yesterday? She wasn't in touch at all." He looked quizzically at Clive.

Clive exhaled. "To be honest, I didn't speak to her yesterday. She was following up on a few queries and questions that we had, doing some background checks and a bit of surveillance, but—"

"Surveillance?" Acting Inspector Beauregard interrupted. "She's not very experienced at surveillance, you know. She hasn't got the patience and—"

"Ah, erm," Clive hesitated while he grabbed hold of Archie, who had jumped onto the table and was making a bee-line for the sandwiches, and placed him, wriggling, onto the ground. "I take it she didn't tell you about yesterday evening's mission, although I can't imagine—"

"Yesterday evening? Do you think you'd better tell me about yesterday evening?" Caspar Beauregard sounded tetchy. While accepting that he had been preoccupied with the disappearance of Lord Westleigh's daughter, the murder of Mary Pullman was still his case and he expected to be kept informed of Clive and Alison's activities.

"Yes, of course," Clive replied, now quite concerned that he might have exposed Alison to some unforeseen danger. "I didn't realise Alison hadn't said anything to you." He didn't like telling lies, but he knew that Acting Inspector Beauregard would not have condoned what Alison had agreed to do and had sworn her to secrecy. "You remember when we went see the Reverend Gerald Ashburton?"

"Yes, but that was a waste of time, wasn't it?"

"Mmm, I'm not sure, but you'll remember his neighbour saying he always went out on a Wednesday evening and that he looked shifty. Well, Alison agreed to follow him yesterday evening. I couldn't do it because I was on duty here and anyway he's met me and might have recognised me. It didn't seem too tricky a task and she was willing enough. I mean we are only talking about keeping an eye on a retired vicar in Stowbrook on a Wednesday evening. All the same, I'd feel happier if I knew where she was and what's wrong with her."

"Me too! I'll try and make contact when we've finished here." Giving no indication that he intended to finish in the near future, Acting Inspector Beauregard reached out for a prawn sandwich and took a generous bite.

"Anyway, have you found out anything that might help us?" Clive asked, keen to change the subject and anxious to avert his gaze from the piece of prawn that had attached itself to the front of the acting inspector's shirt.

"What? Oh yes." Caspar Beauregard's displeasure at Clive's bit of subterfuge had been assuaged by the gargantuan spread in front of him and he paused as he loaded several more sandwiches onto his plate while Jamie Coulton, distracted and distant, returned with an assortment of drinks which he placed on the table with none of his usual delicate finesse.

"Well, I re-checked my notes," the acting inspector continued when Jamie was safely out of earshot. "And, as I mentioned, Mary Pullman did make a formal complaint about her neighbour, Martin Carslake, spying on her and taking photographs. We interviewed him and confiscated his camera and computer, but we found nothing remotely incriminating so we couldn't take any further action. But I have turned up something interesting about Dean Footner."

"Tell me more!"

"Well, the woman you've met who calls herself Tracey Footner isn't in fact his wife; they've never married. Her real name is Tracey Croxton. But Dean Footner has been married before and the two eldest children are his by that marriage. Apparently his wife left him because of his violence. The local social services people were threatening to take his kids into care at one time, but nothing came of it."

"Mmm. Well, that confirms that Dean Footner can be violent." Clive tried to sound more interested than he was in Acting Inspector Beauregard's less than startling revelation. "Have you been able to confirm his alibi for the weekend that Mary Pullman was murdered, and have you searched his workshop?"

"We've searched his workshop. He wasn't very happy about it, but all we found were model aircraft kits and some tools. The manager of the caravan site in Radholme has confirmed that the family were staying there when they said they were. But there is a small cafe on the site – a burger and chips kind of place – and, interestingly, the staff on duty remembered seeing Tracey and the kids eating there on the Saturday and the Sunday – they were quite boisterous, apparently – but there was no sign of Dean. So he could easily have sneaked back from Radholme at the time Mary Pullman was murdered; the trouble is we don't have any sightings of him at all that weekend, so…"

Clive scratched his head, removed Archie from the table for the second time and waited until his colleague had taken another large bite out of his sandwich before he spoke. "So Dean Footner could still be a suspect – he may have no alibi, but you've got no evidence. Have you found anything else of interest?"

Mercifully, Caspar Beauregard finished chewing before he replied. "Well, you were right about Gregory Pullman. Gareth Adamson did purchase his house through Blaby and Quixhill, the estate agents that Gregory Pullman used to work for. I tried to find out if he had handled the sale, but the woman in the office was most unhelpful. She got quite evasive and said she would have to speak to Mr Quixhill, but he wasn't around at the time and she said she'd phone me back, but—"

"Mmm, now that is interesting. Gregory Pullman was most adamant that he'd never heard of Gareth Adamson, which, under the circumstances you describe, seems a little unlikely. I wonder what he's hiding. I think someone will need to speak to Mr Quixhill as soon as possible."

Acting Inspector Beauregard was still chewing on the remains of one sandwich while he was lifting another one from his plate. He looked across at Clive through doleful, heavy-lidded eyes.

"Clive, I was wondering if you might speak to Mr Quixhill, or perhaps ask Alison to when she finally surfaces. It's just that this Lucy Jeffries business – whatever it turns out to be – is taking up so much of my time. I will tell you one more thing, though, that you might find interesting. Gareth Adamson has just put his house on the market through Blaby and Quixhill."

"Has he now?" Clive seemed genuinely surprised. For a moment he paused and watched with a mixture of admiration and aversion as Caspar Beauregard continued his rapid, untidy demolition of a chicken salad sandwich. "Alright, I'll talk to Gareth Adamson again, but we do have a problem. I'm happy enough to continue to help with the investigation, but we've got a big coach party here at the moment and it is very important that we lavish plenty of attention on them, so I'm going to be too busy to spend much time on the investigation in the next few days. You're tied up with Lucy Jeffries' disappearance and we don't know how long Alison is going to be off for, so I'm going to have to ask you a couple of favours."

The detective sighed – it was a sigh so heavy that the whole of his gaunt body seemed to rock – and quickly swallowed his mouthful. "I'll see what I can do," he replied half-heartedly.

Clive, meanwhile, removed Archie from the table for the third time. Archie squawked his protest and, upset by what he perceived to be Clive's repeated, unreasonable interventions, wandered off in search of an alternative pastime. "I've been having another look at the photographs of the crime scene, where Mary Pullman's body was found, and there's something that doesn't look right. I don't want to say too much at this stage, but I remember you saying that the pathologist was puzzled by some inconsistencies and I wonder if you'd allow me to have a word with him."

"Yes, I suppose so, although I should tell you that he is not our usual pathologist – she's on holiday at the moment – and I don't think he's very used to dealing with murder victims. I don't know what you're puzzled about and it might help if—"

Clive held up a hand. "I'm sure if you mentioned me to him and explain that I'm helping you with your enquiries, he'd be happy to help."

"Mmm, I'll see what I can do."

"Good – and one last thing. As you know, Mary Pullman was researching her family history when she disappeared and we have her notebook, admittedly incomplete, with loads of entries about her family forebears. Now I haven't got the time, or indeed the knowledge, to go through them, but I know a professional genealogist. She was involved in my last case in Inglemouth. She's not working full-time at the moment – she has a very young daughter – but I'm sure she could help to make sense of Mary Pullman's notes. Of course, she'd need a fee; maybe your consultancy fund could stretch to something?"

"Now hang on a minute," the acting inspector protested. "We've got some money, but it's not a bottomless pit. I'd have to justify her involvement in the investigation and get authorisation and—"

"Are you close to making an arrest?"

"Well, no."

"Well, there you are then. She lives in Surrey. I'd like to pay her a visit with Mary Pullman's notes and see what she has to say."

"Well, alright, I suppose, but I don't want to waste time and money going down any blind alleys and you must keep me informed and—"

"Good, then I'll arrange to go and see her tomorrow if I can…" Clive paused and looked up as Simon Verwood wandered out of the conservatory and headed slowly towards the rose garden. He seemed unsteady on his feet and weaved a slightly erratic path across the lawn. "He's started early today," Clive thought to himself as Simon meandered away.

*

It was late into the afternoon when the 'Stately Homes of Britain' coach party returned to the hotel and the tour participants eased themselves, slowly and creakily, from the coach and straggled wearily to their rooms. Ostensibly, the late-afternoon finish was to allow them time to "freshen up" before dinner, but in reality it offered them the opportunity to rest their sore feet and have a bit of a nap after a hard day's sightseeing.

For Miranda Bellamy, this daily hiatus represented a welcome bit of free time. True, there was some paperwork to complete and final arrangements for the next day's visit to be confirmed, but this was, nevertheless, an eagerly anticipated opportunity to relax for a while without having to be on duty, maybe to settle down in her room with the latest family saga by her favourite author, Jim Brownsage. She wasn't too thrilled, therefore, when Clive intercepted her as she wandered through the foyer. Although she smiled politely, her expressive eyes betrayed her irritation.

"I'm sorry to bother you, Miranda, but I wonder if I could have a brief word. It won't take a minute, I promise." Clive tried to reassure her as she cast longing glances in the direction of the staircase that led up to the sanctuary of her room.

"Is it about Saturday?" she asked doubtfully, remembering Clive's warning that the planned visit to Chartfield Castle might be in jeopardy.

"Not directly," Clive replied, equivocally. "Can we go into the dining room? There'll be nobody in there at the moment." Looking confused and suspicious, Miranda reluctantly followed Clive and sat down opposite him at a table in one of Clare's imaginatively designed alcoves. "No, no," Clive continued. "As far as I know, your visit on Saturday will be okay. I think the police are now looking elsewhere for Lord Westleigh's daughter. No, it's just that we were talking yesterday about Julia Cockrell."

"Yeees." Miranda sounded wary; the mention of Julia Cockrell's name usually meant trouble in one form or another.

"You see, I don't think I mentioned yesterday that I'm doing a bit of consultancy work for the local police. They've got a couple of complex investigations going on at the moment, including the disappearance of Lord Westleigh's daughter, and they're a bit understaffed so I was asked if I would help—"

"Yes, and?" Miranda's unease was increasing with every word that Clive uttered and the haunted look in her eyes had returned.

"Anyway, you don't need to know the details, but one of the lines of enquiry I'm pursuing at the moment involves some family research that someone was doing. I've got their notebook, but, frankly, it looks quite complicated and I can't spend as much time on it as I'd like; besides, I'm not a qualified genealogist. And I remember you saying that Julia Cockrell isn't able to work as much as she'd like at present and I wondered if she might be interested in helping me. The police will pay for her time."

"Oh, I see," Miranda's demeanour lightened considerably. Smiling spontaneously, she reached into her bag for her mobile phone. "I'll have her number here somewhere." A few deft finger movements followed. "Yes, here it is. Do you want to make a note?" She handed the phone to Clive, who hastily scribbled down a number on the back of a table napkin.

"Thanks. I'll give her a call later on. Shall I say I've spoken to you?"

Miranda shook her head. "Probably best not to – she doesn't usually respond well at the mention of my name. She's always a bit suspicious of anything to do with me after my, er, my, er, my relationship with Trevor."

*

Clive had just finished talking with Miranda, who had disappeared up the stairs towards her room with an impressive turn of speed, when Alison Pawlett walked slowly into the foyer. The dark glasses which she was wearing only partially disguised the heavy bruising on her face. Her nose and lips were swollen and there was a hint of congealed blood around her nostrils. Her dark hair, normally heavily lacquered and sleek, was dishevelled and grubby, and there were spatterings of blood on her denim jacket.

It was Clare, bustling between the kitchen and the dining room, who saw her first. She stopped abruptly and stared incredulously at the bruised and bloody apparition that confronted her.

"Alison? My God, what's happened?"

Alison Pawlett stumbled slightly and leant against the wall for support. She tried to say something but managed only an inaudible mumble. Clare looked around, desperately hoping that Clive, or any other form of assistance, might instantly materialise, but no-one came.

"Look, er, you'd better come into the office. I'll get some help."

"No! No help! I don't want any help!" Alison Pawlett forced the words out through her swollen lips, her voice croaking with emotion. Half-fearing that she would pull away, Clare took her gently by the arm, led her slowly into the office and guided her to a chair. Once Alison, distressed and shaking, was settled into the chair, Clare drew up another chair and gently raised her hands towards Alison's face. Alison flinched.

"May I?" Clare asked and, meeting no resistance, gently removed Alison's dark glasses, revealing the full extent of her injuries. Not only was her left eye badly bruised, but it was swollen so much that it had virtually closed.

"My God, Alison, you need to see a doctor. I'll just..." Clare reached for the phone, but Alison grabbed her hand.

"No, I don't want to see a doctor; I'll be fine..." Alison protested unconvincingly, her words slurring with the effort of forcing them through her swollen lips.

"Okay, okay, no doctor. But we'll need to patch you up a bit. Wait here!" Clare disappeared and, after a few moments, returned with a bowl of water, some paper towels and a first aid box. She dipped a paper towel in the water and, as she started to gently dab at Alison's sore face, she repeated her earlier question.

"What's happened, Alison? Who did this to you?"

Alison Pawlett winced and jerked her head backwards as Clare continued dabbing her wounds. "I, I need to ask you a favour," she stuttered.

"Ask away," Clare replied uncertainly as she continued to tend Alison's sore and puffy face.

"I, I can't go home..." Alison hesitated as she looked up apprehensively to see Clive enter the room, having been alerted to Alison's dramatic arrival and battered appearance by Clare as she searched for the first aid kit.

"You mean your...?"

Alison gave a half-nod and winced. "Yeah, my partner, Colin, the bastard!"

"My God!" Clare repeated. "Have you reported this to anyone?"

"No, no, I haven't and you mustn't either, I beg you. Things are bad enough already. No, no, the thing is, I've got nowhere else to go. I've got no family round here these days and if I stay at any of my friends' houses, he'll come and find me. But he doesn't know about this place and I just wondered if you might have a room available for a few days, just until I can make alternative arrangements. I'll pay my way and everything."

With an expression that ranged from shock to outrage, Clare glanced across at Clive, who had perched on the edge of the desk. He made it clear with a smile and a benevolent hand gesture that he was happy to leave arrangements in her hands.

"The thing is," Clare replied, "the hotel is more or less full at the moment. We've got a coach party in and then it's the bank holiday weekend and..." She looked anxiously at Alison, trembling and hunched pathetically on her chair, and glanced at Clive again, who pointed a finger towards the ceiling. "But, um, we do have some rooms up in the attic that some of our staff use sometimes when they need to stay over. They're not up to the standard of our guest rooms, I'm afraid; they're fairly basic, but if you don't mind that—"

"No, no, I'm sure that'll be fine. I'm so grateful." Alison Pawlett tried to smile but found the effort too painful.

"Incidentally, I should mention that one of the rooms up there is in use for much of the time." Clare exchanged glances with Clive again. "But I'm sure the occupant won't bother you at all."

"I'm so grateful," Alison repeated weakly, fingering her cracked and swollen lips.

"Okay, that's settled then. I'll get Jamie to prepare the room for you." Sensing that Clive urgently needed to have a confidential chat with Alison, Clare began to leave the room, allowing Clive to slip into the chair she had vacated.

"I don't suppose I could have a drink?" Alison asked feebly as Clare was about to depart.

"Yes of course," Clare replied. "What would you like? A hot coffee or a strong cup of tea?"

"A vodka; a large one, if possible."

Clare looked across at Clive again. "Okay, one large vodka coming up."

Once Clare had left the room, Clive leaned across and spoke quietly to Alison.

"Your injuries, Alison; were they inflicted yesterday evening?"

Alison nodded while she continued to dab her swollen eye with the damp paper towel.

"In that case, I think you'd better tell me what happened, if you're up to it. What you tell me will go no further if that's what you want."

Alison nodded again and sniffed. "Yes, yes, I need to tell someone."

Clive leaned back in his chair. "When you're ready then, and do stop if it's all too painful."

Alison Pawlett began her account quietly and haltingly, often stopping between words as though struggling to recall the events of the previous evening, or uncertain whether she could continue with the harrowing narrative, or simply finding the effort of speaking too painful. She described how she followed Gerald Ashburton to 'The Old Vicarage', she mentioned seeing some other men going into the building, she avoided any reference to her enforced comfort break and then recounted the start of her brisk march back towards Vernon Court.

"And as I was walking back," she concluded, shakily, "I heard footsteps behind me as though someone was following me. I felt a bit spooked and I didn't want to turn round, so I just kept walking. And then my phone rang; it was Colin, my partner, or should I say ex-partner. I slowed down to answer it and as I did so, Gerald Ashburton strode briskly past me, raised his hat and said something – I didn't catch what he said because I was trying to make out what Colin was saying on the phone. But as I carried on walking, I could still hear footsteps behind me, so I turned round and there was Colin, right behind me, and, and… that's when he did this."

"He beat you up? But why?"

"When I'd stopped shouting and crying, I think Colin realised he'd gone too far. He'd been in 'The Old Vicarage' himself and when he came out, he saw me scuttling away. He obviously thought I'd been spying on him, so he followed me, determined to have it out with me, I suppose. For some reason, he decided to phone rather than call out to me and then, when he saw Gerald Ashburton walk past, raise his hat and say something, it was too much for him. He hates other men talking to me – he gets so jealous – and—"

"Your partner's done this sort of thing before?"

Alison nodded. "He was on his last warning."

"And did you go home with him?"

"God, no! I've finished with him. I spent the night in my car, nursing my wounds and trying to collect my thoughts. Anyway, I went back home this morning after Colin had left for work and gathered up as many belongings as I could –

some clothes, my laptop, that sort of thing – loaded them into the car and drove away." Alison Pawlett paused briefly to dab at her wounds. "But while we were shouting at each other in the street last night, Colin let slip some information about 'The Old Vicarage'. It seems Colin's brother Dean used to work there as a bouncer."

"Dean?"

"Dean Footner. He works for Richard Edgton now."

Clive whistled quietly to himself. "Yes, I've met Dean."

"Anyway, it turns out that 'The Old Vicarage' is now what they call 'a gentleman's club' for members only. It's called '*The Dog Collar*' for fairly obvious reasons. From what I can make out the ground floor is, basically, a casino. They've got roulette wheels, gaming tables, fruit machines. But upstairs, some of the members are entertained by lap dancers and there are also a couple of bedrooms where the entertainment becomes a little more intimate."

Clive whistled to himself again. "I see. And Gerald Ashburton and Colin Footner are both members?"

"Yes, and Richard Edgton too, it seems. That's how he first recruited Dean, apparently. I didn't ask what Colin got up to when he was there and how much money he spent, but I've drawn my own conclusions."

"And do the police know about this place?"

Alison Pawlett shrugged. "Well, I certainly didn't know about it and nobody's mentioned it. I'll have to mention it to Dick, erm, Acting Inspector Beauregard, of course."

"Yes I suppose you will," Clive agreed grudgingly. "Listen, Alison, I'm so sorry about what happened. I didn't expect this—"

"Oh, no, it's okay. Please don't feel guilty. My face is a bit sore, but I'll heal – no, the really important thing for me was that I found out what Colin was really like and I'm glad I did."

"What do you think you'll do now?" Clive looked up as Clare returned, a look of intense concern on her expressive face, and placed a large glass of vodka beside Alison before quietly leaving.

Alison Pawlett shrugged. "Well, I definitely can't go back home. No, no, I think I'll probably ask for a transfer away from here when I can."

"Yes, of course. Clare was right, you know, you really should report what happened to you." Clive stared hopefully at Alison, but she said nothing and shook her head. "Of course, I can't make you." Alison shook her head again, sufficiently vigorously to convince Clive that there was nothing to be gained from belabouring the point. He hesitated for several moments before speaking and his demeanour became more earnest. "Alison, I'm afraid I must ask you about something else and I'm sorry to do so when you're like this."

"What is it, Clive, what's the matter?"

"You see, I was doing a bit of research earlier today, trying to turn up anything that might help us find Mary Pullman's killer, and I thought it might be useful to find out a bit more about the circumstances surrounding the sale of Fearnley quarry to Richard Edgton."

Alison suddenly became angry. "What the…?" she protested as loudly as her injured face permitted. "You had no right to—"

"Oh, I had every right to do so. Everything I found out is in the public domain – it's just a matter of knowing where to look. And do you know what I found? Of course, you do. I found out that Richard Edgton bought the quarry from a company called Hackleton Holdings and I found out that the registered directors were N W and S L Pawlett. Is there anything you want to tell me, Alison?"

Alison Pawlett sniffed, took a swig of vodka, wiped some moisture from her eyes, winced slightly and then stared resolutely at the floor. "Do I have any choice?"

"I think you know the answer to that."

Alison Pawlett nodded, almost imperceptibly. "Norman and Stephen Pawlett are two of my uncles. They'd run Fearnley quarry for many years and then they suddenly sold it to this businessman with a dodgy reputation called Richard Edgton. I don't remember exactly what was said at the time, but it was common knowledge within the family that they'd sold it under duress to Richard Edgton and at a fraction of its true value. And my uncle Norman was so angry and stressed by the whole affair that he suffered a fatal heart attack soon afterwards. I was a raw constable working in London at the time, but I was so angry at what Richard Edgton had done that I vowed that I would try and get even with him if I could. So I put in for a transfer here and have spent much of the last two or three years trying to find the evidence – any sodding evidence – that would be enough to convict him of some crime or another, but I never have – yet!"

"And your relationship with Colin Footner?"

Alison Pawlett took another swig of vodka. "Another sodding cock-up! When I began investigating Richard Edgton, I discovered that Dean Footner was his chauffeur and one of his loyal henchmen. I also discovered that he had an unattached brother, Colin, and I figured that if I could get close enough to him, I might get to hear something that would help me nail Richard Edgton. So I found out which pub Colin liked to frequent and I turned up there one evening, pretending that I had been stood up, and engaged him in some trivial conversation or other. To gain his trust, I did some mild flirting and one thing led to another and before I knew where I was… I mean, I was in a strange town, I didn't know anybody and, for a while, Colin was great – friendly, helpful – and then…" Alison Pawlett paused, sniffed, took another more modest swig of vodka, dabbed her eyes and breathed deeply. "And the worst thing is, I never did find out anything juicy about Richard Edgton."

Clive, meanwhile, was also fighting with his emotions. On the one hand, he felt genuinely sorry for Alison Pawlett and the mess she had landed herself in; on the other, he was angry that she had behaved so unprofessionally and so secretively.

"Does Dick, er, Acting Inspector Beauregard know about this?" he asked after a moment or two of reflection.

"No, I'm sure he doesn't. I suppose you're going to have to tell him, aren't you?" Alison whimpered.

"To be honest, Alison, I'm in a bit of a quandary. If I were still a serving detective inspector, I'd be taking you off this case immediately and probably suspending you. Your family links to Fearnley quarry, your obsession with Richard Edgton and your relationship with Colin Footner could all jeopardise my enquiries. I mean, if you ever did manage to build some kind of case against Richard Edgton and he stood trial, he would doubtless employ a top-class lawyer and you can imagine what kind of a field day he would have at your expense. As soon as the judge heard about your, er, personal interest, the case would be thrown out."

Alison Pawlett drained her glass and slammed it down on the desk before slumping forward in her chair and holding a paper towel across her face. "So what are you going to do?"

Clive tugged his earlobe. "I have a deal to offer you. In the light of what you've told me, it would no longer be appropriate for you to be part of Acting Inspector Beauregard's official investigation into Mary Pullman's murder or the disappearance of Lord Westleigh's daughter, especially if Richard Edgton is implicated in either of the two. So I suggest that you continue to report sick for the next few days and you keep a very low profile. I'm prepared to offer you free board and lodging during that time, but in return I will also need your help. Tomorrow, I'm hoping to go and see a genealogist in Surrey and over the weekend, I'm going to be very tied up with the coach party here and, it being a bank holiday, things are going to be pretty hectic, so I'm not going to have much time to continue with the investigation. Now, there are quite a few lines of enquiry that need following up and I'd like you to do it, as soon as you feel up to it. All the work can be done using your laptop or your phone – you'll need to be discreet – and if Dick asks, I'll fob him off with some platitude or other. But if your enquiries lead you towards Richard Edgton, you must back off, or Dick'll have to know. And when our investigations are finished, I'd advise you to put in for a transfer and move a long way away from Richard Edgton and his sleazy associates. Do we have a deal?"

"Do I have a choice?"

"Depends on whether you want a career as a detective."

"Well… alright, I suppose." Although Alison Pawlett's reply lacked enthusiasm, there was at least an acknowledgement, albeit grudging, of what was needed. "I can't bear the thought of sitting around here all day licking my wounds, feeling sorry for myself and having to occupy my time. What are the lines of enquiry you want my help with?"

Clive reached a notepad and pen from his desk and placed them neatly in front of Alison.

"For a start, I'd like to find out about Mary Pullman's will. We've heard various stories about how much money she had squirrelled away and who might have inherited and who might not, but we don't really know. I'd like to know what her will says – perhaps you can put a bit of pressure on the family solicitor."

"I've got some information on Sarah Tildesley, if it helps. I've been digging around," Alison interrupted, suddenly warming to her task.

"Have you? Tell me more!"

"Well, as we already know, up until about a year ago she ran her own hairdressing salon in Bailbridge, but, basically, it went bust and she had to close it. She's divorced and her ex-husband pays her maintenance for their two children, but that's about the only money she's got coming in. But here's the interesting bit; up until she disappeared, her mother was making regular payments to her – £300 a month was going into her bank account – but the payments stopped when she disappeared. Now Sarah Tildesley has got behind with her mortgage repayments and the bank is threatening to repossess her house."

Clive exhaled sharply. "So, basically, getting an inheritance from her mother could be an absolute godsend. Does she have an alibi for the day her mother disappeared?"

"Not really; she claimed she was looking after her children all day, but I don't think we have any witnesses. I'll check the notes we made at the time."

"And does she have an alibi for the day when we think her mother was murdered; round about the 12th or 13th?"

"Same again!"

"That's excellent work, Alison. So now the next step is to find out if she really was looking after her children all day and, if she wasn't, what she was actually doing on those two critical dates."

"Leave it to me; I'll see what I can do."

"And I'd like some more information on Gregory Pullman. His neighbour said he might have been violent towards Mary Pullman. Perhaps you can do a background check to see if there is any record of violence – domestic violence especially – and maybe talk discreetly to some of the other neighbours."

"I'll try!" Alison Pawlett fingered her face gingerly as she made some notes.

"And according to Dick, erm, Acting Inspector Beauregard, Gareth Adamson bought his house through Blaby and Quixhill, the estate agents that Gregory Pullman used to work for, so it seems likely that his claim not to know the house or Gareth Adamson is spurious. Dick, erm, Acting Inspector Beauregard hit a brick wall when he spoke to a lady in the estate agent's office. It seems Mr Quixhill is the person you need to speak to, but, by the sound of things, you're going to have to prise the information out of him."

"I'll have a go."

"Good, and talking of Gareth Adamson, I understand that he's just put his house on the market – with Blaby and Quixhill, of course – and I'd like to know why."

"I'll do what I can."

"And did his neighbour, our friend Dean Footner, ever get a key to Gareth Adamson's house cut? He says not, but it might be worth checking with any local locksmiths."

"I'll ask around."

"And forgive me for going a bit off piste, but I'd also like a background check done on one of my own team, Jamie Coulton, but, please, please, be discreet."

Alison Pawlett tried to smile, but the effort clearly hurt her damaged face. "How long are you expecting me to be off sick for?" she asked, with a hint of mischief in her voice.

"Oh, you'll be right as rain next week, I'm sure. And one last thing, and I hope this isn't too painful for you, I'd like to know more about the Reverend Ashburton. We haven't worked out yet why Mary Pullman had written his address in her notebook and I'm sure there's something not right there. I think it would be worth running some background checks.

Where was his last parish? Why has he moved here? Has there been anything dodgy going on?"

Alison tried to smile again, but the pain was too intense. "I do have a bit more information for you, as it happens. Earlier on today, while I was nursing my wounds and feeling sorry for myself, I found out who is running *The Dog Collar* club. Her name's Gabrielle and she calls herself the chatelaine. But I'm sure she doesn't own the place – I think she's only 'front of house'. My hunch is that she's actually working for Richard Edgton."

Clive stared at Alison. It was a hard, intense stare that left her in no doubt what he was thinking.

"Yes, alright, alright," Alison conceded grudgingly. "It might have nothing to do with Richard Edgton, but this afternoon, when I started to feel a bit better, I took a bit of a gamble and phoned Gabrielle. I explained that we were trying to track down a lady that used to visit Gerald Ashburton every week until last April and we thought she might have worked at the club. Anyway, I struck lucky. Gabrielle seemed quite happy to co-operate with the police, which surprised me a bit given that what she's doing is probably illegal. Anyway, she told me that she remembered one of the call-girls who used to work there – she was called Natalie; probably her professional name. And it seems Gerald Ashburton took a particular shine to her and they arranged for her to visit him every Wednesday afternoon. He paid her well, apparently, and there was never any trouble, but he always insisted that she disguised herself so that no-one would realise he was being visited by a call-girl. And then, according to Gabrielle, last April, she just disappeared. She didn't show up at the club any more, she stopped answering her phone and there has been no sign of her since… I wonder, would you mind if I took a break? My head is hurting quite badly."

Fifteen

Friday 25 August

Clive didn't have to drive to Surrey to meet with Julia Cockrell. He could have sent her an email with the relevant attachments and spoken to her on the phone. Then he could have spent the day at work in the hotel, dealing with the usual daily routines and being regularly interrupted. Clare would probably want to discuss something with him, or seek his opinion, Debbie would probably come to complain about a guest who had said or done something inappropriate and Simon could very easily have another hissy fit about Ralph Dalton. And then, of course, there was Alison Pawlett; put into an unexpectedly vulnerable position by Clive's discovery of her family interest in Fearnley quarry, she was suddenly revealing a kind of doe-eyed enthusiasm that might require careful channelling.

But Clive needed time to think, free from distractions and interruptions. The investigation into Mary Pullman's death was proving to be far more complicated and time-consuming than he had expected; there were too many people with a motive of sorts, too many people with the opportunity and too many people who were not telling the complete truth, on top of which he still did not have an explanation for the time-lag between her disappearance and subsequent murder or fully understand how and why she ended up in Gareth Adamson's back garden.

When he worked for the police, Clive did a lot of his best thinking in the car, so he reasoned that up to six hours spent travelling to and from Surrey would give him his best opportunity to make some sense of it all. So he waited for the last members of the coach party to finish their breakfasts and clamber aboard the coach bound for Wickmorstead Hall. He then helped to clear the last of the breakfast crockery from the tables before making his final preparations to leave. Armed with Julia Cockrell's address and telephone number and an annotated road atlas, which he always carried with him on long car journeys in case his notoriously unreliable "satnav" device let him down, he had just picked up his car key and was heading towards the car park when his mobile phone rang. It was Martin Carslake.

Receiving an uncharacteristically abrupt response from Clive and sensing that he had not picked the most opportune moment to phone, Martin Carslake began with a stumbling apology. "Er, I'm very sorry to bother you, but you did ask me to call you if I remembered anything of interest about Mary Pullman."

"Yes, that's right, I did." Normally Clive would have been delighted to receive any titbit of information, however trivial, that might assist his investigations, but he was so preoccupied with his drive to Surrey on unfamiliar roads and his meeting with the emotionally brittle and mercurial Julia Cockrell, that he attempted an uncharacteristic sidestep. "Have you spoken to Inspector Beauregard?" he asked as he strode towards his car.

"Er, no, I haven't. I'd prefer to keep it a bit less official, if you know what I mean."

"Go on!"

"Er, well you remember that Mary Pullman reported me to the police, complaining that I'd been taking photographs of her when she was flaunting herself at her bedroom window?" He paused expecting a response from Clive but was greeted with silence. So, after a momentary hesitation, he continued. "Well, er, when the police first called round, they were merely responding to Mary Pullman's complaint."

"Yes, I remember," Clive replied as he opened his car door and slid into the driver's seat. "You denied you'd been taking photographs. The police confiscated your camera but they didn't find anything suspicious and the matter was dropped."

"Ah yes, that's right, but I'm afraid I've got a bit of a confession to make. You see, I did take some photographs of her but they weren't on the memory card that was in the camera when the police called – the photos were on another card which I thought might come in handy one day, so I'd hidden it away before the police arrived. Anyway, after you'd been to see me last Sunday I started thinking and, knowing that you were now dealing with a murder, I thought I'd take another look at the photos on the card."

"And…"

"And there's something on one of the photos that I think might be of interest to you and I was wondering—"

"But you haven't told the police that you took these photographs?"

"Er, no, I haven't. I didn't want to be accused of being a bit of a weirdo or anything. It's all a bit awkward, really, isn't it? Do you see why I'd prefer to speak to you?"

"The thing is, Mr Carslake, if there is something on your memory card that might be relevant to our murder enquiry then Inspector Beauregard will need to be told."

"Yes, I suppose so, but I'd still prefer to talk to you first."

"Okay, so tell me what was on your memory card that is so interesting."

"I can't, I can't. I mean, I need to show you, if that's possible."

Clive cursed under his breath. "Unfortunately, I'm just about to drive down to Surrey for an important meeting and I'm in a bit of a hurry. I suppose I could call in and see you on my way back? It'll probably be late afternoon if that's alright, and I won't be able to stay long. If I'm not back well before the evening meal, I'll be in big trouble."

"Yes, that'll be fine. I'll be here, so I'll see you then."

*

Alex Jeffries drummed his fingers impatiently on the table. His manner and attitude were much as they had been when Acting Inspector Beauregard had last seen him, except that he now seemed more agitated. His stubble was longer and thicker and his wavy dark hair seemed more unruly now that it was no longer constrained by a cap.

"Thank you for coming in," Acting Inspector Beauregard began as he sat down opposite Alex Jeffries. "I thought it might be easier to talk here at the police station rather than at your place where we might be overheard or you might get interrupted and…"

Alex Jeffries looked around the shabby interview room with obvious distaste and pointedly studied his expensive wrist watch. "Yes, errm, well if it will help get my darling Lucy back, I'm happy to help, but I hope it won't take long. I'm very busy, especially without Lucy to… well, you know."

"I'll try and be brief, and to be honest, Mr Jeffries, it's a bit of a sensitive issue. You see, when we started to talk to some of the estate workers about your wife, we got quite a strong impression that they thought your wife might be having an affair. Her groom, Tom Chewton, was mentioned. Now—"

"What are you saying?" Alex Jeffries protested volubly. "My darling Lucy having an affair? That's an outrageous suggestion!"

"Of course we haven't discussed any of this with Tom Chewton yet, although we will have to at some stage. And I suppose we could ask Lord Westleigh if he knows anything about—"

"Now, now, hang on a minute." Alex Jeffries was normally a man who repressed his emotions, but now he was clearly ruffled. "Let me be straight with you."

"I wish you would!"

"Errrm, you see, after she had our second child, Lucy just seemed to… well, errm, Lucy just seemed to lose interest in sex – always complaining that she was too tired. But I later discovered that it was just sex with me that she had lost interest in. I walked into the stable block one day and discovered Lucy and Tom, errm, well, I think you can imagine. We had a monumental bust-up and I, errrm, threatened to walk out, but when we'd both calmed down we decided we'd stay together, firstly for the sake of our children, secondly for the sake of our business and thirdly for the sake of Lord Westleigh. He's had a few tragedies in his life and we didn't really want to cause him any more grief. So, these days, we have what I think is described as an open marriage. I don't ask too many questions and neither does Lucy."

"There's also been a suggestion that you might be having an affair with your nanny."

"Has there really?" Alex Jeffries answered, sarcastically. "You know the Chartfield estate must have more gossip-mongers and spreaders of groundless rumours than anywhere I've known. But let me tell you that nothing could be further from the truth. It is, errm, possible, of course, that I haven't been, errm, entirely celibate since Lucy, errm, since Lucy sought comfort elsewhere, but I'm not saying any more than that and anyway, I don't see what any of this has to do with Lucy's disappearance."

"But you must admit that it gives you a motive for getting rid of your wife and—"

Alex Jeffries was not given to outbursts of anger. Instead, he set his jaw more firmly and spoke through nearly clenched teeth, giving his voice a rasping quality. "Now look, Inspector, that is an outrageous suggestion and I resent the insinuation. I refuse to answer any more questions without my solicitor, so you must either let me go or caution me in her presence. What is it to be?"

*

The small, elderly, white hatchback looked strangely incongruous, parked on the spacious drive of the Cockrells' house in semi-suburban Surrey. Although there was, superficially at least, nothing exceptional about the house, its prime location, generous dimensions and understated elegance suggested that the owners enjoyed a comfortable lifestyle.

Julia Cockrell welcomed Clive with little outward enthusiasm and ushered him through the spacious entrance hall and into the large, tastefully decorated, contemporary-style lounge. An open panelled door led into what was clearly a "state-of-the-art" kitchen with an impressive array of fitted cupboards, gleaming work surfaces and appliances surrounding a solid, well-proportioned pine table. Julia gestured towards a white sofa where Clive was obviously required to sit, his feet buried in a plush black and white rug, while looking out onto the carefully tended back garden. In a matching white armchair, an elderly grey tabby cat stretched, yawned and opened one eye as the stranger sat down and then, as though suddenly affronted by his unannounced arrival, leapt from the chair and disappeared into the hall, in search of quieter accommodation upstairs.

"Grace, my daughter," Julia began, uncertainly, "has just been fed and has gone to sleep, so we should be alright for a while, but you never know."

Julia Cockrell was much as Clive remembered her. Her long blonde hair, liberally streaked with grey, tumbled freely over her oval, gaunt, pale face. Her lips were thin and her eyes alert and suspicious. She was wearing a check blouse and beige trousers. She sat down opposite Clive in another of the white armchairs, crossed her legs and grasped her knee tightly with both hands.

Clive coughed self-consciously. He was not especially skilled at small talk, particularly with people that he hardly knew, but he felt that it would be somehow discourteous to launch straight into the purpose of his visit without at least observing some basic pleasantries. "How's your husband, Trevor, these days? He wasn't in great shape when I saw him last."

Clive noticed Julia Cockrell tighten the grip on her knee. "Oh, er, he's, he's fine; he's working hard as usual; always dashing backwards and forwards between his two conference centres, but he seems happy enough."

"Good! I had hoped I might see him today."

Julia Cockrell emitted a quiet, mocking laugh. "Huh, I don't expect he'll be back till quite late. He'll want to make sure everything is in good order before the long weekend." Julia went to say something more but, instead, fell silent and gazed thoughtfully at the floor.

Clive coughed again. "Well, it's good of you to see me at such short notice."

"No problem," Julia Cockrell replied with uncharacteristic warmth. "It's nice to be able to talk to an adult for once. I'm afraid Grace and Rosie – that's our cat – are not particularly good conversationalists, or listeners for that matter, and Trevor is never—"

"No, no, I suppose not. Good. Well, as I mentioned when I phoned, I'm doing a bit of freelance work for the local police."

"You're not in the police force anymore?"

"Er, no! I'd had enough of them and they of me, probably. And I'd met Clare and we decided to make a new start. Clare's parents used to run a hotel when she was younger, so we thought we'd give it a go." Suddenly distracted by a stray thought, Clive briefly fell silent and stared wistfully out of the window. "Anyway," he continued at last, "I've been asked to help with a murder investigation and one of the lines of enquiry we're pursuing is the fact that the dead woman, Mary Pullman, was obviously doing some family research when she disappeared. She left behind her notebook, with lots of names and dates, but I haven't got the time or, if I'm honest, the skill to make much sense of the notes. Of course, it might not be relevant, but I'd like to know whether her research could have had some bearing on her murder."

Julia shuddered. "Oh, how unpleasant! Of course, I've come across quite a few instances where somebody has uncovered some dark secrets from their past, but I've never known it result in murder."

Clive reached into his briefcase and produced some photocopied sheets of paper, stapled together, which he handed to Julia, who had opened her laptop. "As I say, her name is Mary Pullman, aged sixty-four. Her maiden name was Hayward. She has two daughters – Sarah Tildesley and Alice

Innes – and one of them has suggested that she was intrigued by her grandfather's middle name and where it might have come from. Sadly, we don't know what it was. Also, there is at least one and possibly more pages missing from her notebook, which could be relevant, and I wondered if you might be able to work out what's missing."

"Ah, yes." Julia nodded wisely as she typed some notes into her laptop. "Middle names can be quite revealing sometimes. Yes, I'll take a look, but obviously I can't promise anything…"

Clive hesitated, hoping that Julia Cockrell would start examining the contents of the copied pages of Mary Pullman's notebook and make some initial observations, but she merely placed them neatly alongside her laptop.

"No, no, of course," Clive replied eventually. "And I know it's a bit of a long shot, but I'd be grateful if you could take a look and see what you can make of it all. The police will pay for your time at your usual rate and I suspect you can unravel most of it without having to travel anywhere."

Julia fixed him with a questioning look. "You know you could have emailed all these to me. You didn't have to come all this way to hand them over."

Clive shifted uneasily in his chair. "No, ah, well, I wanted to hand them over in person and explain the background and, well, I like driving – it helps me to think."

Julia gave a knowing smile without looking up from her laptop. "I see. When do you want my report?"

"If I said 'as soon as possible', would that help?" Clive asked hopefully.

"I'll treat it as my highest priority," Julia replied, "but I don't know what Grace is planning or what Trevor might want us to do at the weekend. He rarely tells me in advance."

There was a weariness about Julia Cockrell's reply and, knowing something of her reputation for capriciousness, Clive looked anxiously at her, fearing that she might yet decide not to risk getting involved, but he need not have worried.

"How exciting," Julia suddenly announced. "I might be helping with a murder enquiry – can't wait to get started."

Though he was pleased that Julia seemed keen to get involved, Clive was feeling frustrated. The journey to Surrey had been worthwhile in a way, and it had certainly helped to clarify some of his thinking, but it had been long and tiring and he had hoped that Julia Cockrell might at least start looking at Mary Pullman's notes and might offer some initial thoughts on what she was hoping to discover. Instead she merely offered a wan smile. After another uncomfortable silence, she was about to say something more when her baby alarm burst into life with the sound of Grace crying very loudly. Immediately, Clive stood up.

"Look, I'd better go. I'm supposed to be on duty in the bar this evening and it sounds as though you're needed elsewhere. Can you give me a call as soon as you've got something – anything – that might help?"

"Of course," Julia replied, casting her eyes anxiously towards the stairs down which the cries were emanating. "Good luck with the M25, by the way. It's always bad on a Friday afternoon, but with the bank holiday weekend…"

Just as he started his car, Clive's phone rang.

"Hello, Dick!" Frustrated by the paucity of information that his visit had yielded and fearing a slow journey home, he greeted his colleague less than effusively.

"Hello, Clive. I'm very sorry, but I don't think I'm going to be able to offer you much help for the time being. I'm heading back to Chartfield Castle. There's been an important development. Can you call me later?"

*

As he drove through the grounds of Chartfield Castle, Acting Inspector Beauregard could not fail to notice the large crowds and the prevailing sense of bustle. In the distance, he was sure he could hear the sound of large sums of money chinking into Lord Westleigh's substantial coffers. With continuing fine weather, it seemed that the estate was under siege from day-trippers, holiday-makers and coach parties determined to get full value for their hefty admission charges by exploring every available facility and attraction within the castle and grounds before beginning their weary journeys home with an abundance of pleasant memories, empty wallets and full stomachs.

In stark contrast, the atmosphere in the castle library was one of echoing stillness. Lord Westleigh, unaccompanied by any of his usual coterie of loyal followers, greeted Acting Inspector Beauregard with a perfunctory wave of his hand and gestured towards one of the semi-circle of neatly arranged leather-upholstered armchairs that faced the carved marble fireplace. Lord Westleigh himself remained standing, preferring, it seemed, to pace about on the plush woven carpet, pausing occasionally to stand with his back to the fireplace as though expecting a log fire to suddenly roar into life and warm his expensively tailored trousers.

"I'm afraid Anthony won't be joining us," Lord Westleigh announced in his usual calm, clipped tones. "He's showing a coach party around the house; a necessary evil in these straightened times. They were in here a little earlier. And we've got another one tomorrow." Clearly affronted by the regular intrusion of tourists into his inner sanctum, the Earl sighed heavily before reaching for a plain white envelope that was resting on the mantel shelf and handing it to the acting inspector. "This arrived in this morning's post. You need to see it."

The acting inspector carefully examined the envelope. There was nothing unusual or distinctive about it. Lord Westleigh's address had been printed onto a label which was affixed to the front, together with a first-class stamp in the top right-hand corner. At the top, it had been neatly slit open, no doubt by an expertly crafted, antique paper knife. Anxious not to destroy or damage any potential forensic evidence, Acting Inspector Beauregard used only the tips of his fingers to open the envelope and carefully extract a folded piece of plain white paper from within. He slowly unfolded it and read the message:

> "We have your daughter. If you want to see her alive again, it will cost you money and you will have to carry out our instructions. We will be in touch. Do not involve the police or any other third party."

The acting inspector subjected the piece of paper and the envelope to close fingertip scrutiny before speaking. "Well, at first glance," he ventured, "I'd say the envelope and paper are probably the type that you can buy in any decent stationers. It looks as though the note and the address on the envelope have been produced by a standard printer, in a standard typeface, using a standard word-processing software package; so not much to go on there, I'm afraid. The postmark is local."

"Yes, quite," Lord Westleigh replied with a faint hint of condescension. "But at least it confirms my suspicions."

"That she's been kidnapped?"

"Yes, and we know by whom, don't we?"

The acting inspector stifled a grimace. "The trouble is we have no evidence that Richard Edgton is implicated. We've searched all his properties around here and we've not found a trace of your daughter."

"Well, I don't imagine he'd be that stupid. Now obviously I'm not trying to tell you how to do your job," Lord Westleigh observed, disingenuously, "but this ridiculous charade has all the hallmarks of Richard Edgton's modus operandi."

"Yes, quite. Er, I'll need to hang on to this envelope and note. We might be able get a fingerprint or some DNA, but… Who's handled them?"

Lord Westleigh shrugged. "Oh I don't know. Several postmen will have handled the envelope, obviously, and Anthony – he opens all my post – and me, and you."

Caspar Beauregard scratched his head; he was clutching at straws. "Well, perhaps I can arrange for someone to take your fingerprints and those of Mr Granard – just for elimination purposes."

"If you must," the Earl replied, grudgingly. "But any day now, I'll wager that Richard Edgton will be in touch to tell me how much I'll have to pay to get my daughter back. And he'll probably tell me how much more money he'll want before he'll sell the bloody quarry to me. And the way things are looking, I'm going to have no choice but to pay him what he wants. God, what a mess!"

"Well, at least we know what we're dealing with," Acting Inspector Beauregard replied with a particularly disconsolate expression.

"Is that all you can say?" Lord Westleigh asked, clearly unimpressed by the acting inspector's limp platitude.

"Well, obviously, we'll keep a tap on your phone, but it'll be difficult to take any further action against Richard Edgton unless we have new—"

"I see." Lord Westleigh sniffed. "You're right, of course. But I just hope, for your sake, that nothing happens to my darling Lucy as a result of any negligence on your part. I mean, can't you at least arrange to have someone follow Richard Edgton?"

Ten minutes after Acting Inspector Beauregard had left the aristocratic presence of Lord Westleigh, the chief constable phoned.

*

As Julia Cockrell had warned, the M25 proved to be little more than a continuous, slow-moving traffic jam and it was into the early evening before Clive, hot, weary, frustrated and very late, finally arrived at Martin Carslake's house. As he approached the front door, he could hear the sound of a vacuum cleaner angrily going about its business, but the sound was extinguished as soon as he rang the doorbell.

Martin Carslake was much more scruffily attired than on their previous encounter; he was wearing a crumpled black T-shirt and shapeless jeans and his feet were bare. He was wiping the perspiration from his brow as he greeted Clive.

"I'm so sorry I'm late," Clive apologised a little breathlessly. "It was a difficult journey back from Surrey and I am running rather behind schedule, so I can't stay very long. I should've been on duty back at the hotel by now."

"Oh, that's alright," Martin Carslake replied a little stiffly. "I won't keep you long. My, erm, lady friend is due for the weekend very soon and I'm trying to tidy the place up a bit." He led Clive into a small, sparsely furnished, immaculately tidy room that he obviously used as an office. There was a functional, featureless desk with a computer placed neatly in the middle of it, a bookcase containing various folders and box files, and, in one corner, a closed cupboard.

"I'm sorry about all the cloak-and-dagger stuff, but I thought you ought to take a look at this." Martin Carslake tapped the computer keyboard and then pointed to an image on his screen. "Now, as I mentioned when I called you earlier,

I'm ashamed to say that I did take some photographs of Mary Pullman when she was up at her window, stark naked. I thought that if she saw me, it might stop her doing it again but instead, as you know, she reported me to the police and—"

"I think I get the picture!" Clive replied with a wry smile. He was quite pleased with his feeble pun.

"Anyway," Martin Carslake continued. "I thought I should take another look at the photos, bearing in mind that you are now looking for Mary Pullman's killer. And I found this."

Clive peered over Martin Carslake's shoulder. "Oh, I see what you mean!" The image was an enlarged, grainy photograph showing Mary Pullman, naked and smirking, standing at the window, but, behind her, in the half shadows, was another figure, a man. Only the unclothed top half of his anatomy was visible, but the conclusion was inevitable.

"Wow!" Clive gasped. "One of Mary Pullman's daughters thought she might have been having an affair and it looks as though she was right. When was this picture taken?"

"Nearly a year ago, apparently; according to the memory card, it was taken on Saturday 4 September at around 3.30. I've put the image onto a disk for you. My camera's not especially high-spec, but the police's technical experts might be able to enlarge it a bit more and clean it up a bit." Martin Carslake handed the disk to Clive as though it was some kind of delicate ancient artefact.

"Thank you," Clive replied, taking the disk and slipping it casually into his trouser pocket. "Right, well the man in the background is clearly not Gregory Pullman. He was probably involved with his cricket team and safely out of the way, it being a Saturday. So who is the mystery man?"

"Well, I can't be sure," Martin Carslake replied cautiously. "But I went along to a couple of Mary Pullman's quarry protest meetings – before we, er, fell out so spectacularly – and he was there. I've also seen his picture in the local paper a couple of times and I'm pretty sure it's Richard Edgton."

*

Clare Walsingham was looking uncharacteristically flustered when Alison Pawlett walked uncertainly into the otherwise empty bar. From what she had seen during their brief acquaintance, Clare seemed the epitome of calm efficiency, but her usually pale cheeks were flushed, she was wearing an intense frown and was repeatedly running a hand through her short, brown hair. She was concentrating on preparing an assortment of drinks behind the bar, while muttering something under her breath, and did not immediately see that Alison had walked in. It was only as she was dashing towards the dining room with a laden tray that she suddenly noticed her and stopped abruptly.

Alison Pawlett was no longer wearing dark glasses and had toned down the appearance of her facial wounds with a liberal application of make-up, though her swollen face and lips still bore the unmistakeable traces of Colin Footner's assault. She nodded weakly as she caught Clare's eye.

"Hello, Clare." She spoke in little more than a whisper. "Have I come at a bad time?"

"Yes, just a little," Clare replied with surprising vehemence. "Clive was supposed to be back by now to take charge of the bar but apparently he's been delayed. God knows why he had to drive all the way to Surrey in the first place and I've got no idea when he'll show up. Meanwhile, we've got a dining room full of very hungry, very thirsty people. Let me deliver these drinks and I'll be back."

As Clare dashed off, trying, with limited success, not to spill the drinks, Alison hauled herself slowly onto a bar stool and looked solemnly around the empty bar. The room had been designed with practical considerations rather than aesthetic ones and was liberally furnished with solid settees and chairs, upholstered in a claret material, arranged neatly around a number of low tables. A few unremarkable prints and pictures adorned the pale maroon walls and a television occupied one corner. After a moment or two alone with her melancholic thoughts, Alison looked up to see Clare rushing back into the room.

"Sorry about that, Alison, but things are just a bit hectic at the moment," she panted. "We've got forty dinners to serve, we're one member of our team down and Chef is getting very stressed and shouting a lot." She bustled behind the bar and busied herself preparing more drinks as she continued to talk. "So how are you today? You look a bit better than you did yesterday."

"Oh, I feel a bit sore and I've got a hell of a headache but, you know… I've been doing a bit of research for Clive, which has been quite illuminating, and I've been out walking for a while and thinking and—"

"Look, I'm very sorry, Alison," Clare interrupted, "but I've really got to deliver these drinks. If he's finished serving the main courses, I'll ask Jamie to come and keep you company for a while, but don't let him flirt with you. His flirting gets him into a lot of bother."

"Huh, I'm really not in the mood for that. Er, I don't suppose I could have a drink, could I?"

Clare was about to head towards the dining room with her loaded tray. "Oh God, Alison, I'm so sorry! How rude you must think me. It's just that I'm trying to do several things at once and… but that's no excuse. What would you like – a vodka?"

"A vodka martini, if it's possible."

Clare smiled. "Shaken but not stirred, I imagine. I'll definitely send Jamie in to see you. He's far better at cocktails than I am. Of course, if Clive were here…" Clare disappeared towards the dining room, holding tightly to her tray and muttering again.

Alison sat alone and brooding for a couple of minutes before Jamie Coulton glided into the bar, smiling his effusive smile and flashing a near-perfect set of brilliantly white teeth. "One vodka martini coming up," he announced in a slightly camp, affected voice.

Jamie made his way behind the bar, where he made an elaborate performance of mixing the cocktail, and delivered it with a theatrical flourish. "There we are. Can I get you anything else?" The question, innocent enough, seemed heavy with innuendo the way Jamie asked it.

"Er, no, no thanks," Alison stuttered, half-turning away. "I'll be fine with this."

Still smiling, Jamie Coulton leaned casually on the bar and looked at Alison. In sharp contrast to his harassed employer, he exuded a kind of languid serenity.

"You're with the police?" he asked.

"That's right." Alison Pawlett's reply was terse.

"You're working with Clive, er, Mr Walsingham?"

"That's right."

"What are you looking into?" Jamie Coulton posed the question in a way that suggested he had more than a passing interest in the investigation.

"I can't tell you anything more," Alison snapped, primly.

"No, no, of course not! I just wondered. Um, I don't suppose it's easy being a policewoman. I mean it can't be easy sometimes, you know, making friends or anything." As he spoke Jamie Coulton was gradually inching closer to Alison across the bar.

"No, it's not!"

"Well, if you're ever feeling lonely, you know, perhaps—"

Alison turned to face Jamie Coulton and pointed to her battered face. She was angry.

"You see these cuts and bruises?" Although she was not shouting, her voice had a new intensity. "They were done by a man – a man I thought I could trust. So do you think I'm going to allow myself to be chatted up by someone I hardly know? Do you have a regular girlfriend?"

"Well, I, um, I…" Jamie Coulton's calm composure was deserting him. "Well, um, yes, I suppose so, but—"

"Then you should be ashamed of yourself. And does your girlfriend know you've done time?"

"What?" Jamie Coulton backed away towards the rear of the bar, his mouth agape. "What do you mean?"

"You've done time for theft."

"How did you find that out?" Jamie Coulton spluttered.

"I'm a police officer; I make it my business to find out. I mean, stealing money from old ladies is quite despicable, isn't it? Do Clive and Clare know?"

"I, er, nnno, I don't think so, they've never said anything and it was a few years ago. You won't tell them, will you? Please don't tell them!" The unruffled calm with which Jamie Coulton usually conducted himself had given way to unrestrained panic. He was about to say something more when Clare returned to the bar to take over from him. His disappearance was rapid and undignified.

"Sorry about this," Clare apologised again as Jamie rushed past her. "I think Jamie and Debbie can handle things in the dining room from now on and they know where to find me, if necessary." She sat down on a bar stool next to Alison. "I hope Jamie wasn't too much of a pain. He's just had a bust-up with his girlfriend and she's walked out on him. His behaviour can be a bit strange, a bit erratic at the moment. I hope he wasn't chatting you up."

Alison Pawlett nodded. "I think he was using a hoary old chat-up line or two, but it's not a problem, really. I'll let you know if he becomes too much of a pain."

"Make sure you do." She stared at Alison Pawlett with a familiar intensity in her grey-green eyes. "So have you reached any conclusions after your walking and thinking?"

"What? Nah, not really," Alison replied, her voice returning to a tremulous whisper. "It's very kind of you and Clive to allow me to stay here for a few days till I can get things sorted out and I'm very grateful. I'll probably go back to work on Tuesday and, you know, talk to a few people; that sort of thing. I might find out if there's the possibility of a transfer or, failing that, find somewhere safe where I can stay for a while."

"You know, it's not for me to interfere," Clare replied with a look of acute concern. "But my advice would be to talk to someone about what happened to you. I mean, you might be finished with Colin – and I hope you are after what he's done to you – but he could do the same to someone else."

"Yeah, I know, but it's not easy. Colin can be very intimidating. Hell, I'm not easily intimidated normally, but he's scared the shit out of me, I don't mind telling you." Alison hesitated for a moment or two while she battled with her delicate emotions. "I'm sorry, but I'm afraid I'm feeling a bit fragile at the moment. Huh, I never thought I'd hear myself say that but—"

Her train of thought was suddenly interrupted by a high-pitched scream and the sound of raised voices coming from somewhere outside. Clare and Alison rushed from the bar, through the conservatory, passing scattered groups of confused and curious diners, and out onto the terrace. Across the lawn, where the rose beds ran close to the walled garden, in rapidly fading light, they could just discern a small group of people bending over something and gesturing agitatedly. Shaking off her self-pitying torpor, Alison Pawlett raced across the lawn. Clare, however, had dressed more formally, as she always did for her stint of serving at the tables and behind the bar, and her tight skirt and high heels did not equip her well for a high-speed gallop across the lawn. Having turned her ankle on the uneven lawn and half-stumbled, she was lagging some way behind the detective constable. Up ahead, Alison pushed her way through the small group of people, whom she presumed were members of Miranda Bellamy's coach party, and stumbled across a middle-aged man with a straggly mane of silver hair, writhing on the ground and clutching the left side of his lower ribcage. His pink shirt was heavily stained with fresh blood which was dribbling through his fingers and trickling onto the ground where he lay.

"I'm the police," Alison Pawlett announced grandly to the assembly, all her old assertiveness suddenly returning. "Please move back."

As Alison was bending over the man, Clare finally arrived, limping and gasping for breath. "My God! It's Simon!" she panted. "What's happened?"

"It's that maniac Ralph Dalton," Simon shrieked, his face contorted by a combination of pain, shock and outrage. "I told you he was bloody trouble. He's just attacked me with a knife. Oh God! Oh God! I'm bleeding to death! Somebody help me! Please, somebody help me!"

"Which way did he go?" Alison asked firmly, ignoring Simon's dramatic entreaty.

"Over there!" Simon screeched as he pointed a shaking finger in the direction of the nearby car park. The sound of a roaring car engine and squealing tyres could be heard disappearing down the road.

"Clare, can you call an ambulance, please?" Alison's question sounded more like an instruction. "And look after this man as best you can. If there is anybody here who's trained in first aid, perhaps you can help. Everyone else, can you please return to the main building? There is nothing more you can do here and this is now a crime scene." Taking complete charge of the situation, Alison Pawlett pulled her mobile phone from the pocket of her denim jacket, clutched it to her ear and marched quickly towards the car park.

Clive had passed the speeding ambulance, sirens blaring, as he approached the hotel at what he thought was nearly the end of his long and tiring day. Darkness had descended and, as he stepped quickly from the car, all he could discern were some shadowy figures moving about on the terrace and some inquisitive faces peering out from the windows of the still-lit dining room. "What the hell has happened?" he shouted as he sprinted towards the terrace, where Clare and Miranda Bellamy were deep in conversation.

"Ah, at last! I think you'd better come into the office," Clare suggested forcibly, as she turned and led the way. "Will you excuse us, Miranda? Perhaps you can tell Alison where we are if she needs us."

"So what the hell has happened?" Clive asked as soon as Clare had closed the office door and sat down.

"It's Simon. He's been stabbed by Ralph Dalton, down by the walled garden."

"Holy shit! No! Is he badly hurt?"

"Difficult to say; he's lost quite a bit of blood, and was not being especially brave, but from what I could see, the wound was in his side rather than anywhere vital. It certainly didn't stop him shouting and screaming as they took him away. We'll know more when they've assessed the damage, I guess."

"Holy shit!" Clive repeated. "And Ralph Dalton?"

"He was in his car and away before anyone realised what had happened. Debbie said he'd checked out a few minutes before he attacked Simon."

"Did anyone see the attack?"

"Not as far as I know. The coach party were all in the dining room when it happened. A few people sitting by the windows heard the commotion and ran to investigate, but the attack had already taken place – and it was getting dark."

"And the police are involved?"

"Oh, yes; in the formidable form of Detective Constable Alison Pawlett. She'd been in the bar drinking, getting in the way and feeling sorry for herself, and then, as soon as she realised what had happened, she was charging around all over the place sealing off the area where Simon was attacked, trying to trace Ralph Dalton's car, taking statements, talking to the ambulance crew, keeping people out of the way and generally throwing her weight about."

"And did Simon say anything coherent before they took him away?"

"He said plenty, but nothing very coherent. He just kept saying that Ralph Dalton was trouble and he'd warned us about him and he needs to be found before the same thing happens to somebody else."

"Mmm, and do we know anything about the weapon? Has it been found?"

"You know, you sound just like a detective inspector I used to know!"

"Sorry – force of habit, I'm afraid."

"Chef says one of his kitchen knives is missing, but he's got no idea when it went missing or who took it and there's no sign of it now. We think Ralph Dalton must have taken it with him."

Clive sat back in his chair, stretched his long legs out in front of him and exhaled loudly. "God, what a day!"

"It hasn't been too great here, actually." There was an edge to Clare's voice which Clive only detected when she was angry. "We've got a coach-load of demanding guests to look after, Alison Pawlett moping about the place and getting in the way, Jamie behaving quite strangely, Chef having a major tantrum, and now this business with Simon. And where have you been? Couldn't you have emailed Julia Cockrell and stayed here to lend a hand?"

Clive looked crestfallen. "Everybody keeps telling me that and, of course, you're absolutely right. I'd no idea this was going to... and I'm very sorry – I made the wrong decision. Has anyone looked in Ralph Dalton's room since he checked out?"

Clare sighed heavily. "No, I don't think so. It's about the only thing Alison hasn't done yet."

"I'd better take a look then."

Clive rose nimbly from his chair and strode off, leaving Clare alone in the office, suddenly feeling enervated, numb and still rather angry. A few minutes later, Clive was on his way back, dangling the key to Room 25 casually from his right hand, when he was intercepted at the bottom of the stairs by Alison Pawlett.

"Clive, I'm glad you're here at last." Constable Pawlett made her remarks sound like a reprimand.

"Yes, sorry I'm so late; bit of a wasted trip and a terrible journey back. Clare's put me in the picture."

"Good! Unfortunately nobody here seems to have witnessed what happened. And Ralph Dalton has disappeared without trace. I've been trying to track down the address he gave your staff at reception, but it looks as though it was false and his car is registered to a hire company. I'm trying to find out more. What do you know about Ralph Dalton?"

Clive recoiled slightly at the relentlessness of Alison's narrative. "Very little, like everyone else, it seems," he replied. "I've just been up to his room, but he's cleared it out. He's left nothing behind."

"I hope you didn't touch anything." Alison saw Clive's censorious look. "Sorry, of course you didn't; I was forgetting. Obviously we'll need to get our forensic people to go over it."

"Of course, I'll make sure no-one else goes in, but it seems that Ralph Dalton is a bit of a mystery to us all. Debbie at reception was a bit spooked by him when he first checked in. He hadn't booked in advance, although he claimed he had, and he seemed quite evasive. Simon had a bit of a fit every time he saw him – he kept warning us he was trouble, but he wouldn't say why and I can't ask people to leave just because our histrionic gardener throws a wobbly every time he sees them. Anyway, in an attempt to placate Simon, I tried to find out a bit more about Ralph Dalton at breakfast one morning, but it didn't get me very far. He just said that he was here on business – he didn't say what business – and that he was probably going to be checking out on Friday, er, today, which of course he did in rather spectacular fashion. I must say he didn't seem especially sinister or dangerous – just a bit reserved. Look, I need a drink; can I get you one?"

"No, not now! I've had one already and I'm on duty," Alison Pawlett admonished. "But if I were you, I'd try and smooth things over with Clare; she's not best pleased with you for being absent when all of this was happening."

"Yes, I've already been made aware of that, but thanks for the warning. I'll probably be in the office if there's anything I can do to help."

Acknowledging that Alison had taken complete, unequivocal charge and was unlikely to yield any part of the investigation to anyone else, Clive went into the bar to open a bottle of white wine and retrieve two glasses. Sitting at the bar, he found Miranda Bellamy in animated discussion with the loquacious Jamie Coulton, who was probing gently about her background and interests. "It must be difficult to make friends when you're travelling around so much," he heard Jamie say. "But if you ever feel lonely…" Jamie stopped talking as he saw Clive approach and, sensing that his continued presence was neither welcome nor needed, glided serenely out of the bar. Miranda looked up and smiled nervously as Clive went behind the bar.

"Miranda, I'm glad I've found you," Clive said, a little gushingly. "I'm very sorry about this evening's little incident. I hope that it won't stop your company from using us again."

"What?" Miranda sounded surprised. "Oh, definitely not! Most of my clients seem to think it's the best thing that's happened all holiday. They'll be disappointed if you can't arrange something similar tomorrow."

"Talking of which, I wonder if I could ask you a favour tomorrow?"

A familiar look of anxiety spread over Miranda's expressive face. "Oh well, I don't know. I am working tomorrow and—"

Clive tried to smile reassuringly. "Oh, it won't take more than a couple of minutes, and it's not dangerous in any way, I promise you."

"Well, I suppose I owe the man who got my attacker put away a small favour."

"Good, I'll catch you later and thank you, Miranda, that's very understanding of you. And don't let Jamie chat you up, by the way; he can be very persistent if you let him."

"Don't worry about that. I find a well-aimed knee in the groin usually gets the message across."

Chuckling, Clive picked up the wine bottle and glasses and strode briskly out of the bar. As soon as he walked into the office and saw the piercing look in Clare's grey-green eyes, he knew that she was still angry. He coughed self-consciously, smiled weakly, sat down and poured two glasses of wine.

"You do want this hotel venture to succeed, don't you, Clive?" Clare asked, pointedly.

"Yes, of course I do," Clive replied, defensively.

"Only the last few hours here have been an absolute nightmare, what with trying to cope with a hungry and demanding coach party, offering tea and sympathy – without much of either – to Alison and then the stabbing. And where the hell have you been when I needed you most? Bloody miles away playing at being a bloody policeman again!"

Clive held up both hands in a gesture of supplication. "Yes, I know, I know, and I'm truly sorry, Clare. I realise now that it was a mistake to allow myself to get so involved in all of this. I let my curiosity get the better of me and I shouldn't have. And my journey today wasn't as useful as I'd hoped it would be, so it's done neither of us any favours. The trouble is Dick is still more or less fully committed to the disappearance of Lord Westleigh's daughter, which I suspect will turn out to be a kidnapping, and then there's Alison; well, you've seen Alison. I'm not sure how much help she's going to be. So it's a problem, really. I mean, I ought to tell Dick that I can't spare him any more time, but it's kind of difficult to let the case go at the moment..."

Clive had run out of things to say. He slumped forward in his chair and closed his eyes. Eventually, it was Clare who spoke.

"I know you and I suspect that you're working on a couple of theories and I know you won't rest until you get to the truth, however long it takes, so we'll just have to make the best of it, won't we? Mind you, Simon's stabbing has been the best thing that could have happened to Alison. One minute she's in the bar full of maudlin self-pity and the next minute she's back to her bossy, domineering best."

"She is that. She told me off for going up to Ralph Dalton's room in case I touched or disturbed something." The room fell silent for a couple of minutes while Clive and Clare sipped their wine and mulled over the events of the last couple of hours.

"I'm puzzled, though," Clive announced at last. "What was Simon doing down by the walled garden when he was attacked? I mean, it was nearly dark and I don't ever remember him being there in the evening. He's usually either getting pissed in the bar or demolishing a bottle of Scotch behind a closed door somewhere. So what on earth was he doing?"

Clare shrugged. "I don't know, but I tell you something else that was odd. When I bent over him—"

"Oh, sod it! Sorry, darling," Clive interrupted. "I've just remembered that I was supposed give Dick a ring this evening when I got back. He was busy at Chartfield Castle when I spoke to him earlier, but he asked me to call him later. I won't be a minute." He reached for the phone.

"Fine, fine, fine," Clare repeated unconvincingly, as she slapped her hand down heavily on the desk. "Do you want me to leave?"

"No, no, you might as well stay and listen to what's been happening." He dialled the number and waited a moment or two for his call to be answered.

"Dick? It's Clive; sorry it's so late – it's been a bit hectic since you phoned earlier. Is it a good time to talk?"

"Not especially," came the terse reply. "Me and my, er, partner are in a restaurant at the moment. Have you heard that Lord Westleigh has received a note from the kidnapper about his daughter? It sounds more and more like Richard Edgton is behind it."

"No, but I guessed as much. We've had our own little drama here as well. Alison may have spoken to you."

"Alison? No! I thought she was off sick."

"She is, or at least she was. It's just that she's staying here at the moment – she's got some problems at home, I think – and was here when Simon, our gardener, got stabbed by one of our guests. Look, can we meet up for a word tomorrow? There are a few things I need to update you on. All I will say for the moment is that I think you may be right about Richard Edgton after all. I might have fresh evidence that links him to Mary Pullman."

"And I have some more information for you. Gerald Ashburton has disappeared."

Sixteen

Saturday 26 August

As the bank holiday weekend got underway, the weather, benign for so long, was changing with a vengeance. Showing mercurial malice, the day dawned with brooding, menacing clouds gathering overhead.

Clive was abnormally restless. The events of the previous day, particularly Martin Carslake's dramatic photographic revelation and Ralph Dalton's violent and as yet unexplained attack on Simon, had left him feeling increasingly confused while, at the same time, Clare was constantly reminding him, quite forcibly and – he could not deny – quite correctly, that he was supposed to be running a hotel. So, with Acting Inspector Beauregard due in an hour and Miranda's coach party safely on their way to Chartfield Castle, he had decided to set aside some time to catch up on his emails, pay some outstanding invoices, order fresh supplies and confirm some recent bookings. With these tasks in mind – though not with his mind on these tasks – he was striding resolutely towards his office with a fresh mug of coffee in his hand when he was waylaid by Alison Pawlett. Her hair had returned to its sleek, severely combed style, her thin lips were liberally covered in bright red lipstick and a generous application of eye shadow concealed the worst of the bruising, although some areas around her nose and cheeks remained visibly discoloured and swollen. She had eschewed her usual denim outfit in favour of a grey hoodie and black combat trousers.

"I've got some news on Ralph Dalton," she announced conspiratorially.

"You'd better come into the office, then," Clive replied, unenthusiastically, as he led the way.

There was no use denying that he had been neglecting his hotelier duties of late and Clare's displeasure at his recent laxity was all too obvious. Normally, his inquisitive nature would have been aroused by Alison Pawlett's tantalising pronouncement, especially when faced with a tedious hour of routine office tasks, but he needed to demonstrate to Clare his unwavering commitment to their joint venture.

"I don't want you to think that I'm not interested in what you have to say," he continued defensively, as he sat down opposite Alison Pawlett and took a swig of hot coffee. "Far from it, but Dick, er, Acting Inspector Beauregard will be here in an hour and he will want to hear your news and I am rather—"

Alison Pawlett wrinkled her nose and winced. "Um, the thing is, Clive, I think Colin may have broken my nose," she said while fingering it gingerly. "It's been too swollen and sore to touch until this morning, but now it feels funny and it's moving about a bit oddly. I think I should go the hospital and get it checked. And anyway, I am supposed to be off sick and I'd prefer not to be here when Dick, er, Acting Inspector Beauregard arrives. He's bound to start asking awkward questions and I'd rather not, you know, have to explain."

"You should've gone to the hospital straight after the incident, you know," Clive admonished.

"I know, I know, but I wasn't really thinking straight and, to be honest, I didn't think any serious damage had been done, but..." She looked at Clive with a coy, submissive expression that seemed totally out of character.

"Alright, alright! You'd better tell me what you know and get yourself to the hospital. I'll offer your apologies to Dick and try to explain."

"Thanks, Clive, I appreciate that. Anyway, the thing is, I've spoken to the car hire company that Ralph Dalton used and, apparently, he gave the name of Henry Carmichael. He hired the car on Thursday 17th August, paid in cash, produced a driving licence in the name of Henry Carmichael and gave the company an address in Bramstone. Now I've traced the people who live at that address and spoken to them. They confirmed that Henry Carmichael used to live there before they moved in, but that was several years ago and they don't have a current address for him – they thought he might have moved to Holland, but they were very vague. The car hire company said that Ralph Dalton, or Henry Carmichael if you prefer, has hired his car until next Wednesday, so obviously we'll keep the place under surveillance and the company has said that they will contact us as soon as he tries to return the car."

"Where is the car-hire company based?" Clive asked.

"Fleetdale."

"Mmm. That must be, let me see, forty miles or so away?"

"Yes that's right," Alison Pawlett confirmed, "but it's close to the airport, a main line railway station and the motorway, so it doesn't really help us much in working out where Ralph Dalton, or Henry Carmichael, lives or how he travelled to Fleetdale."

"Exactly!" Clive agreed gloomily. "So Ralph Dalton, or whoever he is, gave a false name and address, and he has now disappeared without trace."

"It certainly looks that way. I'll get a missing person search organised, check the passenger lists at the airport and see if we've got any potential images from the various security cameras dotted around, but I'll need to get a detailed description of him from the people here, especially you and Clare."

"Yes, no problem. You know where to find us."

Clive pursed his lips and emitted a low whistle. As fast as he tried to extricate himself from the increasingly labyrinthine investigations, another complication arose. But Constable Alison Pawlett hadn't finished.

"And I've got some more news," she announced triumphantly.

"Have you?" Clive tried to hide the tone of resignation in his voice. "Tell me more!"

"I finally managed to speak to Mr Quixhill, although he was reluctant to say much until I mentioned that we were investigating a murder. Apparently, around the time that Gareth and Elizabeth Adamson bought their house in Morstock, Mr Quixhill got two or three complaints from people who were trying to sell their homes through Blaby and Quixhill. It seems they complained that they thought somebody had been in their house while they'd been out at work and, well, had been using their bedroom and bathroom – you know, things had been moved or the bed clothes weren't as they left them or they could smell a perfume that nobody in the house used. Anyway, Mr Quixhill was concerned enough to carry out a bit of discreet surveillance and he discovered that Gregory Pullman would occasionally meet up with a female colleague and they would go into a house together and, er, well, spend quite a bit of time there while the owners were out. Mr Quixhill was about to confront them when the female member of staff suddenly resigned and moved away and, after that, there were no further reports of any problems. He said he didn't challenge Gregory Pullman at the time because he had no proof and he was good at his job and, reading between the lines, he wanted a quiet life."

"Well, well, well, Gregory Pullman, the randy old bugger! Who'd have thought it? It's obviously not just at cricket matches that he scores!"

"I don't know about 'randy old bugger' – dirty bastard, more like!" Alison Pawlett replied, primly.

"Yes, quite. But, it's no wonder he was so evasive when I asked him if he knew Gareth Adamson's house; it was probably one of the venues he used for his illicit trysts. I wouldn't be surprised if he'd got keys cut to quite a few of the houses he was trying to sell."

"I wonder if Mary Pullman knew," Alison Pawlett mused.

"Possibly, but we may never know. I'm certainly seeing Gregory Pullman in a new light, though, and that definitely raises his status as a suspect, especially if his wife did know and confronted him about it. That might also explain why things turned violent between them, if Martin Carslake is to be believed. We're going to have to pay Gregory Pullman another visit. Anyway, that's excellent work, Alison! Now, I hope you won't think I'm being rude, but I really do need to…" Clive pointed towards an untidy heap of papers littering his office desk.

"And I've found out some more about Sarah Tildesley," Alison Pawlett continued obliviously.

"Really? Have you? You have been busy. I don't know how you've found the time." Clive was sounding weary.

"Yes, as we knew, it was the school Easter holidays when her mother disappeared and it was the summer holidays when she was murdered but, on both occasions, her children happened to be spending some time with her ex – I've spoken to him – so she was on her own with no alibi."

"Really? Now that is interesting. When we went to see her, she told us that she was looking after her children on both occasions. Now, if I remember correctly," Clive shuddered slightly as he recalled the hair-raising journey to and from Sarah Tildesley's house, "her house was just off the high street and she would have needed to drive down it to get almost anywhere. Now I'm pretty sure I saw CCTV cameras at the end of the high street – maybe there are some at both ends."

Alison Pawlett smiled weakly, winced and fingered her nose again. "I'll get somebody onto it."

"Excellent, and now I really must get on—"

"And I've been in touch with all the local locksmiths I can find, but nobody has any record of Dean Footner getting a key to his neighbour's property cut, so we're no further forward on that one."

"Never mind, we've got some really good new leads there, well done! But if you'll excuse me, I must—"

"And I've tried to find out why Gareth Adamson has put his house on the market, but I haven't been able to speak to him and he's not returning my calls."

"Isn't he? I'll be going to the hospital a bit later to see Simon, so I might take a small detour to Morstock and see if he's in."

"I could do it. I'm going to the hospital and—"

Clive held up his hand. "Whoa, whoa! You've done enough! You should go straight to the hospital now because you might have to wait a while and it's important that they look at your nose as soon as possible, so I'll deal with Gareth Adamson, and now, if you'll excuse me, I really must—"

"And I've done a background check on Jamie Coulton," Alison Pawlett continued, oblivious to Clive's protestations.

"Have you? And...?"

"And he does have some form; not recently, admittedly, but he has done time for theft. Stealing old ladies' handbags seemed to be his speciality and—"

Clive emitted a heavy sigh. "Has he, indeed? Okay, now you get yourself to the hospital and I'll deal with Jamie Coulton."

Alison Pawlett had only vacated the office a minute or two when there was knocking at the door. Clive recognised the pattern of small knocks getting gradually louder and cursed.

"Come in, Debbie!"

The door partly opened and Debbie's round, suspicious face appeared.

"I'm sorry to bother you, Clive. Is this a good time?"

"No, not really! Inspector Beauregard is due shortly and I really do need to—"

"Only I thought you ought to know that some more money has gone missing and—"

Clive emitted another deep sigh and slumped back in his chair. "You'd better come in, Debbie, and close the door."

Debbie waddled importantly into the room and sat down heavily. Her expression was knowing and smug. "I thought you should know that I've been going through yesterday's takings and we're thirty pounds down. And I'm sure that the money that's gone missing has been taken from the till in the bar."

"And do you know who's taken it?"

"Well, I'm not a hundred per cent sure, but I caught Jamie skulking around in the bar early yesterday evening, just when everyone had gone into dinner, and I thought I saw him take something from the till. He said he was preparing some drinks for one of the diners and scuttled off, but, after he'd gone, I went round behind the bar and noticed the till was open."

"I see!" Clive scratched his head. He couldn't help feeling that it was too much of a coincidence that Debbie should accuse Jamie Coulton of stealing money only minutes after Alison Pawlett had mentioned that he had a criminal record for similar activity. "But you didn't actually see Jamie take the money."

"No, no, I didn't, but I'm usually a pretty good judge of these things – I was right about Ralph Dalton, wasn't I?"

"Yes, yes, you were, but I'm a bit puzzled. I mean, I know Jamie's been acting a bit strangely these last few days, but if he is taking money, then why now?"

"Well, I hear that his girlfriend has walked out on him, so maybe he's suddenly got financial problems. He'll miss her contribution to the rent, that's for sure!"

"Maybe, but are you sure this is an inside job? I mean, we know that Ralph Dalton was up to no good, so could he have taken the money? It's only since he arrived that money's started to go missing."

"I suppose," Debbie conceded grudgingly. "But he'd need to be pretty clever and pretty devious."

"Or pretty desperate! Did you see anyone else coming out of or going into the bar at around the same time you saw Jamie?"

"I wasn't spying, you know," Debbie replied huffily.

"No, no, of course not, but I just wondered if you might have seen anyone—"

"Well, Clare was dashing in and out getting drinks for the diners and I saw your lady detective friend wander in just after I'd caught Jamie in there. Of course, you should've been there, but…" Debbie suddenly stopped talking, no doubt suspecting that she may have said too much.

"Yes, Clare's already made that point quite forcibly. Look, Debbie, I'm very busy right now, but you're right to draw this to my attention and I'll try and tackle Jamie about it later on and—" He paused as there was another knock at the door and Clare burst in.

"Sorry to disturb you both," she announced, chirpily. "But there's a consignment of wines, beers and spirits being delivered that you need to sign for, Clive."

*

By mid-morning, the threatened deluge was well underway, peppering the parched, baked ground with stinging shafts of rain. Rivulets of cold, malevolent, water began to gush and swirl along any exposed hard surface.

Some minutes later, Acting Inspector Beauregard arrived at the Follycombe Hotel on his bicycle. He was drenched, though not, on this occasion, from perspiration. His hair was soaking wet, matted and clinging to the contours of his head. Water trickled gently down his cheeks and his shoes made a gentle sloshing noise as he walked. Stifling the urge to giggle at the sight of the bedraggled policeman wheeling his dripping bicycle around the side of the building, Clare found him a towel to dry himself on and some ill-fitting and unfashionable clothes that had been left behind by a previous guest and not claimed.

"It wasn't raining when I left home," Acting Inspector Beauregard observed ruefully as he settled into an armchair in the otherwise empty bar, while continuing to dry his hair.

"I'll make you a hot drink. Coffee?"

"Y-yes, please, that would be good, thank you," he stuttered through chattering teeth as he dropped the towel in a crumpled heap on the floor beside him.

As Clare left the bar, she exchanged amused glances with Clive, who had just arrived, having taken delivery of the latest consignment of alcoholic beverages. Clive wandered over to where the acting inspector was sitting huddled up, shivering in his chair, studied him closely and laughed loudly. "Dick! I love the clothes. Have you just come from a jumble sale?"

"Er, nno, nno," the hapless detective spluttered. "Your wife found me these clothes to change into. I got rather wet coming here."

"You didn't cycle in this weather, did you?" Clive asked, knowing the answer already but somehow savouring the acting inspector's discomfiture.

"Afraid so! I suspected rain was on its way, but I didn't think it would be this bad so soon."

"So much for a copper's instinct!" Laughing again at the plight of his waterlogged guest, and hating himself for doing so, Clive sat down opposite him and stretched his long legs out.

"So, have you been in touch with the hospital this morning?" Clive asked. "Do you know how Simon is?"

"Ah, yes. I've been to see him; that was before it started to rain. They think he's going to be okay – eventually. The knife wound is a nasty one, though; it's not very deep, so no vital organs were damaged, but the knife was very sharp and his wound is quite a big, jagged one. It was more of a slash than a stab. The real problem is that he's lost quite a lot of blood and they're keeping him on a drip and under observation for the time being. It's too early yet to know when he'll be released."

"Mmmm, it's a bad business. Clare and I are planning to go and see him as soon as we can get away."

"Good and while you're there, perhaps you can pump him for a bit of information on why he was attacked and what he knows about Ralph Dalton. I've not been able to get anything coherent out of him so far, but he might be more forthcoming with you."

"Probably still hungover when you saw him," Clive observed caustically as Clare came back into the room, followed closely by Archie. She was holding a tray with two mugs of coffee which she placed on a table beside the two men.

"Ah yes, that's what I was going to tell you last night before we got distracted," Clare announced. "Just after he'd been stabbed, I bent over Simon to examine his wound and I couldn't smell any alcohol on his breath. Now normally at that time in the evening, he smells like a distillery. I thought it odd. Anyway, I'll go and get some cakes; I take it you'd like some cakes?" Acting Inspector Beauregard nodded enthusiastically. Archie, meanwhile, was settling down on the acting inspector's discarded towel.

"So he was probably sober when Ralph Dalton attacked him. Now that is odd!" Clive reflected. "I've hardly ever known him sober at that time in the evening and I don't ever remember him hanging about down by the walled garden at that time – it's almost as though he was expecting Ralph Dalton to show up."

"What do you know about Ralph Dalton?" Acting Inspector Beauregard asked as he wrapped his hands around the warm mug of coffee.

Clive tugged his earlobe. "Not very much! We know that he was here on business – or at least that's what he told us – but we don't know the nature of it. We know that he hired a car, we believe that he used a false name and we know that Simon was terrified of him."

"He used a false name?" Acting Inspector Beauregard sounded surprised.

"Yes, Alison, er, Constable Pawlett has dug out quite a bit about him."

"Constable Pawlett?" The acting inspector managed to sound both confused and miffed. "I thought she was still off sick."

"Oh, She is, she is. She got badly beaten up the other night and is not in great shape – she's at the hospital this morning getting her nose fixed. But I think I mentioned that she's staying here at the moment; some problems at home, I gather. I'm sure you know all about that. And, of course, she was here when Simon was attacked last night so she took charge of matters. I must say, she was very impressive under the circumstances. Apparently, Ralph Dalton used a driving licence in the name of Henry Carmichael, but we haven't been able to trace him yet."

"But Alison hasn't mentioned any of this to me. I mean, I knew my colleagues had been called to an incident here yesterday evening, but I had no idea that Alison had—" the bewildered acting inspector bewailed.

Clive smiled an indulgent smile. "Oh, I think she wants to keep busy and she probably thought you had your hands full with the kidnapping of Lord Westleigh's daughter. I'm sure she'll bring you up to speed as soon as she can. When she returns from the hospital, I'll ask her to give you a call. Anyway, you said last night that the Reverend Ashburton had disappeared."

"Ah, er, yes, that's right. His neighbour phoned – you know, the one we met. And she said there's been no sign of him since Wednesday evening. That's the night that I understand Constable Pawlett followed him." There was a barbed edge to the acting inspector's comments. He couldn't disguise his annoyance at her for withholding information from him, with Clive's obvious encouragement.

"Couldn't he have just gone away for a few days?" Clive asked, ignoring the obvious resentment in the acting inspector's voice.

"That's what I said, but she was adamant. She said that he would've told her if he was going away. He didn't go away very often but, whenever he did, he always liked her to keep an eye on his place. Anyway, I sent someone round there and there were a couple of days' newspapers on the front door mat, together with some uncollected post and no sign of life. Under the circumstances, we thought we should run some checks and it turns out there is no such person as the Reverend Gerald Ashburton."

"God, not another one!"

"Apparently, yes! We spoke to a Church of England official and they'd never heard of a Reverend Gerald Ashburton; they have no record of anyone by that name qualifying as a vicar or running a parish or holding any office; as far as they're concerned, he doesn't exist. We're trying to get hold of the company that built Vernon Court to find out who originally purchased number two. But the company has gone out of business and it is the bank holiday weekend and…" He shrugged apologetically.

"Mmm. Well, you've certainly got me involved in a tangled web, Dick, thanks very much! Clare'll be delighted, especially if you keep eating all her cakes."

"Did I hear my name?" Clare announced as she entered the room carrying a plate piled high with cakes and pastries, which she placed on the table beside the coffee mugs.

"Yes, I'm sorry everything's getting so complicated," Dick replied as he leaned forward in his chair and, in one swift movement, scooped up a chocolate éclair from the plate. "And on top of all this, I've still got Lord Westleigh's daughter to find. Did I tell you he'd had a note from the—?"

"You did."

"And, of course, he still suspects Richard Edgton. If only I had some proof."

"Talking of Richard Edgton," Clive replied enigmatically, "I've got something here that might be of interest to you." He reached into his jacket pocket and produced a paper copy of a photograph, which he brandished. "I went to see Martin Carslake yesterday – he phoned and asked if he could see me. Anyway, it turned out that he had, after all, been taking pictures of Mary Pullman waving it all about at the window. But when he studied the photos in more detail, he saw someone else, apparently naked, in the background. Tell me who you think that is." Looking smug, he handed the sheet of paper to the acting inspector, who paused to look at it with the chocolate éclair held halfway between his plate and his mouth.

"Bloody hell! That's Richard Edgton!"

"Yes, that's more or less what Martin Carslake said. The story we've been getting from everyone we've spoken to is that Mary Pullman was fighting Richard Edgton's plans for the quarry and couldn't stand the man and yet, judging by that photo, I'd say she was quite friendly with him, wouldn't you? Maybe that explains why she was buying new clothes and dyeing her hair."

"Yes, yes, it would," Acting Inspector Beauregard confirmed, waving his chocolate éclair about excitedly. "Honestly, I don't know what is going on, but I think it's time we pulled Richard Edgton in. I think we've got enough evidence now and—"

Clive Walsingham held up a restraining hand. "I wouldn't advise it, Dick. If, as you suspect, he's behind the kidnapping of Lucy Jeffries, then pulling him in now might put her in danger. No, no, at the moment, what you've got is no more than circumstantial. I'd suggest you put a discreet watch on him and wait for things to happen. I'm sure they will."

Clare, meanwhile, had been surreptitiously studying the photograph over Acting Inspector Beauregard's hunched shoulder. "Sorry, but I couldn't help noticing there's something printed on the photograph in the corner," she observed. "It says '4 September 3.30'."

"Yes, that's right," Clive confirmed. "That's when Martin Carslake took the photograph – Saturday 4th September, last year."

"God, I remember Saturday 4th September. Do you remember, Clive? We'd arranged a 'Wedding Fayre' here and it poured with rain nearly all day. A bit like today."

"Did it really?" Clive suddenly seemed strangely interested in the weather. "So there would have been no cricket that day – it would've been rained off. Now that is very interesting. Dick, would you mind if I speak to Gregory Pullman again?"

*

It was just after lunch when Clive and Clare left the Follycombe Hotel with the intention of visiting Simon Verwood in hospital. As he drove, Clive seemed preoccupied and brooding – Clare fancied that he was gripping the steering wheel more tightly than usual and he was strangely quiet. The only sound was the rhythmic swishing of the windscreen wipers.

"So, um, how's the investigation going?" Clare asked, hoping that Clive might unburden himself. "Have you worked out whodunit?"

"Mmmm. No, that's the problem, really," Clive replied distractedly. "I've got plenty of theories, but the list of suspects keeps getting longer."

"Would it help if you told me about it?" Although she hated seeing Clive so introspective and withdrawn, Clare's motives were not entirely altruistic. Her curiosity had been aroused.

"I'm sorry, darling! I know I'm not being much company at the moment. I just need a breakthrough of some kind and then I'll be fine."

"Meanwhile?"

"Meanwhile, we've got Gregory Pullman, the husband. He admits that he and his wife weren't close but claims there was no-one else. And yet we're now pretty sure that Mary Pullman was having an affair, which he almost certainly knew about, while he was also indulging in a bit of hanky-panky with one his colleagues at work. And then, there's their daughter, Sarah Tildesley. She is out of work, she is trying to bring up two kids on her own and she is seriously strapped for cash. Up to the time Mary Pullman disappeared, she was giving her daughter a sum of money each month, presumably to help her out, but when that stopped… Maybe Sarah Tildesley knew she would inherit a fair amount of money in her mother's will. And she doesn't have an alibi for either the date her mother disappeared or the date we think she was murdered. She lied to us about having to look after her kids when they were actually staying with their father.

"And then there is everyone's favourite villain, Richard Edgton. Dick and Alison both desperately want to build a case against him, but there's no evidence of his involvement. There is certainly something funny going on, though. We were led to believe that Mary Pullman was a sworn enemy of his, you know, campaigning against his plans for the quarry and then you saw the photograph of them both naked in her bedroom."

"I did. But surely, either way, he has a possible motive."

"Certainly, and one of his heavies, Dean Footner, lives next door to where the body was found. I've met him and, let me tell you, he would be more than capable of taking care of his boss's business, if you know what I mean. He claims that he and his family were on holiday in Radholme at the time Mary Pullman was murdered, and it's true that his partner and kids were seen there, but he doesn't seem to have been with them very much. And then there's the Reverend Gerald Ashburton, or at least that's what he calls himself. It looks as though Mary Pullman was due to visit him, for some reason, the day she disappeared. We know he frequents a dodgy 'gentleman's club' in Stowbrook and now it turns out that his name is bogus and he's conveniently disappeared. And, of course, we shouldn't discount her neighbour, Martin Carslake – the one who took the pictures of her. There was clearly no love lost between the two of them. And he was determined enough to take photographs of her up at her bedroom window that he went out into his garden in the pouring rain to do so."

"So, that's all quite straightforward, then. Clive, where are we going? This isn't the road to the hospital."

Without any explanation, Clive had strayed from the usual route to Carlow Valley Hospital and was heading towards Morstock. "There's one more suspect, and I need to speak to him. It's not much out of the way and shouldn't take long. His name is Gareth Adamson."

*

The door to Gareth and Elizabeth Adamson's house creaked open a small amount and Gareth Adamson peered out nervously, his eyes blinking uncertainly and his balding pate reflecting the watery, overcast afternoon light.

"Hello, Mr Adamson," Clive greeted him amiably. "You may remember I came to see you about the death of Mary Pullman. I'm helping the local police and I wondered if you could spare me a few minutes of your time."

Gareth Adamson glanced over his shoulder into the dark interior of the house. "Er, well, it's not very convenient at the moment. I have a visitor and—"

At that moment, the door was pushed wide open and a large, swarthy, muscular man brushed past Gareth Adamson. "It's okay, don't mind me," he said gruffly. "I was just leaving." Clive stood back as the man jostled past him, without acknowledging his presence, and strode towards the neighbouring house belonging to Dean Footner. He walked past an estate car that was parked outside, rang the bell and was quickly admitted.

"Was that Richard Edgton?" Clive asked, recalling the image he had seen on Martin Carslake's photograph.

"That's right," Gareth Adamson acknowledged without adding any further information.

Clive looked up at the leaden sky as heavy spots of rain continued to fall. "Errm, would it be possible to come inside, just for a couple of moments; it's pretty damp out here."

Gareth Adamson stood aside to allow Clive to pass but made no attempt to usher him into the living room. Instead he stood resolutely by the front door, fidgeting with the buttons on his beige cardigan. "I'm afraid my wife isn't here. She's working this afternoon – at the local supermarket." Gareth Adamson sounded as though he was hoping that his wife's absence in some way excused him from talking to Clive.

"Ah, yes, I remember you saying," Clive continued. "Look, I'm sorry for the intrusion, but I'd heard that you'd recently put your house on the market and I was curious to know why."

Gareth Adamson shrugged. "It's no secret, there's no mystery. We only moved here in the first place to be closer to Fearnley quarry, where I worked at the time, but there's no prospect of that re-opening – certainly not as a quarry – I can't seem to find any work around here and whatever attraction this place might once have had, it pretty well disappeared the day I discovered a body in the back garden. And before you ask, Richard Edgton was here to make me an offer – a very generous offer, as it turns out, well above the asking price – which I have just accepted."

*

"Well, I certainly didn't expect to bump into the legendary Richard Edgton," Clive admitted as he drove away. "I wonder why he's so keen to buy Gareth Adamson's house; it's not exceptional in any way."

"Apart from the fact that Mary Pullman was found dead in the back garden," Clare replied. "Is that just a coincidence?"

Clive snorted. "You never know and that's the trouble. There's so much I don't know. I mean, I still don't understand where Mary Pullman was between the time that she disappeared in April and when she turned up dead in Gareth Adamson's back garden a couple of weeks ago."

"Do you think she'd been kept locked up somewhere?"

"Mmmm, it has been suggested, but then we know that she regularly had her hair dyed by her daughter, Sarah. Now, if you were keeping her locked up somewhere, for whatever reason, would you go to the trouble of cutting and dyeing her hair?"

"Probably not, unless—"

"So," Clive interrupted. "If she was held locked up somewhere from when she disappeared to when she was murdered – just over four months – her hair would have grown by maybe two or three inches and her grey roots would be very visible. And yet, when she was found, her hair looked to have been recently styled and dyed and there was no hint of grey. So if she wasn't locked up somewhere, where has she been? There have been no sightings of her or her car, nobody has touched her bank account, there's been no activity on her mobile phone, nothing."

Clare laughed. "Maybe somebody's been keeping her body in a freezer."

"Yes, maybe…" Clive paused as he glanced in his rear view mirror. "Err, I don't want to worry you, Clare, but I think we're being followed."

"No! Are you sure?" Clare asked, her voice sounding tense.

"Well, do you remember seeing a rather posh estate car parked outside the house next door to Gareth Adamson's; the house that Richard Edgton went into?"

"Yes, I vaguely remember a car of some sort, but—"

"Well," Clive interrupted again. "I think it's been following us ever since we left Gareth Adamson's place. And it has two men in it – almost certainly Richard Edgton and Dean Footner."

"Are you sure?" Clare asked again.

"I'll soon find out." Without warning, Clive suddenly turned off the main road and drove down a narrow, winding country lane. At a minor junction, he turned left and, after a meandering drive down a tree-lined, pot-holed lane, returned to the main road, a little further back. Clive glanced in his rear-view mirror; the estate car was still following them. "Yup, he's certainly following us," Clive announced as he continued towards the hospital, casting ever more frequent glances in his mirror.

"What do we do now?" Clare asked, trying to sound calmer than she felt.

"Nothing," Clive replied casually. "We'll drive to the hospital, as planned, and see what happens."

The estate car continued to follow Clive and Clare as he turned into the hospital entrance, but when he reached the visitors' car park and looked around, it was nowhere to be seen.

"It's alright, I don't think we're being followed anymore." Clive spoke with quiet assurance as he manoeuvred his car into a space. "I can't see the estate car anywhere around."

"Phew, thank God for that," Clare replied. "What the hell was that all about?"

"I can't be sure, but the people who were following us were not particularly subtle. I mean, it was easy enough to see that they were following us and they made no attempt to conceal the fact. So, either they wanted to know where we were going but weren't too bothered about being seen, or they were putting on a show to try and frighten or intimidate us in some way."

"Well, they certainly did that, but why? Why would they do that?"

"Why indeed. It looks as though everyone's favourite villain, Richard Edgton, is more involved than I first thought he was."

*

Carlow Valley Hospital was an austere-looking, red-brick building originally constructed as a Victorian workhouse. It had towering red-brick walls, small windows and a steeply sloping roof of black slate. Inside, a series of piecemeal refurbishments had given it the appearance of some more modern hospitals – utilitarian and functional but essentially colourless and cheerless.

It was mid-afternoon when Clive and Clare made their way into the main vestibule and, after a couple of enquiries of the permanently harassed reception staff, they located Simon Verwood at the far end of a small ward of six beds. He looked faintly ghost-like in his white hospital gown with his dishevelled, silver hair and his unusually anaemic complexion. He was still attached to a drip and was propped up on a couple of brilliantly white pillows, with his eyes closed. He jumped visibly when Clive spoke to him but kept his eyes closed.

"Ah, Mister Clive and Mrs Clare, is it?" he mumbled drowsily as he half opened his eyes. "Have you come to collect me?"

"Collect you? No! The doctors haven't said when you can go yet," Clare replied firmly.

Suddenly alert and animated, Simon sat bolt upright, his bloodshot eyes wide open, his mane of silver hair flopping over his forehead and his hands trembling. His voice had returned to its normal resonance. "But I've got to go. I must go. It's not safe in here," he boomed.

"What on earth do you mean?" Clive asked, quizzically.

"He was here earlier." Simon pointed a shaking finger towards the door.

"Who was?"

"Ralph Dalton! He was here. I'd been dozing and then I heard a noise and, as I came to, I saw him creeping towards me. He had one hand behind his back and his face was kind of contorted into a terrible scowl. Well, naturally I called out and hit the panic button, and he turned and ran. He must've come to finish what he'd started last night."

"My God! How awful for you!" Clare sympathised. "When did this happen?"

Simon shrugged. "Oh, I'm not sure. Time drags in this dreadful place and I'd been dozing – it was probably two or three hours ago."

"And did anybody catch him?" Clive asked, more in hope than expectation.

"Oh, no, of course not," Simon snorted disdainfully. "The nurses are a bit stretched at the best of times, but especially at weekends, and by the time someone came, he'd got clean away. I think they had a quick look round, but there was no sign of him. To be honest, I don't think they took me very seriously. I think they've decided that I'm just a hysterical old drama queen."

"Did anyone else see Ralph Dalton? Did they see him arrive or leave?" Clive asked, keen to avoid being drawn into a dialogue about the histrionic tendencies of his maimed gardener.

Simon Verwood gave a forlorn shrug. "Not that I know of; everyone in this ward was either asleep or reading or exchanging minor inconsequentialities with a visitor. Today's a busy day for visitors. There are people coming and going all over the place. I don't imagine anyone gave him a second glance."

"Have you told the police? They could ask to check the security cameras for any sightings of Ralph Dalton."

"The police?" Simon sounded scornful. "No, of course not! Somebody was here this morning, though; had a French sounding name – Bonaparte or something."

"Beauregard. Acting Inspector Beauregard."

"Yes, that's the chap – miserable bugger! He kept asking all sorts of questions about Ralph Dalton. What did I know about him? Why was I so scared of him? Why did he attack me?"

"And?"

"And I told him nothing." He suddenly reached out and grabbed Clive's sleeve. "Look, Mr Clive, I've got my reasons for being frightened of Ralph bloody Dalton, not least the fact that he attacked me, but I'm not prepared to say any more. I'm in enough trouble already and I don't want to make it worse."

"But you'll have to say something sooner or later; otherwise, you could be charged with obstructing the police."

"Look, Mr Clive, all I need is to get out of this dreadful place. I don't feel safe in here. Then, once I'm out of here, I might be able to make the necessary arrangements... I might be able to take care of things a bit." He winked conspiratorially at Clive.

"But obviously we need to catch Ralph Dalton before he does any more damage. Can you tell us anything that might help – where he lives, for example?"

"I've no idea, I'm afraid," Simon Verwood replied unhelpfully, his eyes suddenly focused on the floor.

"We think he might be using an assumed name. Do you know what his real name is?"

Simon Verwood fell silent for a moment or two as though carefully considering his reply. "He used to call himself Harold Plant," he replied at length, "but I couldn't say whether that was his real name."

"And you're not going to tell us anything else that might help?"

"I'm so sorry, Mister Clive and Mrs Clare. I know I'm making life difficult for you both and you've been so kind to me since you took over the hotel, but I really can't tell you anything more – I've probably said too much already. But when I'm finally allowed out of this godforsaken place, I'll deal with Ralph Dalton and you need not worry any more about it."

*

"Are we being followed?" Clare asked timorously as they were driving back from the hospital along the serpentine country lanes that led to the hotel.

Clive checked in his mirror. "No, no, it's okay, we're not being followed."

Clare fell strangely quiet for several minutes before suddenly saying, "Poor old Simon!" Although not normally inclined to be particularly sympathetic towards Simon Verwood, his frequent histrionics or his destructive drinking habits, she sounded genuinely concerned. "It must be at least twenty-four hours since he's had a drink; some kind of a record for him, I should think. No wonder he's not in the best of moods. Still, you did get another name out of him – Harold Plant. Do you think that's worth pursuing?"

Clive laughed. "Maybe, but I can't help feeling that Simon is playing games with us. Still, I'll make some enquiries about Harold Plant when we get back, just in case he's telling the truth."

"You've lost me, I'm afraid, but if he is playing games, just you wait till I get my hands on him." Clare's brief feeling of compassion for Simon had quickly faded.

"Oh, I don't think you'll have long to wait," Clive replied. "He's so agitated and difficult that I should think either the hospital will get rid of him very soon, or he'll discharge himself. Meanwhile, until Simon is properly fit, I'm going to ask Jamie to take on some of his responsibilities in the garden. We need to make sure he's not in the bar or at reception unsupervised until we find out a bit more about the missing money that Debbie has reported."

Deep in thought, Clare again fell silent for a while as she tried to unravel the increasingly complex chain of apparently unconnected developments. "I wish I knew what was going on, but I suspect you know more than you're admitting, don't you?" she suddenly asked, accusingly.

Clive could feel Clare's piercing stare, but he just grunted. "Maybe, but there are still too many loose ends for my liking, too many things I don't yet understand. Every time I think I'm getting closer, something else happens that throws me off the scent again."

As Clive and Clare drove into the hotel car park, a vehicle suddenly pulled out in front of them and accelerated quickly away, its tyres squealing on the tarmac. Clive recognised it as the estate car that had followed them to the hospital earlier.

"There you are; you see what I mean!" Clive added with more than a hint of frustration. "But don't worry about it, Clare. Like Simon, I think they're just having a little game with us."

"We've just seen two men drive out of the car park in something of a hurry. Do you know what they were doing here?" Clive asked Debbie as he strode up to the reception desk looking perplexed.

"Yes, I think so. They turned up unannounced. The older guy, well dressed, quite burly, did all the talking. He didn't say who he was, but he was quite a smooth talker in an oily kind of way. He just said that he'd heard good reports of the hotel and was thinking of booking it for a business conference and he asked if he could look around. Now I reckon I'm a pretty good judge of character and I didn't like the look of him – he seemed very shifty to me. So I asked Jamie to show them around while I pretended I was going into the office to prepare a folder of information for him."

"But there's a pile of folders already prepared," Clive protested.

"Yes, I know. So while Jamie was showing them around, I sneaked out into the car park and had a look at their car."

"And?"

"And I've written down the registration number," Debbie announced proudly as she presented a piece of paper to Clive. "And I noticed that they've just come from the hospital. They had a Carlow Valley Hospital car park ticket attached to the windscreen."

"And did they say or do anything else?"

"No, not really! When Jamie brought them back into reception, I gave them the folder and the big man thanked me and they left."

Clive pursed his lips and emitted a low whistle. "I see," he said. "I wonder what they really wanted and I wonder what they were doing at the hospital. Thank you, Debbie, for your detective work. And talking of which, have you seen Constable Pawlett recently?"

Debbie shook her head. "No, she went out this morning and I haven't seen her since."

*

Later that evening, Clive was in the crowded bar busily plying drinks to the erstwhile staid and sober members of Miranda's coach party. Many of them seemed intent on an evening of relative revelry before they left in the morning and were filling the air with a hubbub of excited conversation and occasionally raucous laughter, when Miranda wandered in. She was looking relaxed and smiling, seemingly gratified that her party's visit to the Follycombe Hotel had been so obviously successful.

Clive looked up as she approached the bar. "Ah, Miranda, can I get you a drink – on the house?"

"Oh, thanks, Clive. Just a glass of your house white would be good."

"Coming up; and how was your trip to Chartfield Castle today?"

"Oh, the trip was fine, thanks; a bit wet at times, but everyone seemed to enjoy themselves – no-one got lost or did anything daft. Anthony, our guide, seemed a bit distracted – he wasn't quite his usual thorough self – but otherwise okay, thanks. And I've got a copy of the guidebook you wanted and the answers to the questions you were asking and—"

"Oh, that's excellent. Thank you so much. I hope you didn't have any problems?"

"No, the place was heaving. No-one was paying much attention to what I was doing."

"Good, so tell me—"

Clive was interrupted by his mobile phone ringing. He looked at the screen and cursed under his breath. "Excuse me a moment, Miranda, I'll have to deal with this. Hello, Dick, what can I do for you?"

"Hello, Clive." Acting Inspector Beauregard sounded even more saturnine than usual. "I've just had a call from the hospital and I thought you ought to know."

"My God, is it Simon? What's happened?"

"Simon? No, no. It's Inspector Morris. He's… he's dead!"

Seventeen

Sunday 27 August

Clive and Clare Walsingham were determined to bid farewell in person to Miranda's coach party as it left the hotel after an early breakfast and set off north on the next leg of its intensive cultural odyssey. The coach company's booking would represent a lucrative form of income for the hotel if it became a regular one and they were keen to demonstrate that they were good hosts – visible, attentive and friendly – right up to the point of departure.

"I hope your group has enjoyed the last few days," Clive said, as Miranda prepared to board the coach at precisely nine o'clock.

"Oh yes, it's been great, thanks," Miranda enthused, smiling broadly. "The food, your hospitality and everything has been first-class. I shall certainly be reporting favourably to the company and I'm sure we'll be back. And the little incident the other night was the icing on the cake."

Clive smiled. "Mmm, I can't guarantee to provide that again; except at our murder mystery weekends, of course."

"Oh well, never mind; but I do want to know how things turn out with your investigations and whether you catch the guy who attacked your gardener. You will let me know, won't you?"

"Of course, and thanks for your help! And have a safe journey!"

Suddenly Miranda wrapped her arms around Clive's neck and planted a kiss on his cheek. "See you next time," she called as she boarded the coach.

As he stood on the entrance steps watching the coach pull away, waving goodbye with one hand and instinctively wiping the smudge of lipstick from his cheek with the other, Clive began to feel uncomfortably cold. He shivered, looked up and noted the odd small patch of pale blue sky peeping timorously between the grey, brooding clouds. Maybe, he reflected, if the sun made an appearance, however fleeting, the day might prove to be more agreeable, climatically at least, than the previous one. In other ways, however, it promised to be just as complicated, fraught and uncertain. A few minutes earlier, Simon Verwood had phoned to announce, formally and loudly, that the hospital was discharging him, to declare that he didn't want to stay there one minute longer than was necessary and to ask if someone could "be a sweetie" and drive over and collect him. A couple of minutes later, Acting Inspector Beauregard had called to say that he had important news and was coming straight over. Clive frowned – Clare was not going to be pleased.

"Clare, darling?" Clive asked awkwardly as they turned away from the chill breeze and headed swiftly indoors. "I wonder if you'd mind collecting Simon from the hospital. Dick's on his way over with some important news and I'll need to be here when he arrives and then Alison and I have got a meeting with Gregory Pullman and his daughter and—"

Clare narrowed her eyes and wagged an admonishing finger in Clive's direction. "Oh, Clive! Honestly, do I have to? I mean, can't he make his own way back? He can call a taxi or something."

"I know, I know," Clive apologised. "But he has been stabbed and I feel kind of responsible and I did promise we'd collect him. Obviously that was before Dick phoned, but—"

"Alright!" Clare snapped. "I'll do it, but I'm agreeing to collect Simon under protest. You know what'll happen; I'll only have him whining and wheedling all the way back about how painful his wound is and how badly they looked after him in hospital and what a bastard Ralph Dalton is, and asking if the police have caught him yet and so on and so on. But I suppose you've got to be here when Dick turns up; I accept that, grudgingly, so I'll do what I have to do. But I need to know how much longer all this is going on for. I mean, we are trying to run a hotel and you did promise that you'd be around all the time when the coach party was here and—"

"I know, darling, and I'm so sorry. When I agreed to help, I'd no idea the case was going to be so complicated and that Dick was going to abandon me while he worked on the aristocratic kidnapping and that Alison was going to get herself beaten up and Simon was going to get stabbed and—"

"Alright, alright! I get the picture. But just remember we're here to make a profit, so go easy on the cakes! Incidentally, have you found out anything about Harold Plant?"

Clive shook his head. "No, nothing at all, although I have worked out that 'Harold Plant' is an anagram of 'Ralph Dalton', so either it's another one of his aliases or Simon made it up to confuse us."

"Well, I just hope for Simon's sake that he's not deliberately trying to confuse us."

*

Clive helped Clare into her car and waved her off before turning and marching briskly back into the hotel. As he passed the reception desk, he paused briefly and spoke to Debbie.

"Have you had time to check yesterday's till receipts yet? Has any more money gone missing?"

"Yes, I've had a look and, as far as I can tell, nothing went missing yesterday," Debbie replied. She sounded disappointed.

"Good, good – that's something at least." Fearing that Debbie was about to say something more, Clive scuttled into his office and closed the door firmly behind him. He had just logged onto his computer and was thumbing through the pile of invoices that required his attention when he heard an urgent knocking at the door. Cursing under his breath, he rose from his chair and opened the door to find Alison Pawlett, breathing hard but looking triumphant.

"Alison, how are you? I didn't see anything of you yesterday."

"Nnno, I'm sorry," Alison Pawlett sounded evasive as she wandered into the office. "I had to wait for ages at the hospital and when I finally got back, I wasn't feeling all that well, so I went upstairs for a while and lay on the bed. I must've dozed off and—"

"And how is your nose?"

"My nose? Ah, yes, it is broken apparently, but there are no complications so it should heal alright."

"Oh well, that's something. I don't suppose you happened to see Richard Edgton while you were at the hospital?"

Alison looked puzzled. "No! Why, should I?"

"No, no, not really. It's just that Clare and I drove over to the hospital to see Simon and, as we were driving, I realised we were being followed by Richard Edgton – he was being driven by Dean Footner. I didn't see him when we parked at the hospital, but he turned up here later on, before we got back, and Debbie noticed a hospital car park ticket on his windscreen. We saw him driving away from here at some speed just as we arrived back. It spooked us a bit and I'd quite like to know what he was up to."

Alison pulled a face and then winced. "Yes, of course; how strange. They'll have security cameras at the hospital. I can take a look to see where he went."

"Yes, that would be good, if you get the time. Meanwhile, did you get my message?"

"Yes, I did, and everything's arranged, although I did encounter some resistance. I'm just off to collect Sarah Tildesley, and Gregory Pullman is expecting you. But there are a couple of things I thought you might like to know before we meet up later."

"Do tell," Clive encouraged, sensing that Alison was feeling pleased with herself.

"Well, I managed to have a word with Mary Pullman's solicitor yesterday, while I was hanging around at the hospital. He wasn't too pleased to be contacted at home on a Saturday and really didn't want to give me any information, but I explained that we were investigating a murder and that if he withheld what turned out to be vital information, you know – the usual thing. Anyway, it turns out that Mary Pullman left just over £400,000 in her will."

"Wow!" Clive exclaimed. "That's not bad for a retired bank clerk. And did he tell you who the main beneficiaries were?"

"He did. Apparently, she left nothing to her husband and, apart from a couple of very minor bequests, the vast bulk of her estate was to be distributed equally among her children."

"Wow!" Clive repeated. "Among her children? So Sarah Tildesley is due to inherit a substantial sum of money. That'll certainly be handy for her. I wonder if she knows."

"And talking of Sarah Tildesley, you asked me to check the security cameras in Bailbridge."

"Yes, and…?"

"And on both the day that her mother disappeared and the day we think she was murdered, we have images of Sarah Tildesley's car driving away from Bailbridge around 1.30 in the afternoon and returning just after six o'clock."

"But no sightings in between?"

"Sadly, no! This area is deemed to be low risk, so we're not blessed with too many cameras."

"That's a shame. Which way was she heading?"

"She was driving towards Stowbrook."

"Which is in the same direction as Buckham."

"Exactly, and when we checked the camera's film over a longer period, we discovered that she made the journey quite regularly – not always at exactly the same time, but there were usually about four or five hours between her leaving Bailbridge and returning. And, as far as we could see, she was always on her own in the car."

"Mmmm. Now that is intriguing. But if she was involved in her mother's disappearance and subsequent murder, it doesn't explain the long time-lag between the two events and where Mary Pullman had been all that time? Still, it looks as though you'll have plenty to discuss with Sarah Tildesley on the journey. Incidentally, Dick, er, Acting Inspector Beauregard is due here shortly. Do you want to stay and hear what he has to say?"

"Err, no thanks," Alison Pawlett replied emphatically. "I really think I should be on my way. The traffic might be heavy this morning."

*

Chastened by the previous day's drenching, Acting Inspector Beauregard had driven to the Follycombe Hotel. An air of profound melancholy hung over him like a heavy pall as he hauled himself slowly from his car, sneezed loudly and plodded with a laboured gait and hunched shoulders into the bar, where Clive was waiting for him. He lowered himself slowly into a bar chair, peered at Clive through heavy eyes and emitted a strange, mournful sound that was somewhere between a moan and a sigh.

Clive studied him for a moment, hoping that the depth of Acting Inspector Beauregard's mournfulness might have been sufficient to ruin his appetite but, when Jamie Coulton appeared with a plate of cakes, grinning broadly as usual and followed by Archie, his tail raised expectantly at the prospect of a tasty snack, there was a distinct, if fleeting, uplifting of his spirit. He sneezed again.

"I'm sorry, Clive." Acting Inspector Beauregard spoke with an unusually nasal timbre. "I think I'm going down with a cold."

"I don't imagine the drenching you got yesterday helped much," Clive replied unsympathetically, a malicious smile playing at the edge of his lips as he edged his chair a few inches further away from his visitor. "I was very sorry to hear about Inspector Morris," Clive continued in what he hoped were suitably reverential terms. "That must have been a great shock to you."

"It was," Acting Inspector Beauregard replied slowly. "I've hardly slept a wink all night what with this cold and… I really thought they'd stabilised his condition and he was out of danger."

"So what happened, if you don't mind me asking?"

Acting Inspector Beauregard emitted another strange, mournful sound. "Nobody seems very sure, really. Apparently, he seemed okay during the day and then one of the nurses doing her rounds discovered that he'd just stopped breathing. They tried to revive him, but it was too late. They're doing some tests to try and find out what—"

"Well, I'm so very sorry," Clive repeated.

"I'm devastated. He was so good to me; I feel he taught me all I know," Acting Inspector Beauregard announced dramatically, his shoulders heaving with emotion.

"Which isn't that much!" Clive thought to himself. "You said you had some important news for me," he said in a desperate attempt to change the subject.

Acting Inspector Beauregard peered at Clive with confused, heavily lidded eyes. "Did I? Oh yes, of course. We've found Richard Edgton's fingerprints all over the envelope that the ransom note to Lord Westleigh was sent in."

"Did you? That was remarkably careless of him, bearing in mind what a ruthless and calculating villain he appears to be," Clive replied, sceptically.

"I suppose it was," Acting Inspector Beauregard conceded, "but there's no mistake; they were definitely his fingerprints. And there's more – much more! When Richard Edgton reported the break-in at Fearnley quarry, I got our forensic people to take a look inside the two small outbuildings that he was using, and guess what they've found? They've found some fibres that look as though they have come from riding breeches and some hairs. Some are human, we're checking to see if they've come from Lucy Jeffries, and the others are horse hairs; the same colour as the horse Lucy Jeffries was riding when she was kidnapped."

Clive exhaled, a look of puzzlement spreading across his face. "Hang on a minute, Dick. If I've understood you correctly, Richard Edgton himself reported the break-in at the quarry – odd behaviour, don't you think, if he'd been holding Lucy Jeffries there and knew you might search the buildings and find some incriminating evidence?"

"Nah, not really," Dick Beauregard replied dismissively. "Richard Edgton knew we were going to get a warrant to search the place anyway, so he got rid of most of the stuff he didn't want us to find – I saw him and Dean Footner do it – then tried to throw us off the scent by staging a burglary. I reckon he must have overlooked some of the little incriminating bits of forensic evidence that we found, or he thought that his henchmen had made a better job of removing the evidence than they had."

"Yes, but—"

"And," Acting Inspector Beauregard was scarcely able to quell his excitement, "there was this large trunk on the floor of one of the buildings and inside were some old quarrymen's clothes and, right at the bottom, we found a blue coat, just like the one that Mary Pullman was wearing when she—"

"And were there some hairs on it?"

"There were, and if they're a match for Mary Pullman's, then bingo! Anyway, the important thing is we've got the bastard at last! As soon as I've finished here, I shall drive over to his place and arrest him."

"Excellent!" Clive replied unenthusiastically, before pausing for a moment while Dick Beauregard bit into his large slice of lemon drizzle cake. "Did you know, by the way, that Richard Edgton is planning to buy Gareth Adamson's house? He's made an offer that Gareth Adamson has accepted."

Acting Inspector Beauregard spluttered, causing himself to choke on the cake and resulting in a sustained bout of coughing followed by a loud sneeze. "No! How did you find that out?"

"Gareth Adamson told me," Clive replied while brushing some cake crumbs from his mauve trousers.

"Well, I wonder why Richard Edgton has done that."

Clive was unable to stifle his sense of mischief any longer. "Maybe there are more secrets in the house that he doesn't want us to find out about. Maybe they left some clues behind when they dumped Mary Pullman's body. Maybe there are some more bodies buried in the garden that he doesn't want us to know about. After all, his thuggish factotum, Dean Footner lives next door."

The shroud of melancholy seemed to lift again from Acting Inspector Beauregard's shoulders. "Well, thank you for that, Clive. I shall enjoy asking Richard Edgton about that. Perhaps we'll have to dig up Gareth Adamson's garden and—"

"And has Lord Westleigh had any further news about his daughter and her whereabouts – another ransom note, maybe, or a phone call?" Clive asked, determined to change the subject before he was overcome by a bout of giggles.

Acting Inspector Beauregard sneezed again. "No, not yet!"

"So you still don't know where Lucy Jeffries is or when the next ransom demand will arrive or what it will say?"

"Er, no, not yet!"

"And you're still planning to arrest Richard Edgton?"

"Yes, I am – I'm not prepared to wait any longer, especially after what you've just told me. I'm going to bring Richard Edgton in for questioning."

"Well, good luck with that, Dick!"

*

Clive hadn't relished the prospect of being driven by Alison Pawlett at breakneck speed along the narrow country lanes that led to Buckham, so he had suggested that she drove over to Bailbridge to collect Sarah Tildesley while he made his own way, at a more sedate pace, to Gregory Pullman's house. Alison Pawlett had advised Clive to expect her and Sarah Tildesley at eleven thirty and, if previous form was anything to go by, she would be punctual to the second, so he planned to arrive at Gregory Pullman's house a little earlier – there were some things he wanted to discuss before his daughter arrived.

Although he was expecting Clive, Gregory Pullman seemed no more pleased to see him than on his previous visit and, with obvious reluctance, ushered him into the tidy living room and gestured towards a chair. Clive noticed his cricket score book, together with an impressive collection of pencils and erasers, neatly arranged on the table under the window.

"I hope this won't take long," Gregory Pullman began, pointedly studying his watch. "We've got a big cricket match starting at one o'clock and I need—"

"Yes, I know! You need to be there in good time because you're scoring."

"Yes, but…" Gregory Pullman's voice tailed away.

"This shouldn't take long at all," Clive reassured him. "There are just a couple of issues relating to your wife's death that I need to clarify."

Gregory Pullman scratched his head. It was a habit that Clive recalled from their previous meeting. "I've told you everything I know," he announced solemnly, as he fidgeted in his chair.

"Ah, well, that's not quite true, is it? I mean, for a start, you denied knowing Gareth Adamson and his house in Morstock, and yet it was your estate agency that handled the sale."

"Was it? I, er, I, er, don't remember that particular transaction. I've handled a lot of sales over the years and can't remember many of them in detail."

"So you're still telling me that you have no knowledge of Gareth Adamson or his house?"

"I, er, I might remember it if I had a look through the files, but no, I'm afraid not." He shrugged apologetically.

"Well, you might like to know that Detective Constable Pawlett has had a very interesting conversation with Mr

Quixhill. Apparently around the time Gareth Adamson bought his house, Mr Quixhill was getting reports that someone had been using some of the houses on his books for, shall we say, extra-mural activities – extra-marital activities, if you prefer. Now he could never prove anything, but he was pretty sure that a female colleague who resigned shortly afterwards had been up to no good and he was pretty sure who she'd been up to no good with."

Clive paused and studied Gregory Pullman. He had the same look of evasiveness that Clive remembered from his previous visit. "Is there anything you want to say?" he asked.

Gregory Pullman scratched his head. "Nnnoo, I don't think so. I'd heard the rumours that were flying around at the time, but I'm afraid Mr Quixhill must be mistaken if he thought I was involved in any way. His memory isn't very reliable these days."

"Of course," Clive continued, "you could have had some spare keys cut so that you and your, er, colleague could visit these houses without anyone in the office knowing. And one of those could have been the house that Gareth Adamson bought."

Gregory Pullman slowly removed his heavy spectacles and examined them for some imaginary defect. "I think you must have a very vivid imagination, Mr Walsingham, that's all I can say. I can assure you that there is not a shred of truth in anything you have just said."

"Alright, let me turn to another matter. We're pretty sure that your wife was having an affair with Richard Edgton in the months leading up to her disappearance. Did you know about that?"

Gregory Pullman looked surprised. "What? As I said, you obviously have a very fertile imagination, Mr Walsingham. I'll admit that I was pretty sure she was having an affair with someone, but Richard Edgton? Good God, no! You must be mistaken!"

"We've got photographic proof. We know that he was with your wife in her bedroom, in a state of undress, let us say, on the afternoon of Saturday 4th September last year."

"Photographic proof, you say?"

"Yes, but I can't tell you anything about the source of the photographs."

"You don't need to – I think I can work it out."

"The point is, Mr Pullman, that if you knew your wife was having an affair with Richard Edgton, then—"

"Hang on, hang on!" Gregory Pullman replaced his glasses and spread his hands out in front of him. "I can assure you I knew nothing about this so-called affair. And besides, if, as you say, it was a Saturday in September, then I would have been with the cricket club, so—"

"Not on that afternoon, you weren't. It rained pretty heavily for much of the day and your match was called off around lunch time, so you could have come back here and caught them—"

"Hang on, hang on!" Gregory Pullman repeated himself. "Look, I knew she was having an affair of some kind. She bought lots of new clothes and was forever having her hair done by Sarah. And, of course, I came home from cricket early sometimes, either because of rain or an early finish and, occasionally, I'd see a strange car parked outside – a very posh one – but, in truth, I didn't want to know any more – it wasn't of any great importance to me what she did with her life – so I'd just turn tail and head for the pub until the coast was clear."

"We've also had information that suggests there was, er, some violence between you and your wife. If you'd discovered she was having an affair, you could have lost your temper and—"

"Hang on, hang on!" Gregory Pullman repeated himself again. "You really don't want to believe everything that Martin Carslake tells you. He's had it in for us for years—"

"Who said anything about Martin Carslake?" Clive interrupted.

"You didn't have to. Let me tell you, Mr Walsingham, that Martin Carslake has as fertile an imagination as you do. He'd like to believe that there were all sorts of, erm, unpleasant things going on between me and Mary, and it suited him to think so, but I'm afraid he's made it all up."

"But knowing that your wife was having an affair could be a motive for—" Clive broke off as he heard a knock at the front door. Looking puzzled, Gregory Pullman rose slowly from his chair, wandered into the hall and opened the front door. "Sarah! What the hell are you doing here?" he exclaimed. Clive meanwhile looked at his watch. It was exactly eleven thirty.

"It's alright," Clive called from the living room. "I asked my colleague, Constable Pawlett, to bring your daughter over here."

"But what about the children? Where are the children?"

"Don't worry, Dad!" Sarah Tildesley spoke quietly and, ostensibly, calmly, but her voice had a tenseness which suggested that she was anything but calm. "They're with their father this weekend. They'll be fine. But I'm hoping this won't take long."

"That depends," Clive added cryptically as the two new arrivals manoeuvred around the small room, easing themselves into the only available chairs. "There are one or two issues I need to discuss with you. My colleague, Constable Pawlett, has been doing some research into Mary Pullman's will and your finances."

"I really must object—" Sarah Tildesley protested, her voice no longer quiet or calm but harsh and shrill. Clive, however, was in no mood to be interrupted.

"You'll have time enough to object when Constable Pawlett has finished," Clive said firmly. "Constable Pawlett, over to you!"

"Thank you," Alison Pawlett began in an assured, business-like voice. "We've been doing a bit of research, Sarah, and we believe you're in a difficult position, financially. We know that your hairdressing business went bust last year and we know that the bank is threatening to repossess your house."

Gregory Pullman leapt to his feet with surprising agility for someone whose lifestyle seemed to be almost entirely sedentary. "Sarah! Why didn't you tell me?"

"It's alright, Dad! It's not as bad as it looks. I've got a part-time job now – while the kids are at school – and I'll settle what I owe with the bank."

"I take it your part-time job is in the Stowbrook area?" Clive asked innocently. "Your car regularly makes a journey in that direction."

Sarah Tildesley looked suddenly flummoxed and she hesitated. "Er, er, yes, that's right." She looked anxiously at her father and then back at Clive, who seemed disinclined to pursue the issue any further.

"Anyway," Alison Pawlett continued, "we've spoken to Mary Pullman's solicitor about her will. It seems she left just over £400,000."

"That's quite a sum for someone who worked as a bank cashier and who retired several years ago. Would anyone like to explain?" Clive asked.

Sarah Tildesley sighed. "Well, I did mention 'Grandad's little legacy', as our mother called it – but I didn't know how much it was. And, of course, my mother didn't always occupy such a junior position at the bank; she was a senior financial adviser for some years." As she spoke, she began to make the kind of random, extravagant hand gestures that Clive had noticed on his previous visit when she was being evasive.

"Anyway," Alison Pawlett continued again. "It appears that Mary Pullman left nothing to you, Mr Pullman, and that her money was to be divided equally among her children. So, under the terms of your mother's will, you would stand to inherit a significant amount of money. I should imagine that would come in very handy, wouldn't it?"

Sarah Tildesley gave Constable Pawlett a frosty stare from behind her rimless spectacles. "I can't deny it," she admitted. "But that doesn't mean I murdered my mother."

*

Acting Inspector Beauregard arrested Richard Edgton and took him in for questioning at around 11.45am. Richard Edgton vehemently denied any involvement in the kidnapping of Lucy Jeffries, protested at his outrageous treatment, made a few threats about the Acting Inspector's "increasingly uncertain future" and, within five minutes, had summoned his solicitor, Duncan Brewham. When his fury had abated a little, he made it clear that, until Duncan Brewham arrived, he was not prepared to answer any questions.

Around twelve noon, Lord Westleigh's private phone rang. He answered it immediately in his normal formal, business-like way. "Hello. Patrick Westleigh speaking."

"Dad, it's me, Lucy!" Her voice sounded shaky.

"Lucy, darling, thank God! I've been so worried about you. How are you, where are you?" Lord Westleigh's tone, less formal and impersonal now, was fearful and anxious.

"Dad, I'm okay – I've not come to any harm or anything – but I can't say any more. I've got a very important message for you. You must listen carefully. If you want me back alive and well, you must be ready to hand over £750,000 in used, untraceable notes tomorrow. Sometime tomorrow, you will receive further instructions on where and when to hand the money over. You are to come in person and alone. You are not to involve the police or any other third party."

"But, Lucy, darling, that's preposterous. How am I supposed to get… hello, hello!"

The line had gone dead. Acting Inspector Beauregard's colleagues, who were monitoring all of Lord Westleigh's incoming calls, managed to trace the call to a "pay-as-you-go" mobile phone, which had been switched off as soon as the call had ended, but they could not trace who made the call or where it was made from.

Leaving a protesting Richard Edgton and his solicitor in the hands of the custody sergeant, Acting Inspector Beauregard leapt into his car and headed for Chartfield Castle. He arrived, breathless and perspiring, to find Lord Westleigh pacing the carpeted floor of the library, his hands clasped tightly behind his back. As usual, Anthony Granard was lurking obsequiously in the background, his spectacles perched precariously on the end of his aquiline nose and a look of deep concern in his alert blue eyes. Lord Westleigh did not offer the detective a seat.

"You've heard the news?" Lord Westleigh demanded of the harassed policeman.

"Yes, that's why I'm here. I came as soon as I—" Acting Inspector Beauregard sneezed loudly.

"Bless you! And I'm told that your so-called surveillance experts couldn't trace the call." There was a heavy hint of sarcasm in the Earl's clipped tones.

"It's always a problem with 'pay-as-you-go' phones, but it couldn't have been Richard Edgton who was responsible for the call – he was in police custody at the time," the acting inspector replied defensively.

"I did not, for one moment, suppose that it was Richard Edgton himself who made the call, but I'm damn sure it was one of his many, thoroughly unpleasant henchmen, acting on his instructions, who forced Lucy to make the call. She sounded very frightened!" The Earl of Westleigh moved towards the hapless acting inspector and inclined his head slightly, as though inviting him to comment, but the acting inspector just sighed and shrugged.

"Well, okay," Lord Westleigh continued, "you'll forgive me, *Acting* Inspector, if I say that I do not have much confidence in your ability to bring this matter to a satisfactory conclusion, so this is what I propose to do. By the morning, I will have assembled three quarters of a million pounds in used notes and I will then await further instructions from Richard Edgton or one of his henchmen. I will then do what he says, hand over the money and get my darling Lucy back. And it would be much appreciated if you and your team didn't go bungling in and putting my darling Lucy in any danger. I'd like you to keep well out of the way and make sure that Richard Edgton, or his appointed emissary, is not prevented from handing over my daughter, if you understand what I mean."

"I do understand," Acting Inspector Beauregard replied uncertainly, "but we do have Richard Edgton in custody and quite a bit of forensic evidence linking him to the kidnapping of your daughter. I reckon if we put a bit of pressure on him, we'll get a confession out of him before—"

The Earl snorted contemptuously. "Huh, I'm not sure you know the kind of man you're dealing with. Over the years, Richard Edgton has successfully pulled the wool over the eyes of a great many more senior and, if I may say so, far more competent police officers than you. So if you want to let him run rings round you for an hour or two today, that's fine, but I doubt you'll be able to hold him for much longer – his solicitor will see to that. And once you've let him go, please stay out of the way. I don't want you interfering and messing this up. Just remember that, over the years, a number of people who have crossed Richard Edgton have disappeared or turned up dead, like Mary Pullman, for example."

*

As Alison Pawlett drove Sarah Tildesley back to Bailbridge at breakneck speed, the silence in the car was oppressive. Whether it was the result of what had been said during the interview with her father or the fright that Alison's driving had engendered, it was clear that Sarah Tildesley was stiff with tension, her left hand tightly gripping the door handle, her narrow lips pressed firmly together and both feet anchored rigidly to the floor. Whatever the cause, however, Alison was not prepared for the whole journey to be undertaken in funereal silence.

"So," Alison Pawlett ventured at last. "I didn't know you had a job. Since your hairdressing business went bust, you've been listed as unemployed. I hope the taxman knows about your job."

"Ah, erm, yes." Sarah Tildesley was gripping the door handle so tightly that there was no scope for her usual ostentatious hand gestures. "I've, erm, only recently started. I intended to tell the authorities, of course, it's just..." Her voice tailed off.

Sensing her passenger's discomfort, Alison Pawlett pressed on with her interrogation.

"Well, we know you've been making the journey back and forth to Stowbrook since at least April. I should've thought five months was plenty of time to tell them." She paused, hoping for a response from Sarah Tildesley, but she just stared resolutely ahead. "What sort of work are you doing? Is it hairdressing again?" Alison Pawlett asked, hoping that a slight change of tack would elicit a more detailed response. It did.

Sarah Tildesley continued to stare resolutely ahead. "Er, no, no – it's quite embarrassing, really! I don't suppose you will have heard of it. It's a club called '*The Dog Collar*'. My mother got to know the woman in charge when she was working at the bank. I don't know how—"

Temporarily stunned by Sarah Tildesley's shock admission, Alison Pawlett had to turn the steering wheel sharply and brake hard, as her car began to career rapidly towards a roadside hedge. "You mean Gabrielle?" she asked once she had regained control of her car.

"Yes, that's right. You know her then?" Sarah Tildesley gulped.

Alison nodded emphatically. "Oh, yes. I know Gabrielle, I know '*The Dog Collar*' and I know what goes on there."

"Oh, no, no, no!" Sarah Tildesley shrieked in protest. "I don't have anything to do with what goes on upstairs. I don't think I'd make much of a living at that kind of thing. No, no, I work in the casino at the tables. I'm a croupier – I think I must have inherited my mother's gift with money and numbers. I only work a couple of afternoons a week when my neighbour's available to pick up the kids from school, but the money's very useful."

"You're paid in cash, I assume."

"Y-y-yes, but I will let the taxman know, I promise, and I'd rather word about this didn't get out. I've got two young kids and things are difficult enough for them as it is and—"

Alison Pawlett smirked. "Let's hope I don't have to tell anyone, then."

*

The combination of a hotel full of demanding guests, an unexpectedly complex and time-consuming police investigation and countless interruptions of varying relevance and importance had done nothing to ease Clive's depressingly long backlog of emails awaiting a reply, or his mounting list of outstanding administrative tasks so, as soon as he returned to the hotel, he marched into the office, closed the door and set to work.

After about five minutes, Clare put her head round the door. "Just to let you know that I've brought Simon back from the hospital and, as I feared, he whinged and moaned all the way back."

"Thanks, darling, and I'm really sorry you had to do that. Where is he now?"

"Oh, he seemed quite keen to go up to his room to rest – he said he was feeling faint. I didn't stand in his way. He still seems very shaky and very nervous, so I suggested he stays in his room until he feels better. He kept asking about Ralph Dalton; where is he now, have they arrested him yet? I take it there's no further news?"

"No, not as far as I know. Dick didn't mention anything when he was here. He loves your lemon drizzle cake, by the way, even though he made a bit of a mess of it."

Clare had only been gone for about two or three minutes when the phone rang. It was Alison Pawlett, who, judging by her breathless tone, was eager to speak to Clive.

"I've just dropped Sarah Tildesley back at her place," she panted. "And, on the journey back, she told me that she worked part-time at *The Dog Collar* club."

"No! Really?" Clive replied, rendered close to speechless by Alison's news.

"And, what's more," Alison added excitedly, "Sarah Tildesley told me that she only worked in the casino as a croupier, but I thought I'd give Gabrielle, the 'chatelaine', another call. At first she was reluctant to say very much, but when I reminded her that we were dealing with a murder enquiry and suggested that the police might want to take a closer interest in what went on at 'The Dog Collar', she became a bit more forthcoming. Anyway, it turns out that Sarah Tildesley has a professional name – 'Tilda' – and that she does in fact work upstairs. Apparently she is very strict, if you know what I mean."

"I get the picture," Clive replied, "although I'm having some difficulty picturing Sarah Tildesley as a dominatrix."

"It seems she's very popular. She has quite a list of wealthy clients who pay her well for her services including, according to Gabrielle, 'a toffee-nosed young man called Alex who lives up at the castle.'"

"Alex?"

"Alex Jeffries, Lord Westleigh's son-in-law!"

*

The sight of Richard Edgton, large, intimidating and bristling with indignation, arms folded across his muscular chest, sitting next to Duncan Brewham, smaller, calmer and unquestioningly loyal to his boss, keenly observant and with an encyclopaedic knowledge of the law, was not one to put Acting Inspector Beauregard at ease.

He coughed self-consciously and blew his nose loudly before beginning his cross-examination. "Err, there are two matters I want to ask you about. The first is the kidnapping of Lucy Jeffries, the daughter of Lord Westleigh."

Richard Edgton exchanged pointed glances with Duncan Brewham, raised his eyes skyward and sighed with frustration. "Yes, I know who she is, but how many times must I tell you, *Acting* Inspector, that I've got nothing to do with the kidnapping of Lord Westleigh's precious daughter? Now, I'm due to fly out to America for a few days on Tuesday and I've got a lot to do before I leave, so unless you're going to charge me with anything—"

"Only the thing is," Acting Inspector Beauregard continued, trying hard to conceal any hint of triumphalism in his increasingly croaky voice, "we've had our forensic people taking a close look at the ransom note that was sent to Lord Westleigh and we've found your fingerprints all over the envelope that it was sent in."

For an instant, Richard Edgton looked puzzled. He blinked momentarily before he leaned forward and fixed Acting Inspector Beauregard with a menacing glare. "Oh, have you? How very convenient for you!"

"And, furthermore, when our forensic team examined the outbuildings at Fearnley quarry, where you claimed to have had a break-in, they found fragments of cloth that almost certainly came from a pair of riding breeches that Lucy Jeffries was wearing when she was kidnapped, they found horse's hair which matches that of the horse she was riding and they found some strands of human hair which they are still examining for DNA but which are likely to have come from Lucy Jeffries." He glared back at Richard Edgton and smiled a self-satisfied kind of smile.

"My God! You'll stoop to anything to pin this kidnapping on me, won't you? So which of your officers planted the evidence? Hang on a minute – I bet Lord Westleigh's ransom note was handed to you and I bet there were none of your colleagues present at the time. Oh dear, Dick, don't tell me it was you who doctored the evidence!"

"None of my officers planted or doctored the evidence and nor did I. In fact, I resent the insinuation," Acting Inspector Beauregard retorted, a little churlishly and probably unwisely.

"So tell me, Dick, you've had your men crawling all over my offices, all the property that I own within a thirty mile radius, all my land. Have you found Lucy Jeffries anywhere? Only if you haven't—"

"Oh, I think we've got more than enough evidence to make a case," Acting Inspector Beauregard replied smugly. "And then, of course, there's also the investigation into the murder of Mary Pullman."

"Oh, I see. This should be interesting. Make a note, Duncan."

"You see, we've discovered that Mary Pullman's neighbour took some pictures of her while she was standing naked at her bedroom window."

"The filthy pervert!" Richard Edgton exclaimed, half-chuckling.

"And it turns out that one of them is particularly interesting. Our technical people have enlarged it and cleaned it up a bit and guess who we've seen standing behind her, naked, at least from the waist up." He pushed a copy of the photograph in question towards Richard Edgton before sneezing loudly.

Richard Edgton stared at the photograph for several seconds before replying. When he finally did so, it was with less assurance than usual. "You can't always believe what you see, Dick. It's easy enough to fake photographs these days. I'm sure your technical people would have the necessary expertise."

"Oh well, in that case I'm sure you won't mind if we show this photograph to your wife and ask her where you were on 4th September last year, when it was taken."

"Now look here." Richard Edgton glared at the acting inspector and half rose from his chair before Duncan Brewham's restraining hand on his shoulder persuaded him to sit down. "Alright, alright, it is possible to conclude from the photograph that, maybe, I had a brief, um, liaison with Mary Pullman, but even if I did, it doesn't mean I killed her."

Acting Inspector Beauregard blew his nose loudly on a crumpled, grey handkerchief before replying. "No that's true, but it does look suspicious, doesn't it? I mean, we've been sold this story that Mary Pullman was nothing more than a minor irritant to you, that you hardly knew her and yet, all the time, you were having an affair which you chose not to mention to us."

Richard Edgton was rattled in a way that Acting Inspector Beauregard had not witnessed before. Large beads of sweat were breaking out on his forehead and he kept clenching his fists into tight balls. "Look, I didn't want this business getting out. It'd make me look pretty stupid, wouldn't it – me having an affair with a woman who was supposedly leading the campaign against my plans for the quarry? And I certainly wouldn't want my wife to find out. But it's no crime and it's certainly no motive for murder."

"Not necessarily, I agree, but one of Mary Pullman's daughters told us that she suspected she was having an affair. She often wrote the letter 'G' against dates in her diary, usually at times when her husband would have been out of the way."

"What are you trying to say? 'G' could stand for anything."

"It could, I agree, but it could be you that she was referring to, couldn't it? Although you are known as Richard Edgton, your real first name is George, isn't it?"

"Well, yes, but I never use George. I prefer to use my middle name – Richard."

"That's true up to a point, I suppose, but your initials 'GRE' are embossed on your briefcase and your limousine has a personalised number plate with the letters 'GRE' on it, so you're not exactly hiding that fact that your first name isn't Richard. So maybe Mary Pullman preferred to use your first name and maybe the letter 'G' in her diary refers to you and, if it does, then your affair lasted quite a long time and you met pretty regularly. So what happened? Did she want more from the relationship than you were prepared to give? Did she try to blackmail you? Did she threaten to tell your wife? Or did you try to end the affair and did she—?" Acting Inspector Beauregard sneezed again and half-turned away as he reached for his handkerchief.

"Look, look, I don't know anything about her diary or what she wrote in it. All I know is that we just had a bit of a fling for a while and that's all. I don't know if she was seeing anyone else and I don't much care! My wife and I are... well... we're not close, let's leave it at that. And then I met Mary Pullman when she started getting steamed up about my plans for the quarry – she came to see me to tell me what she thought of me – and, strangely, we found we had quite a lot in common. She was strong-willed; I like that quality in a woman, and after we, er, started our little liaison, she merely kept up the pretence of opposition so that no-one, not least her family, would think that there was anything untoward going on."

"But it could be just a ploy, couldn't it?" the acting inspector persisted. "You try to charm one of your most vocal opponents so that eventually she'll be won over. And if that doesn't work, then you can always arrange for her to be eliminated and..." Acting Inspector Beauregard allowed himself the rare pleasure of another self-satisfied smile. "There is something else we found at the quarry. In that same building where you store your museum exhibits, we found a large trunk which had old quarrymen's clothes in."

"Yes that's right," Richard Edgton replied suspiciously. "We had clothes made especially to dress the dummies in."

"And at the bottom of that trunk we found a blue jacket that exactly matches the description of the one that Mary

Pullman was wearing when she disappeared and guess what! We found some human hairs on it and—"

"Now, listen…" Richard Edgton began angrily, pointing his index finger aggressively at the detective before becoming strangely lost for words. Acting Inspector Beauregard used the unexpected hiatus to press home his advantage.

"Why are you buying Gareth Adamson's house? Is there something about Mary Pullman's murder in the house somewhere that you don't want us to find out about? Are there other bodies—?"

Richard Edgton thumped the desk in anger. "If I told you why I'm buying the house you wouldn't believe me."

"Try me!" Acting Inspector Beauregard suggested.

"Look, I really don't think I have anything more—" Richard Edgton began before the door to the interview room opened and the duty sergeant appeared.

"Erm, sorry to bother you, sir," the duty sergeant announced sheepishly, "but it's the hospital on the phone; they'd like to speak to you urgently. It's about Inspector Morris."

*

Clive Walsingham had been sitting in his office for over an hour, finally making inroads into his backlog of paperwork and emails but quietly wishing he was striding out on a golf course somewhere, the scent of freshly mown grass filling his nostrils and the delicate sound of birdsong drifting down from the canopy of trees lining the fairways. Then the phone rang. It was Dick Beauregard.

"Hello, Dick," Clive greeted Acting Inspector Beauregard with scant enthusiasm, although he couldn't pretend that his call wasn't a welcome distraction. "Are you missing me already? Are you planning to come over and demolish another plate of cakes?"

"Don't be flippant, Clive," the acting inspector admonished gravely, his voice sounding more gravelly and scratchy than usual. "There have been a number of important developments and I thought you should—"

"I'm sorry, Dick, I didn't mean to sound flippant – it's just that… well, I'm trying to run a hotel here and, at the moment, it's not easy. When I offered to help you, I didn't realise that things would get so complicated and so time-consuming. Clare is, quite rightly, extremely annoyed that I'm not pulling my weight around here, especially as we've been very busy, my gardener has recently been assaulted by one of our guests and Alison, who you kindly assigned to help me, is still recovering from her injuries and not really—"

"No, of course, I understand. I mean, if you'd rather not be involved anymore, then obviously I'd understand—" the acting inspector whimpered, before sneezing resonantly down the phone.

"No, I'm sorry, Dick, I didn't mean to sound so negative any more than I meant to sound flippant. You've just called at a bad time, but I'll try and see it through now; I'm too heavily involved to back away. Let's have your news."

"Well, I've brought Richard Edgton in for questioning. I haven't made much progress with the Lucy Jeffries kidnapping yet; he's not admitting anything despite the forensic evidence. But he has admitted that he was having an affair with Mary Pullman which he didn't want us, or anyone else, to know—"

"Mmm, but that doesn't mean he killed her, of course. Are you still holding him?"

"You betcha, although his solicitor is making a fuss! I'm still awaiting the DNA analysis of the human hair we found at the quarry, but if it turns out that we've got hair from Lucy Jeffries and Mary Pullman, I reckon I'll have enough to charge him and he knows it. And on the subject of Lucy Jeffries,

Lord Westleigh had a call from her earlier on. It was from an unidentified 'pay-as-you-go' phone and it sounded as though she was reading from a script under duress. The kidnappers want three quarters of a million for her release and will be in touch tomorrow with the final instructions."

"I take it the call was made after you'd taken Richard Edgton in for questioning."

"Yes, but that doesn't mean he's not involved. It was probably one of his hit-men who forced Lucy Jeffries to make the call."

"Of course," Clive replied, trying to sound non-committal.

"And, as if that wasn't enough," Acting Inspector Beauregard continued morosely, "I heard from the pathologist at the hospital a little earlier. He wants to treat DI Morris's death as suspicious. He reckons he was suffocated, probably using a hospital pillow or some other—"

"Bloody hell! So it could be murder!" Clive winced at the obviousness of his statement. "It's a bit of a long shot, but might the elusive Ralph Dalton have had something to do with it? Simon said he saw him acting suspiciously at the hospital yesterday."

"Did he? Simon didn't say anything to me when I saw him. Excuse me…" Dick Beauregard turned away from the phone and blew his nose loudly.

"That sounds like quite a cold you're brewing there," Clive observed unsympathetically.

"Oh, I'll be alright," Acting Inspector Beauregard replied nasally and with little conviction.

"Anyway," Clive continued. "I don't imagine Simon would've said anything to you – he doesn't like the police very much for some reason. But when we went to see him yesterday, he told us he'd seen Ralph Dalton trying to creep up on him. He raised the alarm and the aforementioned Mr Dalton scuttled off. Simon was vague about when this all happened, but I suspect it was sometime after you left."

"Oh well, it's a new lead of sorts," Acting Inspector Beauregard replied half-heartedly. "Although I'm not sure what Ralph Dalton's motive would be – we don't know of anything that links him to DI Morris."

"But we don't really know anything about Ralph Dalton, do we? We don't even know for sure what his real name is."

"I suppose so. The trouble is, although they've got security cameras at the hospital, half of them aren't working – they've reduced their maintenance budget, the usual story – so it would've been possible for people to come and go without being filmed if they'd used the side entrance. We've looked at the footage that we have got and we've not found a single image of anyone behaving suspiciously during the late afternoon, which is probably when DI Morris was killed, or at any other time come to that. We did see Constable Pawlett arrive during the morning, although we don't know when she left – and we saw you and Clare arrive and leave. Curiously, we also saw Alex Jeffries arrive during the afternoon, but we don't know why he was there or who he'd come to see and, again, we didn't see him leave."

"Mmm, that's the second time his name has cropped up today – it might be worth talking to him again. You should also know that when Clare and I went to visit Simon yesterday, we were followed all the way to the hospital by Richard Edgton and Dean Footner. We're pretty sure they parked at the hospital, but I don't know why. They might have gone inside – it might be worth checking."

"Oh, I will, I will. Obviously DI Morris made some enemies – it's inevitable in this job – and one of them would have been Richard Edgton—" Dick Beauregard sneezed twice.

"Yes, I thought of that too, but... Anyway, you may not have found many helpful images on the security cameras, but did anyone at the hospital see anyone behaving suspiciously at all?"

"No. The place was full of visitors most of the day and the nurses were rushed off their feet, working flat out, so no..." Acting Inspector Beauregard fell silent and snuffled. Clive thought he could hear his shoulders convulsing under the weight of a particularly dramatic shrug. "Oh, there is one more thing," he announced at last. "We had a phone call from Gerald Ashburton's neighbour to say she saw him returning early this morning and he was looking furtive and smuggling a woman into his house. She couldn't see who it was."

Clive whistled quietly to himself. "Mmm, that is interesting."

"I, er, I don't suppose you could call round and see him, could you? I'm so tied up with these other matters and, as you can hear, I'm not feeling great. You can take Alison with you."

"Alison is still off sick," Clive reminded him. He didn't want Dick Beauregard to know what his constable had been doing. "In any event, I'm supposed to be catching up on my admin. Clare'll kill me if I go out on police business again." Clive's protest sounded half-hearted.

"Only you did say that you'd see this affair through to the end and I'll make sure you're generously recompensed, especially as it is a Sunday."

Clive sighed. "Okay, okay, I'll do it. I've got to admit I'm curious about Gerald Ashburton, who he really is, who he's smuggled into his house, and why and what he really knows about Mary Pullman. But I'll have to spend a bit of time here first so that I can show Clare what a lot of work I've got through before I go out again. I'll go and see him later this afternoon, if that's okay."

*

The Reverend Gerald Ashburton opened his front door barely a few inches and peered out with alert, suspicious eyes, at his two visitors.

"Hello, I'm Detective Constable Pawlett," Alison Pawlett began, brusquely. "And this is my colleague, Clive Walsingham."

"Ah, yes, I know who you are," Gerald Ashburton replied, triumphantly. "Mr Walsingham has been here before and I do believe you, young lady, might have been spying on me last Wednesday."

"May we come in?"

Gerald Ashburton cast a nervous glance over his shoulder. "Ah, well, I'm afraid it's not very convenient at the moment."

"It won't take long," Constable Pawlett replied as she pushed her way past Gerald Ashburton, causing him to half-stumble backwards against the door, marched into his living room and looked around. "Are you on your own?"

"Now look here—" Gerald Ashburton began, showing a rare flash of irritation.

"I'm really sorry about Constable Pawlett," Clive apologised as he wandered languidly into the lounge. "You see she was subjected to a violent assault just after you walked past her last Wednesday evening; you may have seen or heard something, although you didn't stop to help her. We wanted to talk to you, but, unfortunately, you disappeared rather mysteriously immediately afterwards. Constable Pawlett would be especially interested in knowing where you've been for the last couple of days and who you really are. You see, we know there is no such person as the Reverend Gerald Ashburton. And, of course, we are still investigating the murder of Mary Pullman, so you can see why my colleague is keen to speak to you. And, as there doesn't appear to be anyone else here, maybe now would be a good time to get some answers."

"Yes, I see," Gerald Ashburton replied uncertainly, chewing the end of his index fingernail and suddenly looking considerably older and frailer than when he had marched briskly past Alison Pawlett on their previous encounter. "You'd better take a seat, I suppose." He gestured weakly to a couple of armchairs.

"Where would you like to start?" Clive enquired of the bogus clergyman as he tried to stretch out his long legs in the cramped confines of the small living room.

"Look, I had absolutely nothing to do with this woman's murder," the Reverend Ashburton protested vehemently. "I've done some bad things, I'll admit, but murder isn't one of them."

"Well, perhaps you can start by telling us who you really—" Clive's question was interrupted by the sound of a high-pitched sneeze coming from behind the closed bedroom door. Alison Pawlett immediately sprung to her feet and, ignoring Gerald Ashburton's feeble protest, disappeared swiftly into the bedroom, emerging a few moments later with a young woman at her side. She had a pale, frightened face, a look of fear in her deep brown eyes, a slightly red nose and short, dyed blonde hair. She was wearing an ill-fitting man's dressing gown, tied so carelessly around her waist that it was clear she was naked beneath it.

Clive averted his gaze from the young woman – not perhaps as quickly or as completely as he should – as she struggled to prevent her shapely anatomy from spilling out of the flimsy confines of the loosely fitting dressing gown. He looked quizzically at Gerald Ashburton. "And this is?"

The Reverend looked ashen-faced. "And, er, this is, er, Natalia. I'm afraid she, er, has a bit of a cold."

"I'd noticed. There seems to be a lot of it about. And who is Natalia?"

"The chatelaine at 'The Dog Collar' said you'd befriended one of the girls who worked there," Alison Pawlett interrupted chirpily. "She said her name was Natalie."

"Oh, did she? Yes, this is her," Gerald Ashburton conceded contritely. "It's Natalia in her native country, or Natalie."

"But the chatelaine said that she disappeared in April," Alison Pawlett continued. "And she said she'd heard nothing since. So what happened?"

"Perhaps Natalia would like to tell us herself?" Clive suggested, giving him an excuse to subject the snuffling young woman to closer scrutiny.

"English no good," the young lady muttered rather nasally and without much conviction.

"Perhaps I should tell you," Gerald Ashburton suggested. "Natalia comes from Eastern Europe; you don't need to know exactly where, but it's a troubled part of the world. She's part of quite a large family – she has three brothers and one younger sister. Unfortunately, her brothers are not nice people; they're into drugs and pimping and all manner of rackets. When she was fifteen, they forced Natalia into prostitution. Some of her clients were extremely unpleasant, but if she tried to defy her brothers, they became violent towards her. For three years, her brothers did exactly what they wanted with her, but, when she reached eighteen, she managed to get away and moved over here."

"Where she worked as a prostitute," Clive added, cynically.

"Yes, true, but it's not like it was for her back home. She's very good at what she does – I can vouch for that – but over here she is well looked after, Gabrielle sees to that, and she earns good money, most of which she is allowed to keep. And I confess that I've become a regular visitor to 'The Dog Collar' and, over time, I got very friendly with Natalia. Eventually she agreed to visit me once a week, when she'd, er, well, when she'd look after my requirements, as it were, and do a bit of tidying and cleaning for me while she was here. Gabrielle knew all about it and I paid Natalia very well for her time and trouble."

Natalia nodded enthusiastically. "Gerry is very nice man."

"And then," Gerald Ashburton continued, "back in April, she got word that her mother was very seriously ill and not expected to live very long. She didn't want to go back home, of course, and face her brothers, but she felt she had to go and see her mother before it was too late and perhaps try and help her younger sister, who was being controlled by her brothers in the same way that she had been. And then, once she got back, the inevitable happened. After her mother died, her brothers tried to force her to take her mother's place. They insisted she look after them, you know, do all the cleaning, the shopping, the cooking and other stuff as well."

"But when I spoke to Gabrielle," Alison Pawlett interrupted, "she said Natalie had disappeared and she didn't know where she'd gone or what had happened to her."

"Ah, well, as I said, Gabrielle looks after her girls very well; she's very protective. I think it was probably only Gabrielle and me who knew what had happened to Natalia, but she would never betray a confidence, least of all to the police." He shot Clive a wry smile.

Clive reciprocated. He knew that Gabrielle was not quite as protective and discreet as Gerald Ashburton believed, but he kept his thoughts to himself. "And now she's back here. So what's happened?" Clive asked.

"I got the odd message from Natalia when she was back home, but she was frightened that her brothers would find out and wouldn't be pleased, if you know what I mean, so she couldn't say or do much. But she bided her time, made her plans and, eventually, a few days ago, she finally got the chance to escape. She headed straight to the airport and, when she got there, she texted me and asked me to meet her when she landed. So I did. I left this place in something of a hurry and headed for the airport, arriving in time to meet her flight. We stayed at a hotel by the airport for a couple of days. She was – she still is – terrified that her brothers will come looking for her, so I decided that she could stay here with me until Gabrielle and I can find her somewhere safe to stay."

"Gerry, he look after me," Natalia confirmed with an emphatic nod of the head.

"I take it the hotel you stayed at will confirm your story?" Alison Pawlett asked suspiciously.

"I expect so, but we didn't use our real names. I called myself Byron Shelley – I've always liked the romantic poets."

"And while we're talking of aliases," Clive observed. "Would you like to tell us what your real name is?"

The bogus clergyman gave an exasperated groan and glanced up at the ceiling, as though expecting some kind of divine intervention. He groaned again. "Yes, I suppose I should really. It's right that you know. My real name is Gerald Buckland and I am, or rather was, a fully ordained priest."

"What happened?"

"Ah well, I'm afraid I was embezzling church funds. I had a contact on the inside at Nicholls Bank and she became adept at secretly moving money from various church accounts to my own account, for a fee, naturally. But what I didn't know was that she was providing similar services for a significant number of other people and, when she finally got caught, she spilled the beans. The church held a formal enquiry and, of course, the outcome was inevitable. A few years ago, I would have been 'defrocked', as the papers like to say. The terminology is a bit different these days, but the outcome is the same."

"I wonder if I can guess the name of your inside contact at Nicholls Bank."

The Reverend shook his head in a gesture of resignation. "It was Mary Pullman, of course."

"And she was due to visit you the day she disappeared?"

"If you say so, but I can assure you I never met the woman. We spoke on the phone a few times but that was it and after our little 'arrangement' ended, I had no further contact with her."

"Why were you embezzling funds?" Constable Pawlett asked sternly.

"Ah well, I'm afraid my wife had expensive tastes – clothes and jewellery mainly… as did my mistress… well, both my mistresses, actually. And then there was the gambling. I loved gambling, still do. The trouble is I'm not much good at it. But I get by. I inherited quite a bit of money when my wife died and I live fairly frugally these days… apart from the call-girls and the casino, of course. When I moved down here, I wanted to make a fresh start, so I took the name Ashburton. The village of Ashburton in Devon is only a few miles north of Buckland, so it felt quite neat, quite apposite."

"And where was your last parish?" Clive asked.

"Oh, miles from here, you probably won't have heard of it. It's a little village not far from Cambridge."

*

Clare was waiting for Clive when he and Alison Pawlett arrived back at the hotel in the late afternoon. She wasn't standing aggressively in the foyer with her hands on her hips, but she was hovering by the reception desk and the look on her face suggested that Clive's homecoming was not going to be especially welcoming. Immediately spotting Clare's thunderous expression, but pretending to ignore it, Clive sniffed the air thoughtfully as he walked through the foyer.

He sensed that Peter the chef, relieved of the tiresome burden of producing wholesome but predictable food for the recently departed, wholesome, predictable coach party, was planning to unleash at least one of his more exotic and experimental dishes on the limited number of residents who were planning to dine at the hotel that evening.

"I could murder a pizza," Clive announced as he pecked Clare on the cheek. "Judging by the smells coming from the kitchen, I should think our guests will be reeking of garlic for weeks."

Clare gave a wan smile. "You should be careful what you wish for, Clive, especially when using words like 'murder.'"

"And will you be joining us for dinner tonight? Do you fancy a pizza?" Clive asked Alison, still feigning obliviousness to Clare's barbed comments and tetchy mood.

"Err." Alison Pawlett hesitated for a moment before she caught Clare's eye. "Err, no thanks, Clive," she said at last. "I'm going upstairs for a while and then I'll be making some more enquiries and then I'll see how I feel. But I'd say that there are a few things you and Clare need to discuss, and I don't want to get in the way."

As Alison made her way upstairs, Archie the cat came hurtling down, skulking low to the ground with his ears back and a scared look in his eyes. Alison had to take swift evasive action to avoid tripping over him.

"Sorry about that, Alison," Clare called after her. "I've not seen Archie come down the stairs like that before. Something must have frightened him."

"That's odd," Clive mused. "There's only Simon up there and although he moans about Archie damaging his flowers, he's always made him very welcome."

"Mmmm," Clare replied, "but Simon is behaving a bit strangely at the moment, even by his standards."

"Yes, that's true." Clive could defer the inevitable no longer. He looked at Clare apprehensively and recognised the look of intensity in her grey-green eyes as a harbinger of trouble. "You said 'murder' might not be the right word to chose, but maybe it is, if you're contemplating mariticide."

"Don't tempt me!" Clare retorted tartly. "While you've been swanning off on some wild goose chase – pardon my mixed metaphor – we've had a lot of clearing up to do after the coach party, which I thought you might have been around to help a bit more with, Jamie has been getting under my feet saying that he needs to speak to you urgently, Julia Cockrell phoned about half an hour ago, saying she'd got some important information for you and perhaps you could phone her as soon as you get in and, to cap a brilliant day, Chef has handed in his notice with immediate effect."

Clive gasped. "He's done what? Why?"

"The official reason is that he's bought the restaurant near the square in Stowbrook – the one that closed down two or three months ago – and he's going to open his own business there. Unofficially, he made it clear to me that he feels 'his creativity is being stifled' here because we only want him to do traditional food and we don't allow him to experiment enough."

"He's not said anything to me," Clive protested.

"He might have done, if he'd had the opportunity," Clare retorted.

Clive took Clare by the hand and led her into the office. He closed the door, wrapped his long thin arms around her slender body and kissed the top of her head. "Clare, darling, I'm so sorry about all of this; it's all got a bit out of hand, I'm afraid. I'll talk to Chef later on and try to persuade him to change his mind."

"It's too late, Clive! He's used all his savings and a whopping bank loan to buy his new restaurant, so he can't back out now."

"I see! Oh well, that's that, I suppose. His timing could have been better, though."

"To be fair to him, which isn't easy, he could have given in his notice earlier, but he said he didn't want to cause a problem while the coach party was here."

Clive sighed. "Oh well, that's jolly decent of him! So, there's nothing more to be done for the moment, I suppose. After the bank holiday, I'll advertise for a replacement. But, for now, I'll need to speak to Julia Cockrell and then I'll be available for the rest of the day, I promise."

Clare looked up at Clive with an earnest, weary expression. "And tomorrow and the day after?" she asked.

"Ah well, I'm afraid I can't be sure, but I think I'm making progress at last. I'm just not entirely sure what Dick is up to and whether he's helping or hindering the process, and Alison's a bit of a loose cannon."

Clare remained in Clive's comforting, protective embrace, enjoying the warmth of his closeness. Eventually, she looked up at him. "You'd better call Julia Cockrell while I ring for a couple of pizzas. Chef won't be pleased, you know!"

"Huh, I hardly think it matters now," Clive replied testily.

As Clare was about to leave the room, there was a tentative knocking at the door. Clare opened it to find Jamie Coulton standing outside, looking uneasy.

"Errr, I wonder if I could have a brief word, if it's not too inconvenient." Jamie's tone lacked its usual silky smoothness.

"No, it's not really convenient," snapped Clare. "But Clive has turned up at last and he's not done much to help all day, so I'm sure he can spare you the time."

Clive raised his eyes to the ceiling and sighed again as Clare disappeared, slamming the door behind her. "You'd better sit down, Jamie," he said with a resigned expression.

"Er, yes, er, thank you." Jamie eased himself awkwardly onto the spare office chair. "I feel I need to offer you an explanation."

"Is this about the missing money?" Clive asked pointedly. He wasn't in the mood for prevarication.

Jamie looked puzzled. "Missing money? What missing money?"

It was Clive's turn to look puzzled. "Debbie tells me that some money has been disappearing from the tills over the last few days and I thought—"

"No, no, I, errr, I didn't know any money had gone missing. No, I, err, I don't know anything about that."

Although Jamie seemed less than convincing in his protestation of innocence, Clive had no actual evidence that he had been embezzling funds and felt it might not be altogether diplomatic to mention Debbie's suspicions.

"So what have you come to tell me?"

"Well, err, I know I behaved very badly last weekend, getting drunk and ending up in a police cell and you came and bailed me out and everything and I was a bit evasive about what happened at the time, but I can tell you now."

"Please do!"

"You'll probably remember that Zoe walked out on me because I was late getting home a couple of times and she assumed that I was seeing somebody else and I couldn't tell her who I'd seen and why. Well, I can now. The truth is, err, that I met Pete a couple of times and—"

"Pete?" Clive looked mystified.

"Oh, sorry! Peter, or Pierre, as he prefers to be known, your chef!"

"Oh, him!"

"We met in my local pub, the King's Arms, because he didn't want anyone to know what was going on and he swore me to secrecy. Then he told me in confidence that he was planning to open up his own restaurant in Stowbrook and he offered me a job. He said he wanted me to run the front-of-house operations, you know, meeting and greeting, running the bar, serving at tables, that kind of thing. He said he knew I'd be good at it. Well, it all came completely out of the blue and I said I was flattered but I needed time to think about his offer, but he wouldn't let me discuss it with Zoe, or with you, or with anyone. Anyway, it's all out in the open now – he's told you he's leaving, so I don't have to keep the secret anymore."

"I see," Clive replied uncertainly. "This has all come as a bit of a shock. You said he'd offered you a job, but you didn't say if you'd accepted."

"Well, after a bit of soul-searching, I've decided to turn his offer down. I like working here and I don't want to leave and then there's… Anyway, I've decided to stay."

Clive narrowed his eyes and looked directly at Jamie. Although he didn't really want to lose two members of his team in one evening, Jamie's departure might have proved to be a blessing if he was, in fact, to blame for the money going missing. "Well, that's good news, Jamie," he announced with little conviction. "Have you contacted Zoe?"

"Ah, er, well, that's a bit difficult at the moment – she's not returning my calls – and I'm thinking I might wait a while before I try and make contact again. And if you need an extra pair of hands in the kitchen while you're trying to find a new chef, then I'm quite happy to help. I've learnt a bit from Pete over the years."

*

It was quite late in the evening when Clive finally got round to phoning Julia Cockrell.

"Julia? Hello. It's Clive Walsingham here. I'm sorry I wasn't around when you called and I'm sorry it's so late. It's just been one of those days."

"No problem," Julia replied with surprising alacrity. "Clare explained. I just wanted to give you an update on my research. I haven't made quite as much progress as I would've liked. Grace has been a bit demanding and Trevor insisted we had a leisurely pub lunch and… well, anyway. But then I imagine you've been able to get quite a lot of background information from Vernon."

"I beg your pardon?" Clive sounded puzzled.

"Vernon! Vernon Court. I saw his name written in the margin of Mary Pullman's notebook."

"Vernon Court is a person?"

"Yes, he's a genealogist, like me. You mean you didn't know?"

"But, but…" Clive spluttered, seemingly unable to comprehend what Julia Cockrell was telling him. "We've been investigating an address in Stowbrook – 2 Vernon Court."

Julia laughed. "Yes, I joked with him once that his name sounded like an address. But surely you would've found him on the internet. He's got a website like me."

Clive coughed nervously. "Well, it was Clare who looked up Vernon Court on the internet, but she's very thorough and she sets high standards – I'm sure she wouldn't have missed him. She said she'd found several addresses but she didn't say anything about a person."

While Clive had been talking, Julia Cockrell had begun working on her laptop. After a few seconds of frenetic keyboard activity, she stared at the screen and her mouth fell open. "Well, that's just weird," she announced. "I've entered 'Vernon Court' in the search engine and it hasn't found him. It's as though all references to him have been erased for some reason—"

"Tell me about him," Clive urged, his fabled analytical powers beginning to reassemble themselves in his befogged brain. "It sounds as though you know him well."

"Oh, no, I wouldn't say that; he's just an acquaintance, really. Because he and I are doing the same kind of work, our paths cross occasionally – or at least they did. I haven't seen him for a while, mainly because I'm stuck in this damned house most of the time. I think he's originally from South Africa. As I recall, he first came over here to be with his girlfriend – I can't remember her name, but I think she came from a very well-connected family. Anyway, they broke up after a while and I thought he'd go back to South Africa, but it seems he stayed over here. As I recall, he spent some time working for one of those firms that tries to trace the heirs of people who have died intestate, but the last I heard, he'd gone freelance, although—"

"Where does he live?"

"Somewhere in London, I think, in a flat or bed-sit. That's not much help, is it?"

Clive smiled. "Not really, but it's a start."

"Ah, but he will be a member of the major genealogical societies and he'll be registered with some of the big record offices, especially those in London. Someone will have his address."

Clive closed his eyes and slumped forward in his chair, almost banging his forehead on the desk. Julia Cockrell's affirmation that Vernon Court was a person rather than an address had left him temporarily bewildered and extremely annoyed that so much time and effort might have been wasted pursuing a retired clergyman who, for all his shady foibles, probably had nothing to do with Mary Pullman's disappearance and subsequent murder. Caspar Beauregard, who had never given much credence to that particular line of enquiry, would be depressingly smug when he found out. On the other hand, the revelation that Mary Pullman might actually have been meeting a professional genealogist on the day she went missing made Julia Cockrell's promised research all the more tantalising.

"I suppose," Clive reflected as stoically as he could, "the entry in Mary Pullman's notebook could have meant that she had engaged Vernon Court to do some research for her and that she had arranged to meet him at two o'clock on the day she disappeared – hence '2 VERNON COURT'. Her husband recalled her leaving the house just after lunch, so that would fit."

"Yes, I guess so," Julia agreed guardedly. "But I'm worried that Vernon's website has disappeared. I hope nothing's happened—"

"Look, I'll try and track Vernon Court down. Can I ask you to describe him to me?"

"Yes, yes, of course, although it is a while since I last saw him. Let me see; he is probably in his late thirties or early forties, average height, quite slim. When I saw him last he had quite long, light brown hair."

"Did he wear glasses?"

"He did for reading, I think. They had quite heavy frames, as I recall."

"You said he came from South Africa originally. Did he speak with an accent?"

"A slight one, yes, but it wasn't always that obvious—"

"Alright, we'll try and track him down. Meanwhile, have you got any other information for me?" Clive asked hopefully.

"Ah, oh yes. I have some. What I like to do, when I'm doing family research, is to start with the current family members and work back in time – it's usually easier to make the ancestral links that way. So I've been concentrating mainly on Mary Pullman and her immediate family."

"And…?"

"And did you say that she and her husband Gregory had two daughters?"

"Yes, that's right, Sarah and Alice."

"So you don't know that they also had a son, Geoffrey?"

"What? Well, I suppose I had a slight suspicion from something someone said, although Gregory Pullman has never mentioned a son and neither have his daughters. What happened to him?"

"I don't know where he is now, but, as far as I can tell, he's still alive – he'd be about forty-two."

"How interesting!"

"And I hope you'll forgive me, Clive, but I strayed slightly from my remit because I was intrigued by the mysterious figure of Geoffrey Pullman, so I did a bit of digging and I came across a newspaper article – it was from the *Carlow Valley Gazette*. It goes back about eight years, but it was a report of an incident that took place at the public conveniences in Stowbrook. The article described it as an 'act of gross indecency' and named Geoffrey Pullman as one of the individuals involved."

"Holy shit! So maybe that's why the family don't talk about him! You said that Geoffrey Pullman was one of the individuals involved. Was the other individual named?"

"He was. It was somebody called Simon Verwood!"

*

Clare was sitting up in bed, reading a book when Clive finally pulled back the duvet and, yawning, hauled himself slowly into bed.

Clare looked across at Clive. There was less intensity in her eyes now and she acknowledged his arrival with a gentle nod and a slight smile. "Is it okay if I finish my chapter? That is, if I can get through it without nodding off." It was a familiar request which Clive greeted with benign amusement.

"No problem," he replied. "As it happens, I just need a few minutes to finish a bit more research." He coughed nervously. "Erm, by the way, did I mention that I'm going to see Gregory Pullman and his daughter again in the morning? Alison's making the necessary arrangements."

Clare slammed her book shut. "No, Clive, you didn't, as well you know. Honestly, I really need to know when all of this is going to end. When are you going to stop playing at being a policeman? Only I'd quite like to have my husband back and helping to run this hotel."

"This'll be over very soon, darling, I promise. We've made a lot of progress today – I think. I know a lot more than I did a few hours ago." He reached for the guidebook to Chartfield Castle, which Miranda Bellamy had obtained for him and which had been languishing on his bedside table, and started flicking through the pages.

Slightly embarrassed by her uncharacteristically petulant outburst, though still inwardly annoyed, and regretting that she had slammed her book shut without first noting the page that she was on, Clare thumbed through her book to find the passage she had just been reading, glanced across and gave Clive a quizzical look. "Hello, you taking an interest in history all of a sudden?"

"No, not really!" Clive replied, as he continued flicking his way through the lavishly produced guidebook. "There are just a couple of things I'm curious about." He turned the page to reveal a full-length glossy family photograph. "Oh, look! Here's a picture of the Earl of Westleigh with his arm around his daughter, Lucinda – very cosy. And sitting next to them is his son-in-law, Alexander Jeffries."

He waved the photograph under Clare's nose, but she gave it only the most cursory of glances.

"Ah, here it is!" Clive announced triumphantly as he turned another page.

"Here what is?" Clare was sounding tired.

"Here in this book; the Earl of Westleigh's family tree!" Clive pointed excitedly at a complicated-looking chart that covered a double-page spread in the guidebook. "Do you know what the Earl's family name is?"

Clare frowned. She was weary and not really in the mood for a late-night quiz, but there was something gnawing at the back of her mind. "Hang on a minute! Yes, I think I do. One of Miranda's coach party said something. He was very boring and I wasn't really listening, but I think he said it was a religious name of some kind, Prior or Abbott or something—"

"Monck."

"Yes, that's it – Monk."

"Yes, Monck – spelt with a 'c'. But look here!" Clive waved the book under Clare's nose and stabbed his finger at a small piece of text. "Look at that!"

Clare studied the text intently for a moment or two before she spoke.

"Blimey!"

Eighteen

Monday 28 August

Although Clive Walsingham remained a devotee of the full English breakfast, he would occasionally eschew its delights if Clare's regularly good-natured prodding of his expanding waistline and mild joshing became more persistent, as they had done of late. So, whenever she was around and taking a keen interest in his dietary regime, he tended to start the day with much lighter fare. Today, for example, his breakfast comprised just a poached egg and a slice of toast.

There was no fixed venue for his breakfast. Sometimes, if he was especially busy, he would take it into his office while he worked. Occasionally, if Chef was suitably preoccupied, he would eat perched on a stool in a corner of the kitchen and, once in a while, he and Clare would dine together in their private rooms. Today, however, he was breakfasting with both Clare and Alison in a quiet, discreetly screened corner of the dining room which was normally reserved for their use. There, they could eat and talk without being observed or overheard.

While Alison Pawlett slowly stretched out her arms and yawned before tackling her croissant and coffee, Clive turned to Clare, who was chewing her way slowly through an unappetising-looking bowl of muesli. Still reeling from the verbal lashings she had given him on the previous evening, Clive was looking forward to a bit of gentle teasing at her expense.

"Clare, do you remember looking up Vernon Court on the internet?" he asked innocently.

Clare stopped chewing and looked puzzled. "Yes, why?"

"It's just that when I spoke to Julia Cockrell yesterday, she said that Vernon Court was a person – a fellow genealogist, in fact."

Clare's jaw dropped, the spoon fell from her hand and clattered into the dish. "You're kidding!"

Clive shrugged. "That's what Julia said and I've no reason to doubt her. The trouble is that when she searched for him on the internet she couldn't find him. I imagine you didn't find him either?"

"No, no, I didn't," Clare replied, defensively. "I mean I was looking specifically for an address, not a person, but I'm sure I would've noticed if a person called Vernon Court had popped up."

"Yes, quite." Clive puffed out his cheeks and turned to Alison, who was staring at him in disbelief, the hand holding her croissant suspended motionless halfway between the plate and her mouth. "So there's another mystery for you, Alison. If Vernon Court exists and is a genealogist, why is there no trace of him on the internet? Julia Cockrell thinks he lives in London somewhere and that he'd be registered with various record offices and family history organisations. So can I suggest you get someone to check him out, especially as Mary Pullman might have been planning to meet him on the day she disappeared?"

Alison Pawlett quickly replaced her croissant, uneaten, on her plate, gulped down several mouthfuls of coffee and stood up.

"Bloody hell, Clive, that's a bit of a shocker! You mean we've been wasting our time investigating the mysterious clergyman?"

"It certainly looks that way, although, as you know, he'd had some dealings with Mary Pullman. I'm rather afraid you got beaten up for nothing."

"Not necessarily," Alison Pawlett replied phlegmatically. "I found out some things about Colin that I needed to… Anyway, this is no time for self-pity or recriminations, I've, er, I've still got a few contacts in the Met from when I worked in London. I'll try and get hold of someone."

"Thanks, Alison!" Clive called after her as she headed rapidly towards the stairs. "Is everything arranged for our interview with Gregory Pullman and Sarah Tildesley?"

"Yup!" she called back over her shoulder. "Ten o'clock at Stowbrook police station."

*

The gloomy, dispiriting interior of Stowbrook police station reinforced Clive's passionate dislike of such places and his determination never to set foot in them again. The interview room, with its single, narrow window, soulless grey walls, dismal, utilitarian furniture and stale smell, did nothing to lift his spirits.

"I really must protest at our treatment," Gregory Pullman was complaining repeatedly but with no great conviction, as he had done since the interview began. "We told you all we know yesterday, so there was absolutely no justification in dragging us here today. It is a bank holiday, after all, and I've got—"

"I expect you're scoring for Buckham Village cricket team later on," Clive interrupted.

"Yes, that's right, and—"

"Well, we'll try not to keep you long, but, unfortunately, you didn't tell us everything you know yesterday, did you?"

Gregory Pullman and Sarah Tildesley exchanged nervous glances. "Didn't we? I'm sure we did." Gregory Pullman protested again.

Clive smiled indulgently. "You see, when DC Pawlett spoke with your family solicitor about your late wife's will, he said that the money was to be divided equally among her children. Interesting phrase that one, isn't it? He said 'divided equally *among* her children' not '*between* her children', so I commissioned a bit of research and it transpires that you and your wife did in fact have three children, Alice and Sarah, which we know about, but also a son, Geoffrey. But then, why am I telling you this? You already know."

Sarah Tildesley, who had been maintaining a sullen, tight-lipped silence, gave her father a frosty look from behind her rimless spectacles. "Dad, we've got to own up."

Gregory Pullman shook his head, swallowed hard and took several deep breaths before speaking. "Geoffrey's been a huge disappointment to us, to me. He was such a bright pupil at school, all the teachers thought so. We quite thought he'd go on to university and then follow his mother into the banking profession. But then, out of the blue, he announced that he'd had enough of academic studies and he wanted to train to be a landscape gardener. Well, Mary's always been very keen – sorry, was always very keen – on gardening, so, after our initial shock, she, we, encouraged him, helped him with his fees and the like, and how did he repay us? I believe the modern term is 'cottaging'. Now it's no secret that I'm a very traditional, conventional kind of man, but I'm not some kind of puritanical bigot. I think I could have coped with my son being gay, eventually – it was just the way he flaunted it, as though he was deliberately trying to provoke me with that defiant look that he inherited from his mother. So, finally, after the court case, which I'm sure you know about, I told him I didn't want anything more to do with him."

"So what happened to him?" Clive asked.

Sarah Tildesley adopted another of her extravagant hand gestures, almost dislodging her spectacles in the process. "Geoffrey moved to Holland – I don't know what, or who, first attracted him – but he ended up working in a gay bar in Amsterdam."

"I must advise you," Constable Pawlett announced, rather pompously, "that withholding information from a murder enquiry is a very serious offence. Given what you've told us, Geoffrey Pullman has got to be a prime suspect and—"

Sarah Tildesley shook her head emphatically. "No, no, I know Geoffrey wasn't involved. When my mother disappeared he was working in Amsterdam, as he was around the time you think she was murdered."

"So you've kept in touch with him?" Alison Pawlett asked, while trying to stifle another yawn.

Sarah glanced uneasily at her father. "Yes, I have; he is my brother, after all. And I know my mother kept in touch. Whenever Geoffrey had a long weekend off, he'd come over and meet up with my mother – normally when he knew my father would be out of the way at his cricket club or some such."

"So the entries in her diary with the letter 'G' against them were when she planned to meet up with Geoffrey?" Clive asked.

"Yes, that's right."

"So where is Geoffrey now?"

Sarah Tildesley's alert eyes darted quickly between her father and Constable Pawlett. "Er, well, when he heard about my mother, he, er…" Her words tailed off.

"Err, I wonder," Clive said. "Mr Pullman, if I could ask you to leave the room for a moment or two. There are a couple more questions we need to put to your daughter. Constable Pawlett will show you where you can wait and then we'll arrange a lift home for you."

"Yes, but, hang on a minute—" Gregory Pullman began to protest before Alison Pawlett grabbed him firmly by the arm and escorted him from the room. Clive narrowed his eyes and stared at Sarah Tildesley while he waited for Alison Pawlett to return. Sarah Tildesley, for her part, fidgeted uncomfortably on her chair and stared blankly at one of the stark, grey walls.

When Alison Pawlett returned a few moments later, Clive resumed his questioning. "Err, the thing is, DC Pawlett has been making a few enquiries about the nature of the part-time work that you do, and it's not quite what you've told us, is it?"

"I don't know what you mean," Sarah Tildesley protested weakly.

"So you're happy if we tell your father then—"

"Okay, okay." Sarah Tildesley waved her arms about theatrically. "Although I don't see that this is relevant to anything."

"Let's hope you're right." Clive turned to Alison Pawlett, who was yawning again. "Perhaps you'd like to tell Mrs Tildesley what you've discovered."

"There's really no need," Sarah Tildesley replied, brusquely. "You've obviously done your homework. I do, er, work upstairs at 'The Dog Collar' club. I, er, have my speciality."

"So I believe," Clive replied with a valiant attempt at keeping a straight face. "I'd be interested to know how you got into this, er, particular profession."

Clive thought he caught a glimpse of a defiant smile on Sarah Tildesley's lips. It seemed to be a family trait. "It was while I was at my hairdressing salon," she replied. "A woman came in one day and we started chatting and then suddenly, out of the blue, she mentioned that she worked at *The Dog Collar* club. I'd never heard of it and I was quite shocked when she told me what she did. But then she mentioned, casually, how much money she earned and it got me thinking. I mean, I knew I'd have to close my salon before long – it was haemorrhaging money – and I couldn't rely on hand-outs from my mother forever. The trouble was I needed to keep up the mortgage repayments and look after the kids and I didn't have any qualifications or anything, so later, when she came in again, I asked her about the possibility of working there. She put me in touch with Gabrielle, one thing led to another and I started work there."

"And I imagine none of your family knows what you do?" Clive asked.

Sarah Tildesley shook her head emphatically. "No, absolutely not, and I'd like to keep it that way."

"And the money's good, from what you've just said," Alison Pawlett added.

"I get by. I have some very rich clients and they pay well."

"Including Alex Jeffries?" Clive asked.

"Err, yes, but how did you—"

"Tell me about Alex Jeffries."

"But surely he's got nothing to do with my mother's death!"

"It's just a line of enquiry; you do need to tell us all you can."

Sarah Tildesley briefly waved her arms but less energetically than before. "There's not much to tell, really. Alex is a regular visitor; he visits most weeks, he's got plenty of money and he pays me well. He's not very demanding – I'm not sure he likes women all that much. He's quite submissive, really, if you know what I mean. He takes a good beating, pays up and goes home."

"Does he talk to you much about himself and his private life?"

"Does he? I can't stop him sometimes. He often complains about his wife and how she's got the hots for half the men on the estate. He moans about his father-in-law and what a bully he can be. He complains that he's having to work too hard and never gets any thanks and he's got no mates that he can go out and have a drink with – he's quite a miserable bastard, really!"

*

As Clive and Alison left the interview room, Clive turned to his colleague. "When you take Mrs Tildesley home, you'd better have a good look around – see if there's any sign of a visitor. And don't forget to check the garage."

As Alison Pawlett turned to leave, more languidly than usual, she yawned again. "You okay?" Clive asked solicitously. "You're yawning a lot this morning."

"Yes, sorry," Alison replied. "I didn't get much sleep last night. The couple in the next room were arguing about something most of the night."

Clive's raised his eyebrows in surprise. "The couple in the next room? Are you sure? There is no couple in the next room. There's only—"

"I assumed it was Jamie and his girlfriend," Alison replied.

"No, no, he lives down in Crowdale and anyway, his girlfriend has, er, moved out, at least for the time being. But tell me, did you hear what the couple were arguing about?" There was a sudden urgency in Clive's voice.

"No, no, I didn't. I had a pillow over my head most of the time. The woman seemed to be crying at times, but the only thing I heard her say clearly was when she shouted something like, 'This can't go on; it has to stop.' She shouted it several times, but that's really all I heard—"

"Oh, shit, shit! That explains why Archie…" Clive exclaimed as he headed rapidly towards the door that led from the police station to the car park. "Look, I've got to phone Dick and then dash back to the hotel. I'll call you later!"

*

It was nearly midday when the Earl of Westleigh's private phone rang. He had been expecting the call all morning and had been pacing the floor of his study for some time, his chubby hands clasped firmly behind his back, stopping only to glance up occasionally at the large ormolu clock on the mantelpiece. He was quick to answer.

"Hello, Dad!" Lucy's voice sounded strangely disembodied and devoid of emotion.

"Thank God! Lucy, darling, how are you?"

"Oh, still in one piece, but for how much longer now depends on you, Dad! Have you got the money?"

"Yes, yes, I've got the money. It hasn't been easy, but I've got it."

"Good – listen carefully. You are to drive to Fearnley quarry with the money. You are to go alone and you are to arrive at the quarry entrance at one o'clock. When you arrive, wait by the entrance and you will receive further instructions. Have your mobile phone switched on and come alone!"

"Yes, but… Lucy! Lucy!" The line had gone dead.

Within five minutes, Acting Inspector Beauregard had received the news. He went immediately to the cell where he had been holding Richard Edgton and unlocked the door. Richard Edgton's appearance had changed. His blue and white striped shirt, usually crisply laundered, was crumpled and open at the neck. His hair, normally sleekly styled, was bedraggled and his erstwhile smooth facial contours bore the shadowy evidence of more than twenty-four hours of stubbly growth. His demeanour, ordinarily one of powerful, overbearing control, was subdued.

For all his ragged appearance and relatively subdued manner, however, he had lost little of his spirit. He rose quickly to his feet and took a couple of paces towards the acting inspector. "You took your bloody time," he announced in a strident voice.

"You're free to go," Acting Inspector Beauregard informed him, rather grudgingly. "We have new information on the kidnapping of Lucy Jeffries."

"I should bloody well hope so," Richard Edgton stormed, his rage re-kindled. "I've got a plane to catch tomorrow and, thanks to you, I'm running desperately behind schedule. Don't think you've heard the last of this."

"There's been a development at Fearnley quarry, a potential hostage situation. I'm on my way there now and I think you should come with me."

"Do you know, Acting Inspector, I think I've had enough of your company for the time being? So, if you don't mind, I'll make my own arrangements to get to the quarry. I'll see you there."

*

Clive's car came to a screeching halt in the hotel car park. He jumped out, slammed the car door shut and sprinted towards the hotel, the sudden physical effort providing a sharp reminder of how unfit he had become. His face had a rubicund hue and globules of perspiration were forming on his forehead as he bumped into Clare who was chatting with Debbie in the foyer.

"Clare, Clare," Clive gasped. "Have you seen Simon today at all?"

Clare exchanged puzzled glances with Debbie. "Simon? No, why, should I? It is a bank holiday and he is supposed to be recovering from his injury and—"

"Only I didn't see his old banger in the car park. I need to check his room."

As Clive dashed behind the reception desk, nearly knocking Debbie over in his haste, reached into a drawer and grabbed a key, Clare stared at him with bewilderment. Even when he was under pressure, Clive normally displayed a languid calm that bordered on indolence, but now, suddenly, he seemed to be in the grip of a serious and unexplained panic attack.

"Clive, what on earth's happened? What's going on?" Clare called after him as he raced up the rear stairs, taking them two at a time. She followed him as quickly as her shorter legs and fashionable shoes permitted and found him standing in Simon's room, breathing heavily and staring uncomprehendingly around him.

The room was far less lavishly furnished than the guest rooms. Against one of the magnolia-painted walls was a single, unmade bed. On the opposite wall was a wooden wardrobe and drawer unit, separated by the door that led into the bathroom and toilet. Although the room was basic, the view, through the dormer window down across the Carlow valley, was impressive.

"Look at this!" Clive exclaimed, gesturing excitedly. "I've just come back from Stowbrook police station where I've been talking with Alison and she was complaining that she had been kept awake half the night by a couple arguing in this room, Simon's room. But look at it! There's nothing here. It's been cleared out; there's just the furniture left. It looks as though the bed has been slept in, but there are no clothes, no personal effects, nothing." Still trying to comprehend what he was seeing, Clive suddenly disappeared into the small bathroom. "It's the same in here," he shouted. "I'd guess someone's had a bath this morning, but there's nothing in here, no toiletries, no towels, nothing!"

Clare sniffed the air thoughtfully. "You know, it doesn't smell as though Simon's been in here much recently; there's not the usual stench of sweat and stale whisky. Actually, it smells refreshingly fragrant."

"Exactly, exactly! Clare, can you do me a favour? I've got to dash out again, I'm afraid, but can you check that address in the village that Simon was living at? He told me he'd been thrown out – something about the lease expiring – but I'm just wondering—"

He paused as the shrill ringtone of his mobile phone interrupted him. "Damn! Hang on a minute. Hello." Clive spoke with an uncharacteristic terseness.

"Hello, Clive, it's Julia, Julia Cockrell; have I called at a bad time?"

"Hello, Julia! Now that rather depends on what you've got to tell me, but I must admit I am in a bit of a hurry."

Julia sounded disappointed. "Oh, alright, I'll try and be brief. I've been doing a bit more research on Mary Pullman's family tree and I've discovered what her grandfather's middle name was—"

"Don't tell me, let me guess – it was 'Dalton'!"

Julia sounded even more disappointed. "Yes, but how did you—"

"It's a long story, but I'll tell you later, Julia! You are an absolute star, by the way. But right now, I must dash. I'll call you later."

Clive rang off and began racing back down the stairs. "Can't stop now," he called back over his shoulder to a still bewildered Clare. "I've got to phone Alison and then I've got to go out, but I shouldn't be long. Wish me luck!"

*

"Ah, I'm glad you've called," Alison Pawlett began, breathlessly. "I've found out something!"

"Is it important?" Clive asked, sensing a frisson of excitement in Alison's voice.

"My contacts in the Met have come up trumps," she announced triumphantly. "I've got some news about Vernon Court."

Clive tugged his earlobe. The "Vernon Court" debacle had been something of an embarrassment, prompting an all-too-vivid recollection of a similar mistake he had made some years ago with a gentleman called Maurice Dance, and he preferred not to be reminded of his error. If Alison did have news about the vanishing genealogist, however, he needed to know.

"Okay, go ahead," he replied with muted enthusiasm. "But keep it brief – there's something I'd like you to do."

"Well, as soon as I left you at breakfast, I got in touch with one of my former colleagues in the Met and he's traced Vernon Court's last known address. As your contact mentioned, he is registered with a number of family history organisations in London. Anyway, my contact went round to the address – it's close to where he's based. It's officially called an apartment, but it's really only a pretty bleak bed-sit by all accounts, but he couldn't get an answer. Anyway, he managed to track down the landlord and I've spoken with him on the phone. He said that Vernon Court was a tenant until a few months ago and then he started to fall behind with the rent, so the landlord went round to the bed-sit and found it empty. It had been completely cleared out. There was no sign of Vernon Court or his belongings. The landlord knew he'd originated from South Africa, so he just assumed he'd done a bunk and gone back there – he didn't leave a forwarding address or any clues as to his whereabouts. Eventually the landlord re-let the bed-sit and he's never heard anything more from Vernon Court."

"Did he say when Vernon Court disappeared?"

"He couldn't be precise about the last time he spoke to him, but it was early May when he went round to the flat and discovered he'd left."

"Mmm, so he could have disappeared around the time that Mary Pullman disappeared."

"Very likely, I'd say. I'm trying to get passenger lists from all the aircraft that fly to South Africa, but I'm wondering if something more sinister might have happened to Vernon Court, so I'm trying to establish if any unidentified bodies matching his description have turned up since April, but no luck so far."

"And there have been no leads and no sightings of him since April?"

"None, as far as I know, but then nobody's been actively looking for him."

"No, of course; thanks Alison, that's really helpful. I'm just waiting for a couple of things to fall into place and then I suspect everything's going to kick off. Are you still prepared to work with me on this?"

"You bet!"

"Okay, let me tell you what I'd like you to do."

*

Richard Edgton's estate car slowed to a halt at the entrance to Fearnley quarry. There were three vehicles parked in front of the main gates; one was an expensive Land Rover, which he assumed had come from the Chartfield estate, one was a dark grey saloon car and the other, a battered, mud-spattered, elderly maroon hatchback which he thought he might have seen in the Follycombe Hotel car park. Following the alleged recent break-in, Richard Edgton had arranged a temporary repair to the perimeter fence, but it had clearly proved insufficient to cope with that day's determined intruders, who had opened up a large hole in it and, he assumed, made their way inside.

Dean Footner got out of the car, strode importantly over to the main gates, unlocked them, hauled them open, returned to the car and, squeezing it between the parked vehicles, drove it a few yards to the front of the main building, where he pulled up. Richard Edgton alighted slowly from the car, his eyes alert and suspicious, winced slightly as he eased his heavy frame into an upright position and exhaled sharply as he was immediately buffeted by a lively, cool breeze and a steady, depressing drizzle blowing spitefully into his face. He stood motionless for some moments, a muscular hand held up in front of his eyes to shield them from the elements, and squinted up along the side of the hill. The hillside was pockmarked with the scars of decades of quarrying. Here and there, steep precipices of bare limestone fell into shallow, muddy lakes. Elsewhere, the escarpments were riddled with tunnels and caves where generations of quarrymen had hacked into the hillside in search of the best stone. As he surveyed the largely desolate scene, Richard Edgton could just make out a couple of figures standing in front of one of the main quarry tunnels, probably three hundred yards or so from where he stood.

"This might be a trap. Give me ten minutes," Richard Edgton barked at Dean Footner, "and if I haven't returned, come after me and make sure you've got something suitable to defend yourself with."

Richard Edgton winked knowingly at Dean Footner, turned into the wind, buttoned up his coat and strode carefully along the rising, uneven track, picking his way over the loose stones that scrunched under his feet and around the many murky puddles that littered the route towards the tunnel. After several minutes of clambering over the rough surface, he arrived, a little breathless, at the tunnel entrance, where he was confronted by two waterproof-clad men, one significantly taller and older than the other, each armed with a shotgun which they were pointing ominously towards the dark interior of the tunnel. Just inside, huddled against a dark, dank wall, trembling and crying, was a young lady whom Richard Edgton assumed to be Lucy Jeffries. She was still wearing the riding clothes that, presumably, she had been wearing when she disappeared. Next to her, with a protective arm around her shoulder, was the unmistakeable profile of Lord Westleigh. As protection against the predictably malevolent bank holiday weather, he was wearing a full-length raincoat and tweed cap. Facing them, cowering against the opposite wall, was the gaunt hangdog figure of Acting Inspector Caspar Beauregard, a look of desperate anxiety in his heavy, watery eyes.

"Ah, Richard Edgton, I presume," the older of the two men announced gleefully. "I didn't think Lord Westleigh and Dick whatsit would come on their own. It's getting quite crowded here. You should've brought a bottle and some sandwiches!"

"Yes, I'm Richard Edgton, as well you know, but would you mind telling me what you're doing on my property and what the hell is going on?" Seemingly undeterred by the sight of the two men steadfastly pointing their shotguns at the occupants of the tunnel, Richard Edgton stood with his feet apart and his chest thrust out in a clear gesture of defiance.

"I'll tell you in a moment," the man replied, "but first I'm afraid you're going to have to join the others in the tunnel." He waved his shotgun at Richard Edgton in a menacing, erratic way and gestured towards the tunnel entrance.

"Now look here—" Richard Edgton began, his defiance beginning to falter as he stared down the barrels of the firearm.

"Better do what he says," Lord Westleigh interrupted. "He means business, I think!"

"Alright, alright," Richard Edgton conceded, raising his hands in the air, as the man continued to brandish the shotgun in his direction. "I'm going, but I'd still like to know what's going on!"

"So would I," Lord Westleigh boomed from within the shadowy confines of the tunnel. "Simon, what the hell is going on?" he demanded of the older of the two shotgun-wielding men.

Favouring Lord Westleigh with a look of utter contempt, the man advanced a couple of paces towards him. "Shall I tell you, Patrick, shall I tell you what's going on? What's going on, Patrick, is that I have had enough of doing your dirty work. Ever since I can remember, it's always been me, your baby brother who's had to do your dirty work, and there's been plenty of it over the years, hasn't there? Well, we couldn't have the squeaky-clean reputation of the 33rd Earl of Westleigh besmirched by any hint of dodgy dealing or scandal or malpractice, could we? So who has to carry out your dirty work? Your long-suffering kid brother, that's who!"

"I paid you well enough to do what you did," the Earl snarled. "I didn't hear you complaining about that. You know, you really should be grateful, Simon – I could have disowned you after some of your, erm, some of your behaviour, but I didn't."

"And do you know why you didn't disown me? I'll tell you – it's because I'm too damned convenient. You pay me, not as much as I deserve, and I'll do your dirty work, no questions asked. That's the deal, isn't it? Well, not anymore! You paid me right enough, and I could cope with it when it was just a matter of evicting a defaulting tenant or sacking an embezzling employee. I've served in the army, I can look after myself, but then it all got much worse, didn't it? I had to 'arrange' those two so-called fatal 'accidents' here so that Richard Edgton, your fellow troglodyte, would be forced to close this place and you could buy him out cheaply. I killed two people, Patrick, just so you could get one over on Richard Edgton! And then there were the murders of Mary Pullman and Vernon Court. And who had to dispose of the bodies? Simon Verwood, your bloody fall-guy and Tom Chewton, your daughter's trusted groom." Simon Verwood pointed a shaking hand towards the young man who was standing at the far side of the tunnel, pointing his shotgun towards its occupants with a distinct lack of enthusiasm.

"So where will it all end, Patrick?" Simon asked, his voice growing ever more manic. "Well, I'll tell you, Patrick – it ends right now. While I was in hospital recovering from my stab wound, they ran some blood tests and it turns out I've got chronic liver disease – all those years of hard boozing have finally caught up with me. The damage is done, you see. There's no cure and the specialist wasn't very optimistic about my chances of seeing in the new year. And I do not want to spend my last few months as your glorified errand boy and reluctant hit-man, Patrick, so it ends now. And when this is all over, I just want to spend the rest of my time quietly somewhere with my... with my boyfriend."

Suddenly alerted by the sound of loose limestone shards scrunching beneath a heavy foot close behind him, Simon

Verwood wheeled round to see Dean Footner, creeping towards him, with what appeared to be a pick-axe handle raised threateningly above his head.

"Oh no you don't!" Simon Verwood shouted before firing his shotgun at the approaching figure. Dean Footner let out a groan, dropped the pick-axe handle and fell backwards onto the ground where, after several convulsions, he lay motionless. From within the tunnel, Lucy Jeffries screamed, the sound echoing chillingly around the limestone walls of the quarry. Amongst the men, however, there was only a stunned silence. There could be no doubting that Simon Verwood was deadly serious and that they were in mortal danger.

Satisfying himself that Dean Footner no longer posed a threat, Simon Verwood turned back towards the tunnel and waved his shotgun at the occupants in a wild, agitated way. "Nobody should ever creep up behind me like that," he shouted to no-one in particular. "I was trained to deal with that kind of thing in the army. I learnt a lot of useful stuff in the army before… well, before, I left. That's where I learnt to fly helicopters, wasn't it, Patrick?"

"You obviously didn't learn about re-fuelling them, though, did you?" Lord Westleigh shouted defiantly. "I mean, all you had to do was drop Mary Pullman's body here in the quarry for the police to find, but you couldn't even manage that, could you? Oh, no, you started getting low on fuel, so you had to turn back and jettison her body in some poor bloke's back garden. Some welcome back from holiday that was for the poor bugger!"

Simon was becoming steadily more frenzied, constantly shifting from one foot to the other, his eyeballs bulging, and brandishing his shotgun ever more wildly. "Look, look, I, I, we… Tom and I, we didn't mean to drop her into that chap's garden. We were aiming for the school playing field behind his garden, but the light was fading, our fuel was running out and, and… okay, we made a small error of judgement."

"And you flew so low over Willowmere Heath that you spooked the horse that Detective Inspector Morris was riding and put him in hospital. I'd have thought Tom of all people would have warned you not to do that, knowing how the horse might behave, but obviously not. And then, to add insult to injury, you got it into your stupid, addled head that Inspector Morris might have seen who was piloting the helicopter so, when you discovered he was in the same hospital as you, you decided to murder him, just in case he came to and remembered what had happened."

"That's right, you can sneer all you like, Patrick, but let me tell you a little secret that'll wipe the smile off your sanctimonious little face. When I broke into the buildings here to plant the evidence to incriminate Richard Edgton, just as you instructed me to, I discovered something very interesting. I found a locked cupboard and, when I prised it open, I found some sticks of explosive and some detonators. That's something else I learned about in the army; how to handle explosives. So the bad news for you four unfortunate people is that I have rigged up the explosives in the tunnel and I have a detonator here and, in a moment, I'm going to activate it. Then there will be a massive explosion, the tunnel will collapse and you will be buried alive and it will be goodbye to you and a fresh start for me."

"Me?" Lucy Jeffries shrieked. "Me? You're going to kill me as well? Why? I don't understand. I've gone along with this ludicrous kidnap stunt. I've let you shut me up in that pokey little hotel room. I've gone along with your mad scheme, and now you're going to…"

Lucy Jeffries began to sob uncontrollably as her father's protective embrace tightened.

"Lucy, Lucy, dear sweet Lucy. I really don't want to do this," Simon Verwood replied, disingenuously, while flourishing his shotgun in an increasingly crazed manner, "but I have no choice. You see, as I said, I want to spend however long I've got left with my boyfriend, my lover, the only man I feel comfortable with and, you see, dear Lucy, he just happens to be your husband, Alex."

"Alex?" Lucy squealed. "My Alex and… you? How could you? No, I don't believe it! It can't be!"

Simon shook his head sadly. "I'm afraid it is true, Lucy. From the moment he first met you, he tried to convince himself he was straight and I rather think he thought he'd succeeded for a while, but, sadly for you, that wasn't the case. I'm sure you must have heard the rumours that Alex was seeing somebody else; well, that somebody else was me. And do you know, my dear Lucy, that the only person who bothered to visit me in hospital, apart from Inspector Bonaparte over there and my employers, was Alex? And that's the problem. You see, I'm being selfish for once in my life and now I want Alex all to myself, so I'm afraid—"

At that moment, Lucy Jeffries emitted another piercing scream which so distracted Simon Verwood that he didn't hear the footsteps approaching behind him.

"Simon, put that gun down!" The voice, firm and authoritative, caused Simon to jump and wheel round. Clive Walsingham was hot and panting and not feeling as authoritative as he sounded, and the sight of a shotgun barrel being waved in his direction halted his progress.

"Oh, Mr Clive! I was just talking about you. What a shame you had to turn up and ruin things. You've been so good to me since you and Mrs Clare took over the hotel and I really don't want to harm you, but, unfortunately, you now know far too much about what I've been up to and you wouldn't leave me in peace if I let you go, so I'm afraid you're going to have to join the others in the tunnel."

With his bloodshot eyeballs bulging manically in their sockets, he pointed the shotgun threateningly in Clive's direction and gestured towards the tunnel entrance. Clive raised his hands above his head and walked slowly and reluctantly into the tunnel.

"Don't be so bloody stupid," Richard Edgton suddenly called out from the gloomy interior of the tunnel. "Do you think I'd be stupid enough to—?"

"Enough, enough!" Simon called out. "I've had enough. Time to say goodbye!"

While Tom, the groom, continued to stand reluctant guard over the hostages, Simon slowly and deliberately activated the detonator. Lucy Jeffries screamed.

Nineteen

Monday 28 August, afternoon

An eerie, ghostly silence descended on the small group of damp, bedraggled and deeply shocked individuals as they each tried to make some sense of what had happened. Having failed to trigger the promised explosion, Simon Verwood stood motionless, staring disbelievingly at the malfunctioning detonator and trying to fathom the cause of its failure. Lucy Jeffries continued to sob uncontrollably, her father's arms now placed so protectively around her shoulders that her face was completely buried in his aristocratic chest. The Earl of Westleigh had lost his hitherto impregnable veneer of authority and suddenly seemed older and more vulnerable. He stared at his errant brother through uncomprehending, hurt eyes. Acting Inspector Beauregard also blinked uncomprehendingly through his heavy, red-tinged eyes, the events of the last few minutes having destroyed the painstaking but flawed case that he had built against Richard Edgton. Not wanting to attract Simon Verwood's attention in any way, he was also battling against an almost overwhelming desire to sneeze. Clive Walsingham moved slowly out from the canopy of the tunnel and looked anxiously beyond Simon towards the main gates while Richard Edgton started to chuckle before he too advanced a few paces out of the tunnel.

"You didn't really think that I'd keep live explosives locked in a cupboard in an outbuilding in a deserted quarry, did you? Have you any idea how volatile they'd become?" Richard Edgton mocked Simon as he continued to walk slowly towards him. "What you found were all dummies – we were going to use them in the museum. I thought you would have spotted that, being an army man." He took another pace and then stopped abruptly as Simon suddenly raised his shotgun and pointed it at him.

"Don't come any nearer," Simon shouted. "The explosives may not have worked, but we've got enough ammunition to take you all out, so stay right where you are." Simon took quivering aim at Richard Edgton, who instinctively dived behind the nearest rock. Simon was about to fire when Acting Inspector Beauregard finally sneezed, loudly, the noise reverberating around the limestone walls of the quarry. Momentarily distracted, Simon lowered the shotgun and, as he did so, he was struck violently on the back of the head by a pick-axe handle wielded with great force and delivered with a sickening thud. He dropped unconscious to the ground and lay motionless while Alison Pawlett dropped the pick-axe handle and quickly secured Simon Verwood's limp wrists in a pair of handcuffs.

"That was cutting it a bit fine, Alison," Clive observed casually, though his heart was beating fast, as he walked from the tunnel, dusting himself down, and snatched the shotgun that Tom Chewton, his spirit broken, allowed him to take without resistance.

"Yeah, sorry about that," Alison Pawlett replied glibly. "It took me a bit longer than I thought to persuade Geoffrey Pullman to come with me. I had to put my foot down a bit."

Clive shuddered at the prospect.

"I've locked him in the car," Alison continued as she observed Acting Inspector Beauregard's dumbstruck inactivity with barely concealed contempt. "I'll call an ambulance, then, shall I, sir?" she shouted.

"I think you'd better," Clive confirmed quietly. "Dean Footner is still breathing, but there's quite a lot of blood seeping from his chest and I expect Simon'll probably need some first aid when he comes come round. That was one hell of a wallop you gave him!"

"Yes, thank you!" Alison replied, cheerfully. "I just imagined it was Colin standing there!"

As they awaited the arrival of the police back-up unit and the ambulance, members of the group stood silently around, still unable quite to comprehend what had happened and unwilling, or unable, to speak about it, the gloomy damp weather closed in, giving the quarry a ghostly, spectral-like appearance, and Acting Inspector Beauregard finally stirred himself into action. Absently wiping his nose with the back of his hand, he wandered uncertainly over to Clive, who was watching Alison Pawlett administering emergency first aid to the still prostrate Dean Footner while Simon Verwood slowly regained a shaky consciousness.

"You'll think I'm such an idiot," Acting Inspector Beauregard confided. He paused, hoping for a swift contradiction from Clive, but none came. "But it's difficult to concentrate when a shotgun's being pointed at your—"

"Of course it is, Dick." Clive smiled.

"I mean, I've just heard that Simon Verwood is the brother of Lord Westleigh, whose family name is Monck – I don't understand."

"I only found this out yesterday, Dick, so don't feel too bad. The previous owner of the hotel wasn't a great record-keeper, so we didn't know much about Simon's background. Apparently, as a result of a dynastic marriage a couple of hundred years ago, the Moncks, Lord Westleigh's direct ancestors, incorporated the surname of Verwood into the family arms and became Verwood-Moncks. I suspect Lord Westleigh found the double-barrelled name a bit cumbersome when he went into business, so he simply called himself Patrick Monck, Earl of Westfield, or just plain Patrick Westfield. Simon, on the other hand, maybe to distance himself from his brother or maybe because his brother instructed him to do so, simply adopted the first half of the family surname, Verwood."

"I see," Dick Beauregard replied. "Or at least I think I do. So, from what I've just heard, did I gather that Simon Verwood dropped Mary Pullman's body from a helicopter?"

Clive smiled again; it was an indulgent, slightly smug smile. "Yes, that's quite right, you did!"

"But there were no injuries on her body, which there would have been if she'd been dropped from a great height. And her body had been arranged so very neatly and… and it makes no sense."

Clive continued to smile, while resisting the temptation to give his snuffling colleague a condescending pat on the head. It was time to tell Dick Beauregard what he knew. "Ah, well you remember the pathologist being confused by what he called 'some irregularities'?" Acting Inspector Beauregard nodded uncertainly. "And do you remember me studying the photographs of the area where Mary Pullman's body was found?" The acting inspector nodded again. "Well, for a while, I couldn't work out why the grass around Mary Pullman's body was so green when we were in the middle of such a hot, dry spell of weather and when the householder had been on holiday for two weeks. So I spoke to the pathologist and he confirmed what I had been thinking." Clive paused momentarily, partly for dramatic effect and partly to study Dick Beauregard's increasingly befuddled features. "And we concluded," Clive continued, "that when Mary Pullman's body was dropped from the helicopter, it must have been encased in a solid block of ice – improbable though it sounds, it's the only explanation that makes any sense. The block of ice would have cushioned the fall, thus preventing her body from being damaged when it hit the ground and, as it gradually melted in the sun, the water freshened up the grass around the body. That would also explain why the body looked so tidy, as though it had been deliberately placed there. And the pathologist confirmed that, because Mary Pullman's body thawed slowly from the outside, the rate of decomposition of some of her internal organs was slower than he would normally have expected."

"Good God!" Acting Inspector Beauregard stood gaping at Clive in disbelief. "But why go to the trouble of freezing the body?"

"Ah, I'm probably not the best person to ask," Clive replied modestly. "But I suspect that Mary Pullman was actually murdered on the day she disappeared in April and frozen in ice immediately afterwards and that Lord Westleigh was simply waiting for the right time and the right opportunity to dump her body."

"But how? Why?" Dick Beauregard asked, his face a picture of utter bewilderment.

Clive waved a dismissive hand. "Dick, you have to ask yourself who has a controlling interest in a major frozen food company and will therefore have access to an industrial refrigeration unit? And Miranda Bellamy, the manager of our recent coach party, had a snoop around Chartfield Castle and discovered an ice house that looked as though it had been modernised; the perfect place for storing a body. And who owns a helicopter? And if you strip a dead body naked, dispose of the clothing – apart from any you might want to use to incriminate somebody else – and freeze the body in a block of ice, then you are getting rid of a lot of potentially damaging forensic evidence. And once you've frozen the body, you can, in theory at least, dispose of it whenever and wherever you want – as long as you own a helicopter. Of course, as you heard, they hadn't planned to drop the body in Gareth Adamson's back garden – the original target was Fearnley quarry. Now I imagine you'd have got very excited if Mary Pullman's naked body had turned up in Richard Edgton's quarry – that would have just about sealed your case against him – but we now know that Simon Verwood screwed it up. He was running out of fuel and panicked. He had to abort his flight before he could get to the quarry and, on the way back, decided to dump the body in the school playing fields, where it probably would've lain undetected until the start of the new term, but he couldn't even get that right."

"Oh, of course, I get it now," Acting Inspector Beauregard announced as though suddenly overcome by some profound revelation. Then, as Lord Westleigh began to walk away, a protective arm still around his shaking, sobbing daughter, Acting Inspector Beauregard cleared his throat. "Errrm, Lord Westleigh, I'm arresting you for the murder of Mary Pullman and Vernon Court and the abduction of Lucy Jeffries."

"Don't be stupid, man!" Lord Westleigh snapped as he continued to walk away. "You've seen and heard what's happened. Your constable has got your man; whatever he did had nothing to do with me!"

*

Dick Beauregard and Clive Walsingham stood and watched as a small procession of official vehicles taking Dean Footner and Simon Verwood to the hospital and Lord Westleigh and Tom Chewton to Stowbrook police station turned out of the quarry entrance.

"I wonder," Dick Beauregard spoke quietly as though his voice was beginning to fail, "would you mind sitting in on my interview with Lord Westleigh? I'm not feeling too great, my voice is starting to pack up and he'll be difficult to pin down."

Clive's eyes continued to follow the vehicles as they left the quarry and began the climb along the side of the hill and into the swirling mist. "Thank you, Dick, but no! I never want to see the inside of another police station ever again and Clare will kill me if I'm gone for much longer. No, no, you've got all the evidence you need, but there is one more thing you might want to raise…"

*

Without his large, brown-framed spectacles and with his parched fair hair cut much shorter, presumably by his sister Sarah, Geoffrey Pullman looked rather different from his "alter ego" Ralph Dalton, although his bright yellow trousers still seemed uncomfortably tight and his demeanour remained aloof and wary.

Clive ushered him and Constable Alison Pawlett into the hotel bar, closed the door firmly behind him and gestured to a table in the far corner.

"Acting Inspector Beauregard can't be here at the moment. I'm sure you'll appreciate that he's rather busy elsewhere. But he has given me permission to have a word with you; this is all quite informal. I understand you've been released without charge."

Geoffrey Pullman pulled a face and glanced nervously at Alison Pawlett. "Yes, I suppose so, although they've told me I might still face charges of some kind and they've taken away my passport, so I can't go back to Amsterdam just yet. If I don't get back soon, I'll probably lose my job."

"I'm sorry to hear that," Clive soothed. "Leave it with me and I'll have a word, you know, to see if I can expedite things for you. Meanwhile, can I get you a drink?"

"Ah, er, just a mineral water. I don't drink – Simon's put me off booze for life."

"Okay. Leave it to me." Clive strode behind the bar and quickly produced three bottles of mineral water and three glasses. "Mineral water alright for you, Alison?" Constable Pawlett hesitated for an instant before nodding her reluctant assent. "So tell me," Clive continued as he sat down and opened the bottles. "How did you first meet Simon Verwood, or more correctly, Simon Verwood-Monck?"

"Through a mutual friend I met when I was at agricultural college. Simon had a bit of a reputation in the horticultural world at the time – he was running his brother's chain of garden centres – and my friend introduced me to him and arranged for him to give me some work experience. I thought I'd just be given some menial role in one of his centres, but he seemed to take a bit of a shine to me – I wasn't sure why at first. I was a bit naive and uncertain about things then, but it didn't take Simon long to start flirting with me and—"

"And you started a relationship?"

"Kind of, yes, but I soon discovered that Simon could hit the bottle hard and, when he was drunk, his behaviour became quite outrageous – too outrageous for me. The incident in the public lavatory was just about the last straw."

"And it was then that you fell out with your family?"

Geoffrey Pullman took a long sip of water. "Yes, well, my father, really. He's very straight-laced and couldn't come to terms with having a gay son, so I was banished. I was thrown out of the house and effectively ostracised. He told me never to come back. So I moved to Amsterdam and forged a new life for myself."

"But you kept in touch with your mother and sisters."

"Yes, although it was all very hush-hush. We'd communicate by text and email and sometimes, when I'd got a bit of time off work, I'd come over and meet up with my mother whenever my father was out of the way."

"Yes, we saw the initial 'G' against some dates in her diary. It took us a while to work out who the 'G' was. And did your mother tell you about the family history that she was researching?"

Geoffrey Pullman laughed. "Actually, it was the other way round to start with. You see, when Simon got drunk, his guard would drop and he'd start tittle-tattling and betraying what he called dark family secrets. I mean, his accounts were fairly garbled and sometimes too far-fetched to take seriously, but I remembered him telling me about one of the Earl's ancestors, Ralph, who had a bit of a penchant for servant girls – girls who were in service up at the castle. He got two of them into trouble and, very much against the family's wishes, he married them. The first girl was called Jane Dalton – she disappeared without trace shortly after the marriage – and the second was Mary Hayward, which was my mother's maiden name, so I mentioned it casually to her one day and she suddenly got very excited and said she'd do some research."

"And did your mother tell you what she found out?"

"Some of it, yes, but she enjoyed her little secrets. She did tell me that she was certain her grandfather, Frederick Dalton Hayward, was the son of Mary Hayward and Ralph Verwood-Monck. His middle name was obviously some kind of recognition of, or homage to, Jane Dalton."

"But you said that Ralph married Mary Hayward, so surely your grandfather should have been called Frederick Verwood-Monck?" Alison Pawlett asked as though not entirely convinced by Geoffrey Pullman's account.

"Ah, well, I think that's the nub of it. My mother suspected that Mary had been bought off by the Verwood-Monck family and that she and Frederick had been handsomely rewarded for their silence and for conveniently omitting the family name from Frederick's birth certificate. She couldn't prove it, of course, but my mother often talked about her grandfather's 'little legacy'. I believe she engaged the services of a professional genealogist to try and get proof."

"Vernon Court?"

"Yes, I believe that was his name."

"So how did your mother and Vernon Court come to get themselves murdered?" Clive asked.

Geoffrey Pullman studied his glass, swilling the water around in it several times before taking another large sip. "I don't know for sure. All I know is that she and Vernon Court were planning to visit Chartfield Castle, armed with the findings of their research. With hindsight, I think she knew that something unpleasant might happen because she sent me a copy of some pages from her notebook which she said were very important and asked me to hide them in a safe place. And then, a couple of days later, she suddenly disappeared."

"And you suspected the Earl of Westleigh?"

"I tried not to, but then I remembered Simon confiding in me that his brother had a rather ruthless, unscrupulous streak and that he sometimes carried out the Earl's dirty work. I thought it was just Simon being melodramatic and over-creative at first, but, when we heard nothing more from my mother, I started to have my suspicions. And then, when my mother's body turned up, I reckoned either Simon or his brother must have murdered her, presumably because of what she knew. So I decided to try and flush them out. I contacted the mutual friend who had first introduced me to Simon and discovered that he was still in touch with him and that Simon was working here at the hotel. So I flew over from Amsterdam, hired a car—"

"In the name of Henry Carmichael."

"Yes, how did you—?"

"We checked with the car hire company."

"Yes, of course. I don't actually know anyone called Henry Carmichael, but, one night, after the bar where I work had closed, we discovered a wallet in one of the toilets. There was nothing much in it – I suspect any money or credit cards had already been removed by whoever stole it. But there was a driving licence in the name of Henry Carmichael. We kept it behind the bar for ages, but it was never claimed so, when I realised that I needed to hire a car when I flew in and that I didn't really want to use my real name, I thought I'd use it. The photograph didn't look especially like me, but once I'd acquired those big heavy glasses and coloured my hair, there was a passing resemblance. The bloke at the car hire company only really glanced at the driving licence."

"So you hired a car. Then what?"

"I drove here and registered as Ralph Dalton, knowing that Simon would recognise the name and realise that I was on to him. And then I strung him along for a while. I made sure that he saw me going from here to the car park and I could see immediately that he knew who I was and why I was here. I took the opportunity to visit my sister a few times while I bided my time."

Clive nodded knowingly. "Yes, you obviously made the impression on Simon that you planned to do. He kept warning me and Clare that you were bad news and suggesting that I ask you to leave. He seemed deeply troubled by your arrival. So were you planning to attack him in revenge for him murdering your mother?"

"What? Me? No, no!" Geoffrey Pullman looked astonished at the suggestion. "I didn't plan to attack him; if I was going to attack him, I would hardly have chosen to do it in your grounds and in full view of a coach-load of guests enjoying their dinner. No, no, I just wanted to confront him and find out what really happened to my mother and who was responsible. So I slipped a note under the door of his shed asking him to meet me on the Friday evening just after I'd checked out. I put my luggage in the car and waited for him down by your walled garden. I planned to confront him, find out what happened to my mother, drive off into the sunset and then tip off the police, anonymously, of course. But then he suddenly appeared from nowhere with this strange, demented look in his eyes. He came charging at me wielding a knife. I'd half-expected that he might pull a stunt like that, but I keep myself pretty fit and I'm a good few years younger and more agile than Simon, so I was ready for him. I must admit I don't exactly know what happened next, but I do remember grappling with him and then pushing him over and, the next thing I knew, there was a big blood stain on his shirt. He was still holding the knife, so I guess the wound must have been self-inflicted, either deliberately or accidentally, but, either way, I wasn't going to hang around. I snatched the knife to stop him doing any more damage either to him or me and fled the scene. As I left, I could hear him shouting and screaming that he'd been attacked."

"Well, that explains why Simon was uncharacteristically sober that night; he was obviously planning to attack you. What happened to the knife?"

Geoffrey Pullman shrugged. "Oh, I dumped it in some undergrowth beside a country lane somewhere. It was dark and I don't know the area very well so I'm not sure exactly where—"

"And where did you go after the attack?"

"I went and stayed with my sister, Sarah, which is where Constable Pawlett found me. I was planning to go back home tomorrow, but—"

"And I take it you went nowhere near the hospital over the weekend?"

"What? No, nowhere near, why should I?"

Clive shrugged. "No, no reason – it was just something that Simon said."

"I'll need you to make a statement," Alison Pawlett interjected, ignoring Geoffrey Pullman's question and Clive's reply. "Can we do it now?"

"I don't see why not," Geoffrey Pullman replied. "The sooner we complete the formalities, the sooner I can get my life back."

Geoffrey Pullman stood up and grasped Clive's hand in a surprisingly firm handshake. "Thank you for the hospitality. Your hotel is excellent, by the way, apart from the gardener."

"Thank you," Clive responded. "And what will you do about your mother's research? Will you pursue it?"

"Nah! Whatever claim my mother thought she had against the Monck-Verwoods for diddling her grandfather out of his rightful inheritance, I doubt she would have won any court case and it would have been very expensive, very stressful, very complicated and, knowing what we now know, very dangerous. No, I'll just content myself that Lord Westleigh got his comeuppance in the end and settle for whatever my mother left me in her will."

*

In the drab, bleak surroundings of the police interview room, the Earl of Westleigh seemed less confident and bombastic. He fidgeted continuously with his signet ring, from time to time he would look across at his solicitor, a balding, scholarly looking man with round horn-rimmed glasses, as though seeking assurance and, when he spoke, his voice no longer bore the rich, composed timbre with which he usually commanded an audience. Instead, it had a tremulous, faltering quality.

"As I keep saying," he was saying, "the deaths of Vernon Court, whoever he was, and Mary Pullman were nothing to do with me." Although the Earl tried to sound suitably outraged that anyone could doubt his integrity and try to sully his hitherto impeccable reputation in this unjustified and dishonourable way, he was lacking his usual powers of persuasion. "Must I remind you again, Acting Inspector, that I was out of the country when Mary Pullman's body turned up?"

Acting Inspector Beauregard slowly cleared his husky throat before speaking. "But you heard what your brother said at the quarry – we all did." He was frustrated. He no longer had any doubt of Lord Westleigh's culpability, but the Earl was clearly not prepared or willing to admit anything.

"Loud and clear, thank you!" the Earl replied, making no attempt to conceal his contempt for Dick Beauregard. In his eyes, the detective was little more than a still raw detective sergeant who had been temporarily promoted far beyond his limited ability. "But whatever my brother did, or says he did, he did not do it with my approval or connivance. I'm afraid he's always been a bit of a maverick, but, sadly, he gets worse when he's had a drink or two. And he's frequently had a drink or two."

"So do you deny that Mary Pullman and Vernon Court came to see you on 5th April?" Acting Inspector Beauregard persisted.

The Earl spread his hands out on the desk in front of him. "I'm a very busy man, Acting Inspector. Lots of people want to come and see me for one reason or another, but my personal secretary, Anthony Granard, vets them all carefully and very few actually get to meet me in person. Often, Anthony will receive visitors on my behalf. Occasionally, even Simon will do the honours if he's around and sober. But I'm afraid I don't remember those two. Why would they want to visit me?"

Acting Inspector Beauregard paused to blow his nose. "We think Mary Pullman believed she had uncovered an, er... an irregularity in her family tree which suggests that her grandfather might have had a legitimate claim to have succeeded to the title of Earl of Westleigh, instead of your grandfather."

The Earl waved his aristocratic hand dismissively. "Oh, there are irregularities, as you put it, in most aristocratic family trees – not everything was done by the book – but that's not grounds for murder."

"Of course, it's possible that Mary Pullman may have been intending to try and extract money from you in exchange for her silence."

The Earl threw his head back and laughed; it was a hollow, slightly sinister laugh. "Hah, that's rich! Well, as I have already said, I have no recollection of meeting this woman."

"But your brother says—"

"My brother is a complete waste of space and you really shouldn't believe a single word he tells you. I've done my best for him over the years, I really have, but he is a hopeless case. I mean, he talks proudly about his army record, but he never mentions the embarrassing incident with the good-looking young officer that would have led to a court martial if I hadn't intervened. As it was, he was discharged for being 'temperamentally unsuited' to army life. I tried hard to give him a fresh start; I put him in charge of running my chain of garden centres and he did quite well for a while until he started to hit the bottle and I had to relieve him of his duties. And then, of course, we come back to his other 'activities'. Now don't get me wrong, Acting Inspector, this family has had its share of pink sheep over the years, but Simon was just so indiscreet and flagrant. 'In your face', I think is the modern idiom. I mean, he couldn't take his latest boyfriend back to his place to… do whatever. Oh no, he had to go and get himself arrested in a seedy public lavatory, for God's sake. I've worked damned hard to be a successful businessman, but it hasn't been easy with Simon doing his best to besmirch the family name whenever he got a chance. I mean, supposedly murdering a couple of innocent visitors and then kidnapping your brother's daughter are not exactly acts designed to enhance the family reputation, are they?"

"He says you paid him to carry out your dirty work."

The Earl was sounding increasingly exasperated. "Look, I paid him an allowance so that he could try and mend his ways – waste of time, of course! Most of what I paid him went straight into the coffers of a certain Scottish distillery."

"So you knew nothing about the two murders or the kidnapping of your—?"

The Earl tutted loudly, gave an irritated sigh, leaned forward in his chair, planted his elbows firmly on the table and gave the acting inspector an intimidating stare. "Absolutely not – I've already told you! I suppose I can see why he might have been trying to frame Richard Edgton. It is well known that I hate the man – jumped-up little… and Simon probably thought he was doing me a favour in his own misguided way, but as I keep saying—"

"But there is one little mystery I'd like your help to solve," Acting Inspector Beauregard interrupted. It was time to show his hand. "Correct me if I'm wrong—"

"Oh, I will, don't worry about that, Acting Inspector!"

"You see, the thing is, you received a phone call from your daughter at midday yesterday, Sunday, and during the course of that phone call, she told you, for the first time, that you were going to have to pay £750,000 to get her back alive…"

"Yes," the Earl replied warily.

"But we've been in touch with your bank, Nicholls, and they've told us that you made a special arrangement to withdraw £750,000 in cash on Saturday morning – at least twenty-four hours *before* you got the phone call. So how did you know that you were going to require that amount of money?"

The Earl glanced furtively at his solicitor and fidgeted with his ring. "I, er, well, I expect somebody had said, er—"

"You see, I reckon you had a detailed plan worked out. You must have known that Richard Edgton was flying to America tomorrow, so, for the plan to work, it had to be carried out today. Now you knew we were bugging your phone so, at a pre-arranged time, your daughter would phone and tell you to deliver the ransom money to Fearnley quarry. Then all you had to do was lure Richard Edgton to the quarry on some pretext or other and, with a bit of luck, we'd turn up just in time to find your daughter in the cave, and you handing over a case with £750,000 in it to Richard Edgton. And then we'd discover that he was due to leave the country tomorrow and that, coupled with all the other evidence that you've manufactured, would just about wrap up the case against him. And if, for some reason, Richard Edgton didn't walk into the trap that you'd set, there would still be enough evidence to nail him – a suitcase with £750,000 left in the cave together with some convenient proof that your daughter had been there; a coat button, or a handkerchief or a piece of jewellery, maybe."

"Yes, but—"

"But then things started to unravel. For your plan to work, it was necessary for Simon to set up the phone call from your daughter, giving details of the amount of the ransom, either on Friday evening or early on Saturday morning. That would have just given you enough time to arrange the cash withdrawal before the bank closed for the bank holiday weekend. But then Simon, your ever reliable brother, got himself stabbed in a fight with Geoffrey Pullman on that Friday evening and was in hospital all day Saturday, and in no position to carry out the plan.

"But you couldn't afford to delay the plan. If the so-called handover of your daughter in exchange for the ransom money hadn't taken place today, Richard Edgton would have been on his way to America before it happened and the case against him would look a bit flimsy. So you gambled on raising the cash, as originally planned, on Saturday morning. Unfortunately for you, by the time your daughter finally made the critical phone call, Richard Edgton was already in our custody. Meanwhile, of course, Simon, scared by what the hospital doctors had told him, decided to rebel and blow the whistle on you and your devious schemes! What a mess!"

His voice temporarily enfeebled by his lengthy soliloquy, Acting Inspector Beauregard sat back in his chair and succumbed to a paroxysm of violent coughing.

Lord Westleigh, meanwhile, smiled a sinister smile and waited for the acting inspector to recover. "But that doesn't prove anything, does it, Acting Inspector?" he asked innocently. "I expect Anthony Granard will tell you that he had advance warning that the amount would be three quarters of a million and—"

"Oh, Anthony Granard has already told us that he's prepared to testify against you, as are your brother and your daughter and your son-in-law," Acting Inspector Beauregard croaked.

"But, but—"

"And then, of course, there's the question of the ring…" Acting Inspector Beauregard was sensing, for the first time, that he had his prey in his sights and was going for the kill.

"The ring, what ring?"

"That signet ring on your little finger that you've been constantly fiddling with," Acting Inspector Beauregard continued in little more than a hoarse whisper. "You see, it's amazing what modern-day pathologists can uncover with all the advanced techniques and hi-tech gadgetry available to them. These days, they can often identify the tiniest of marks and indentations caused by each individual finger around the neck of a victim who's been strangled. Would you be surprised to know that, in such cases, they can identify even a small indentation made by something on the little finger of the murderer? Something very like your signet ring, for example. I've been in touch with the pathologist and he confirms…"

"Ah, well, of course I expect my dimwit brother wears a similar ring."

"He doesn't actually – never has. He's a gardener and is forever getting his hands dirty, so he avoids wearing any rings. But if the pathologist could examine your ring then maybe he'll be able to confirm that the marks on Mary Pullman's neck are a perfect match and—"

Lord Westleigh smiled ruefully and sat back in his chair. "I wonder if I might speak with my solicitor, in confidence. It shouldn't take long."

Acting Inspector Beauregard feigned irritation at Lord Westleigh's request, but he was, in truth, happy to escape the rigours of the interview for a few minutes in order to imbibe copious amounts of water, irrigate his nasal passages and equip himself with a generous supply of throat lozenges. On his return, he found the Earl in a strangely mellow mood.

"That's it, it's all over! I've heard enough!" the Earl declared calmly, raising his hands in a gesture of surrender. "The game, as they say, is up. I shall hand over control of my companies to Lucy and keep Anthony on the payroll so that he can keep an avuncular eye on her and assist her with her divorce from that wretched scumbag, Alex. And I shall spend my retirement at Her Majesty's pleasure, where I shall write my memoirs and become something of a celebrity jailbird."

Acting Inspector Beauregard could feel his heart racing. "So are you confessing to the murders of Mary Pullman and Vernon Court?"

"I am confessing to the manslaughter of Mary Pullman and Vernon Court. It's been a good game – quite a bit of fun, in its way – but it's over now. I made a very silly mistake and under-estimated you. You've been smarter than I expected – much smarter!"

"So what really happened?"

Lord Westleigh sighed. "You know, it wasn't really about Mary Pullman's somewhat spurious claim to be directly descended from the rightful heir to the Westleigh family fortunes. I mean, she may have had some kind of genuine claim, but she'd never have got to court; we'd have threatened her, or bought her off – that's how the family has been doing business for years. No, no, it was about money, as it so often is. I don't know if you realise this, Acting Inspector, but for some years Mary Pullman was employed by Nicholls Bank as a senior business adviser to many of its more powerful and wealthy clients, including yours truly. Officially, she was supposed to advise us, in confidence, on legitimate investment opportunities and advantageous funding streams that might be available to us – schemes that could make our money go further, or reduce our tax liability, you know the sort of thing. But there's often a thin dividing line between a legitimate opportunity and a dodgy scam and, it turns out, she was helping me, and lots of others, it seems, to make money through some extremely dodgy scams – a bit of insider trading, questionable offshore bank accounts, tax avoidance schemes, embezzling money from dead clients' accounts, misappropriating funds, you name it. Well, eventually the taxman started to take an unhealthy interest in what was going on and the bank rumbled what she had been doing, but the directors were put in a difficult position. If they exposed what she had been up to, there would have been a lot of adverse publicity, their reputation, and that of their bank, would have been badly damaged and a lot of big investors would have withdrawn their money, so they did a deal instead. In exchange for Mary Pullman giving her bosses a list of all the clients who, thanks to her, were involved in dodgy deals, they'd keep quiet about her involvement. They moved her to a lowly clerical job, on the pretext that she wanted a less stressful job, and allowed her to retire early and fade into obscurity. But her whistle-blowing cost me a lot of money; all her dodgy scams were closed down and I was forced to go legitimate. I had a monumental tax bill to settle and, one way and another, lost millions, and I do mean millions. Naturally, it all made me very angry.

"I'd heard that she'd retired, but I had no idea what became of her until I happened to look in Anthony's appointments diary and recognised her name. And so, when she arrived with her co-conspirator, Mr Court, I confronted her about all her scams and the subsequent whistle-blowing that had cost me so much. And do you know, she showed not one iota of remorse? She said it was all my fault and that I should not have allowed her such a free rein with my money and that my accountants should have spotted what was going on. And then she just smirked at me. Well, I'm ashamed to say, I just lost my temper. I remember putting my hands around her throat and shaking her and the next thing I knew, she was on the floor, motionless. And, of course, her friend Mr Court had seen what had happened, so he had to be dealt with as well."

"What happened to his body?"

"Fish food, I should think. Simon loaded his body into the helicopter and dropped him out at sea somewhere, well away from the coast. I sent some of my people round to clear out his flat and my technical people hacked into his computer and erased his website, and got rid of as many references to him as possible. Effectively, they made him just disappear."

"But why the charade with the ice? Couldn't you just have got rid of her in the same way you got rid of Vernon Court?"

"Of course we could, but where's the fun in that? No, no, I had a hunch that Mary Pullman's body might be useful to us at some stage, so we froze her. It had always worked so well in the past. But then my stupid brother messed it up!"

"You mean you've done it before?"

The Earl gave a knowing wink. "Oh, we hatched the idea some years ago when I first acquired a controlling interest in the frozen food business. I thought it was a brilliant idea, but I'm admitting nothing. Let's just say you might want to take a closer look at your list of missing persons. You see, by freezing the body in a block of ice, we can preserve it for as long as we want in our specially adapted ice house and, with the aid of the helicopter, dump it whenever and wherever we want. It means a body can turn up in the most unexpected of places, weeks, or even months, after the individual has been, er, shall we say, eliminated? And it throws your boys and girls completely off the scent. In the case of Mary Pullman, we thought we'd hang on to her body for a while – at least until you had lost interest in your 'missing person' search. My original idea was to return her to her grieving husband by dropping her in her own back garden, but then I discovered that she was a very loud and committed opponent of Richard Edgton's plans for Fearnley quarry and, as I've been itching to get back at that bastard for some time, I hatched a plan to implicate him. Simon was going to wait until we had a spell of hot weather and I was safely out of the country – the perfect alibi – and was going to take the chopper and drop Mary Pullman into the quarry. The ice would soon melt in the heat and an anonymous tip-off to your boys would result in her body being discovered. Then, when you conducted a search of the quarry buildings, you'd come across some of her clothing which Simon had managed to plant there and Richard Edgton would've had a lot of explaining to do. But, of course, the idiot got it wrong. He was running out of fuel, so he had to abort his flight and ditch her body. And if that wasn't bad enough, he flew so low over Willowmere Heath that he spooked the horse your inspector was riding and—"

"But your brother would have needed an accomplice. He couldn't have flown the helicopter and dropped a heavy block of ice at the same time."

"Oh, that was Tom, the groom. I imagine you've already got him in custody. When I first took him on, he was a bit of a hothead, always getting into fights and petty crime, but he was very good with horses. Fortunately, he was always quite happy to help us with some of our shadier business, for an appropriate fee, of course."

"I see. And what happened to Mary Pullman's car?"

"Well, somehow it found its way into a scrap yard, where it was crushed. You won't find any trace of it now, nor of the other bits and pieces she had with her."

"And the kidnapping of your daughter?"

"Do you know, I have hated that man, Richard Edgton, from the moment he moved into this area. Up until then, I'd pretty well got the run of the place. I could use my name and my influence to get my own way whenever I wanted. But then he tried to muscle in on my territory and my schemes and, frankly, became too much of a nuisance. I'd thought about eliminating him for a while, but that thug of his, Dean, was always getting in the way, so eventually we planned to frame him. When Simon made a mess of dumping Mary Pullman's body in the quarry, we came up with Plan B, the kidnapping of my daughter. While I was conveniently out of the country, Anthony invited Richard Edgton to Chartfield Castle, ostensibly to make an offer on my behalf to buy the quarry. It was a deliberately niggardly offer that we knew he'd reject, but we got his fingerprints on the envelope, which is what we wanted. Then we 'arranged' the kidnapping of Lucy. Simon squirrelled her away somewhere, then he broke into the quarry buildings and left traces of Lucy's hair and clothing. He left Mary Pullman's coat as well, figuring that while that piece of evidence alone might not be enough to convict Richard Edgton of her murder, it would certainly make life uncomfortable for him.

"The plan then was for you to find Richard Edgton's fingerprints on the envelope that contained the ransom note and Lucy's hair in the quarry building. Then, Lucy's phone call would lead us both to the quarry, where we'd discover her and you'd arrest Richard bloody Edgton just as he was planning to leave the country, apparently with a briefcase full of used notes. And he'd be out of my hair at last. It was all going so well until my idiot brother got himself hospitalised when he should have been organising Lucy's final phone call. And then, of course, as we now know, he just flipped. I should add, by the way, that Lucy was a party to the charade, though probably not entirely willingly."

The Earl paused, glanced at his solicitor and swallowed hard. "So what happens now?"

"You'll be formally charged with the murders of Mary Pullman and Vernon Court and the kidnapping of your daughter. You will make an application for bail, which we will oppose and—"

The Earl gave another cold, sinister smile. "And you'll be formally promoted to detective inspector and spend the rest of your career looking anxiously over your shoulder."

*

Richard Edgton grasped Clive Walsingham's hand and held it in a bone-crunchingly strong grip.

"Welcome," he oozed. "I'm so glad you could make it. Can I offer you a drink?" He released Clive's hand and strode over to a large cabinet containing an impressive array of expensive alcoholic beverages, cut-glass decanters, tumblers and wine glasses.

Clive examined his hand and waggled his fingers gingerly, seemingly surprised that no long term damage had been done, and exhaled. "No, no thank you. I've got to get back to the hotel shortly. I'm on duty and Clare thinks I've been neglecting my responsibilities recently. She's right, of course."

Richard Edgton laughed as he poured himself a large brandy; it was a deep, throaty laugh that echoed around the plush furnishings of his office. "Women often are. Well, I for one am really grateful that you've been neglecting your hotel duties. I think it's mainly down to you that I've been released without charge. Dick Beauregard seemed convinced that I was responsible for the murders and the kidnapping and pretty well every other crime that occurred on his patch." He waved his hand towards the same low-slung aluminium-framed chair, upholstered in a vivid red fabric, which had so discomforted Acting Inspector Beauregard. Strangely, although Clive Walsingham was several inches taller than the Acting Inspector, he seemed better and more comfortably suited to the strange angle of the chair.

"Oh, I just let the evidence point me in the right direction," he observed modestly. "But there are a couple of things I don't quite understand."

Richard Edgton sat back in his expansive office chair and took a sip of brandy. "Fire away!" he commanded amiably.

"Why were you following me on Saturday and why did you visit my hotel?"

Richard Edgton laughed again. "Yes, I thought you'd seen me – you can still behave like a detective when it suits, can't you? You see, I'd heard that you were involved in the murder investigation – Dean told me – and I knew that Dick Beauregard wanted to nail me for it and, as I don't have a lot of confidence in Dick's objectivity, I thought I'd tail you for a while to see if you were following any leads that might prove my innocence. When I bumped into you coming out of Gareth Adamson's house, it seemed like the perfect opportunity."

"And I led you straight to the hospital where I was visiting Simon Verwood!" Clive replied, laughing.

"Exactly! I checked to see who you were visiting and, when I realised, I didn't bother to hang around. Instead, I went to look over your hotel while you were out of the way. It's got an excellent reputation and I always like to check out the competition."

"And?"

"And, I was most impressed. Your lady on the reception desk was a bit formidable, though."

"Ah yes, that would be Debbie – very efficient but not one to suffer fools gladly. She came with the hotel and we're still working on her 'customer care' skills."

"And the other thing you don't quite understand?" Richard Edgton seemed keen to move the conversation on, satisfied that he had told Clive all he needed to know about his activities on Saturday.

"Ah yes. I heard you're buying Gareth Adamson's house – at least that's what he told me – and I was curious to know why."

"Oh, there's nothing sinister about that. Gareth Adamson had clearly been badly shaken by coming back from holiday and finding a body in his back garden, and I'd always felt a bit guilty about having to make him redundant when the quarry closed, so I made him a good offer. To be honest, I don't quite know what I'll do with the house now. Dean's family is quite large and, as the kids grow up, they'll want more space, and I did wonder about knocking the two houses into one to give him more elbow room and maybe allow him to expand his model aircraft hobby. He's completely obsessed by model aircraft. I'm convinced the only reason he took his family to Radholme for a few days was so he could attend the model aircraft rally that they had there that weekend. But what the future holds for him, I don't quite know." Richard Edgton paused and looked reflective. "Mind you, the Adamsons' other neighbours, Mr and Mrs Holt, are quite frail now and I doubt that they'll be able to go on living there for much longer. I might make them a generous offer as well and then, if you include Dean's place, I'll effectively own a block of three houses. Now that does offer some real development possibilities."

Clive shuddered. "Have you heard how Dean is?"

"Mmmm? No, not really. It's very early yet. He's critical but stable apparently. I gather that none of his vital organs suffered too much damage, so he should pull through, eventually, although he may not recover completely. It seems that Simon Verwood isn't quite the crack shot he claims to be. Is it true, by the way, that he hid Lucy Jeffries in one of the rooms at your hotel while he pretended that she'd been kidnapped? That would be ironic, wouldn't it, after Dick and his men had turned over all my property within a thirty-mile radius, looking for her?"

Clive gave an embarrassed giggle. "It is true, I'm afraid. Simon rented a place in the next village, but he was usually so drunk by the end of the evening that I let him crash out in one of the attic rooms we let the staff use in an emergency. He did all his own cleaning and laundry – that was the arrangement – so we never really had much cause to enter his room, and he could come and go via the old servants' staircase, so we never really knew whether he was in residence or not. Then he told us that he'd been thrown out of his place in the village – he claimed the lease had run out – so I let him have unrestricted use of the attic room until he could find somewhere else. Except, of course, as we now know, he hadn't been thrown out of his place and he just wanted to use our room to accommodate Lucy Jeffries. She must have been up there all the time he was in hospital, but we were very busy downstairs and didn't hear or see anything unusual. And, to cap it all, Simon started pinching money from the till so that he could buy food for her. He was a good gardener, though, when he was sober."

As he was talking, Clive had been gazing out of the large picture window at the eighteenth green, no more than a few paces from the River Carlow. "Wow, that's some view you've got there!" he enthused.

"Not bad is it?" Richard Edgton smiled smugly as he took another sip of brandy and settled so far back in his large office chair that he seemed to be at risk of toppling over backwards. "I hear you're a bit of a golfer."

"Yes, although I don't get much time these days. How did you know?" Clive replied defensively.

"I make it my business." He looked at Clive with a self-satisfied expression. "Look, I owe you a favour. How would you and your wife like free membership of our golf club here?" He glanced around the desk at Clive's legs stretched out in front of him. "I see you already have the correct attire – bright yellow trousers!"

Clive crossed and uncrossed his legs as he considered Richard Edgton's tempting offer. "I hope you're not offering me some kind of inducement."

Richard Edgton held his large muscular hands out wide in a gesture of innocence. "I've no need to do that. You know, despite what you've heard about me, I am a legitimate businessman and everything I do is perfectly legal. Now I'll admit that, in my younger days, when I was trying to make a living in some of the rougher parts of London, not everything I did would have stood up to detailed scrutiny, but since I moved here, everything I have done has been kosher. Take the quarry, for instance; when I bought it, the limestone seam in the hillside was virtually exhausted and, despite what you may have heard, I made a good offer to the Pawlett family. I liked the brothers – they were no businessmen, but I liked them; they looked after their people well. I was really very sorry to hear about Norman."

Richard Edgton fell silent and brooding for a moment or two before continuing his narrative. "Anyway, I tried to keep the quarry going, not least because a lot of people's livelihoods depended on it, and I might have succeeded, for a time at least. That was until the two fatal accidents; I never really believed they were true accidents – it was all too convenient – but I couldn't prove anything. Anyway, they pretty well put paid to the quarry. Then, when Lord Westleigh scuppered my plans for the quarry museum, I realised what he was up to. He bought off the planners, used his considerable influence to persuade one of the big financial backers to withdraw and fought my plans for a theme park tooth and nail in the hope that he could eventually buy the quarry from me at some ridiculous knock-down price.

"Of course, the more he tried to sabotage my plans, the more determined I became to thwart him. Now, thanks to you, it looks as though he's going to be out of the way for a few years so I can go ahead with my plans at last. It'll be so good for the area; a boost for tourism and the local economy." Richard Edgton formed his hand into a fist and gently punched the air.

"There were some things you kept at the quarry that you didn't want Dick to see, though, weren't there?" Clive asked, feigning a look of innocence.

Richard Edgton threw his head back and roared with laughter. "Now you mention it, there were a few files going back several years that I didn't want Dick to see. They involved some highly dubious transactions which were arranged for me by a certain senior financial adviser working for Nicholls Bank. But I bore no grudge against the lady – I should've checked her advice more carefully – and I settled what I owed. I think me and Mary kissed and made up particularly well, don't you? But you can imagine what Dick would've thought if he'd found her name among those old records, and I couldn't afford to take that chance."

Clive glanced at his watch and stood up. "I hope you'll forgive me, but I really ought to be getting back. Thanks for the invite, and I shall certainly keep an interested eye on developments with the quarry. Is that why you're flying to America tomorrow?"

"I was, but I've postponed the trip. It didn't seem quite right to go just at the moment, what with Dean and everything else that's happened."

Richard Edgton stood up, grasped Clive's hand and held it in another vice-like grip. "You know, I've heard a lot of very good reports about your hotel, and I've seen for myself how well you're doing. Of course, you are taking some of my custom, including one particularly profitable coach booking, so I'd be prepared to make you a very good offer for it if ever you wanted to sell. I hear your chef is leaving, by the way. That'll be difficult for you."

"Yes, but how did you know?" Clive asked suspiciously.

"As I said earlier, I make it my business; that's how you stay ahead of your competitors."

"Are you saying—?"

"And before you start accusing me of something – Dick Beauregard was very good at that – no, I had nothing to do with your chef's decision to go. But, for what it's worth, we recently saw several very good candidates for the position of sous-chef here at Carlow Bridge and there were a couple that, I think, might make a very good hotel chef. I'll email you with the details."

"Well, that's very—"

"And don't forget the offer of free membership to my golf club."

Twenty

Later in the week

There was an unmistakeable jauntiness about Acting Inspector Beauregard as he strutted onto the hotel terrace carrying a bicycle helmet under his arm and sporting a red T-shirt and tight black lycra shorts. Archie, who had been snoozing in a quiet, sunny corner of the terrace, was so alarmed by the sight that with, a rare show of athleticism, he raced for cover, hurtling across the acting inspector's path and causing him to half-stumble and crash into one of the many chairs that populated the terrace.

Barely stifling a chuckle, Clive winked at Constable Pawlett, now dressed in her familiar denim, and made a show of studying the sky intently. "Do you know, I think it might rain later," he observed mischievously.

Rubbing his knee where it had collided with the terrace chair, panting slightly and perspiring profusely, Dick Beauregard flopped onto the chair that he had just crashed into. "No, no! It won't rain today. Today is a lovely day! And even if it does rain, today is still a lovely day!"

Clive winked at Alison Pawlett again. For a moment, he thought about not asking the question that Dick was desperately wanting him to ask, but, in the end, he relented.

"I must say, your cold seems a lot better, but there's something else, isn't there? So tell me, why is today such a lovely day?" he ventured at last.

"He's confessed!" Dick Beauregard replied breathlessly. "The Earl of Westleigh, no less, has confessed to the murders, or at least the manslaughter of Mary Pullman and Vernon Court. Apparently, the main motive was money. He believed that Mary Pullman had swindled him out of a lot of money when she was a senior investment adviser at Nicholls Bank. And, even more exciting is the fact that he might have murdered someone else, maybe more than one – I don't know who – but he hinted that he'd used the body in the block of ice method before and that he'd had his ice house specially adapted to store the blocks of ice in."

Clive's face had a tendency to betray a flicker of emotion even when he wanted to present an image of enigmatic and cold detachment. He smiled – he couldn't help it. "Did you mention the pathologist and the impression of the signet ring?"

"I did, and I think that was actually the clincher. He pretty well surrendered after that. I'm so grateful, Clive! That was a brilliant suggestion of yours – absolutely brilliant – and he fell for it! He obviously believed that the pathologist *had* found an impression of his ring."

"Oh well, that's good! I'm glad my suggestion worked."

"How did you know about the Earl's signet ring anyway?"

"Oh, I saw a picture of him in his overpriced souvenir brochure and I spotted his ring. It seemed such a chunky piece of jewellery that I thought the pathologist could have found an impression of it on Mary Pullman's throat or neck. Anyway, how's Simon?"

"Oh, still a bit bruised after Alison whacked him. He's confessed to being responsible for the two so-called accidental deaths in the quarry and the murder of DI Morris. He's also admitted planning and carrying out the fake kidnapping of Lucy Jeffries and disposing of the bodies of Mary Pullman and Vernon Court. And he's admitted breaking into Fearnley quarry, planting the evidence and nicking the dummy explosives and detonator, plus, of course, the shooting of Dean Footner, but he's angling for a deal at the moment. He's quite willing to testify against his brother, but he wants some kind of mitigation in return. He keeps saying that he knows something about the death of Lord Westleigh's wife twelve years ago and hinting that it wasn't suicide. I'm not sure what good it'll do; if the doctors are right, he could be dead before the case comes to court and—"

"Yes, that was a bit of a shock," Clive agreed. "I mean, we all knew he was an extremely heavy drinker, but he seemed indestructible. And I had no idea about Simon and Alex Jeffries; that was a real shaker."

"Yes, that was a bit of a revelation," Acting Inspector Beauregard agreed with an emphatic nod of his head. "When I originally spoke to Alex Jeffries, he told me that it was Lucy who had lost interest in sex, but, as we now know, it was Alex who had lost interest in his wife."

"You know, Dick, if things hadn't worked out for you and you hadn't made any arrests, I was thinking of offering you the vacant post of hotel gardener, but I don't think I could have lived with those shorts, and anyway, I expect you'll be rewarded for your excellent work; a permanent post of detective inspector, perhaps?"

Dick Beauregard was momentarily distracted by the sight of Clare and Jamie Coulton arriving with two plates, one piled high with an assortment of sandwiches and the other containing the usual expansive array of cakes. "Well, there are processes to go through, but I've been given to understand…" he said rather diffidently as he eyed the sandwiches being placed on the table in front of him.

"And you, Alison, what's your future?" Clive asked.

Alison Pawlett had been sitting quietly at the table listening to the exchange between Dick Beauregard and Clive without once offering a comment. "Dunno," she replied enigmatically. "I've got some difficult decisions to take…" She paused as Jamie Coulton placed the plate of cakes in front of her, brushing against her shoulder as he did so and grinning broadly. A half-smile flickered briefly across Alison's still-bruised face as she looked up at the grinning Jamie.

"I don't suppose I could stay here for a little bit longer?" Alison asked, her cheeks turning slightly pink. "I've got nowhere else to go for the moment and… obviously I'll pay my way."

Clive exchanged glances with Clare. "Alison, of course you're most welcome to stay here for a while longer while you sort yourself out. I'm glad you're enjoying our hospitality. Besides, I don't think Simon will be using his room again and I'm thinking Inspector Beauregard would like you to stay on and—"

"The chief constable is very pleased with Alison's work, even if some of it was, er, a little unorthodox," Acting Inspector Beauregard interrupted with uncharacteristically fulsome praise.

Clare took Jamie Coulton, who was loitering close to Alison's shoulder, by the arm. "Come along, Jamie. We've got work to do, let's leave these good people in peace." She tugged hard at Jamie Coulton's arm and almost dragged him into the conservatory only to return, moments later, leading a thin, nervous-looking woman out onto the terrace. The woman had long fair hair, streaked with grey, and was wearing a pale green blouse and slightly baggy denim trousers. Clive looked up and rose quickly to his feet. "Julia! How wonderful to see you. Glad you could make it. Where's Grace?" He pulled out a vacant chair and invited her to sit down.

Looking ill at ease, her eyes darting rapidly from one person to another, Julia Cockrell arranged herself carefully in the chair, fidgeting for a few moments until she felt comfortable. "Oh, Trevor's looking after her. We agreed – or rather I agreed – that it's about time he took a turn. It'll be good for him; he needs to delegate more and Grace will make sure he does. I'm sure he'll cope for a couple of nights; at least, I think he will. He knows where to find me." She paused to look around at her new surroundings. "What a lovely place you have here."

Clive inclined his head in appreciation and introduced Julia Cockrell to the detectives. "Clare, can you spare the time to join us?"

Clare fixed him with one of her intense stares, her grey-green eyes displaying a warmth that had been missing in recent days. "I'd love to. I'll just go and organise Jamie to take Julia's luggage to her room and bring the drinks and I'll be right back." While Clare disappeared inside, Julia carefully opened the laptop she'd brought with her.

"I take it you'd like me to tell you a bit about my research," she asked, as she carefully positioned the laptop on the table in front of her so that she could easily read from it, adjusting the angle slightly to ensure that the screen was shielded from the direct rays of the sun which had made a welcome return now that the bank holiday weekend had come to an end. She had just finished and was resting her gaunt arms in her lap when Clare returned.

"Good, good!" Clive rubbed his hands in anticipation. "I invited Julia here today partly so that she could collect her generous fee from the police," he looked questioningly towards Dick Beauregard, "and partly to tell us about her research into Mary Pullman's family history and the Earl's dark secrets."

Clare rubbed her hands together, in subconscious imitation of Clive. "Oh, good! A nice juicy scandal!" She paused as Jamie, still grinning, returned with a tray of coffee and a jug of fruit juice which he deliberately placed, with due ceremony, in front of Alison Pawlett, brushing against her shoulder again as he did so.

"Can I pour you a coffee, Julia?" Clare asked, while gesturing to Jamie that it was time he left.

"Yes, thanks. Black please, no sugar." Julia sounded tense and apprehensive, and Clive began to wonder if his invitation to her had been worth the time and effort, particularly as she declined to take a sandwich from the plate as he passed it round, but he need not have worried.

Julia cleared her throat a little self-consciously and began her narrative. "I suppose we should start with Ralph Verwood-Monck. He was born at Chartfield Castle in 1870 and was the heir to the title of Lord Westleigh. Now it seems that young Ralph had a bit of a penchant for servant girls and, in 1890, he married one of the servants at Chartfield; a girl called Jane Dalton. I think it is safe to assume that she was pregnant at the time. Anyway, soon afterwards, the marriage was annulled, almost certainly because Ralph's family disapproved of it and because Ralph had been under twenty-one at the time of his marriage. If he had married Jane Dalton without parental approval, which seems likely, they would have had sufficient grounds to get it annulled. Intriguingly, Jane Dalton then completely disappears. She doesn't appear in the 1891 census either as Jane Dalton or Jane Verwood-Monck and nor does any baby that she might have had. My guess is that they had both died. I can't find any record of their deaths, but registration records at that time were not totally reliable or comprehensive. Jane's death might have been in childbirth or as a result of one of the many virulent diseases that were around at the time, but, of course, there could have been a more sinister reason – we can only speculate."

"How do you mean?" Clare asked, wide-eyed with astonishment.

"Well, while Jane Dalton was alive, it would have been difficult for Ralph to re-marry. The normal conditions of annulment were that neither party could re-marry, but if one party were to die, then, of course, the rules changed. But, as I said, we can only speculate. What we do know is that, in 1896, Ralph went through a marriage ceremony with another servant girl called Mary Hayward. Now I imagine that his family may have tried for another annulment, although it's not easy to see what grounds they could have used, especially as Ralph was now twenty-six and even a family as powerful as the Verwood-Moncks would have had some difficulty making a case. What I can tell you is that I can't find any record of an annulment. All I know for sure is that, six months after the marriage, Mary Hayward gave birth to a boy whom she called Frederick Dalton Hayward. She was still calling herself Mary Hayward and she didn't name the father on Frederick's birth certificate, but the choice of 'Dalton' as his middle name was obviously significant – a subtle tribute to Ralph's first 'wife'."

"So it was on the basis of this evidence that Mary Pullman thought her grandfather was the legitimate heir to the Westleigh estate," Clare asked, eagerly.

"It seems so," Julia replied guardedly. "It's pretty clear that Ralph was legitimately married to Mary Hayward, although his family may well have put pressure on her to deny it. They might even have told her that her marriage *had* been annulled and she would probably have been none the wiser. In any event, I should imagine they paid her well for her co-operation. That's probably why she used her maiden name on Frederick's birth certificate and why Ralph's name was not recorded."

"So what happened to Ralph, Mary and Frederick?" Clare asked, eager for some more hints of scandal.

"Well, it looks as though Ralph's family finally married him off to an heiress called Alice Godolphin in 1900."

"But hang on a minute. You said that he was legitimately married to Mary Hayward?" Clive asked, his analytical mind quickly getting to the nub of the problem.

"Yes, that's quite right; it's pretty clear that Ralph's marriage to Alice Godolphin was bigamous, but the Verwood-Moncks would have had a lot of power and influence and been able to pull a few strings. But, you can see why Mary Pullman got so excited."

"So what happened next?" Clare asked.

"Ralph and Alice had a son, William, born in 1902, and a daughter, Matilda, born in 1904, but by the time of the 1911 census, they were living apart. I don't know what happened to Mary Hayward – it is not an especially uncommon name and the trail went cold. What I do know is that, after the start of the First World War, both Ralph Verwood-Monck and Frederick Dalton Hayward joined up. Frederick, as we know, survived the war, but Ralph was killed at Passchaendale and it was his son, William, who inherited the title of Lord Westleigh in 1919. He married Olivia Goddard in 1931 and it is his grandson, Patrick, who is the present Earl of Westleigh. Frederick Dalton Hayward, meanwhile, married Ann Pritchard and, as we know, they had a granddaughter, Mary Hayward, later Mary Pullman."

"So Lucy Jeffries and Geoffrey Pullman are related?"

"Yes, I guess so – distantly, I suppose. Obviously I can do some more research if you want me to go further and then, of course, there are also Vernon Court's notes. Have you been able to track him down?"

Clive exchanged nervous glances with the detectives and there followed a brief, uneasy silence which was finally broken by Alison Pawlett.

"I got in touch with my colleagues in the Met and they tracked down Vernon Court's last known address. As you suggested, he was registered with a number of family history organisations in London. Unfortunately, he disappeared around the same time as Mary Pullman."

"And we now know," Acting Inspector Beauregard added, solemnly, "he was with Mary Pullman when she was murdered and, because he saw what happened to her, I'm afraid…" He broke off and shrugged.

"What? You mean…? Omigod, how awful!" Julia Cockrell's lips tightened and she began to fidget with the buttons of her pale green blouse.

"But don't worry, Julia," Clive soothed. "The murder of Mary Pullman seems to have much more to do with her dodgy financial activities than with her family research. It was poor old Vernon Court's misfortune that he happened to be an unwitting eyewitness to the murder. But obviously, we don't want to stir up a hornet's nest, so it might be as well if you don't mention your research to anyone."

Julia continued to fidget with her buttons. "Oh, yes, yes, absolutely. My research is always confidential and is the property of whoever commissioned it – once I've been paid, of course!"

*

Through the open bedroom window, the sound of distant birdsong wafted up on the gathering breeze from the river valley below. From the ground floor, the telephone could be heard ringing before being swiftly answered, no doubt, by the ever-efficient Debbie in her usual brisk manner. From the floor above, there was the muffled sound of an animated female voice, followed by the sound of a man laughing.

Clive continued to rest his head between Clare's pert, slightly damp breasts, as he brushed a bead of perspiration from his contented brow.

"I'm going to need a new gardener," he announced, as he gave one of Clare's nipples a gentle tweak.

"Yes," Clare agreed while absently stroking Clive's thinning hair. "But the main gardening season's coming to an end. I expect Jamie can keep an eye on it until the winter sets in; I think he's going to need some kind of outdoor activity to keep him occupied. And, in the spring, you can advertise for someone new or we can contract it out. I hear Chartfield Garden Centres do contract work."

"I'll bear that in mind." Clive laughed.

"Mind you," Clare said, thoughtfully. "I'm more bothered about finding a new chef at the moment."

"Ah, I might have found someone for that job, courtesy of Richard Edgton. Did I tell you, by the way, that he's made a generous offer for this hotel?"

Clare suddenly sat bolt upright, causing Clive's head to jerk backwards onto the pillow. "He's done what? I hope you didn't accept!"

Clive laughed as he allowed his hand to wander between Clare's naked thighs. "No, of course I didn't. No, no, we seem to be making a success of things here, so let's keep at it."

Clare leaned back, closed her eyes and sighed. "Phew, so you are serious about carrying on with this venture?"

"Deadly serious!"

Clare placed her hand firmly on Clive's wandering hand and held it in a tight, restricting grip. "So in future, you're not going to allow yourself to be distracted by police investigations that Dick Beauregard can't handle."

Clive laughed. "No, absolutely not! I promise…!"

He felt Clare release her grip on his hand and he was about to allow it to wander again when he was suddenly made painfully aware that he had forgotten to close the bedroom door properly. Without warning, the door was pushed open and Archie marched in, with his tail far more erect than anything Clive could manage at that precise moment. With a triumphant mew, he jumped onto the bed and landed heavily on an exposed expanse of Clive's naked flesh, to which he attached himself with his razor-sharp claws.

As soon as Clive had finished shouting, first with pain and then with rage, his mobile phone rang. With his flesh still smarting, he answered it. He recognised the morose voice immediately.

"Hello, Clive, it's Dick Beauregard here. We've just found a body and I wondered…"